'Malky' Dalgleish is one of 40 Highl[...] at the battle of Dunbar and sent to [...] Shields. What follows is a rattling y[...] times of poor Tyneside fishers, fish wives, keel men and p[...] If you like a salty tale – love in the sand dunes, sweat in the salt houses, riding-the-stang and dodging the press gang, you'll enjoy this book. If you are interested in how the Poor lived in 1650 (by their wits, mainly) you'll learn something too.

Robert Colls, author of *This Sporting Life: Sport and Liberty in England, 1760-1960*

Following his trilogy vividly chronicling the life of ordinary people on Tyneside in the early 20th century, John Orton gives us an arresting re-creation of life around the mouth of the Tyne in the mid-17th century during Oliver Cromwell's Commonwealth. The story he tells of five Scots lads working and looking for love in a world of indentured labour, press gangs and smuggling, will not only grip readers with a particular interest in the history of the North East. He wears a blue bonnet will be source of fascination and pleasure for anyone who wants to know how human beings much like themselves fared in a world that was radically different.

John Gray, author of *Feline Philosophy: Cats and the Meaning of Life*

First published in Great Britain as a softback original in 2022

Copyright © John Orton

The moral right of this author has been asserted.

Editing, design, typesetting and publishing by UK Book Publishing

www.ukbookpublishing.com

ISBN: 978-1-915338-34-1

HE WEARS A

BLUE BONNET

John Orton

Also by John Orton:

THE FIVE STONE STEPS
(A tale of a policeman's life in 1920s' South Shields)
2014

BLITZ PAMS
(Police Auxiliary Messengers)
2016

A CHILL WIND OFF THE TYNE
2018

All published by *ukbookpublishing.com*

HE WEARS A
BLUE BONNET

Malky Dalgleish and four highland Scots, who befriend him on the battlefield at Dunbar, arrive in South Sheels in November 1650, as indentured servants to work in the salt-panns. After Cromwell's victory in the battle, they had been marched from Dunbar to Durham in the infamous death march, the survivors of which were sold by General Haselrig; mostly to work in the colonies in the New World, but forty to go to Sheels. This is the story of five Scots lads who work and suffer in the salt-panns. Malky and Davey find love of a sort with two Sheels lasses, and also become involved in smuggling from the caves of Harton and Marsden; Niall escapes to work on the keels; little Dougie, the boy fifer, is not strong enough for the work in the panns and is taken into service; Tomag distils his own *usquebah* (whisky).

He wears a blue bonnet gives a grim but authentic account of life in a riverside township at the mouth of the Tyne during the years of the Commonwealth: with tales from the salt-panns, from the keelmen of Newcastle, from the toon-end of Sheels where the fishers live, and from the ale-houses. The Parliament forbade any frivolous or immoral activities and miscreants were whipped in the Market Place - and folk fled to their homes when they heard the drum of the press gangs on the high and low ways of Sheels - but life went on.

John Orton, whose *Tyneside Trilogy – The Five Stone Steps, A Chill Wind off the Tyne and Blitz PAMS* – tells of life of ordinary working people South Shields in the first half of the twentieth century, now recounts the lives and struggles of the folk of Sheels in the 1650s, when the town, as we now know it, was at the beginnings of its rise to become a major port, and centre for heavy industry.

LIST OF
ILLUSTRATIONS

The Keel Row

As aa cam thro Sandgit,
Thro Sandgit, thro Sandgit,
As aa cam thro Sandgit,
Aa heard a lassie sing.
Weel may the keel row,
The keel row, the keel row,
Weel may the keel row,
That ma laddies in.
He wears a blue bonnet,
Blue bonnet, blue bonnet,
He wears a blue bonnet,
An' a dimple in his chin.
Weel may the keel row,
The keel row, the keel row,
Weel may the keel row,
That ma laddies in.

The Keelman's Widow's Lament

Aye now I've seen yer bonnie lad,
Upon the sea I spied him,
His grave is green, but not wi' grass,
An' ye'll never lie beside him

(Both traditional.)

NOTE TO READERS

He Wears a Blue Bonnet is set in the 1650s. Old and dialect words that may not be readily understood appear in italics the first time they are used in the text, and are defined in the glossary at the end of the book. Some of the words in common 17th century usage may appear on the coarse side now, so apologies in advance if sensibilities are offended. The Sheels characters all speak with a local accent, as King's or Queen's accepted pronunciation did not come in until the nineteenth century. Fore and surnames are spelt as they appear in documents of the record at the time, and all characters are fictitious even if they share a name of a man or woman of Sheels of that time.

CONTENTS

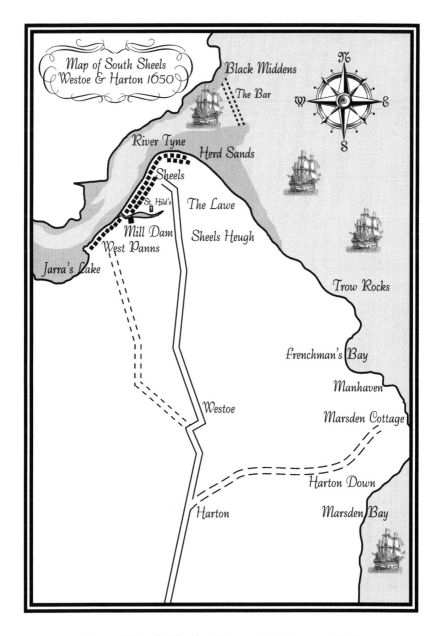

Map of South Sheels, Westoe, & Harton, 1650

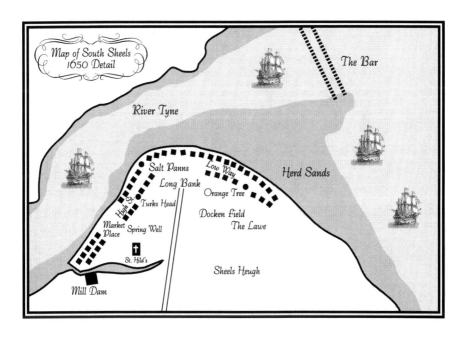

Map of South Sheels 1650 (detail)

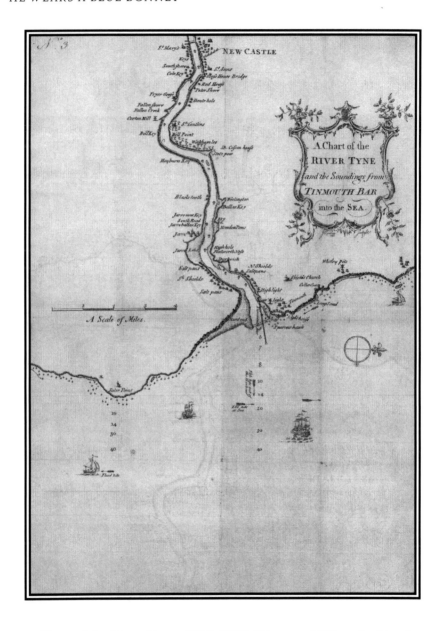

Chart of the River Tyne, 1700-1750 (Tyne and Wear Archives)

PART I

CHAPTER ONE

Young Malky Dalgleish was in a state of high excitement. He had not slept a wink and had little appetite for the thick *porritch* that was their usual breakfast, taken after the lengthy grace delivered by his father, Archibald, a Covenant minister. Auld Archie, as the lad called him, but only ever behind his back, was a thin stick of a man, nearly bald and with a grey unsmiling face stuck in a mask of misery, until the eyes lit up in ecstasy as he prayed to the glory of God.

Malky kept his eyes in his bowl determined to do nothing that might lead his father to change his mind. His younger brother and two sisters took after their father and sat well behaved and silent at the table. Archibald was to join the other Covenant ministers who were to accompany General Leslie to lead the Scottish army against Cromwell's parliamentarians. When he had first told his son that he was to come with him as his clerk, Malky had whooped with such irreligious joy that his father had stepped back to the mantel, taken the martinet off its hook and whipped the lad round the face, once on each cheek.

"If ye let your passions overtake ye again, Malcolm, then ye will stay at hame, and lose this opportunity to witness the glory of the Lord when his forces smite the enemy."

2

Breakfast over, his mother had waited until her husband had left the room, to drag her Malky to her and nearly squeezed the life out of him, tears flowing down her rosy cheeks. She was a handsome woman, full bodied and full of life, or tried to be, without incurring her husband's displeasure. It had not been easy for her to move to Edinburgh from their home in Blairgowrie, away from all her friends and family, but Archibald had been one of the first ministers to take the Covenant. He had spent more and more time in Edinburgh, and when he had been invited to become one of the ministers at St. Giles, he finally decided to move his family south. It had also meant that Malky had fewer opportunities to sneak out of the house to go fishing at Kinloch near his grandparents' house and run wild with the highland lads of his own age. He now attended the church school and when he returned home his father insisted that he continued studying Latin and Greek, but Malky's heart was not in it.

He at last escaped his mother's arms and ran outside to the yard where the stable lad had readied their mounts. His father had a sedate palfrey, Malky a half wild pony that he had brought with him from Blairgowrie. He was to lead the pack mule that carried their provisions. His father came out, at last, and they were away. They both had long cloaks against the constant drizzle. Archibald wore his wide-brimmed outdoor hat, and Malky sported a blue bonnet with the band tied in a bow at the back in the highland style.

Cromwell, who had been besieging the city throughout a dismal and wet August, had finally given up and retreated to Dunbar where the hoped-for provisions from England would reach him. Leslie's cavalry harried them all the way as the rest of the great Scottish army followed. The Covenant ministers rode near the head of the long columns, just behind General Leslie and his commanders. It was not easy going and the columns soon splintered as they made their way along the narrow and muddy trails that led from Edinburgh to Dunbar. The slow going meant that they had to spend the first night in an improvised camp in fields beside the way near Hadynton. The small number of tents that had been brought on the officers' pack horses was just enough for the General, his staff and the covenanters, but there was no bedding and little food other than what they had brought themselves as emergency rations.

Archibald's face was set in even more misery as usual as he sat in his wet clothes in a freezing tent eating the slabs of cold porritch and the *bannocks* his wife had prepared for them, but to Malky it was a great adventure. He had left the tent to piss and as he stood downwind with his legs astride, he heard the sound of singing coming from a nearby tent. He had rarely heard any Scottish airs or even psalms since he had come to the strictly Presbyterian Edinburgh, where even a friendly smile would be condemned as levity of spirit. He was about to sneak over when he was overtaken by two black-garbed figures who strode past him with a determined step and pulled open the tent flap. The sound of singing voices stilled and was replaced by harsh words of warning of what would befall frivolous idolaters. Malky had heard it all before and returned to his own silent tent.

They broke camp at first light and struck out without first taking breakfast. The lad managed to munch at some of the remaining bannocks before they set off. Outriders had returned the day before and they were no more than a few hours' march from the outskirts of Dunbar. General Leslie rode off at speed with his cavalry to scout for a good position from which they would attack the English. It was late morning when the army arrived at Doon Hill where the General had led them.

The hill was a good mile and a bit from Dunbar, and from its summit they could see the dispirited English army shivering in the open – only Cromwell and his generals had tents. The rest of the Scottish army arrived in the afternoon. Once encamped, with ditches dug and mounds thrown up, they were in an impregnable position. Although most of the men had tents, the food supplies were still held up on the muddy trails. It was not of immediate concern as it was the practice of the Scots to fast for two days before a battle to put them into a fighting mood. The officers and the Covenant ministers in the General's headquarters felt no such impulsion, and ate well that night with boiled beef, *neeps* and fresh-baked bannocks. Leslie held a council of war the next morning, a Saturday. Malky followed his father into the large central tent with orders to take a note of what was said. He wore a black jacket over his waistcoat, and would have blended in with the other ministers and clerks were it not for his highland bonnet. Malky had just turned seventeen and was a big lad, stockily built with broad shoulders and strong shanks. Wavy chestnut locks fell nearly to his shoulders, his nose was straight and his lips were full, but his most striking feature were his eyes: one was blue, the other chestnut.

The colourful martial clothing worn by Leslie and his generals was in contrast to the stark black gowns of the ministers, but their trade was war and they were accepted for what they were. As he stood beside his father holding his wax tablet at the ready, Malky's eyes crossed with two men standing close to the General and who were staring at him. The older man was tall and thickset with a patch over one eye and a deep scar that ran down that side of his face. His youthful companion had curled black hair, sported a moustache and wore a richly embroidered blue coat trimmed with ermine, and scarlet breeches.

"A clerk in a highland bonnet," he called out in good humour.

"He is my son," said Archie. "We have not lang moved from Blairgowrie to Edinburgh. He used to run wild wi' the other laddies when he should have been studying the scriptures."

"And ye didna' think to let him fight wi' us, so he could use his wildness to smite our enemies?" replied the officer.

"Ach, he's still a boy and his mother would no' have allowed it."

The older man now spoke. "I knew auld Geordie Drummond when he first took the barony. We used to hunt and fish round Kinloch."

Malky was eager to join the conversation. "Aye, it's good fishing at Kinloch. Ma mother was born there and ma grandparents farm a good bit of land roond there."

General Leslie interjected. "Interesting as your reminiscences of hunting and fishing are, Johnny, we are here to talk of battle."

The younger man spoke quickly and quietly to Malky. "Do ye speak the Gaelic?"

"He does," replied Archie, "and, to his shame, far better than his Latin."

"Just a minute, Davey," the one-eyed man said to Leslie. "May I introduce myself, Pastor Dalgleish. I am John Douglass, commanding a regiment of dragoons and this is my trusted second, Captain Robbie Colquhoun. My dragoons act as messengers during battle, but all of my messengers are lowlanders. There are still a small number of highland regiments in our army, mostly infantry." He paused and looked at the covenanters. "Your Government's commission purged most of them – so be it. But it means that a messenger who can speak the Gaelic, and pass an order on direct to the men if needed, would be a great boon. If we have here a lad who can read and write and also speak the Gaelic, then it is his duty to join Douglass' dragoons."

Malky could not believe his ears. He had been whipped by his father when he had dared to suggest that he should volunteer to join the new army, but now he took his chance. "I will," he shouted, perhaps a little too enthusiastically for some of the strict Presbyterians. "I can speak the *erse* and have a half wild pony that can run like the wind."

Auld Archie was about to interject, but was forestalled by a look from the leader of the covenanters whose own two sons had joined the new army. He said nothing.

"Then we will have ye, Malky me-lad," said Colonel Douglass. "Go with Captain Colquhoun after our meeting and

7

ready yourself for battle. We will no doubt be attacking the morrow while Cromwell's men are still in disarray."

This was too much for Archibald Dalgleish. "I didna' raise objection to him becoming one of your messengers, but he will nae fight on the Sabbath."

The next day was a Sunday. The other Covenant ministers were as one to support Pastor Dalgleish, and there followed a heated discussion. Leslie and his officers were clear and confident that an immediate attack against an unready enemy would lead to certain victory, but the Covenant ministers would not budge. To them it would be a sacrilege for their forces to take the field on the holy day, and there were those with sons in the army who asserted that their offspring would refuse any orders to do so. Leslie gave in. It was only the first setback for a General, who knew as much about war from his years serving the Swedish King, as the covenanters knew of the Bible. If he could not attack straight away, then he favoured a strategy of staying atop Doon Hill and sending out his cavalry and dragoons to harass the enemy. Their position was impregnable, and if the English were goaded to attack they would be thrown back, and they would meanwhile starve looking at the empty sea off Dunbar. But once again the covenanters prevailed and it was agreed that they would move to the fields on the bottom slopes of Doon Hill on the Monday and prepare for a pitched battle on Tuesday the 3rd September. Leslie was not too disheartened. His officers and men were in better shape than the English and he was certain that he would prevail.

Malky fetched his pony and then accompanied Robbie Colquhoun through the forest of tents to where the dragoons were camped. As they walked along, Robbie told the lad that John Douglass often talked of a bonny lass that he had met at Kinloch.

"She had fair hair with a touch of red, smiling eyes and a soft bosom. She was as taken to Johnny as he was to her, but he had to leave her when he left Blairgowrie to ship out to Sweden where he was to join David Leslie. He learned later that the lass had fallen pregnant and had been married to the local pastor, who had agreed to wed the lass to save her from shame, and for his part, to receive a healthy dowry in land." Robbie paused. "Before he lost his left eye at the battle of Wittstock when fighting the Germans, he was known for having two eyes, each of a different colour. One was blue and one was chestnut – just like yours, Malky."

The lad slowed his step and pulled his pony to a halt. "Are ye saying that he's ma Da'."

"Weel, he thinks sae from the way he looked at ye when ye came in behind miserable auld Archie. Ye'll get no special treatment, mind, but if ye do weel in battle he'll want to keep ye by him. He's nae other sons – apart from the odd bastard in Sweden."

"Ye mean I'm just a Scottish bastard?"

"Aye, but he could acknowledge ye as his son. He had real feelings for your Ma'."

They walked on in silence for a while and then Malky asked, "What did the Douglass mean when he said there were only a few highland regiments left?"

9

"We lost many stout highland men at the battle of Preston a few months ago, but we had enough left to form a good number of regiments. But then the covenanters set up their blasted commission to ensure that the army matched their own high standards. They kicked oot any soldier who had loose morals, who swore or who drank to excess. I've rarely met a highlander who did not chase a bonny lass, drink the *usquebaugh* until he was legless, and curse the Good Lord when his bottle ran dry."

Malky started laughing and Robbie joined in. "We lost most of the clan regiments. When the highland chieftains left, their men left wi' them. But we also lost lowland Scots as well and nearly 3000 men in all – hardened soldiers. The new recruits that replaced them were nowt but useless clerks and ministers' sons, who had never seen a sword, much less used one."

"But I used to practise sword play on ma Granda's farm, when I stayed there in the summer to help with the harvest. He said that every highland laddie, even a minister's son, should know how to fight," said Malky.

"Ach, I didna' mean ye, son."

The quarter-master was not happy when the captain arrived with a new recruit.

"I dinna' what ye expect, Captain, if ye canna' organise things any better. I'm here reet enow, but my stores are not. I brought the oatmeal and the mutton on oor own ponies so we'll feed, but there's nae spare uniforms or muskets." He leant forwards and thumbed Malky's jacket.

"That's good quality cloth, laddie, and it'll keep ye warm enow - and your boots look sound. If ye keep yon bonnet on yer heed we'll knaw ye're *ane* of oor's." He chuckled.

"He's going to be a messenger so he'll still need a cross-belt. He's not had any training yet, so he'll carry a sword and not a musket," answered Robbie. The quarter master grumbled but eventually handed over a well-worn cross belt with buckles, a leather pouch and a sword. "It'll need a good sharpening but it's solid enow."

Malky Dalgleish received little welcome from the dragoons whose tent he was to share. It meant one more to occupy their already cramped space, and one more to eat their already stretched rations. Malky did not let on that he still had cold porritch and bannocks in his satchel. If the battle was a long one, he might need sustenance on the hoof. He'd had little knowledge when he joined them of how a dragoon was different from any other cavalryman, but he soon learned that they were mainly used for scouting, or harrying. When they fought, they dismounted and used musket or sword. As a messenger he would normally be on his own, and did not need to be part of any of the units who fought together.

After a Sunday of never-ending sermons they did little the next day, until orders reached them to ready themselves to move out. It took a long time but by early evening General Leslie's troops had left the security of Doon Hill and marched down to the plain where they set up camp in their battle formations ready for the morrow. They had taken station on the south bank of the Brox Burn – it was a fast-running stream with sloping banks and would be difficult to cross from either side if under fire. Douglass' dragoons were on the far east of the

11

army, nearly on the sea shore. They were very much a reserve force behind Montgomerie's cavalry near the road where the burn was easily fordable. Once they were encamped Captain Colquhoon sent a corporal to fetch young Dalgleish with his pony.

The Colonel and his officers were readying themselves to mount their horses. Robbie Colquhoon greeted the corporal in his usual casual manner.

"We've found quarters in one of the farmsteads on the other side of the hill and are staying there the nicht. General Leslie wants his officers to have a good sleep and a hearty breakfast before the fighting starts. Ye, corporal, and yer brithers, 'll keep order and see the men are up and in formation after their gruel and ale on the morrow. I'm taking Dalgleish as a messenger so that he knows where we're staying if anything pressing should arrive that requires oor attention. He'll be back by nightfall. Come on, Dalgleish, look lively," he cried, as he turned his horse and trotted off.

They had not been long on the road when the Colonel himself dropped back to ride beside Malky. He did not waste time in small talk. "I knew your mother when I was in Blairgowrie, and she and I felt great love for ane another. I could never hae wed a farmer's daughter even if he was a man rich in land. The nicht before I was due to leave I went to say my goodbyes, and that was when we both gave in to oor true feelings. I only learned much later from Geordie Drummond that she had become pregnant, and that auld Dalgleish had seized the chance to take a bonny lass to wife and also to gain some land for himself. I often thought of her and of the bairn, but there was nowt else I could do. The Douglass men have eyes of different colour – it passes down from father to son. Sometimes it may skip a generation but it always comes back. Ye have ma hair and ma stature, but it is by yer eyes that I know ye are mine, and I knew it as soon as ye walked into Davey Leslie's tent behind auld Archie. We'd only ever met in secret, and yer mother told nae ane who the father was. Most supposed that it was a farm lad. For the moment this must remain between us. I hae nae wish to embarrass yer auld man, nor yer mother after all these years, but do well in the battle and I will look after ye."

He spurred his horse away and left Malky to his thoughts. The farmstead was only a couple of miles from Doon Hill, but they were all drenched by the constant drizzle. Malky was not invited in. Captain Colquhoon came over.

"We won't see ye till tomorrow at the camp. There won't be any need for ye to come oot here again. The Colonel wanted an excuse to speak to you personally. Cromwell's caught in a trap and he's naething to do but to wait for us to spring it." As Malky turned to ride away, Robbie shouted after him. "And tell the corporals to make sure the men cover their muskets with dry cloth the nicht – if they let the fuses get damp, they'll nae flare up the morrow."

By the time Malky had returned to camp he was thoroughly sodden and would have little chance to dry out. He reported to the corporal of his troop and mentioned what Colquhoon had said about the muskets.

"Orders have already been given, laddie, and the captain should know better than to think we need to be told to do what is second nature to us. Oor musketeers are mostly battle hardened, and wouldn't need telling any way. Not like the raw recruits in the infantry. If this weather continues we'll hae little gun-fire to support us, but the pikemen will do the necessary."

Malky slept little in his damp clothes. But he was also in a state of excitement at the thought of going into battle in the morning. He may have nodded off for a moment in the dead of night, but musket shots in the distance wakened him. He quickly pulled on his coat and cross belt, tied on his bonnet and ran to the corporal's tent. The drizzle had died down a little and he could see flashes away to the west. The corporal was standing outside the tent.

"Should I ride to warn the colonel?" Malky asked the Corporal."

"Let's wait a while. We were ordered to send some pickets out by the burn. They may have thought that they saw something, or the enemy might have tried to push them back. Cromwell's army are in no condition to mount a night attack – they'd all droon in the burn." He chuckled.

The flashes died down and quiet returned. Some minutes later the dragoons that had been on picket duty came back. They were not in a happy mood. They had been spotted by some English scouts who had challenged them and then fired their muskets. None were hurt, but as they led their horses up the slope away from the burn they were fired on by Lawers men – their fellow Scots. No one was hurt apart from one or two of the musketeers who were set upon by the dragoons when they reached them.

"They were the new recruits the covenanters had sent us. Their shots had gone way over the *heids* of oor men and they'd wasted a lot of their ammunition. Their fuses will be damp and I'll be surprised if they'll light easily when we attack, and even if they do they must hae used most of their shot already."

Heavy rain started to fall, and a cold wind off the sea was driving it on. "Ye wouldn't be welcome at this time of the nicht, if ye're thinking of riding to tell the colonel. And ye'd likely get lost in the dark. Wait until dawn then head oot. I don't think there's any need, but if ye dinna' gang, and they hear of the skirmish, they'll say they should have been informed."

Malky tried to stay awake as he doubted whether any light would filter through the tent covers in the wet, overcast conditions, but he must have dozed off, as the next thing he knew he was being shaken hard by the shoulder.

"Raise yersel and mount up. They're attacking us. Ride oot to the colonel and fetch him back as quick as ye like." Malky fumbled with his belt buckles in the half dark of the tent, and became aware of the sound of muskets and the shouts and screams of men in the distance. "They're in the cavalry's camp, and if oor lads dinna' rally they'll be here soon enough. Shift yer arse, Dalgleish."

It was only when he was in the saddle and riding as fast as he could in the half dark and driving rain that he realised that he had not had his morning piss. He dared not stop and his trews soon became wetter than they already were as he failed to hold back his waters. He had to slow to a gentle canter after his horse had nearly stumbled twice on the muddy ground. When he arrived, the house was in darkness, but he saw a glimmer of candlelight in a barn where a young lass was milking a cow. Malky hailed her and he then ran over and banged on the shutters. The heavy door opened and a woman in a thick shawl asked what the noise was all about.

"Ye must raise the Colonel Douglass. The army's being attacked, and if ye're not quick ye'll have a troop of Sassenachs at yer door." The words worked and in a few moments Douglass came to the door pulling on his undershirt. Malky just shouted out the words as quick as he could.

"They shot at oor pickets a couple of hoors ago but naught happened. The corporal said no' to bother ye but to come at dawn. But they're already in Montgomerie's camp and they'll be in oors if the lads don't rally."

"Slow down, Dalgleish," the Colonel said, now wide awake. "Ye say that we're being attacked."

"Aye."

"And oor troops were not up and ready before dawn."

"Ye couldna' see it was dawn, Sir. The corporal had to shake me awake."

"Go and help saddle oor horses. I'll talk to Colquhoon and the others."

The horses were in the barn with the cows. Malky started to help the lass with the saddles when his bowels started moving. He didn't want another accident on the way back so he asked the lass where he could go.

"We gang in the fields when we're working or behind the barn but in this weather, you'd best do it ower there." She pointed to a heap of animal manure by the back wall. "And then shovel it in. Naebody will notice. Take some straw for the

16

wiping." He hesitated a little. "Och, don't fash yersel' aboot me watchin'. I've seen what the other farm lads have between their legs many a time."

Malky needed to go quickly so he just squatted by the manure heap as the young lassie watched. When he finished and stood up his wee man was standing to attention. She looked at him and smiled.

"Do ye want me to pull it for ye? That's what the lads make me do when they catch me." The lass could not have been more than fourteen and was well built but with a plain face and lank hair.

Malky was tempted. His wee man was always awfy stiff in the morning but he never dared touch it the way the highland laddies at Kinloch had shown him. It was a carnal sin of the worst sort and he had suffered many a lecture from Auld Archie. 'Ye dinna' only gang to hell but ye become blind and mad as weel.' The lassie took a step towards him and Malky felt himself blushing as he knew he would not be able to resist what the lass was going to do. Then the voice of an angry Captain Colquhoon broke the silence. "Where' the blasted horses, Dalgleish? There's a battle to get to."

Colonel Douglass had decided that he would head over to the farmhouse where General Leslie was staying to make sure that he had heard the news, and would stay with him to decide what action was required.

"He'll probably want to gang to Doon Hill in any case to have a good vantage point to see what's happening on all fronts," mused Douglass, very much to himself. Malky was thinking that they would not see much in this weather, but he said nowt and just spurred his pony onto the way back to the camp. He was to lead Captain Colquhoon who would take charge of the dragoons until Douglass re-joined them.

The rain had turned into a steady drizzle, but the sky was lighter and it was a much easier ride, so long as they kept carefully to the muddy trail. They heard the noise of battle before the coastal plain came into view.

"Holy God," shouted Robbie Colquhoon.

The ground on both sides of the burn was a mass of horse and foot, fighting it out at close quarters. The dragoons had no doubt joined the cavalry to stop the English assault. The English guns on the top of the bank opposite were firing desultorily into the packed ranks of Lawers infantry who were trying to block the attacking force. They were not outnumbered, but were clearly outgunned, and did not seem to be using their own muskets.

"Come on, Dalgleish, that's where we're needed," cried the captain, pressing his mount forward, with Malky following. They had nearly reached the rear ranks when the red-coated English managed to outflank the Scots who broke and ran. Colquhoon charged at a group of English musketeers who were reloading. His horse shied to avoid crashing into the enemy. They saw their chance, and one of them hit the horse in the face with his musket, and horse and rider went down. Malky did not hesitate and galloped full pelt towards the melee. The enemy backed off, but at the last minute Malky pulled his mount up and leapt to the ground. He charged the first man and stabbed him in the throat with his sword. He had put all his weight behind it and the man fell to the ground, drowning in his own blood. The others fell back, still fumbling with their muskets. Colquhoon's mount got to its feet and galloped off. The captain stood up and dusted himself down. Malky whistled for his pony which was looking lost half way up the hill. It came down nervously. Colquhoon walked quietly over and grabbed the reins, leapt into the saddle, and spurred away, shouting over his shoulder. "Well done, Malky, I'll see ye're mentioned to the General. I'm off to join him and get back to Edinburgh, we're finished here."

Malky had little time to reflect on Colquhoon's treachery as two of the English were coming back for him, this time carrying their swords. They had given up on their muskets in the steady drizzle that had dampened their wicks. He was not going to run and instead charged them, letting out a highland war cry. They were seasoned campaigners, and the first one he met with side-stepped neatly, and struck his sword with his own, sending it airwards. His comrade then lunged forward to run the lad though. Malky thought his days were over, when he heard a cry as wild as his own and saw the head of a pikestaff fly past him and embed itself in the chest of his assailant. But it was not over yet as the other man came back at him and nearly had his head off, and would have done so had not Malky managed to parry the blow with his own weapon which was then pushed back onto his head. As he stumbled sideways, he kicked out hard and caught his attacker's knee from behind. The man staggered and Malky gave him such a blow with his sword that his neck was all but sliced through.

The lad who had come to his aid, was struggling to pull out his pike from the now groaning Sassenach's body and Malky put his foot on the man's chest and helped pull the pike free, bringing out with it two of the screaming man's ribs. The pike man stabbed him in the throat to put him out of his agony. He was older than Malky, but not so tall nor well built. His hair was sandy and he had smiling blue eyes. He wore the *plaid*, with a bonnet tied with a bow just like Malky's.

"Ye're lucky I heard yer cry," he said in the Gaelic. "I was ganna leave ye to it, thinking ye were one of these damned covenanters that will get us all killed. Ye'd best come wi' me and join the other lads. I think there's worse to come." His name was Niall *Bahn* 'the fair', and was part of a pike troop in which his brother Tomag also served. Tomag was the elder of the two and a huge man with brown hair and a moustache that drooped down on either side of his mouth.

"Welcome, Malky. This battle looks ower and we've nae officers to tell us what to do, so we're gang' to fall back, but steadily. Ye can stand at the rear and warn us if any ane has got behind us."

Niall laughed and said, "Ach, he'll slice their heids aff before they can get near us," and Malcolm Dalgleish was thenceforward known as Malky the Heid Slicer in the highland troop he now joined.

They were soon in the thick of it with the English rampaging forward, but the highlanders held their line supporting the raw recruits, including some lowland Scots who had flocked to join Sir James Campbell of Lawers' famous highland regiment. They then heard a deep rumble coming towards them.

"Sounds like horses," cried Niall, "the cavalry are on us."

Tomag who had taken the lead as there were no officers in sight shouted to the men.

"When we see them, stop and form two lines. Front rank kneeling, rear rank standing and wi' pikes held firm. A horse willna' run on to a wall of spikes. Ye slice the legs of any that run past, Malky me-lad."

The lowland Scots in front of them just gave up and ran, throwing their useless muskets to the ground. The English cavalry chased them down and killed them.

The highland line stood firm. Some horses urged on by over-eager riders skidded into them and scattered a few pike men, but they soon reformed. The English cavalry rode round them and then the reserve infantry came marching in good order. Those who were facing them were given an order to halt. An English officer walked forward with a white ribbon tied to his sword. A flag of truce.

Tomag left the front rank and walked forward. He gestured to Malky to walk with him.

"I'll only treat with officers," the Englishman called out.

Tomag spoke in the Gaelic and then pushed Malky forward.

"Tomag Deòireach says to tell ye that oor officers like to have a good breakfast before they cam to the field. Ye can wait for them if ye like, but the men will follow Tomag's orders."

The Englishman hesitated a second and then nodded and called out. "Your highlanders are the only ones standing to fight. We can surround you and slaughter you all with the muskets we have kept dry, or you can surrender. You will be taken prisoner and treated fairly."

21

More Gaelic from Tomag. "And will we be fed and given fresh watter, or ale?" Malky translated.

"My own men drink from the brook and have had no solid food for days. If we capture your baggage train then they will eat first. You will only be fed if we have any to give you. You may be hungry but you will not be dead."

Tomag asked for a minute and returned to the men leaving Malky on his own.

"You are a covenanter?" asked the Englishman. When Malky nodded, he smiled and said, "I have fought alongside the Scotch in the past when we were on the same side. Keep the faith, young man. It is not the Lord God who has deserted you, but your officers."

Tomag came forward and agreed the surrender. The pikes, swords, and *ballack knives* were lain on the ground. The prisoners were moved to the rear of the advancing troops and shepherded towards the coast, their numbers steadily increasing. As they trudged along they tried to avoid the dead, the dying and the wounded. Malky passed one young laddie who was screaming in agony, his face half cut away and his guts spilling out of his belly. His hand grabbed Malky's ankle. "Where is God?" cried the lad. "I gave him my Covenant and he promised to protect me." Despite the punches on his shoulder from those around him to move on, Malky stopped and knelt. The lad was little older than he himself – his eyes would now and again shoot up, showing all the white, as he screeched in dire pain. He looked up at Malky, and in a lucid moment he said, "Will ye finish me aff, friend."

Malky did not know what to do, but Tomag who had been marching on came back. He looked around and seeing that no English were looking, he reached under his armpit and drew out his little black knife, the *scian doo*. "Ye'll have to do it, laddie, ye stopped to gie him comfort." He handed the knife to Malky. "In his neck till the blood spurts oot."

Malky knew that he was committing a mortal sin, but as God had deserted the poor lad, then at least he could put him out of his misery. He thrust the blade in deep and then twisted until a spout of blood came out splattering his clothes. The lad looked him in the eyes groaning and gurgling as the blood choked him, and then the pain left him, the eyes blanked over, and he stayed quiet. Malky wiped the blood off the knife on his already bloody sleeve and gave it back to Tomag. They caught up with Niall who took one look at his new, blood-soaked friend and chuckled, "Ye been slicing mair heids aff, Malky."

"He was one of oors," said Tomag in Scots. "He thought God would protect him, but Malky sent him to the skies. We'll do the same for ye, Malky lad, if ye end up with a pike through your guts." Both Tomag and Niall had served with Lawers for a year or so and knew some Scots but preferred to let the English think they spoke only the Gaelic.

Those Scots regiments, which had not already left the field to flee north with General Leslie, surrendered. In little under a couple of hours before breakfast the English had won a battle they had been doomed to lose.

There was a break for a few hours when little seemed to happen. They could see riders bringing food to those who were standing guard, and could only guess that the English had captured the Scottish supply train. Malky, Niall and Tomag, with about a dozen other close companions, stood together under the freezing drizzle. Niall and Tomag would every so often wander off a short way and kneel down to pull the leaves off a wild plant, which they would then chew for a long time before swallowing. Malky followed them and did the same. The bitter leaves of what Niall called *Brigid's plant* and *lus-lus*, but to Malky were dandelion and plantain, were sharp and refreshing but also were wet with the drizzle and helped ease the thirst.

The red-coated Parliamentarian soldiers then started weeding out the old, the boys, the weak, and the wounded who were unlikely to take up the fight again and would be sent back to their homes. They were made to walk if they could to the edge of the field next to the burn and those too infirm or wounded were carried on stretchers. During the rest of the day they were taken away to Dunbar. The others who were mainly young men like Malky and his friends were left to their own devices, and told to be ready to march south the next morning.

When the English had passed the small group of highlanders, they had wanted to take the fife player, wee Dougie, as he was about fourteen and little more than a boy. He clung on to Davey, the drummer, who was by his side. They were cousins of Tomag and Niall and had only joined the Covenant army for this campaign. Davey looked about sixteen or seventeen, and could have fought as a foot soldier, but he wanted to stay close to wee Dougie and had asked to be a drummer. He'd laid down his drum at the same time as his sword but Dougie kept his fife tucked into his belt.

"Dinna' tak me," cried Dougie in Gaelic, and he was about to be manhandled away when Tomag stepped in, grabbing Malky by the arm to speak the Scots. "Can ye no' leave him. Davey is his only kin, and he won't be able to find his way hame on his own."

The English pikeman smelt of ale and was in a hurry. "Ye've got a forced march ahead of ye, we can't have any weaklings who'll slow us down."

"He's a strang laddie, for all his size. Besides we're all kin here and we'll carry him if we hae to." Tomag, Niall and Malky were standing firm.

"Be it on your heads then," the Englishman said, walking off. "If he falls behind he'll get this through his throat," and he made a jabbing motion with the pike.

Tomag said that it would be a forced march without rations and encouraged the lads to stuff their pockets with as many foraged leaves as they could. "It will give ye something to chew on and keep yer mouth moist and will stop you stomach frae shrinking." Tomag had survived two famines and told of men who had gorged themselves on the new grain and died in agony of the flux, while those who had eaten sparely to eke out what they had, survived to tell the tale.

Tomag had sent Malky to talk to one of the English guards and asked if they could take the plaids of some of his fallen comrades, whose bodies were piled up not far from where they stood. The young Englishman was about the same age as Malky with a pockmarked face, and worried eyes. He seemed to hesitate and then Malky said that the Lord would see him as a Good Samaritan if he helped his fellow Christians in need.

"Are ye a Presbyterian?" the Englishman asked.

Malky said he was, 'praise to the Lord'.

"I'll look the other way if you're quick about it, but if an officer comes I'll have to yell at you to leave off."

Tomag and Niall went to work while Malky kept watch, and they returned quickly after their grizzly work, each carrying an armful of plaids. That night in the sodden field, Malky shared what was left of his mother's now solid porritch and bannocks with Niall and Tomag and their cousins Davey and Dougie – the cousins both looked fearsome and cold and fell on the food as though starved. They all gave their thanks, and this small act of generosity by Malky sealed their friendship. They wrapped the plaids of their dead comrades around them and it helped to keep out some of the damp and cold, when they sat back-to-back on the ground and tried to sleep.

Long before dawn they were roused to their feet and told to piss and shit and ready themselves as they would be moving off. They could hear the sound of tramping feet ahead of them and were then moved on themselves. As they left the fields and reached the way, they had to wait until they could take their place in the long column, whose width depended on the width of the trail. As soon as it was light, and they were marching through open country they realised that their escort of mounted dragoons were few in number. They were given no food and water. The intermittent drizzle helped to moisten their lips but when they halted for a break, which was not often, some fell to their knees to lap up water from the puddles in the muddy track. But not the highlanders. They were used to long treks and going without food or water. The bitter leaves they chewed spared them the worst pangs which the lowland Scots were suffering. They would occasionally see one of the dragoons galloping off after a prisoner who had made a run for it, but the chase was usually a short one, and they would then hear a pistol shot as the prisoner was killed. Many still tried when they were passing through woodland or past hedges where they could slip away without being noticed. Once again Tomag warned them against trying their chance.

"We were north of here two months ago when Leslie learned that Cromwell was on his way. We burned or spoiled anything that was growing in the fields and every beast, pig or sheep was sent north for slaughter. The country ye'll need to cross will be like a desert, and ye'll find nae welcome from any of the folk who still live there and survive on what they hid from us. And even if ye manage to walk far enough, ye'll be spotted as a highlander because of your plaid and turned over to the English, who will no doubt give a bounty for your heid."

They marched all day and then on into the night. They could hear mutterings around them, and every so often the sound of feet running into the fields and bushes as many made their escape. The guards could do little as once the escapers had left the road, they had no chance of recapturing them in the pitch black. Malky was the one who suffered most as he was not used to long marches, but if he slowed down, a push in the back from Niall or Tomag would keep him going. Those that fell by the wayside, and who were not helped up by their mates, were either kicked to their feet by a dragoon, or, if that failed, had a knife through the throat to put them out of their misery. Big gaps appeared in the column as groups of men ran off, and the guards would occasionally call a halt to push men forward to keep the marchers compact. It seemed that they had been walking as long in the night as in the previous day, but at last they heard shouting ahead and saw the great walls of Berwick by the light of the torches held by the town's garrison. Red coated infantrymen stood on each side of the road and the column was halted. They then very slowly walked through the town gates and were tolled as they passed through. They went along a wide way until they reached the Market cross where four streets met. They sat on the ground weary and exhausted as town folk came round with pails of water from the public *pant*. They were allowed to drink their fill. Malky had managed to find a space on the ground with his back to the wall of a house and had just closed his eyes to sleep when the Berwick infantrymen started kicking the Sots on to their feet.

"It's nearly dawn and you've got another good march ahead of you," shouted a sergeant.

There were mutterings, and then a group of about thirty men, all lowland Scots and not happy at being ordered about by the king-killing English, stood out from the rest. Their leader was a tall man, with an educated air about him.

"We've marched for miles through the night, with ne'er a scrap of food. We're all exhausted and we're not gangen further until we've been fed and rested." He gestured to his followers and they all sat down. "We'll not move until we're ready."

There were more mutterings among the throng of Scots prisoners.

Niall whispered to Tomag. "We should join them, Tomag. If we all stay doon, they'll no' be able to do onything."

Tomag put his hand on his brother's shoulder. "Just ha'd on a sec, Niall. Let's wait and see."

It was good fortune that they did. The Sergeant shouted out orders and a squad of infantry ran forward with their knives out. The Sergeant grabbed the tall man who had spoken by the hair and slashed his throat open. His men followed suit and the thirty seated mutineers were done to death and left in the Market square as the rest of the prisoners marched on without dissent.

After another two days of forced marching with only a few hours rest at Wooler, they reached Morpeth. They halted at a farmstead outside the town and were allowed to drink from the water troughs before filing into a walled field. After taking their first mouthfuls, and then being hurried on, Tomag motioned to the others to hold back. They slowly mingled back into the waiting men and managed to have a second drink from troughs that had been filled up again with fresh well-water. They heard shouting and the sounds of fighting from the field and an irate farmer was angrily waving his arms and wagging his finger at the officer in charge of the column. When they walked through the gateway into the field they saw men who had been starved of all food for days savagely biting into raw cabbages. They had been put into a cabbage field – not all the cabbages had full heads but they were being eaten roots and all. Tomag once again took charge and guided them as quick as they might to the far corner where there were fewer men fighting over the greens. A group of highlanders sat on the ground by the stone wall with a small heap of the vegetables they had pulled out of the ground. They were chewing slowly away at the green leaves, without the desperation of the lowland Scots. Tomag spoke quietly to them and they said nowt when he bent down and picked out a couple of heads. He knew some of the men, and they were happy to let the five lads share their cabbages – Tomag would return the favour in the future if he could. They spread their spare plaids over the wet ground and sat down. There was more noise as the remnants of the column came into the field and fought with those who had arrived first for a scrap of a leaf or a piece of earth-covered root. The English soldiers left them to it.

Tomag looked round to make sure that none of the English were nearby, then reached into his shirt and pulled out his scian doo, which he had hidden under his armpit, tied with a short cord round his shoulder. Niall did the same and the two of them used their little black knives to slice their cabbages very thinly. They carefully put their knives back and then handed out a small portion of the raw leaf to Malky, Davey and Dougie. "There's nae need to gobble it doon," Niall said to Malky. "Naebody will tak this away frae us. Chew it for as lang as ye can. Ye'll get all the goodness oot, and it won't lie heavy on your stomach."

"Do we eat the roots as weel?" asked Davey.

Tomag sniffed at the earth-covered root. "Smells of shite," he muttered. "I've heard of farmers putting night soil on the ground. As we canna wash them clean we'll only eat the leaves." They stopped the chewing well before they felt full, and would eat what remained the next day.

They were used to being woken whilst it was still dark, and they were herded back out of the field before the dawn.

Malky had heard noises during the night, and the raw cabbage was having its effects on those who had gobbled it down half chewed, roots and all. Some were vomiting and some were squatting to let a watery shite out of their arseholes. They were marched slowly past the troughs so that they could take water. There was just a faint light in the sky as they left the Morpeth farmstead. Malky had taken the chance to speak to one of the English soldiers. At first he said nowt, but after Malky had quietly asked again, and he had looked around to make sure that none of the sergeants were nearby, he whispered that they would reach Newcastle that day and then it was the last march to Durham. As they made off, Malky told Tomag and the others what the lad had said. Davey looked up at Tomag and asked him what they would do to them when they reached Durham.

"I hope they'll feed us first of all, and gie us a chance to recover from the lang walk. They'll most likely press us into their own army and send us to fight somewhere. I've heard of other highlanders being sent to Ireland."

It was not what the lads wanted to hear. They had all been happy to fight the English, but had expected to return home with coin in their pocket after they had been victorious.

They had not gone far when the first men started falling down. Some were dead before they hit the ground. Others were spewing from both ends. They were dragged to the side of the road by the redcoats and left to die in the ditches, but the column marched on. Most of the plaid-coated highlanders were not affected, but even some of these were afflicted by the flux and left behind. Davey pulled Niall's arm and pointed back to where a prisoner who could not go on was being run through with a pike. Those still on their feet as they marched through the Newcastle city gates were a sorry sight, their minds as worn by the death of so many comrades, as their bodies by the relentless pounding of their feet. The rain had fallen constantly that day and they were all drenched through. The Newcastle town-folk at first jeered at the defeated Scots as they paraded through the streets, but then fell silent as they saw the state that they were in. Some fell in the streets but they could not be left to die there, and the soldiers had to carry or drag them to the great church of St. Nicholas where the prisoners would be housed overnight. Water butts had been placed outside the church, but there was no food and they spent a restless night shivering on the bare flags. Malky still had some cabbage leaves to chew and they all huddled together beneath the great arches. None of them had ever seen a kirk so big. They did not sleep much because of the groans of the sick and the overpowering stench of the watery shite that was soon running across the stone floors. The English had them filing out in the pre-dawn dark. It took time as there were hundreds who either would not, or could not move, and who lay in their own filth. Sometimes you could not avoid them and had to trample them rather than fall yourself. The soldiers were reluctant to touch them and so they were left where they were. Once outside the steady drizzle was half welcome as it washed the stench away. They were able to relieve themselves against the great walls while the column formed once more. It was a slow march to Durham as many fell by the wayside and many more only managed if supported by their friends. The plaid-clothed highlanders now marched together and most had escaped the flux so far.

The steep way up the hill to the castle and the cathedral finished off those who were already weakened by the flux and was a trial for those who weren't. Dougie, the youngest of the little band, needed the strong arms of Tomag and Niall, and with such help as the exhausted Davey and Malky could give, to reach the top and to sink down on the ground outside the cathedral which was to be their prison. It was now an empty and disused edifice after the powers of the bishop had been taken away and the clergy who were suspected of having royalist sympathies had been chased from the town.

They were assembled and tolled through the great door and into the freezing cold, cavern-like interior. A dozen braziers had been put along the walls and those first into the cathedral ran to them and stopped any heat from carrying to anyone else. The prisoners settled themselves where they could on the cold stone slabs. Some of the covenanters started to say psalms but they were largely ignored. There was no glory to God in this place. The night seemed endless to the starving men, and once again those with the flux lay in their own filth. Some did not wake up and it was not till the third day that any attempt to take away the dead was made. The soldiers refused to touch the bodies in case they were infected themselves, and the prisoners who could stand were forced to carry or drag the corpses to the great door where pressed townsfolk lifted them onto hand carts and took them away. There were so many afflicted that an officer was called to the gaol. On the morning of the fifth day all those with a fever and who were vomiting and fouling

33

themselves were carried out of the cathedral and taken to the castle where a makeshift hospital was set up.

At Malky's estimation more than half who had come through the doors had either died or been taken to the castle. Those remaining were, in the main, highlanders. Even some of those suffered the bloody flux after the first cauldrons of broth were carried in and ladled out. There was rarely enough to go round and the cups of greasy tepid broth were quickly drunk, but often, came as quickly back up again. Once more Tomag insisted that they took theirs slowly and chewed any lumps of gristle thoroughly. In the evening loaves of hard bread were laid on a bench by the door but the English guards let them fight over it. If you had money or valuables then a guard would take what you had in exchange for a loaf of bread or a pail of coals. Once this became known, the lads on their own were robbed of anything that might pass as currency including their coats, trews, if not spoiled, and boots, and left half-naked. None came to their aid.

A young man, a lowland Scot, who was clearly alone, came over to where Malky was sitting and asked if he could sit down beside him. Malky just shrugged his shoulders. He was a sorry specimen. His greasy locks spilled from under his bonnet and his pale face was scarred with old pocks. He was pale and as skinny as a rake. He was small of build and had sloping shoulders and thin arms. He had avoided the flux as he had been too weak to fight for any food. "Have ye taken the Covenant?" he asked. Despite his forlorn appearance his voice was deep and strong.

"Aye," said Malky, "and little good it has done me. I only came as a clerk to ma Da' but I was put into the dragoons as I spoke the Gaelic, and they needed messengers for the Highland troops."

"Hamish Bruce," he replied. He did not get any further as two men in plaid who had been eyeing him and Malky set upon them suddenly. Malky managed to push his own opponent away and Niall was quickly by his side, but Hamish had little chance against the burly fellow who was pulling his victim's coat off and punching him hard every time he resisted. The smaller man had given up on Malky, and now joined his friend in stripping the clothes off Hamish, who cried out piteously for help. Despite Niall's hand on his shoulder and shouts of 'leave him be, Malky,' the lad's temper was up and he ran forward, kicking the man who had attacked him ferociously in the head, and leaving him lying on the cold slabs spitting blood. The burly highlander who now had Hamish's coat in his hands moved quickly to fend off a blow that Malky had aimed at him and stood to face the young lad.

"Ye'll wish ye'd nae done that, laddie. Leave this ane to me," he pointed to Hamish, "and I'll de ye nae harm."

Malky just rushed at him. His speed caught the bigger man unawares and Malky had him in the back-hold – his chin resting on the other's shoulder, one arm under the man's left armpit the other over his right shoulder and hands locked.

"The back-hold," shouted Tomag, who now stood beside Niall and whose presence kept anyone else from joining the fray. "Oor Malky's the makings of a good highland laddie." Malky had wrestled with the other lads at Kinloch and there

35

were not many who could beat him. He soon had his opponent worried as he held him tight while kicking him in the ankles. He then stamped his right heel hard on the ground, moved his left foot forward and pulled upwards, taking the feet from under the other man, who was soon wheeling round, helpless in Malky's grasp. Malky then heaved with all his strength and the man looked set for a fall on his back. At the last minute, Malky jerked his enemy hard sideways and upwards, unclenched his hands to change his grip so that he held the man upside down and then smashed him head first onto the stone paving. There was a loud crack as the man's skull split and brains and blood spattered the floor where the man lay dead. There was a shocked silence and then Malky grabbed Hamish who had retrieved his coat, and with Tomag and Niall hurried them away from the dead body.

"Weel done, Malky," said Niall. "You're a heid breaker as weel as a heid slicer." He looked at Hamish. "Ye'd better nae upset this ane."

Tomag had chuckled at Niall's words, and Davey and Dougie had smiles on their faces for the first time in a long while as they shouted out 'Malky the heid breaker'. As they sat together away from the dead body that would lay there until an English soldier made the rounds looking for the dead or dying, Tomag said to Malky, "Ye canna save them all, Malky. This is not of your making."

The harassing of the weak went on and some of the more desperate broke into tombs and catafalques to rob the dead, only to let the pestilential humours spread into the already noxious air. Any wooden screens or pews that had not already been taken by the townsfolk were broken up using any loose paving slabs and used as fuel.

Malky lost all track of time in the cathedral gaol. Tomag and the highlanders already knew a few words of Scots and Malky was teaching them more. Although they did not know where they were to be sent, they were certainly not going back to the highlands. Hamish became an accepted part of their group. He had worked as a servant for a *pothecary* in Stirling. He had shown an aptitude for the work and his master had started to teach him his letters so that he could learn more of the trade. One night his master had taken in a travelling Covenant preacher as an act of charity – the man had spoken so vehemently of the duty of all able-bodied men who had taken the Covenant to fight against the king-murdering English, that his master had sent Hamish away the next day to join the local volunteers who were to march to Edinburgh. He said it was wrong of him to keep a lad like Hamish working in his business when he could be fighting for the cause.

The flux showed little sign of easing, but as more died or were taken away to the castle hospital their conditions improved. They managed to have a cup of broth or a piece of bread most days. But then their guards started bringing in milk which was boiled with flour, and giving each prisoner an equal measure. It was meant to stop the flux, which it did, but it also filled their bellies without making them puke or shit.

There was a group of half a dozen lowland Scots who had banded together and would fight off any who came to rob them of clothes or food. They sat just beside the highlanders. On a day, which they were told was a Sunday, they said together a psalm that they knew. Malky was touched by their diligence when they were in such a piteous state, and after a few moments he joined in with them. When their devotions were over, the lad sitting next to Malky gave him a friendly smile. "Ye speak the Scots as weel as the erse then."

"Aye. I was brought up in Blairgowrie. My father's a Covenant minister and we live in Edinburgh noo." Malky paused and looked down. "Or did. I dinna' where I'll end up. I'm Malky Dalgleish."

"Alec Duncan frae St. Monans. We all worked at the salt-panns, and went to the Covenant kirk on a Sunday. The Minister said it was oor holy duty to gang and fight the English wi' General Leslie."

Over the next few days, the two groups became friends. It turned into good fortune when one of the English guards asked if there were any weavers or salt workers. The General wanted some men to be sent up to Newcastle and Sheels to work in the trade there.

"Will we be freed?" asked one of the St. Monans lads.

The Englishman laughed. "You'll be sold as indentured workers. The General needs to get some money back for all he's had to spend to feed you. But at least you won't be sent to the colonies."

Malky had already asked Alec about his work in the panns and had learned enough to tell his highland friends that it was work they could do, and if they were sent to Sheels they might be able to get back to Scotland.

A call went out later that day for weavers, and a dozen men were chosen. The next morning, after they had had their morning milk and wheat porritch, another call went out for salt workers. The St.Monans lads stood up, and so did Malky and his friends as well as some others. They were all marched outside and counted. There were thirty-two.

"We need forty," shouted an officer and one of the soldiers went inside and another eight were pressed into the group.

They had a small escort of dragoons, and were then marched off down the hill, over the bridge and on the road north. This time there were supplies on pack mules and they were not forced on as they had been on the march from Dunbar. They were allowed to halt for rest and food every few hours, and they stopped as night was drawing in at Monkwearmouth in the abbey church. They had beer to drink and bread, boiled bacon and pease pudding for their meal. After a breakfast of porritch and cold bacon they headed north through the flat country. Their destination was clear to see as the black clouds of smoke hung in the air over Sheels.

Alec held his hands over his eyes and then said, "Weel, lads, I reckon there must be more than a hundred panns for that much smoke to be up. Ye ever shovelled coal, Malky?" Malky just shook his head. "Weel, laddie, ye soon will."

St Hild's Church 1760

CHAPTER TWO

They halted at the small township of Harton. There was an ale house by the road with the sign of the *Ship* where the officer watered his horse at the trough. Two good horses were tied to the side of the house. The prisoners were allowed to take water from the public fountain while the officer entered. A servant came out with a tray holding cups of ale for the foot soldiers. Not long after, the officer himself appeared through the front door accompanied by two prosperous looking men, well clothed with heavy wool cloaks to keep out the biting wind blowing from the sea.

The prisoners were assembled and the officer called out to them.

"These men are two of the pann-owners, Mr. Coatsworth and Mr. Milbourn. They will lead us into Sheels and you will be taken to St. Hild's Church where you will be quartered until the pann-owners decide between themselves which of them will take you on." Malky turned to his highland friends and translated the officer's words into Gaelic. One of the pann-owners was watching and spoke to the officer, who told him that some of the highlanders spoke only the Gaelic and that the lad with them would translate. The man dismounted and then walked to where the Scots prisoners were standing.

"Which one of ye is the English speaker?" he asked politely, and Malky stepped forward.

"We call it Scots," he half muttered.

The man laughed. "I am Ralph Milbourn. What's your name, lad?

"Malcolm Dalgleish."

"And how many of ye speak only the Gaelic, Malcolm?"

Malky pointed to his friends. "All those who wear the plaid. But they all know a few words of Scots and I'm teaching them more."

Milbourn looked them over. "Ye all look half starved. Will ye be able to work?"

Tomag asked Malky what the owner of the panns was saying. They had a short conversation and Malky then said, "We were marched for days without food and received little enough when we were held prisoners in Durham. But as highland Scots we willna' shirk work, provided we are fed properly, and have the Sabbath as a rest day."

"I'll try to get some of ye in my panns, and then ye, Malcolm, can tell the others what they have to do, until they've picked up the language."

Malky just nodded and passed on the words to his friends. He had noticed that the man spoke with a deep nasal voice, and that his way of speaking was different from that of the other English soldiers.

The way took them through a village called Westoe where they left the road and were led along a narrow track through fields. The pann-owners led, and they all walked either one or two abreast. The thick black clouds of smoke were now nearly overhead and were being blown inland by the north-east wind.

"We'll nae see the sun if we have to work there," said Niall who was just in front of Malky. They soon came to a burn, and the path they then followed led them to a mill pond with a large building near the bank which held the mills. They could see the rush of water as a sluice had been opened and they heard the sound of the wheel turning. As they passed the large stone building they saw donkeys turning a gin through the open doors of the part of the mill nearest to them.

"Ach, they have a horse mill as well as a water wheel. They must have a muckle of grain to grind," shouted Tomag over the sound of the water and the wheels.

"So let's hope there's soft bread for the salt workers," chimed in Niall.

Their spirits rose somewhat until a young lad who was loading baskets of flour onto donkeys jeered at the marching men as they passed by, and then picked up a handful of stones that he threw at those at the back of the column. Some of the prisoners whelped in pain, as the missiles struck them. The officer halted the column and rode back with the pann-owners. A big man with black hair, bushy eyebrows, and a thick moustache had come out of the mill and shouted to the man to stop. He wiped his hands on his floury smock and walked up to the mounted men. He stood not far from Malky who could make out much of what was said.

"Ye should keep yer lads under control, Cuddy Blackburn," said Mr. Milbourn. "If they harm any of these men so that they canna' work the panns we'll be after ye for compensation."

"Weel, ye'll get nowt from me. Young Jackie Jobling meant nae harm. He'd got a temper that's all, but his fatha' lost his work in the panns when the Scots soldiers turned them all ower, and smashed them when they left. Jackie was lucky that I could *tyek* him on here." Malky was to learn later that the Scots under Leslie had taken Sheels in the civil war, and had all but destroyed the salt-panns as they left, so that they would not compete with the Scottish salters. "And if ye put all these men to work in the panns and send up more smoke then I'll be forst in line at the Vestry court to ask for damages from ye and the rest of the panners. When the clouds drop we can hardly breathe and me flour gets full of black specks. Some of the farmers roond here are gannen to the mills at the Deans and at Cleadon where the air's cleaner, instead of coming here where they should."

He looked the prisoners over. "There's some strapping lads here. Are ye taking them all for the panns or can others tyek one on?"

"General Haselrig's asking twenty pund a man," replied Milbourn. "But that's for a seven-year indenture. We're getting back on wor feet noo, and I'll be putting in more new panns mesel', so I think we'll need most of them. But there's nowt to stop anyone else in the toon taking one. We'll be sorting it all oot at St. Hild's tomorrow."

The miller grumbled under his breath and walked back to his mill and the column moved off.

There was an unsteady looking wooden structure passing as a bridge in front of the sluice gates, which took the path over the mouth of the stream that led from the Tyne to the mill dam. The horse riders dismounted and led their steeds carefully across the bridge which had no rail. The soldiers then pushed and shoved at the prisoners who were told to watch out, as many of the planks were rotten and most were loose. As the first of them reached the other side, they stood round and waited until the others had crossed. It gave Malky and his friends a chance to take in their surroundings. To the west were the chimneys of a multitude of salt-houses that now took up most of the river bank as far as they could see. The thick black smoke slowly curled up into the air. Outside each saltern there was a well with a pump, and sheds and storehouses. On the other side of the narrow way there were cottages and hovels where the salt workers lived. Alec Duncan, the St. Monans salter, was standing by Malky. "There must be hundreds of them, and the salt-hooses are much bigger than the anes at St. Monans. We're gonna' be working oor ballocks off, Malky."

On their side of the mill dam there was a quay, where a ship was unloading its ballast into *wains* that would take it to the ballast hills. The river itself was full of moored ships. They could also see *keels* coming down the river loaded up with coals which they would load onto the colliers. They could see more smoke coming from panns on that side of the dam, but they could not see the salt-houses themselves as they would be further downriver, past the houses that were built along a winding way that ran along the river bank.

The path they then took was steep at first, and narrow, muddy, and rutted. It wound up to a small stone Church. "St. Hild's," cried out Mr. Coatsworth. They all went into the church and stood on the stone flags behind the private pews.

The Curate was expecting them and talked to the officer and the pann-owners. He was a tall man of youngish appearance, but with an arrogant sneer on his long face and tight-lipped mouth.

Not long afterwards a table was carried into the church and the Vestry clerk appeared carrying paper, ink and quills. "Come up to the table and give your names and your home settlements," called out the Curate. "When your time is served we do not want you to be a burden on this parish and you will be sent back to your home town or village. We will also need your occupation before you joined the traitors' army."

Malky translated the Curate's words for Niall and the others. "What language is that?" the Curate cried out. "We shall have no heathen tongues in the House of God."

Malky called out, "We are nae heathens, Minister. I am a Presbyterian and my father is a Covenant minister. I was brought up in the highlands and speak the Gaelic. I was translating your words for my highland friends who still have difficulty with the English."

The Curate was livid. "Well, I will not have it in this church. And you are not to address me unless I ask you to, young man."

Malky just stood there while Tomag and Niall sniggered.

The prisoners went up one by one and gave their names and addresses. Malky took his turn to stand at the table and gave his address as St. Giles, Edinburgh, and his occupation as the son of a minister. The Curate said nowt and Malky turned to leave, but stood just back from the table. He doubted whether the clerk would understand the highlanders' Gaelic version of their names.

"Go back to your place, laddie," said a clearly irritated Curate.

"I can help your clerk with the Gaelic…" He had no time to finish as the Curate shooed him away with his hands. He just turned and walked back to where the prisoners all stood. Tomag was now at the table. When asked his name he replied "Tomag Deòireach".

The clerk looked up bemused. "Could ye say it again, more slowly, please?"

Tomag looked over his shoulder at Malky who just sat stone-faced. "Tomag Deòireach Mac Niall Deòireach," he shouted faster than before.

The Curate looked towards the panners who were trying to stifle their laughter, turned on his heel, and headed to the Vestry at the back of the church. "I have better things to do," he muttered in a whisper that could be heard by those standing at the church-doors, and then called out, "You take all the names Mr. Ashburne, and then we can start on the indentures."

The clerk looked imploringly at Malky, who stared back stony-faced.

Ralph Milbourn walked over to where Malky was standing, grabbed him by the arm and marched him back to the table where Tomag was standing. "Noo, Malcolm, we're not all like the Curate here. He's known for having a poker up his arse. Would ye kindly help Mr. Ashburne so that your friends' names are correctly written doon."

"Aye, of course I will, since ye ask me sae politely. I'll gie him the Scots version. It's Thomas Dewar, Mr. Ashburne."

"And where's he from?"

"Invergarry."

"Ye'll need to spell that for me."

Malky did.

"Ye can read and write then, Malcolm lad?" asked Mr. Milbourn.

"Aye."

Milbourn said no more. The others came up and Malky gave the Scots version of their highland names.

Later in the day two servants from one of the inns in the High Street wheeled up a hand cart with two large cauldrons and flat cakes of bread. One pot contained *dograve* cooked in milk and onions, the other boiled cabbage. The Scots piled the white fish onto the bread and wolfed it down but no one touched the cabbage - the prisoners did not want to be poisoned again. The soldiers had no such reservations and heaped their bread high with the fish and the cabbage. They had ale to drink, but later in the evening they all had great thirst as the fish had not been steeped long enough, and water had to be fetched from the church well for them to quench their thirsts.

They were up early the next morning and given porritch, and bread and honey, with light ale to drink.

The church soon filled with salt-pann owners and others from the town, most coming out of curiosity, some hoping that they might find a servant if there were more than were needed for the salt-panns. Tomag turned to Malky and whispered, "It's like a cattle mart, laddie. We're being sold off like beasts." The Curate and the clerk came out of the Vestry and took their places in front of the altar. The clerk had a pile of papers in his arms which he placed on the table in front of him. "The indentures," called out the Curate.

There was the sound of horses from outside the church, and then one of the soldiers who was standing at the door called out, "It's the General's son."

A moment later the officer called the soldiers to attention as Sir Thomas Haselrig walked through the doors. The eldest son of the Governor of Newcastle was a young man in his early twenties, and dressed richly, but the older man who accompanied him wore sober black cloth. They were both greeted warmly by William Coatsworth and Ralph Milbourn who walked them down to one of the front pews. As they passed Malky and the highlanders Milbourn gestured to them and spoke into the ear of Haselrig's companion. He was of stocky build with a weather-beaten face, and the air of a man you would not like to cross. As Malky would later learn he was Isaac Frost, who had been a sea captain, but now owned half a dozen ships, salt-panns and a quay. He lived at Biddick Hall where Thomas Haselrig had stayed last night.

It was Isaac Frost who began the proceedings. "When we approached Sir Arthur and told him that we were in sore need of servants to work the salt-panns he agreed to supply us with forty men. We agreed to pay twenty pounds a man with an indenture for seven years. For any of the Scots who look more like boys than men we will only pay ten pounds. All coin to be given to Sir Thomas on the conclusion."

The clerk, Mr. Ashburne, spoke. "I have the indentures and have inscribed the name of each prisoner on a blank form which will require the master's name and the signatures. In the time available I only have one of each and would suggest that I shall keep the indentures here and if any dispute should arise then the Vestry court will determine it."

"Agreed," called out one of the pann-owners, anxious to get on.

"I would first wish to deal with the three highland men and a boy, who speak the Gaelic only. They have a companion who speaks Scots and Gaelic and who could translate their master's words into their own tongue. It would make sense if all five were to work at the same panns." He paused a moment and then called out the names. "Malcolm Dalgleish, Thomas Dewar, Neil Dewar, Davey Finlayson and Dougal Fraser, will ye come forward."

Wee Dougie looked small and frail besides the other four.

Ralph Milbourn stood up and looked them over. "I shall take Malcolm, and Thomas and David. My good friend Isaac Frost has three panns next to mine and we share a quay. He will take the other two, Neil and the boy Dougal."

The clerk took the indenture with Malky's name on it and wrote in Mr. Milbourn's, then placed it in front of the lad and handed him the quill. "Make you mark, lad, and be quick about it," said the Curate who had clearly not got over his irritation from the other day. Malky took the paper, held it up and started to read it, mouthing the words quietly. The Curate made as if to snatch it away, but Malky stepped back. "Ma father always said that ye should read over any contract before ye sign." He scanned the sheet, now carefully reading the words out aloud. It was a short form only, and stated the servant was bound to the master for the term of the indenture. In return for the servant's hard labour and good conduct the master would

50

feed and house him. There were mutters of slavery from one or other of the Scots. "The length of the indenture is missing," he said and himself wrote in 'seven years'.

"I was not sure of the agreed term," said the clerk, "I will fill them in as we proceed."

Malky signed, and then the Curate and the clerk witnessed, adding the sealing wax. All the others made their mark in turn as their lives were made over to the salt-panners of Sheels for the next seven years. Those that had signed were placed into two groups - one for the South Sheels and one for the North. Thomas Haselrig then took the clerk's place at the table as each of the pann-owners came forward with their money pouches and paid their coin.

The men and lads destined for North Sheels were marched through the town, first along the High Street and then on the narrow ways down to the toon-end, as it was known. There were houses crammed together in courts and alleys up the side of the hill they called the Lawe, and on the river side were the salt-panns as well as all manner of workshops and sheds, serving the river trade, and quays and landings for the sea-going fishing boats and cobles. Fishing had been the main industry in Sheels before the salt-panners came along.

Some of the women hoyed their piss pots out of the upper shuttered windows on to the heads of the prisoners until the soldiers who were accompanying them threatened them with their muskets. The ferry man had been forewarned and had the ferry boat and the horse boat ready for the prisoners and for the mounts of the salt-pann owners. The rest who were destined for panns in South Sheels were taken by their new masters.

Most of them were walked back on the way they had come and across the bridge at the Mill Dam on the way to West Panns – the name given to all the land occupied by the salt-panns that ran along the foreshore westwards from the Mill Dam. There was a narrow track between the salterns on the one side, and houses on the other, and which led to the Lay Gate. There were ballast hills on the landward side and the salterns stretched all along the river bank as far as Jarra's Lake, pumping out their black smoke which hung in the air.

Malky and his friends were taken in the other direction and along the way into the High Street, and then along the narrow and winding Low Way, until they reached the panns which their masters owned.

PART II

CHAPTER THREE

There was a cold wind off the water as the Scottish prisoners trudged along the riverside way. There were some quays with ships tied up for loading or unloading, and the workmen and merchants looked curiously on as Malky and his highland friends followed their new masters, who were on horseback. Mr. Coatsworth was no longer with them as his panns were on the west of the Mill Dam away from the town. The path was narrow and winding, as houses and workshops had been built with no great pattern or plan. The road widened out at a crossroads into a Market Place as it joined with another from the south. They then followed the High Street with tall houses on both sides. The town's constable greeted the salt masters, as they passed his house.

"They the Scotch prisoners for the panns?"

"Aye, we'll work them hard so I doubt if they'll be any trouble," replied Isaac Frost.

The constable looked at the Scotch lads and brandished his stave. "And if they are then I'll give them a taste of this, and lock 'em in the pillory for a day."

They continued down the High Street and then the way narrowed, and once again became winding as it skirted alleys and courts, some backing onto the river, others up the bank on the landward side. As they rounded a corner they saw the salterns on the open river bank. There were as many as fifty or sixty salt-houses, each holding one or two panns. On the other side of the way were big houses built of brick or stone with slate tiles. These had been the homes of the sea captains, merchants, and wealthy townsfolk – some of the salt-panns had been built on gardens that led to the river bank. Many of these houses were now occupied by the pann-owners.

The tide was low and the shore-line that may have been sandy once was now flecked with the dust of the coal smoke that blackened everything. Large pools of river water, called sumps, were held back by rough mounds of rock and sand, with pipes taking the water into wells near the salt-houses – low brick, stone, or timber and daub buildings with board roofs. As the Scots lads would find out the longer houses held two panns. Dense black smoke pumped out of the chimneys at the rear, or on the side of the salt-houses. Quays and wharves with store houses and sheds were built alongside the salterns. In the distance the highway continued on between old houses crammed together, and on to the toon-end where the fisher folk lived in cottages and houses in streets, alleys, and courts, some along the foreshore but most up the bank.

They halted by the panns where they would work. A keel was moored at the quay and the keelmen were shovelling the coal out of the boat into large wooden barrows. Two men were struggling to push one of the barrows to the salt-house and to keep up with the keelmen who had already nearly filled the second and were shouting aggressively for them to hurry.

"What ye're waiting for lads?" shouted Ralph Milbourn. "That's my coal." Malky translated the words quickly to Tomag and Davey.

"My two can help an' all," called out Isaac Frost. Malky waved Niall and Dougie on with them.

Niall and Dougie helped the two Sheels men, and with four of them on the handles they soon had it moving. It was not far to the salt-house, but then they had to tip the barrow up to empty it on to the heap in the opening on the side of the furnace-house which was in the middle of the two-panned saltern. Wooden shovels were on hand for them to scoop the last pieces of coal out. When Tomag and Malky reached the barrow on the quayside a keel man shouted out, "Weel, I've never seen a highlander in a plaid pushing a coal barra' before!" He had a broad Scots accent. Malky started to translate the words into Gaelic, but Tomag got the drift. Tomag held one of the handles as Malky quickly took the chock from under the wheels, but the barrow did not budge and even with Malky pushing they barely moved it. The keelman who had spoken to them jumped on to the quay and put his shoulder to the back of the barrow to get them moving. He then let them struggle on, and just walked alongside, as the other barrow had not yet been completely emptied.

"Oor job is to unload into the barra's. We canna' do yours as weel. Ye normally need three or four to get it moving, and to help unload. Each barra' holds half a *chaldron* and we carry six chaldrons a *tide*." He helped them again as they struggled to upend the barra', and then started back to the quayside with the empty truck as the five Scotch lads helped the Sheels men shovel the coal as far as they could into the furnace room.

"Are ye the Scotch prisoners frae Dunbar?" shouted another of the keelmen as they started shovelling the coal again into the barrow.

"Och aye, we are," Malky muttered.

"We heard ye'd be coming to Sheels. They'll work ye hard and pay ye naething."

A stockily-built middle-aged man with a red face and a heavy tash was standing by the coal heap. "Dain't hang aboot noo, lads. Ye'll soon get used to it."

"Mayhap," replied Malky, "but the red-coats kept us prisoners in Durham and only fed us slops. We'll need to be fed up to gain oor strength."

"Mr. Milbourn'll feed ye weel. I'm James Jobling, in charge of these panns, and the ones next door. Noo get a move on." He had a slate-board in front of him on which he was keeping a tally of the barrows as each was emptied. "Organise yersels into two teams. One can push the barra's and the other the shovellin'. Ye can change ower after a bit."

Niall was breathing heavily and fell to the ground as they tipped the coals out of the barrow he'd been pushing. Tomag and Malky lifted him to his feet.

Mr. Milbourn had been watching the lads at work and could see that they were struggling. He walked over to his house and shouted something through the open door. Not long after he returned with a pail of ale and a half pint cup and put the pail on the ground beside Jobling. He looked at the tally board. "Let them have a cup of ale each after the next barra' and then after the next three," he said to Jobling, "it will help to keep them gannen'."

When Jobling gave them the nod Tomag was the first to dip the cup and drank it down with one swig. He went to dip it again, and James Jobling stayed his hand. "One cup only, lad, every three barra's." Malky was next and quaffed the ale gratefully. He looked at the board in front of the foreman. "Are ye counting the barra's?" he asked.

"Wye aye I am. The pann-keel carries six chaldrons and wor barra's hold half a chaldron each. Mr. Milbourn marks the slate up and I just cross each barra' off. There should be twelve."

The beer helped them through the task, and also drew the keel-men off their boat when all the coal was gone. "We've worked just as hard," shouted the skipper. Another pail was brought out and they all shared, passing the cup round.

The skipper of the keel was John McGilvray from Peebleshire. He had been working on the pann-keels for a good many years. Two *bullies* and a boy made up the crew.

"Ye'll be seeing a lot of me ower the next weeks. *Ance* the winter weather sets in we can't always take the keels oot so the pann-owners like to get stocked up."

"Sae if the bad weather lasts then we dinna' work?" asked Malky.

"Wye-aye ye de," said Jobling, "we get coals from collieries in Durham by pack pony. It costs mair but the coal burns slower, and after nine boilings ye'll have a lovely fine white salt that we can sell for nearly double the price when the sea lanes open again in the Spring."

"It's rare that that happens," chipped in McGilvray. "The coal-keels..." He stopped and looked out on to the river. A keel was coming downstream fast, piled high with coals held up by planks, and heading further down the river where waiting colliers were anchored. He pointed at it and continued. "They carry eight chaldrons and pile it up like that so it's easier to discharge into the colliers. Mind it's still hard work. A lot of those keels normally lay off in the winter anyway as the colliers won't risk the sea passage. Some do, but a lot of the keel men gang back to the borders or to Scotland for the winter.

"In the pann-keels we stick to the shore and we use oor *puoys* to pole the keel in the shallows. We also take *weys* of salt doon stream to the salt merchants and the fishers."

Niall was looking out over the river and watching the coal keels sail past – some were propelled by oar only but others had a single sail at the bow. He could see the crew on one keel standing on the deck, ready to use the long oar when they lowered the sail and started to move towards one of the colliers. "Och, that laddie's got a blue bonnet like oors, Malky," he shouted.

"Aye there's many a Scots laddie on the keels. Ma brither Angus is a skipper," replied McGilvray.

"It must be a braw life on the keels," muttered Niall.

"It's dangerous and it's hard," said John McGilvray, "but if ye like the outdoors, it beats sweating away among the coal dust for twelve hoors a day."

With the keelmen gone the Scottish lads were walked over to the big houses on the other side of the way. Isaac Frost had ridden away but a much younger man, who could have been chipped from the same block, stood beside Mr. Milbourn, who looked at Malky and said, "Ye and my two other servants will be lodging with me. The other two will stay with Mr. Frost's son, Lewis, he manages his father's panns when he is not away at sea." The other man looked sternly on. "I've explained to him aboot the Gaelic and he's agreed that Neil Dewar and Dougal Fraser will work in the same salt-house as ye so that they can learn the work, and some of the language. We'll swap two of my men who'll temporarily work for Mr. Frost in the salt-houses next door. A fortnight should de. But they'll still lodge in his hoose."

The younger Frost then spoke. "After what the Scots did to wor panns, I was against taking ye on but me Da' said that we had no option if we wanted to get the new panns working. If ye work hard I'll treat you fairly, but if ye give me any trouble ye'll get it back tenfold." He waited while Malky translated his words into the Gaelic – the lads had already got the gist from the tone of his voice.

"Do they have any other claes?" he asked Malky.

"They've got some spare plaids, but they're dirty with blood and mud."

"They wear nowt beneath the plaid roond their legs?" asked Frost.

"Naught," replied Malky.

Lewis Frost turned to Ralph Milbourn. "It'll be too hot for them stoking the furnaces with the top part of the plaid over their showlders, and if they take the plaid off they'll burn their ballocks when they turn roond to shovel the coal, as weel as giving the women a fright." He looked at Malky.

"Tell them to let us have the spare plaids. We'll get them washed and I'll set one of the tailors on to make some breeches for them. We'll then have the plaids they're wearing and see if we can make them into short coats."

Malky explained it to all to the lads who muttered under their breaths, but handed over the spare plaids. Milbourn took his three and headed them towards his house.

Lewis Frost called after them. "After I've fed these two I'll send them in, so Dalgleish can start on their lessons in English before they gan to bed."

Although Malky's home in Edinburgh had an upper floor, the highland lads had only known stone cots with turf roofs, one room, with no windows or chimneys, and an open fire. They looked worried as they entered the small lobby with doors on either side but followed Ralph Milbourn into the kitchen. All the family including the servants and indentured labourers usually ate together at the long table with benches at either side. The central chimney stack divided what had been the great hall and Mr. Milbourn and his wife and children would retire into the parlour on the other side of the house after their meals. Steep wooden steps led up to the rooms under the eaves where they would sleep. The Milbourns had a four-poster bed, but the others slept on wooden pallets with a sackcloth mattress filled with straw. Three women were in the kitchen.

Mrs. Milbourn was a large woman with a sour face who scowled at the Scotch lads, but said nowt and carried on chopping apples at the table. Three young children were sitting in the ashes in the open hearth. A stout woman with fat rosy chops, who seemed to be in charge of the cooking, was stirring a large pot which hung from a rachet hook hanging from the oak beam over the hearth. As well as the open fire, there was an oven built into the wall of the fireplace. A young lass dressed in a black pinafore with a white apron tied round her middle was grating a large loaf of bread. All three women stared at the three Scots.

"These are the new servants," said Ralph Milbourn. "They're indentured to me and we'll feed and lodge them."

"We were expecting them, and I hope ye'll not regret bringing these savages into wor home." There was bitterness in Mrs. Milbourn's voice and it was obvious that she had made her views known before, but Milbourn took no notice.

The cook seemed to side with her mistress. "We dain't want the salt workers in here during the day, Mr. Ralph. They shouldn't be here before six o'clock when they finish their work."

"Aye, weel, it's their forst day, and they've been hauling coals. I'll have some ale, pet. And the lads will take some if there's enough."

The cook muttered something. "Well if they're staying here they can get oot my way and keep themsels to themsels."

The young lass went over to the back of the room and the lads followed. A barrel was on a trestle under the steep wooden stairs. She used the tap to fill a pail and dipped a pewter mug for Mr. Milbourn. She then filled a large earthenware cup into the beer and handed it to Malky. "That's for the three of ye'se, and ye'll only get one mair with your dinner."

"Ye'll normally eat your meal when you finish your work at six o'clock, but today ye can eat with us at four," said Mr.

Milbourn, who drank deeply of his ale.

The sharp ale and the smells of the cooking were putting a keen edge to the lads' hunger, and they said little as they waited to be fed. The grated bread was stirred into the broth stewing in the pot, and the small apple pies that the mistress had made were fried in butter in a large pan after the cauldron was ratcheted up to make room.

Malky always remembered their first meal. As they sat on the benches, the master at the head of the table clasped his hands together and gave the prayer of grace. "Gracious God, we have sinned against Thee, and are unworthy of Thy mercy;" Malky knew the words by heart as this was his father's favourite grace before the meat, and he started saying the words half aloud, "pardon our sins, and bless these mercies for our use,". Milbourn looked up and opened his eyes to see who was joining him but continued the prayer, "and help us to eat and drink to Thy glory, for Christ's sake. Amen." The cook ladled the pottage into a large bowl that was placed before the master. He spooned it out into wooden bowls that were passed down the table - the broth was brown and thick, with onions and neep and the meat of small birds. There were some whole larks. The master picked out two for his own bowl and used the pewter spoon to cut the others into halves so all would have a taste. His wife cut thick slices off the loaf that was in front of her and handed it round.

When everyone was served Ralph Milbourn said quietly, "We dain't normally talk when we're eating, but I'll make an exception for ye lads. Malky, ye can tell them the English words for what they are eating and it'll help them to learn the language." The thick pottage was followed by the fried apple pies and then bread and cheese for those that were still hungry. All the Scots lads helped themselves. When all had had their fill, the master looked at Malky.

"And now we'll have the grace after the meal. Wor new servant Malcolm can do the honours." It was a challenge, said half in mischief, but Malky stood to his feet and said the grace, as he had done many a time at home in his best Scots, "Blessed God, in Thee we live, move and have oor being; make us thankful for Thy mercies; and as we live by Thy providence, help us to live to Thy praise looking and waiting for a better life with Thyself above, through Jesus Christ oor Lord. Amen," and then repeated it in Gaelic, surprising them all. Malky had done as he had been asked, but in his own mind, he was not sure if he wanted to thank a Lord that had put him and his friends through so much pain and woe. He could not but help remember the agonies and despair of the young covenanter on the battle field, who he himself had put out of his misery.

The Milbourns left to go into the parlour with the children, but the bairns all sneaked back in under the common stairs at the back of the room. They wanted to see and hear more of the new servants with their quaint ways, and they were soon trying to teach them English words. The cook, Jenett, mainly ignored them, and sat in a low chair by the fire mending some of the children's clothes with needle and thread. The kitchen lass, Peggy, had cleared away the table and was in the open scullery at a deep sink, washing the pans and dishes. When she had finished she too sat with the Scots men and took a particular interest in young Davey who was about her own age.

He blushed at first as the lass tried to talk to him, but was soon taking sideways looks at her and making her blush in turn. Even the war-hardened Tomag was smiling at the children's antics, and trying his best not to frighten them when he would shout out an English word in anger as he had difficulty in saying it.

Davey and Dougie were good looking lads and would have the lassies chasing after them. They were both different in complexion from Tomag and Niall who had sandy hair and hazel eyes, as did most of the other highlanders in the regiment. The lads' hair was black and wavy, their eyes brown, and their skins dark and swarthy. Malky joked with Niall that Davey seemed to have made a conquest and mentioned his dark good looks.

"Aye, it's nae secret. His Granda' was a Spaniard. Ane of their warships was wrecked off the coast years ago during the great gales, and the survivors came ashore. Most of the folk there were Catholic, and nae supporters of Elizabeth who had cut aff the heid of oor Queen Mary so they took the Spaniards in and gave them shelter. Some of the lairds sent their men oot to hunt them doon and kill them, but they didn't find many. An auld crofter with nae sons but only *dochters*, took in the lads' granda. He had been a soldier and was a strang man who worked hard. He married one of the dochters and took over the croft when her Da died. The lads' mothers are his dochters and take after him - and so do Davey and Dougal. Aye, there's many a black-haired highland laddie noo."

They heard a knocking on the door and Mr. Milbourn went to see who it was. Lewis Frost came in followed by a small man dressed very smartly with a big blue cloak wrapped round him to keep out the cold. He had a young lad behind him who wore only breeches and a jacket with holes in the sleeve and whose teeth were chattering. The lad was carrying the plaids that they had given to Mr. Frost earlier, and he also had some plain clothes folded on top of the plaids.

"This is Jan Gerritson, the tailor. He says the plaid cloth is good quality. He will clean it up himself."

"It is too good a quality to cut up into pieces to make breeches," the little man said. "I will exchange it for some that have seen a little wear," he coughed as though embarrassed, "and whose owners have nae mair need of them."

He looked at Tomag. "You're a big lad. I'm not sure the ones I've brought will fit you. Let's sort the young'uns oot forst. Take your plaids off, lads, and we'll see what we can do." He looked at Davey first and then took a pair of trews from his young servant who was inching towards the fire.

Jenett looked at the lad. "Ye look froze, hinny." She got up from her seat, took the clothes from the lad's arms and pushed him down to sit on the ashes in the fireplace. "Ye should clothe your servants properly, Mr. Gerritson, young Dicken has always been a bit frail. It was good of you to tyek him in when his poor mother passed away, but she wouldn't have let him gan oot in the cauld like it is the neet."

The tailor took no notice and was trying a pair of trews on Davey. The tailor had not realised that he only wore a short shirt under the top part of the plaid, and when he saw Davey's wee man sticking straight out in front, he'd quickly turned him round and shoved him further under the stairs. The lass Peggy had not missed it and blushed a deep red. Tomag laughed heartily and nudged Malky in the side. It was an old story often told round the fire of a long winter evening about the auld highland warriors who found that the full plaid kept getting in their way when they were fighting, and so they took them off, running at the enemy wearing only their shirts with their loins bare to the wind, and putting the fear of God into the foe at the sight of the gruesome weapons between their legs.

The trews were too big but Gerritson took his scissors out and a needle and thread and soon had them fitting as they should. He then fitted out Dougie and Niall. Tomag, however, took one look at the trousers that were meant for him and shook his head, and then talked quickly to Malky. "He says he'll no' get into those, and he's not used to having his ballocks squeezed tight in trews anyway. Can ye no' cut the top of the plaid off and he'll just wear the bottom, wi' a belt roond it to keep it up."

It was the work of a few minutes, then Tomag spoke again. This time for a bit longer. Malky turned to the two salt-pann owners. "Tomag says that with all the plaids you've given the tailor, you should have more in return than some deed men's trews. He says they'll also need a coat that will keep them warm and not freeze like the young lad."

"Ye'll be bringing them some coats then, Mr. Gerritson?" asked Lewis Frost.

"I'll have to see what I can do with the plaid," was all he said.

Tomag then snatched the top part of his plaid that Gerritson had taken and threw it over to Dicken. "Put that roond your shoulders and tuck it in your belt. It'll keep you warm until your master makes you a proper coat," said Malky translating the highlander's words.

Mrs. Milbourn had come through from the parlour with a bottle of wine and poured out three glasses for the men. She looked at Dicken huddled in the ashes. "Bring the boy a cup of ale, Peggy."

"Aye and I'll cut a slice of bread that we can toast on the fire and he can dip it in the ale. That will warm ye up, Dicken."

They would be up at five, and Peggy the maid an hour before, so Niall and Dougie left to go next door with Mr. Frost, and the others trudged up the stairs. There was a pit out the back at the top of the garden with planks over it for them to shit, and they had a piss pot in case they needed it at night. There was a common well further up the bank which the houses in the row shared, and where they could wash in the morning if they wished to. They all shared the one pallet.

Jenett and Peggy slept in the kitchen and would wake every so often to keep the fire going. Jenett banged on their door at five and they got themselves ready as best they could by the light of a rush-tallow torch. They went down to the kitchen and found Jimmy Jobling standing by the hearth with a cup of ale in his hand. Peggy poured them out a cup each as well, smiling at Davey as she did so, and then she went back to pouring some foul-smelling fish blood onto a bowl of oatmeal.

"It'll taste better than it smells by the time we put some onions and some herbs in it," said Jenett. "Peggy'll bring it ower aboot nine o'clock for your breakfast. There's nowt like an oatmeal pudding to keep ye gannen. Ye'll get ale during the day but nowt else to eat until ye get yem at six the neet, so get as much doon ye as ye can."

"Is there any hot watter for a shave?" asked Malky. "We've all nearly got beards noo. We've only got one razor between us and it'll need a sharpening." It was only Malky who had the razor. The others used their scian doos, but they kept them hidden under their armpits and did not want the English to know that they kept them there.

"Give us a look," said Jobling. Malky pulled out his razor. It was a small blade in the shape of a tiny axe head welded on to a short metal stick. Jobling ran his finger along the edge. "There's not enough time noo as we need to get the furnaces lit. There's a sharpening stone in the salt-house, that ye can use and ye can shave tonight. If ye want to have a shave in the morning then ask Jenett to put a kettle on for ye and get up a few minutes early." He finished his ale and got a small shovel from the hearth and carefully put some red-hot coals into an iron pail, with a dirty rag wrapped round the handle. He handed it to Tomag.

"Let's get a shift on before the handle gets too hot. Ye, Malky, carry that one," he pointed to a wicker basket full of chopped wood. "That'll be one of your jobs the neet, to chop up the kindling wood. And ye, Davey-lad, grab an armful of straw."

They went out of the warm kitchen into a cold and blustery November morn. "There's always a cauld wind off the Tyne, me lads." They hurried across the way and into the fore-room of the saltern. Niall and Dougie had come out of the house next door and were just behind them. None of them, apart from Malky, had coats, but they would soon warm up. Another lad about Malky's age was already there.

"That's Walter," said Jobling. "There's three men to a pan. Walter's been raking the ashes oot. That's the job for the first one in." The fore-room, where the coals were shovelled into the furnaces, was in the middle of the saltern and stood between the two rooms that housed each pann. The furnace doors were in the bottom of the walls that separated the fore-room from the two boiling rooms where the panns stood. The dividing walls kept the coal dust and smoke from getting into the brine.

"Here, I'll show ye the panns. There's two in this hoose but we've only been boiling the one, but noo ye're here we'll do the two." He took them up a short flight of stairs, through a door into the boiling room to the left. He put his rush and tallow candle into an alcove and it shed a dim light.

"There's only one torch allowed in the boiling hoose and it stays there – we dain't want any ashes flying aboot and contaminating the brine. When it's light we open the winda's in the roof a bit if we need to do any work in here. The roof's made of boards, and the nails are wood – metal nails rust away in a few weeks once the boiling starts."

The iron panns were huge – twenty feet long and twelve feet wide, and a good fourteen inches deep. The one they were inspecting had a good layer of thick white brine in the bottom. "We started this one yesterday. We boil the watter doon to less than a quarter, seven or eight times till it's thick and ye can see the crystals forming. The first part of the boil's on full heat, but then we simmer it gently so that the crystals are fine. This one's had five boilings – we'll get it gannen and then fill it again twice more before we let it set and take oot the salt. The other pann is new and hasn't been used yet so we'll fill that up as weel and then start the boiling." He turned and called out the door, "If ye've finished raking oot the ashes, Wally, get doon the street to the butchers and fetch a pail of blood."

Tomag and Niall looked at Malky who then said, "Ye're no' making mair *poudin's* for us, are ye?"

Jobling laughed. "Naw, ye needn't worry, lad. We put it in the watter when it first boils to clear it, and then we skim off the scum. One of ye'll have to help me with it."

Jobling first showed them how to fill the panns with sea water from the cisterns. They always kept the cistern full for a while so that any mud or sand could settle, and then they would open the spigot so the water would run down the trough that passed through the saltern wall and into the pann. There was a cistern by each of the boiling houses, and both were filled from the sea water pits by a pump. The first pann had been boiled down so that there was only a few inches of a thick brine in the bottom. Jobling first topped up the pann which already had the thick brine in, by turning the spigot on the trough and letting the sea water flow until the pann was full. He then took them down the steps and across the fore house to the second pann and repeated the process. Once that one was full as well, Jobling took the lads back into the forehouse so that they could light the fires under the panns. Davey and Dougie would get the wood and the straw burning with the hot coals from the bucket they had brought in and Tomag and Niall then took over the fireman's job of shovelling the coal into the furnaces at either side of the forehouse until the coals were glowing red. They then went back into the boiling houses. Jobling shouted

71

to Walter to keep the coals topped up as they needed a good heat for the boilings. The water in the panns was still just luke-warm and the Scots lads watched while Jimmy Jobling carefully poured three ladles-ful of the black beast blood into the first pan and stirred it round. As the fires from the furnace started to heat the water and make the odd bubble appear, a thick scum slowly appeared on the surface. Jimmy let it boil awhile and then went to the back of the boiling house wall and took two long wooden paddles. He handed one to Malky and then with each of them standing on the walkway on either side of the pan, they slowly moved forward holding the paddles so they met in the middle and skimmed off the scum. They then trooped across to the other boiling house and Tomag and Niall did the same with the other pan. After two or three skimmings the brine was clear.

Now that the panns were bubbling away, Jobling let Walter show them how to rake the coals carefully around the brick support in the middle of the furnace which was called the mid-feather. This not only supported the pan but helped regulate the heat. Once the first rapid boiling started to subside, the briny water only needed to simmer gently.

Their spell in the boiling houses had left them soaked through with sweat, and with condensation from the steam. Tomag and Niall were to do the first shift as firemen keeping the furnaces going at a steady burn. It was also necessary for the coals to be raked every so often. If the firemen wanted a spell, or were needed in the boiling house, then the two younger lads, Davey and Dougie, would do it. Raking was not heavy work, but your face and arms took the full blast of the blazing coals. If you raked too fast you might get some red-hot ashes on you. The firemen worked in a small enclosure in front of the furnace. The usual shift was four hours and then two others would take over. When they weren't firing the furnaces, one would be outside on the pump filling up the cisterns and the other would carry the coal baskets, which Dougie filled, from the coal heap to the furnaces. If there were any lumps of coal that were too big they'd be broken with a pick. One of them might be needed in one of the boiling houses to help Jobling or to keep an eye on things if he was away in the other saltern, so they were kept busy.

Malky was the first to be sent outside with Walter who would show him the pump so that he could refill the cisterns. It was hard and backbreaking work as each heave on the pump handle would only project a quart or so of water and the panns needed gallons of it.

"They should get a gin and some donkeys like they have in the West Panns," muttered Walter who was spelling an exhausted Malky, "but they have ranks of salterns ower there, all owned by the same pann-owner and they're pumping all the time. Here with only two or three panns it's cheaper to use a man that they pay six pennies a day to break his back."

They pumped in all weathers. Today there was only an icy wind off the Tyne, and Malky could only imagine what it would be like with rain or snow.

Every so often they'd walk over to the cisterns and climb up the steps at the side to lift off the cover to check the level. When the two cisterns were full, Malky and Walter went back into the forehouse – from the icy cold to the hot and dusty. One

73

of the other lads would do the pumping next time and Malky would have a full spell at the furnace.

The sky was beginning to lighten when the door opened and Peggy came in with two pails.

"Bait time," said Jobling. "Noo, before we eat, we need to rake ower the coals and make sure they're burning evenly before we have wor break. Let the two lads do it, they'll have to get used to it. Take it steady, lads," he called as Davey and Dougie did the raking. Jobling was standing by Dougie who was the smallest. "Put some back into it, lad, ye've got to reach the back coals as weel," he shouted.

Dougie was exhausted, and as he gave one big push his left knee gave way and he fell forward. He would have gone head first through the furnace door had not Jobling leapt forward in a flash and pulled him back by the shirt tails. There was a silence. Then Tomag grabbed the rake that Dougie was holding and finished the raking for him. He said nowt but his face said it all. Jobling looked to Malky.

"Tell your mates that I dain't like seeing the young uns work like this any more than they do, but they've all been bought and paid for and they'll have to get used to the work. Come on, let's have some pudding and ale."

There was one large tankard and after he had taken a swig Jobling passed it round. They all drank deeply. Peggy had brought some bowls, but not enough for everyone and some of the lads had to share. The pudding had been cooked in a cloth and Peggy cut it into large chunks which she deftly put into the bowls. The pudding was black, thick, and juicy with onions and herbs. They used their knives and hands to eat and little was said until Davey shouted out, "What's this?". He spoke in English, holding up a little juicy fruit and Peggy laughed. "It's a raisin. Jenett lets me hoy a handful in if she's got some to spare."

It was then back to work. Jobling would go in to the boiling rooms every now and again to inspect the panns. When the first pann had boiled down enough to Jobling's satisfaction, he took the three oldest lads in to the boiling house so they could see.

"It's thick and you can just see one or two crystals forming. We'll fill it up again with fresh watter to do another boil today, and mebbees just start another. In Sheels we do seven or eight boils before we draw the salt. This pann might be ready tomorrow so we can let it settle owernight and then draw the salt the morrow." He pointed to four small iron pans in each corner. "Once the fresh watter's half way up we tyek oot the scratch pans and get rid of the scratch. It's white earth that comes up when the watter's boiling and we need to get rid of it after each boil or it taints the salt."

Malky took over the coal shovelling as the pann filled up, and his furnace was soon blazing away. He shut the door and wiped his brow while Dougie staggered over with more coal. Tomag had stayed in the boiling house with Jobling to add the blood to the pan when it was just lukewarm and helped with the skimming. They then checked the second pan and decided that it was ready for a second boiling. Niall was struggling with the stoking and was starting to cough, so he went out on the pump with Walter to help him, and Davey was asked to do the stoking. Dougie was unwilling to get too near to the furnace after his accident and kept bringing the coal from the heap to the stokers. He did his best but the work was hard, especially if he had to break up lumps of coal, and he was starting to sag at the knees.

They were all struggling by the end of the day. This time it was just them round the table as the family and the other servants had eaten earlier. They needed their dinner of *umble* pie. The cooked offal in gravy with onions and neeps, under a thick suet crust gave them back some energy, but after they'd finished they just sat at the back of the room worn out. They had little energy to do much, but Peggy came over when she'd finished scouring the pans and sat by Davey saying a few words to him.

They all woke the next morning with sore muscles, traipsed over to the salt-house and forced themselves to carry on with the work. The North wind was fresh and they all felt the bitter cold when they had to go out to the pumps after the heat of the fore-house.

Both panns had been filled up again with fresh water and were simmering away nicely when they heard a shout from outside. Niall, who was on the pump with Dougie, came running in. "It's John again with another keelful."

Jobling and Tomag came out of the boiling house. Jobling stood by the doorway with his tally board. The Scots lads and Walter walked over to the quayside and once the first barrow was full, four of them heaved it away and off to the saltern. Tomag and Malky just got on with it. Niall struggled a little as he had started coughing with all the dust from the furnace room. Davey pulled his weight but Dougie was soon sitting on the ground exhausted and panting. Their ale was brought out and skipper McGilvray and his bullies joined them round the pail when the work was done. He became quite pally with Niall and they seemed to understand each other. The ash clouds were slowly shifting in the wind and black specks were falling into their ale so they moved inside. John told them that he'd be coming down whenever he could before the sea lanes closed.

The next day started with only one furnace going as the other pann was ready for the drawing of the salt. Jobling got Tomag to help him with the work, while the others watched. The salt crystals had set and were a pure white.

"It's like sna'," said Malky as the others nodded.

"Aye," replied Jobling, "it's the finest white salt and the crystals are small. If ye salt fish or meat with that it will last for years. That's why Sheels salt is sought after." First Tomag raked the salt round, then he pulled it all towards the side of the pan nearest them to let some of the brine, still in the salt, drain to the other side. After another hour the salt was dug out and carefully transferred into the salt baskets they had brought from the store-house alongside the saltern. Malky, Davey and Dougie carried the baskets through the side door which was carefully opened and shut behind them, to stop any coal smoke from the chimney from entering the boiling house. Once in the store-house they lifted the baskets and tipped the still damp and hot salt into one of the *drabs*. The drabs were like horse stalls with loose boards at the front so salt could be taken out or put in. The bottom of the drab was built of boards that were step-like with the board at the back higher than the next one and so on. This was done so that the brine still in the salt would drain away until the salt was completely dry and could be taken away for shipment or sale. There was a draining hole in the bottom board and the brine that came out, the *bittern*, ran into a trough that, when full, was lifted up and poured into a cistern where it was stored. It was a long job as Jobling told them that a Sheels pann could produce about fifty-six bushels of salt, just under a ton and a half. An excise man had been sent for and he fixed a seal to each of the drabs once it was full. "They de that to make sure that nae salt evaporates before the weighing when the excise is paid," muttered Jobling bitterly.

The Milbourn and Frost panns did not boil on the Sunday. The owners were both devout non-conformists and would not work their men on the sabbath. The Saturday was often a short day if salt was to be drawn as there was no point in starting a new boil, but there was always some work to be done. The bittern that was not taken away with the salt would harden on the iron pann, and needed to be chipped away from the iron after every three or four drawings. This was a job for the younger lads who would clamber into the pann when it was cold and loosen off the hard bittern, using mallets and iron chisels until the pann was clean.

On their first Sunday, the Scots servants all declined to attend chapel. It had been mentioned a couple of times. The highlanders were all Catholics and weren't going to betray their faith. Malky had no love of the God that had failed to keep his covenant, and now that he had the chance of a new life before him, even one that would start in servitude, he did not want to return to the old ways of the kirk. The chapel that the Milbourns and Frosts went to was in the High Street. It was no more than a room in one of the large mansions which the owner, himself a non-conformist, had converted, after Parliament had allowed freedom of religious expression. Mr. Milbourn told the lads that they were free to do what they wanted but must return for dinner at two. He would be entertaining the Frosts in their parlour and there would be roast meats. The servants would eat in the kitchen as usual.

It was a miserable cold day with a biting wind off the German Ocean and squalls of rain. With no coats to speak of and no cloak between them, they said they would just stay in the house. They needed the rest in any case. Jenett was not best pleased. She was busy with the roasting of fat beef over the open fire, with bacon and veal on higher spits. She and Peggy also had puddings and pies to make.

After their breakfast of *hasty pudding* with raisins and honey, they left the benches and sat under the back steps. Although the fire was blazing away in the hearth, there was a cold draught coming through the windows and the lads were soon shivering at the back of the room. Davey ran upstairs and came down with their blankets – they looked a sorry sight. Jimmy Jobling called in for a cup of ale. He took off his cloak in the lobby and shook off the rain. He had been down to check on the panns.

"Can ye not find them some work to do, Jimmy," grumbled Jenett. "They're making me feel cauld just looking at them. But I cann't have them near the hearth, not on a Sunda'."

"Couldn't one of them turn the spit for ye?" Peggy heard, and said very quickly, "That would be a help for me as well. Davey could do it."

"But there's still the others. And I think they'll be sending the two from next door in when Mr. Frost gans oot to chapel." Jenett put her hands on her hips and then went over to the big wooden dresser. She opened one of the drawers and took out a small leather pouch. "I got the raisins for next to nowt off that Molly Hawes – dain't ask me where she gets them from." Molly Hawes was the widow of a young fisherman who had been lost at sea. She was a big lass with a big gob, and had started hawking fish and whatever else she could find since her husband had perished.

Jobling laughed. "Weel, they say there's plenty of raisin trees roond Frenchman's Bay."

"Anyway, I have a few pence to spare." She counted out two half *groats*, a penny ha'penny and two farthings. "Can ye not take them roond to the *Orange Tree*. They can sip ale and keep warm and get oot from beneath me feet." The sign of the *Orange Tree* was just two doors down and one of the few pubs used by both the panners and the fishers.

Jobling took the pence. "D'ye not kna' that the Vestry court has banned pubs from opening on a Sunda' when there are church services?"

"Weel, tyek them somewhere else." Just then the door opened and Mr. Milbourn came in wearing his Sunday best, followed by Lewis Frost with Niall and Dougie in tow. "I canna' tyek any more, Mr. Milbourn. Jimmy's gan to tyek them off me hands 'til dinner time. I've even had to raid the housekeeping so they can have a cup of ale somewhere with a hearth to keep warm."

"Ye kna' the pubs are closed during worship, Jimmy?"

"Wye of course," replied Jobling with a crafty look on his face.

Mr. Milbourn half smiled and took his own purse out. "Give Jenett back her pennies, Jimmy. Here's sixpence, and ale only. I'll not have them drinking liquor on a Sunda'," he said as he handed over the silver coin. He and Lewis Frost then left to ready their families for the chapel.

Dougie stayed with Davey and they took turns at the spit. It kept them warm and Peggy gave them milk to drink to slake their thirst. When Davey was looking after the meat, Dougie went over to the table and asked Jenett, half in words and half in signs, if there was anything to do to help. She was on the point of giving him some tongue, but he looked so forlorn with his dirty shirt hanging over the old patched trews that were too big for him, tied round the middle with his old belt, that she just smiled. "Aye come on then, lad, we need some neeps peeling and cabbages sliced, and then ye can help wor Peggy with the pastry for the pies." Davey thought he might have missed his chance in getting close to the lass, but on second thoughts he wouldn't want to be laughed at for doing women's work.

The others had followed Jobling out into the cold. They huddled together and kept as close as they could to the walls of the houses to get what shelter there was. As soon as they'd passed the salterns they entered the long row of narrow streets with houses on both sides and were spared the worst of the wind and rain. They passed the crossroads where a path led down to a quay and another up the bank by the ballast hills and then saw the sign of the *Turk's Heed*. Jobling walked past, and then turned quickly straight up a narrow alley by the side of the house. "It's Cripple Foot Lane so watch yer footing," shouted Jobling. The cobbles were uneven, and there were high steps every two paces or so that took you by surprise. There was a court by the rear wall of the pub and they went in. Jobling knocked with his knuckles three times on one of the doors. It opened only a fraction and he half whispered, "I've come for the prayer meeting." The door opened. A young fellow with a squinty eye hurried them in. "I kna' ye, Jimmy, but whe are these lads with no coats and shivering cauld?"

"They're me new panners, and I'll vouch for them," he said, handing the lad a farthing. The young fellow had a rush-tallow torch and led them down a dingy corridor with no windows and then opened the door of what looked like a store cupboard. He gave Jimmy the torch and bent down to pull up a heavy metal ring that opened a trap-door. A blast of hot air and smoke came up. He took the torch back. "Quick as ye like. Ye gan first, Jimmy, and help the lads to get their feet on the ladder." They went down in turn and found themselves in a long oblong chamber. There was a hearth in the middle with burning coals and two braziers at either end. There were no windows in the ceiling and the fires were the main source of light apart from two tallow candles on the walls. At the far end there was another trap in the ceiling which was just open half an inch to let the smoke out. There were a dozen or so men standing or sitting on benches by the walls with tankards in their hands. As they stood round at the bottom of the ladder, a short stout man with side-whiskers and a tash came up with two empty wooden pails. A rope with a hook on the end was lowered down and the lad upstairs pulled up the empty pails. "Ye better bring these back full up and another small one with London gin. Gie me a shout when ye're ready."

The Scots lads made straight for the central hearth and were soon rubbing themselves warm. Jobling paid for their drinks and brought over wooden tankards for them. "John Marledane owns the hoose. He used to sail as mate on the *Oswin*. He doesn't look much noo, but if ye give him any trouble he'll sort ye out all reet." The ale was dark and strong and they gulped down the first mouthfuls with nods of gratitude to Jobling. He knew most of the men there and soon wandered off leaving the lads to themselves. A few moments later the trap opened and the lad started dangling a small pail down. The landlord stood at the bottom of the steps as the pail swung unsteadily towards him. "If ye spill any of that gin, Squinty, I'll take a stick to your arse," shouted Marledane. Tomag handed his mug to Niall and walked over. He was head and shoulders higher than the stout publican and easily reached the pail which he lifted down and handed to Marledane. "Wye thank ye, lad." He took the small pail away and Tomag reached up and got the two larger and much heavier pails to the ground. As he carried the last pail over, Marledane said something to him. Tomag waved Malky over.

"Is he deef?" asked the landlord.

"Nae, he's highland Scot and speaks mainly the Gaelic," replied Malky.

"Tell him I'll not dole him oot any ale noo, or all the other buggers'll be clambering up the ladder to help me, but his next pint's on the hoose." He paused then said, "If he'll help little

Squinty with all the pails until we can open upstairs, he'll have free ale." Tomag had picked up the gist and asked Malky to say that he was happy to help. Jobling had been watching and came over to ask what was going on. He of course kept the purse strings and with the money saved he went on to the gin which came in half pint horn cups. They heard the bells from St. Hild's at noon and not long after, a runner came down from the church. Squinty shouted down the hole that the church was out and they could all come upstairs. Marledane went up first and Tomag lifted up the pails to him.

The others finished their ale or gin and climbed up, some more steadily than others. Then Squinty went down to douse the fires, close the hatch and take back up any empty tankards or cups. The drinkers would leave by the back door into the lane in groups of two or three, and then in by the front door.

The ale house had two rooms on either side of a central chimney. Settles were round the walls and benches and boards on trestles in the body of the rooms. The barrels were at the back and Marledane, Squinty and Marledane's wife served the customers. There was a large clock on a shelf over the fireplace and when it was nearly two the Scots lads stood up from the settle where they were sitting. Marledane saw them and came over with a cup in his hand. He gave it to Tomag.

"Your foreman, Jobling, has been spending the pennies ye saved him with your free ale on getting as much of this doon his throat as he can. Ye have this before ye gan. It'll keep ye warm on the way back." Tomag sniffed it, took a swig and turned his nose up. "It's not the *usquebah*," he muttered as the others all took a drink until the cup was empty. The gin was bitter and the taste of juniper not to the lad's liking. "D'ye ever get any usquebah?"

"Not in Sheels," said Marledane. "Ye'd have to make it yersels," he laughed. "Ye dain't have any cloaks then?"

"I'm lucky I have ma coat," said Malky, "but the highlanders couldn't work in their plaids so they had to give them to the tailor, but they only got auld trews in exchange. But it's not far from the hoose to the saltern."

Niall started to cough. The smoky atmosphere was not doing him any good. He mumbled something to Malky. "He says that they should have at least one cloak for the one who has to do the pumping outside."

Jobling had come over. His face was red and his words were starting to run into one another. "Weel dain't expect owt from Milbourn or Frost. They've not been making much since the Scotch army smashed their panns, and they had to pay twenty pund each for ye'se lot, so they're not gan to want to shell oot any mair for claes."

The rain had eased off but the wind was still biting, and they were glad to arrive back in the kitchen. Jenett and Peggy were both busy laying out the platters to take into the parlour, and Dougie and Davey were sitting on the floor of the hearth. The lads had to go the back of the room where they had shivered that morning, but it was not as cold now. Jenett had cooked a brisket of beef in a pot with onions and neeps, and the master and his guests would have the broth to start their meal with a sop of wheaten bread. When they had finished the broth, the roast meats were taken through with a plate of cabbage cooked with onions and beef dripping. The master would carve the beef, and the meats would stay on the table until they had eaten their fill. Jenett sat the lads round the kitchen table and ladled slices of the boiled beef with what was left of the broth into their bowls. They set upon it eagerly and mopped up what broth was left in the bottom with thick chunks of barley bread. Jenett had kept back some of the veal and the bacon which she had sliced up for the families in the parlour. She put the plate on the table and they all cut pieces off with their knives. Jenett then popped her head round the parlour door and called for Peggy to help her clear the plates away and then take in the sweet pies and custards.

There was still a good half of the roast joint and other meats, but this time Jenett carefully cut only a few slices of what was left over and put it onto rounds of barley bread. "I have to make sure there's enough for tomorrow's dinner. Me and Peggy'll be busy deeing the washing for the week. But not for ye'se lot," she laughed. "Ye're wearing the only claes ye've got."

The left-over pies and custards all but finished the lads off. Davey and Dougie helped the women to tidy away and clean the dishes.

The next morning John Marledane came into the forehouse as they were having their usual breakfast of oat pudding. He bade them welcome and handed over to Tomag a full-length cloak of homespun wool with many a patch. "It's an auld'un I've had for years. Ye can all use it when ye've got to work ootside. I've had a thought aboot the coats as well," he said looking in Jobling's direction. "Ye kna', the ship's masters all keep a *slops* chest with working claes for new crew. As they'll not be sailing for a bit, they might bc willing to lend ye some jackets for the lads, until Gerritson makes their coats from the plaid. I'll ask aboot. A pail of coals or a few cups full of salt would nae doot be very persuasive."

And so it turned out. But Lewis Frost was not happy with the lads wearing sailors' jackets as they would be the first to be taken if a press gang was sent in to recruit for the navy. Although they would normally stop ships coming into the harbour and take men from the crew on board, they would also send a gang into the streets and it was sailors they went for first. If it was a hard press they would take landsmen and boys too. Frost's harsh words to Gerritson did the trick and they soon had coats. Only two were from the plaid and Tomag and Niall had those. Gerritson had kept what he could of the fine quality plaid cloth for other clients who would pay good coin for it.

The lads were worked hard over the next months. The pann-keels only came down occasionally, and when a cross wind was blowing off the land they did not see McGilvray sometimes for a week or so. Pony trains of small coal started arriving from Durham collieries, and by burning the panns for longer, and at a low heat, they made the finest salt, that would earn their masters the fortune they expected from their panns.

CHAPTER FOUR

By December the Scots lads were just about managing the work. They spoke and understood enough words of English to get by, and Niall and Dougie now worked in one of the Frost's pann-houses next door. It only held one pann and Niall and Dougie did most of the work with a hand from Jobling when needed. They did not have to do any pumping as Frost had three panns altogether and a Sheels lad worked the pump for all of them. It did mean though that Niall was in the furnace room for most of the day and his coughing became worse.

Tomag had taken to salt making and would be the one who Jobling called through to the boiling house when he needed any work doing there. The big Scot seemed to understand the process, and when Jobling had to be in one of the other salterns he was trusted to do whatever was needed. Malky had suffered badly with chapped hands and lips as his skin was not as hardened as the highlanders' to the outdoor weather. Going from the heat of the furnace room to the freezing cold and rain when it was his turn at the pump made things worse for him. All that Jenett could do was to give him some fat off the dripping to rub on his sores, and he soon became Greasy

Malky to the rest of them.

The only good thing about the pump work was that it gave him a chance to see what was going on along the way. He would watch the comings and goings. He particularly looked out for the fishwives and hawkers who carried their wares in baskets on their heads, and whose hips swayed as they walked along. One in particular had caught his eye, a shapely blonde lass who often stopped at Milbourn's house to sell something to Jenett. It was that Molly Hawes who sold the raisins. One day, she had seen the young lad in a blue bonnet looking her way and had given him a wave, and now each time she passed and Malky saw her, he would wave back.

Wee Dougie was not cut out for the work. Although women were sometimes employed in the salt-houses to do the ash raking, they were often as strong as men, but they were also careful in what they did. Dougie was not the strongest of lads but he also lacked gumption. One day when he was giving Niall a spell at the raking, his rake caught against the side of the brick feather in the middle of the furnace. Instead of pushing it forward and easing it back, he pulled on it with all his strength and when it came out so did a chunk of burning coal. As he fell back the red-hot lump fell into his lap burning through the thin wool of his trousers. He screamed like a woman and used his hands to push the coal away from his groin, burning them as well. Niall was on him in a trice and pulled him to his feet, shaking away the red-hot lumps, but some small bits remained and they had to take the lad outside, pull his trousers down and pump the cold well water on to him. The screams and shouts had alerted the others and Davey and Malky had ran out to help. It was a poor, bedraggled, whimpering creature that they carried back to the Frost house. Lewis Frost was there when they laid Dougie on the table and inspected his wounds. His fingers were burnt but the worst burn marks were on his belly and his groin – luckily for him his wee man was unmarked, but all small and shrivelled up by the cold.

"The cauld sea-watter from the pump seemed to do him some good," ventured Malky. "Should I get some mair in a pail and we could dab him wi' that."

"It might help," said Frost, "but with a burn you really need some ointment as well. My father kna's a pothecary in Newcastle, but I doubt he'd want to spend any more coin on this arse-worm who's not even earning his keep."

"One of the Scots prisoners we got to know in Durham Cathedral was a pothecary's assistant and he came wi' us to Sheels," said Malky. "He would know what was needed."

Frost looked interested. "Well we dain't want his wounds to fester and have him die on us. Do ye kna' who bought him?"

Malky shook his head. "I'm not sure, it might have been Mr. Coatsworth, but I know that he went to the West Panns. His name's Hamish Bruce."

"Get these men back to the salt-hoose, Jobling, and keep the fires going as best ye can. Can ye manage all reet if I tyek Malky here with me? We'll see if we can find this pothecary." It was a statement rather than a question and Jobling just nodded. Lewis looked at Malky. "Run and get a pail of sea-watter from the pump while I get my horse saddled and we'll gan to the West Panns." Dougie was starting to whine pitifully. "Wrap him up and put him on one of the settles. Keep dabbing the watter on him and give him some ale to deaden the pain. If it does nae good ye'd better try the brandy, but not too much."

With Malky half walking and half running, Lewis Frost rode along the narrow way until he reached the High Street. At the crossroads he headed up the Salt Well Lane. As they passed the well itself Lewis Frost muttered, "It might be worth sending someone up with a pail to bring doon some of the salt watters from the well, they're said to heal all ills.

"Henry Ashburne lives just up the lane," he shouted over his shoulder. "He'll have the indentures and we'll kna' where we can find Bruce."

Ashburne was at home, but the indentures were in the Vestry. He was happy to take them there and they crossed the pasture field to the Church. He was a man of medium build with a soft round face with sharp eyes that were never far from a smile. He hid his bald pate under a hat that was pulled down over his ears. He remembered Malky from the sale at the church and chatted to him pleasantly. When he found Bruce's indenture, it was as Malky remembered, and Hamish had been sold to Coatsworth.

When they crossed the bridge by the mill dam, Lewis Frost dismounted and led his mount carefully over the rickety structure and they entered the West Panns. It was a biting cold day with an icy drizzle, but not much wind for once. The black smoke from the chimneys hung in the air and they were enveloped in a dark fog that was difficult to see through. West Panns was as desolate a place as Malky had seen. The salthouses, the storing sheds and their quays, covered the shore. On the other side of the way stood the cottages where the workers lived. Despite the cold, some women with children stood on the steps of their doorways. There were only a few shops, but several ale-houses where the panners slaked their thirst. There were no common wells, and the workers who lived there relied on the carriers to bring water on donkeys and to buy it at a pant. The water was carried by the women in *skeels*, large wooden pails, which they carried on their heads, and which cost a farthing to fill.

Malky could just make out men working a pump or shifting coal or salt in barrows. As they passed a long range of salt-houses all close together, he saw a donkey pulling a gin to pump the water.

"These are Coatsworth's panns," said Frost. "He has a dozen at least. I doubt if he'll be here himself, but he'll have an overseer." He dismounted and tied his horse's reins to a post. They walked down a narrow path along the side of the salt-house.

"They must have big panns," said Malky as they passed down the way to the side door.

"They're the same size as wor panns, but they have two of them in a line connected to each other. The furnace only runs under the first, and they boil the watter hard. The heat of the metal passes by conduction to the smaller pann, which is lower down. When the brine is ready, they let it pass from the first pan to the second by opening a spigot. It then simmers very gently, giving a fine crystal, and the first pan is filled up again from the cistern. They produce more salt and use a lot less coal, and the salt is of the finest quality. Most of the panns here are nowhere near as well managed, and produce salt with the crystals all compacted together. They mainly sell it to the fishers." They pushed open the door and entered the furnace room.

"I'm Lewis Frost looking for William Coatsworth or his overseer," he called out in a loud voice.

One of the men stoking the furnace nearest to them stood up and wiped his coal smeared brow. He was bare chested and his hair was lank with coal dust.

"Mr. Coatsworth disna' dirty his hands doon here." He spoke Scots.

"Are ye ane of the Scots prisoners frae Dunbar?" asked Malky.

The man came closer. "D'ye no' recognise me then, Malky."

"No' with all that coal dust ower ye, man. But I recognise the voice, Alec." It was Alec Duncan from St. Monans. "We're looking for Hamish Bruce, the pothecary's lad. Wee Dougie's had a nasty accident and has some burns that need attention."

"Hamish's the lad for ye then. He was not pulling his weight and some of the other men were picking on him and stealing his food – and some were deeing other things that I'll no' speak of. The overseer here's Big Rabbie Dunne. He disna' know much aboot salt making but he he's got fists the size of bull's ballocks, and he keeps the men working. He'd had one too many cups of gin one day and stumbled next to a pan. His left hand went into the boiling watter. Ye could have heard his screeches in St. Monans. Young Hamish who was in the furnace room came running. He was the only ane to help Big Rabbie and he made up some ointment with some plants he had been oot picking at Jarra's Lake. Noo he's under Big Rab's protection and if any ane lays a finger on him he gets a belting. He does a woman's work noo, raking oot the ashes, but he can read and write and Rabbie's got him helping with the tallies. He lets him have time aff to gan picking wort, and bark and sic like, and if anyone gets hurt or falls ill he looks after them, and Big Rab takes payment of some sort. If ye gang past all Mr. Coatsworth's panns ye'll find them in the salt store on the quay. We've had a good few drawings of the salt and the excise man is there to collect his coin."

Malky was loth to go after such a brief meeting. "Are ye allowed oot on a Sunday? Ye could cam and see us."

"We have Sundays to oor selves reet enow, but there's naething to do so we just sit by the fire, and keep warm. But the West-panners are not allowed in Sheels anyway. The fishers don't like the panners, and if they saw us they'd knock us senseless and hoy us in the river. There was so much trouble that the court banned us from crossing the bridge. But if ye're aff yoursel on a Sunday call in. We live in the cottages just opposite."

When they reached the salt store, the weighing had nearly come to an end and they stood just inside the doorways as the last bushel of fifty-six pounds was weighed and tipped into the wooden case that held the *wey* of salt. The lid was nailed shut and the excise man applied his seal. It would take two strong men to carry it to any wain or boat. Mr. Coatsworth's steward was there and he counted out the coin to the excise man, Henry Coultheard. He was a man of middle age, well dressed in a deep red dress coat and a heavy, blue fur-trimmed cloak. He had two stout servants with him both carrying heavy cudgels, who would guard him on his way back to the High Street in Sheels where the Parliament's Surveyor of Salt kept his treasury. Coultheard was in name, deputy, but to all intents and purposes, the head of the Sheels excise. After he had left, Lewis Frost walked over to where Coatsworth's steward, and his overseer, Robert Dunne, were standing. He was a big uncouth man just as Alec had described him.

"Good morrow, Mr. Frost," greeted Coatsworth's steward, who knew the Frosts, "how can I help ye?"

"It's probably Mr. Dunne who I should ask." He spoke quickly to Malky, "Is that lad Bruce?" and he gestured to the slightly built youth who was closing the tally books. Malky nodded. "One of my indentured servants has had a serious burning. Young Malky here, who is indentured to Ralph Milbourn, reckons that a Hamish Bruce who was imprisoned with him at Durham was a pothecary's assistant. We wondered whether ye might spare him for a couple of hoors so he can tend to Wee Dougie. He's little more than a bairn, and his whining will keep the whole hoose awake the neet if he's not tended properly."

"He's a good lad is wor Hamish for the burns," said Big Robbie, holding out his left hand and wiggling his fingers. "It's scarred but my fingers aren't all glued together which is what usually happens if you put your hand in the boiling brine." He looked over to the steward. "I'd like to help, and I'm sure so would Hamish, but the ash pit in the middle salt-hoose needs raking oot before tomorrow when we're starting a new boil."

"Is there not a woman in one of the cottages who could do it?" asked the steward.

"Aye. It would be two hours' work, with the adding of the bittern, so I'd have to pay her a penny ha'penny."

Lewis Frost pulled his purse up from his belt. "There's threepence. Ye can buy some drink. I've heard you're partial to the gin."

"He was," said the steward, "but no longer. He sticks to ale noo, dain't ye, Robbie?"

"Wye aye I do. I'm not gan' through agony like that again and Mr. Coatsworth put me on half pay when I could only use the one hand."

Hamish went over to the cottage where he lived to gather up what he might need. He walked alongside Malky with a leather satchel hanging from his shoulder. He was pleased to see his former friend, and they chatted away, giving each other their news as they walked behind Frost's horse. The horse waved its tail and a good dollop of horse manure fell to the ground. "Has your master got a cow for milk?" asked Hamish.

"Ach no, but a farmer brings some doon aff the church meadow and people take their pails in the morning." Hamish stopped and bent down, picking up a good handful of the steaming shit, wrapped it in a rag and put it into his satchel. "Cow dung is best but we'll have to make do, for noo." Malky's face must have given away his surprise at what Hamish had said. "Ach, dinna' worry, Malky – when it's dried oot, it makes a good poultice mixed with dock and nettle."

Malky was sent straight back to the saltern after they had arrived at the Frost house. Just before they finished their work, a lad came in with a message for Jobling. He was in the fore-house checking the coals in the furnaces before they left for the night. "What is it, lad?" he asked.

"Mr. Frost says can he have Malky again and another of the Scots if ye can spare them. The pothie..." the lad couldn't get his tongue round the word, "the healer's got to gan yem to the West Panns and he needs someone to guide him ower the bridge. It's blacker than pitch oot there with the fog. I nearly got lost just crossing the way."

They met up with Niall as they left the saltern, and told him the lad's words. Tomag's brother said that they should go on. He was still coughing and he didn't want to be out in the cold any longer than he could help. His nose was permanently running and his head would spin sometimes if he stood up too quickly.

"I'll gang wi' Malky then, but we'll need lanterns," said Tomag.

"Mr. Frost has them ready. They're auld but they give a good light. They're from Mr. Frost's last ship." The lad had not been exaggerating about the density of the fog, and they had little idea of where they were once they had left the salt-houses. They lost touch with the youngster and then walked into the wall of a house. A door opened further up the street, and they saw a dim light, and then heard a ghostly voice calling their names. They held on to each other and the wall until they reached the Frost house. Mr. Frost was holding the lantern.

"This fog is thicker than pea soup," he laughed. "I dain't think ye'd be safe oot the neet even with a lantern. Hamish can sleep here and ye can tyek him back tomorrow if the fog's gone." He sniffed at the air. "I can small a touch of sea – there's a breeze coming, so it should clear."

Although the fog had gone as Lewis Frost had predicted, it was still black night at half past five when Tomag and Malky set off with their lanterns to escort Hamish over the bridge and on to West Panns. He had washed Dougie's wounds with salt water and applied an ointment that he had brought with him and then bandaged the deeper wounds. He had made up a poultice with the horse dung but left it in the hearth to dry out overnight. When they washed the wounds again the next day they could apply it then. He would come back in three days' time on the Sunday to check the patient and Frost had said that he would be given dinner.

As they walked along the dark way, meeting the occasional worker on the way to the panns, Tomag asked if Hamish had noticed how Niall was suffering with coughing and head colds.

"It's the panners' sickness. I've seen a lot of it. The coal dust enters the nasal passages and inflames them, bringing noxious humours to the heid. And gangen oot from the heat of the furnace room into the cauld, will just make it worse."

He paused a minute, rummaged in his satchel and pulled out an eggshell wrapped in a cloth. "I hae to use egg shells to hold my ointments as I have nae pots or jars. I saw yesterday, Malky, that you have sores, and chaps, on your face and hands. Rub this on at neet and in the morning. It will sooth them, but ye'll have to live with it until the Spring. It's just your work, same as Niall, but in his case I have naething to give. If I could set up as a pothecary, and have a press for oils and a still for liquors, then I could make a balsam that would help, but the pann owners would have to pay. Mr. Coatsworth did mention it the other day as he was beginning to realise that my cures and treatments were keeping men working."

Tomag's ears perked up. "Ye can use a still, Hamish?" The lad nodded. "I miss the usquebah in this cauld weather and it would nae doot do Niall some good. I dinna like the gin they gie ye." The big Scot looked at Hamish. "Would ye know how to make a still for the usquebah?"

"Och, a still's a still – it's just the size that might be different. A pothecary still's quite small as you only want a small amount of liquor, but it all depends how much usquebah you mean to make."

"Ye cam early on Sunda', Hamish, and when ye've sorted young Dougie oot, we'll take ye for a wee walk to the *Turk's Heed*. There's a man I want ye to meet."

Malky missed the talk between Tomag and Hamish with John Marledane, but he had an idea what they were trying to cook up. Although it was a cold January day, there was a very weak sun in the sky and only a few clouds. He and Niall decided to have a walk along the riverside and take a look at the ocean. Niall did not want to go down to the smoke-filled hole under the *Turk's Heed*. He hoped some fresh air might help clear his blocked nose and head. Malky's sores on his face were not so red now after only a few days of Hamish's ointment, and he did not look so greasy. Every Sunday morning, they washed themselves out in the yard with well-water and soap that Jenett gave them. Despite the freezing cold they needed to get the coal dust off their skin and out of their hair. She only allowed them inside into the scullery when it was so cold that the water in the pail froze over and then she would heat some water over the fire.

As they headed down the Low Way past the last of the salt-houses the pathway narrowed. There were shops and inns a-plenty although most were closed with it being a Sunday. On the river side of the way there were alleys leading down to the quays and landings, and any number of sheds and workshops. There were some large houses where sea captains and merchants lived, and behind them, up the bank to the Lawe were many alleys and courts where houses were crammed together. As they neared the river mouth the buildings were smaller and older and there were more landings. This was where the fishers lived. There were a good few folk about, and shops and inns were open despite the Vestry laws. The constable rarely ventured this far away from the High Street.

Some of the sea cobles must have been out that morning as there were piles of fish on the ground and the fishwives were sorting them ready for cleaning and salting. Others were sitting on the ground with their children, mending nets and checking fishing lines.

The two strangers with their blue bonnets were getting some funny looks. The men's faces were hostile, but Malky's chestnut hair and youthful face, and Niall's golden locks and the dimple in his chin, were drawing sideways glances from the young lassies.

"Ye sure it was a good idea to come this way?" asked Niall. Malky paid no notice as his eyes darted everywhere, and then he pulled Niall's arm. "There," he half whispered, looking up a narrow alley leading off the way and up the bank. You could make out, just a couple of doors up, a big lass sitting at the bottom of some wooden steps, gutting fish. Malky walked over and started up the alley. "Och, I thought I might find ye doon here, Molly," he shouted.

The lass looked up. "And whe are ye?"

"Malky from Mr. Milbourn's panns. Ye sell fish to Jenett, his cook, and ye give me a wave when I'm ootside on the pump."

"Well I kna' Jenett, but I dain't recognise ye, all washed up and with nae coal dust on yer *fyece.*"

It was not the welcome that Malky had dreamed about at night but he kept on. "Sundays are the only time I have aff, and I thought we might have a chat or a walk oot if ye wanted to."

"Ye tark funny."

"Ach, sae de ye, lassie," said Niall, coughing and wiping the snot from his nose end.

"We're Scots," said Malky.

"Eeh, are ye those lads who were captured by Cromwell and sold to the pann-owners to work like slaves?"

A small crowd had gathered where the alley opened on to the way and there were murmurs when they heard what Molly had just said. She was known for her big gob and they probably heard all down the street.

Molly looked again at Malky. He was about her age but he had the look of a decent fellow, and not at all like the rough fisher lads who were only ever after one thing, and who she had to slap hard if their hands got too far up her skirts. Not many came back for more.

"Ma friend's heid's full of snot frae the coal dust and he needs to get some sea air, but we dinna' where the best place is to walk."

"Aye, he does look a bit cauld and weepy." She had still been gutting her fish as she talked and put the last one in the basket, kicking the innards with her feet on to the cobbles. "Did ye want to buy a fish or two," she asked.

"Ach, I'm sorry, Molly, I would, but we don't get any wages, just oor keep."

"All reet, Malky, I'll take a stroll with ye'se two but dain't get any ideas."

She wiped her hands on her pinny, stood up, and ran up the steps with her basket which she put inside the door on the small wooden landing, and then came down to stand beside the Scots lads. She was a good hand's width taller than Malky. He had not realised that when he had seen her along the way, but it made no difference. There was something about her that stirred his feelings. He could feel his wee man starting to swell inside his trews, and quickly tried to stop his mind thinking of what lay underneath Molly's pinny.

"I thought ye could show us the way to the Frenchman's Bay," he said as they turned out of the alley.

Two of the men, who had been listening to what Malky had had to say to their Molly, stepped forward. The one who spoke was not that much older than Malky but he was taller, solidly built with big shoulders, muscled arms and strong hands. Like most of the fisher men he had fair hair and blue eyes.

"And why d'yese want to kna' aboot Frenchman's Bay?"

Before Malky could say anything, Molly opened her gob. "It's nowt to de with ye, Georgie. Nor ye, Micky Coulson," she said to the other who was a strapping lad with light brown hair, twinkling eyes and a crooked sort of grin. "And young Malky's not the sort of man who would try anything like ye did, the last time ye caught me in the alley with me basket on me heed and not able to defend mesel."

There were guffaws of laughter. When a fish lass was walking with a heavy basket on her head, it was an old trick for a lad to take his chance to have a feel of her tit or her bum.

Malky wasn't sure what to make of Georgie or Micky.

"We'd heard aboot the raisin trees at Frenchmen's Bay and thought we could hae a look at them."

There was a silence. Molly looked at him as though he was daft and one or two others smirked.

"Raisin trees? What ye're talkin' aboot?" asked George.

"We'd never had raisins afore we came to Sheels and Jenett said she bought some lovely ones frae Molly. She thought they cost so few pennies that they'd come frae the raisin trees at Frenchman's Bay."

There was even more laughter. "Are ye simple or someitt?" asked Molly.

"Well simple or not, he's not ganna walk oot with me little sister, and get her under the raisin trees." Georgie had as big a gob as his sister and everybody was having a laugh.

Micky Coulson stood squarely beside Georgie. "Ye'll have to get past us, Scotchman." His voice was threatening, but Georgie pushed him back.

"This is my business, Micky, and if I hear any mair of ye putting hands on Molly then I'll start on ye next."

A big, old, one-eyed man, dressed in his Sunday clothes and with a thick cloak wrapped round him, stepped in between Georgie and Malky, who stepped back. "We'll have nae fighting on a Sunda', Georgie, and the pubs haven't even opened yet. Let him on his way."

George looked uncertain.

Malky realised, that as Molly's brother, Georgie was unlikely to back off now, and even if he did, he'd be there again when Malky came back to see Molly next Sunday, which he had every intention of doing. He glanced at Molly, but her face gave nothing away.

"Ach, I'll fight him for the way," said Malky, "we often had a wrassling match on a Sunday up in Blairgowrie. Ma hame in Scotland."

"Blairgowrie," said the man who stood between them. "Ye have come a lang way. Weel, we used to like a bit of sport on a Sunda', before the Vestry laid doon the law." He looked round. "But we're not too fashed aboot the Vestry laws doon here in the toon-end. Will ye wrestle him, Georgie-lad?"

"Wye aye, Captain Bowmaker, I will, and when I've finished with him, he'll have to crawl back to the panns and nivver show his fyece here again."

"Make a circle," shouted the captain in his foredeck voice. He looked at the two lads. "And tyek your coats off."

Before he did so, Malky spoke up. "It'll be the back-hold, mind. That's how I wrassle."

Georgie looked blank.

The Captain chuckled to himself. "When I was a fisher lad the keel men would sometimes row doon to the toon-end after they'd unloaded their coal if it was a still day. There was always a couple of pails full in the bottom of the boat, if ye could be bothered to sweep it up. They'd let one of the lassies do it and she could keep the coal in exchange for a salmon, or a few *harrain'*. They were mostly Scots and they would come ashore on the strand. They'd challenge the hard lads like George here to the back-hold. I gave it a try mesel' and even won a couple of throws." He unclipped his cloak and handed it to Molly. "Hold that, lass. What's your name, lad?"

"Malky Dalgleish."

"Reet, Malky, we'll show Georgie-lad the back-hold. Mind, I'm getting auld so we won't gan at it full pelt."

He and Malky stood in the centre of the ring the onlookers had formed on the strand, faced each other, and took their holds. Malky had not realised how barrel chested the captain was and only just grasped his hands behind his back. As Bowmaker rested his chin on Malky's shoulder he whispered in his ear. "Let me win the throw. It'll give Georgie some confidence. When you fight him let him win one throw – ye dain't want to make him look silly in front of his mates." Straight away he tightened his grasp. Despite his age he had a grip of iron and swung his opponent to the left. Malky's feet nearly left the ground, but he straightened his legs and moved so quickly, still to the left, that he could have swung the Captain round and down. Instead he let him steady himself and on the next move, he did not resist too much and felt his feet leave the ground as he swung into the air and onto his back. The Captain did not release his hold and his arms cushioned Malky's back. They stood up quickly and shook hands.

"That's not too difficult then, Georgie. Come forward. I'll be the judge."

When the two lads clinched, Malky had to stretch to get the grip on the taller man. He could feel the iron strength of Georgie's forearms on his back, but was not worried. He pulled his arms down, spread his legs wide and went into a crouch to give himself some leverage. Georgie was trying to swing him as the captain had done, but Malky moved forward swiftly and unbalanced the fisherman who was swung in the air and landed on his back with Malky on top of him. They stood up and Bowmaker stood between them and raised Malky's hand. "Throw the first to the Scot.

"Catch your breath, lads. Reet. Roond, the second."

This time Georgie put pressure on Malky using his extra height and weight. Twice Malky's feet nearly left the ground, but then he moved forward in a repeat of his first move, but he did so slowly and his right foot slipped backwards. His opponent heaved to the right and Malky was flying through the air again, but had time to release his grip and bring his arms over his chest to cushion himself, when Georgie came crushing down on him.

There were whoops from the crowd and shouts of encouragement. The next throw would be decisive. Once again Georgie used his bull like strength to try to unsettle the lighter Scots lad, but Malky used his feet and was soon getting into a rhythm swinging the other from side to side. He moved his right leg as though to give the decisive swing and

Georgie moved his left leg forward, but then Malky brought his right foot upwards behind Georgie's leg at the knee and pulled it back as he pushed all his weight forward. Georgie had no chance and fell backward. He knew he had lost but he kept his grip on Malky whose feet flew in the air over the head of the fisherman. There were gasps in the crowd as they expected the Scot to have a heavy fall, but he loosed his own grip, put one hand out to touch the ground and did a back flip that broke Georgie's hold and landed him on his feet. There were a few grudging cheers. His hand went up as Bowmaker judged him the victor. Malky slapped Georgie on the back.

"Ye sure ye've never used the back-hold before?"

"Nivver."

"Weel, I've had easier contest with lads who've wrassled all their lives. If I come again on a Sunday and ye're no' oot fishing we'll have another go. Ye can practise with your mates."

Georgie smiled. "Aye I will."

"It's my turn noo," said Micky Coulson, throwing his coat to the ground.

"Naw it's not," shouted Molly as she came over. "The family honour of the Naesbitts's at stake. I'm ganna have a go," she shouted and put the hold on Malky, but instead of his chin going on her shoulder it got stuck between her very large tits, which bobbed up and down as she pulled the poor lad from side to side. The crowd was loving it. Bowmaker stepped in.

"That's a foul grip, you're supposed to get the lad on his back, not smother him standing up." There were more laughs as Molly released her hold. Malky had never been as close to a woman like Molly before, and now wanted more.

"I'll call that a victory," called out Bowmaker. "Ye can walk oot with her noo, Malky lad."

"Had on a second," she said and ran back and up the steps to her room.

While she was away Captain Bowmaker was talking quietly to Niall, who was shivering inside his cloak and looking even paler than usual. "Niall here's too cauld to gan walking doon to the sea the day," said the Captain to Malky. "He can come wi' me to the meeting hoose. He needn't join in the worship, but there's always a good fire and he can keep warm." He whispered in Malky's ear, "The meeting hoose is at the sign of the *Orange Tree*."

Molly was back carrying an empty basket under her arm.

"Is that for the raisins?" said Niall innocently.

Bowmaker laughed and Molly walked off with Malky at her side.

They soon reached the river mouth and Molly pointed out the priory at Tynemouth. "There's nae priests there though noo. It's the syem at Durham."

"Aye, I know," said Malky, "we were kept prisoner at the cathedral there."

"Them priests liked their fish and they were wor main customer. Captain Bowmaker's *Oswyn* used to carry full loads of fish doon to Durham, mostly salted. And when it was the harrain' season he was doon there twice a week with fresh fish. He doesn't gan oot with the ship much noo, as he's getting auld."

The tide was out and she pointed over to a stretch of sea-weed covered rocks just below the priory.

"They're the Black Middens and they're completely covered when it's high tide and ships are crossing the bar. If the wind's blawin' a gale it drives the ships reet on to the middens. Ye can watch the sailors drooning but nae one can de owt aboot it, as nae coble would get oot in face of the wind, and if it did it would be swamped in a minute."

They carried on walking along the foreshore. The yellow sands stretched out before them.

After a good mile or so they passed some rocks jutting out into the sea. "They're the Trow rocks," said Molly.

They left the sands to walk behind the rocky outcrop and then clambered down a rocky path to the sands again. She showed Malky the cave they called the Fairie's Kettle. They had to clamber up more rocks but once in the cave they saw a large perfectly round bowl made of stone which was full of water and looked just like a kettle. A spring which spurted from the rock above it kept it full of the purest water.

"Ye can only get to see the kettle when the tide's oot," whispered Molly. "When it's in, it covers the entrance reet up."

"Have ye ever seen the fairies?" asked Malky.

"Naw, but I've heard of those that have. They all die within a year of seeing them. So I wouldn't look too hard."

They climbed on upwards and after a steep ascent they just about managed to get through a narrow opening in the rock that came out in a clump of gorse.

"Not many kna' aboot that, so dain't say owt when we get back."

They then walked along the cliff side until they saw a bay with white sand stretching out below them, beneath the steep limestone rock face. "There's a path doon ower there," she said and they headed towards it. It was little more than a shallow fissure in the rock and in places they had to go backwards on their hands and knees and clamber over rocks. When they both safely reached the sands she said, "And dain't ask me any mair aboot the raisin trees. It's smugglers who bring the raisins in, and lots of other things off the ships. They kna' to anchor off here, and send a boat in with the boxes and barrels that the fishers will pick up. Bowmaker organises it. The customs kna' nowt aboot it."

Malky was more interested in getting close to Molly and whilst he never managed to get his arms right round her, he did manage to kiss her quickly on the cheek. Molly put up with him, but gave no inkling that she shared his wish to become a little more intimate.

Malky's chances of any further canoodling quickly vanished, as Molly pushed him away and told him to look for any driftwood. "If I can fill this basket then I'll have mair than enough for a couple of weeks' firewood, and if ye see owt that looks valuable give me a shout. Ye'll be surprised what gets blawn ashore." With the tide being out they could walk round the cliff edge and make their way carefully over rocks and stones until they found the path that took them up and around the Trow.

Malky had never been beachcombing, but soon had an armful of wood that he could put in Molly's basket as they slowly walked back to Sheels along the sands. When her basket was full, Molly put a small wicker ring covered in cloth on to the top of her head, and with Malky's help lifted the basket onto it. It was heavier than when full of fish but she managed. They were half way along the Herd Sands on the way to the river mouth when they saw a tree trunk – or at least a half of one. It was skinned of its bark and was about a foot across.

"If I could get that yem I could keep warm for a while," said Molly. Malky knelt down, put his hands round it to test the weight and then heaved it up on to his shoulder.

"Ye must be stronger than ye look," said Molly.

"Ach, shovelling coal and pumping sea watter all day gie's ye muscles ye never knew ye had," he replied, but his voice was strained and he walked more slowly as they headed home. He twice stopped to swap shoulders. As they reached the strand and started on the low way, George Naesbitt saw them and ran across.

"Here, gie me one end, Malky." The Scots lad did and they walked together until they reached Molly's home. They carried the log up the steps and lifted the basket off Molly's head.

"Thanks, Geordie," said the Scot.

"It's Georgie," said Molly.

"What did ye say, Malky?" asked the fisher lad.

"Geordie. It's what we call a George in Scotland. It disna' sound so saft as Georgie-boy."

"It disna'," shouted George Nesbitt, laughing out loud as he imitated the Scot. "Weel, that'll suit me." He turned his back on them and walked down the steps and out on to the way. "I'm Geordie from noo on, and if anyone calls me Georgie, they'll get a slap."

"He's as daft as a brush, that one," said Molly, "but dain't think it runs in the family and try owt with me." She looked at

Malky and smiled. "Weel, are ye coming in or not?"

The room was more like a loft and had lines and netting piled up against the walls. There was a small fire in the hearth which backed on to the chimney of the main part of the building. There was a settle against the wall, where a window with scraped horn panes was shuttered over, and a small table. Her bed was in the corner, such as it was, a pallet with a sack stuffed with straw and a woollen blanket and sail cloth as a cover.

Malky was to find out that it been an old loft used for storage and was part of Molly's late husband's family's home. She had moved in with them when they married, but she had soon fallen out with the mother-in-law, and her man had built a hearth and they had moved in. After her husband's coble went missing she stayed on, making what living she could, selling fish and mending nets.

Molly took Malky's hand and pulled him on to the cot beside her. She wound the blanket round them. "It's the only way to keep warm in this place," she said. Malky did not need much encouragement. They were soon finding out other ways to keep warm until Molly said, "Ha'd on, Malky, me man's not been gone that lang, and I'm not ready to get entangled with someone else I hardly kna'. I dain't mind a bit of cuddling but ye're not ganna' get what ye want. At least not the day."

Malky was thinking back to the young farm lass in the barn outside Dunbar. He put his hand gently on to Molly's, and slowly led it to rest on his very stiff and not so wee man.

Nobody knew what exactly went on between Malky and Molly upstairs in the loft, but the lad had to run home as fast as he could so as not to miss his dinner, and many a tongue wagged.

After they had had their meal that day, Mr. Milbourn told them that Lewis Frost had been to see his father, Isaac, at Biddick Hall, about Dougie. The lad was clearly too young and not yet strong enough to pull his weight in the salt-house. The older man had not long been at the Hall and through his contacts with Thomas Haselrig was starting to invite some of the local yeomen and the Newcastle freemen and merchants to his hall for meals. They expected roast meats and he could do with a kitchen lad who could turn the spit to help his wife and the maids. Dougie would go there, and when he was not needed in the kitchen, he could help the grooms in the stable. Dougie did not want to leave his friends, but he had hated his time in the salterns, and was happy to work in the kitchens and in the stables.

CHAPTER FIVE

Jenett had never been happy about having the Scots servants living in the house, and taking up space in what she regarded as her kitchen. She was always yapping on about it to Mrs. Milbourn who in turn got on to her husband. Ralph Milbourn had paid good money for the lads and wanted to keep his eye on them until he was sure they could be trusted not to run off. They were unlikely to get far by land, but there were ship's masters who would take a runaway apprentice or servants as deck hands if he were short of crew, and they would never be heard of again.

They didn't see much of Niall now, as he was usually so tired after work that he had his meal and would go and lie in his bed to keep warm until he slept. Davey and Malky would often find themselves talking about lasses, although neither of them had any great experience. Tomag said they should try to think of something else - a lass would never give in to an indentured servant, as they could never marry, and if the lass had a bairn, she would be up before the Vestry court and whipped in the market place at the back of a cart. The lad might be flogged as well by his master if he was ordered to pay for the upkeep of the bairn. Malky said nothing about Molly, but told them the story of the girl in the barn who pulled off the farm lads. "She

114

wouldna' be whipped for that," said Davey, with a crafty grin on his face.

It was mid-February. There had been a heavy snow, and then a fortnight of frost when the milk from the cows froze in the pail, and it was so cold that you only went outside if you had to. Icy winds blew from the sea up the river, and in the mornings they would run and slide to the salt-house. Poor Niall became so tired and frail that Jobling had had to whip him twice for falling asleep in the furnace room - on Mr. Frost's orders. Tomag had whispered in the foreman's ear before he gave the punishment, and he had barely tickled the lad's back, but they all feared that worse was to come. It was a master's right to punish a servant, but Niall was not unwilling, just unable. The day after the second whipping he fell down as he tried to clamber out of bed. He looked so unwell when he eventually managed to get down the steps that Mrs. Frost sent him back upstairs, and told her husband that he was too ill to work. A few days later the weather changed. The wind died and the snow and ice started to melt under a watery sun. Niall had had three days in bed and then a Sunday sitting by the hearth and was put back to work on the Monday.

John McGilvray was now a regular visitor to the salt-house quay, but the river had still not come fully to life. The keels laden with coals for the waiting ships were few but would be seen more in the coming weeks. In the early season some collier masters would take a chance if the weather looked set fair, and would stick to the coast so that they could make port if a storm was brewing - Yarmouth and London and the Channel ports all needed their coals.

McGilvray always talked to the highland lads and had taken a shine to Niall in particular. He had not seen him for three weeks and was taken aback at how frail he looked. When he was pushing his second barrow, the lad fell to his knees, and had no strength to get back up. John leapt up to the quay and ran over. "Are ye not weel, man?"

Niall started coughing. Tomag and Malky had come over.

"He's not been weel, for nigh on a month noo," said Tomag.

"His heid's full of cauld," added Malky. "He's always coughing and his nose runs oot with snot. He canna shake it aff, and he's tired all the time. He's been whipped twice by Jobling for slacking." John looked up at this remark and then looked over menacingly to where Jobling was waiting for the coals. Malky continued, "Oor friend Hamish, the pothecary, says it's the coal dust that gets into the tubes in his heid, and with working all day at the furnace, he has no chance of improving."

Niall slowly got to his feet but put his hand on John's shoulder to steady himself. "He's no' pushing any mair barra's to-day. I'll get ane of my lads to help ye wi' 'em." He walked Niall back to the quayside, sat him down and then started talking to him.

When the work was done and the ale brought over, McGilvray walked back to the saltern. He looked hard at Jobling and spoke in a cold, controlled fury. "If ye're thinking of giving him a whipping for slacking, then ye'll end up ower the side of the quay yersel."

"It's the master," said Jobling defensively. "If I didn't whip him then he'd have me whipped instead. Mr. Frost's not a bad master, but he wants his money's worth from the Scots lads.

Tomag's already warned me and I just give him a tickle, his skin's barely broken."

"Does yer master know that he'll kill him if he keeps working him like this," cried an angry McGilvray.

Jobling said nowt.

The pann-keel skipper walked off towards the quay and gestured to Tomag to follow him. Malky and Davey tagged along. They all put their heads together.

"If ane of ye went missing what would the master do?" asked the skipper.

"Apprentices are running aff all the time," said Malky. "The master calls oot the constable and the watch, and they gang looking for them, asking if anybody's seen them. Ye see the bills posted on the doors."

"Are yer masters hame this Sunday?" asked McGilvray.

Davey butted in. "Ma Peggy told me they're all gang away to Biddick Hall for dinner with Niall's master's fatha'. She said we might hae a bit of time together after dinna', if Jenett gangs asleep in front of the fire."

"Do ye know any of the Scots lads in the West Panns?" asked McGilvray.

"Och aye, we keep meaning to gang and see Alec Duncan and the other lads frae St. Monans at Coatsworth's panns," said Malky.

McGilvray said a few quiet words to Malky who would tell the others, shook his hand and was then away.

On that Sunday they all sat round the table having breakfast. It was hasty pudding as usual, but was followed by bacon, eggs boiled in cream, and a black pudding that Jenett

117

had made the day before with fresh sheep's blood. After the end of meal grace, given by Malky, as was the custom when they ate together, Mr. Milbourn said that the family were going with the Frosts to Biddick Hall for dinner. The Frosts were taking their cook and the scullion with them to help with the service, as the Coatsworths would be there as well. Niall would have his dinner at the Milbourns' and if they were late coming home then he could sleep upstairs with the other Scots.

Malky then spoke and said that they wished to go to the West Panns to see the Scots lads from St. Monans who had befriended them when they were held captive in Durham, if Mr. Milbourn had no objection.

"None at all," said Milbourn. "I'll give ye the Sunda' ale money, Malcolm. And stay with your Scots friends. The West Panners are a rough lot."

"Ach, we can take care of ourselves, Master," said Tomag, and Milbourn did not doubt the big man.

A carriage had been sent for the two families and they left early, as they would have to take the Westoe road and then pass along the cart way that led to the Lay Gate farm. No cart ever tried to cross the Mill Dam bridge.

As the Scots lads were leaving Jenett said, "And dain't expect any roast meats for your dinner. As the master's away I'm just boiling some sassidges, and there's still half the black pudding left from this morning, and plenty of pease pudding from yesterday, so ye won't gan' hungry."

"Ach, that'll de us fine, Jenett," said Tomag, "and dinna' worry if we're a wee bit late. We've a fair bit of time to make up wi' oor friends frae St. Monans."

"Weel, me and Peggy are eating at the usual time. If ye're not here then ye'll have the sassidges cauld, not that I care," replied Jenett sharply.

Peggy gave a worried look over to Davey, who smiled at the young lassie, as if to say that whatever the others did he would be there on time. He was not going to miss the chance of being alone with Peggy while Jenett was snoozing by the hearth.

They set off along the way. As the salt-panns were not working on the Sunday, there were no thick clouds of smoke over the toon, but the sky was still overcast, there was a light drizzle, and a breeze from the sea was starting to blow up.

"Ach, there'll be some weather the day," said Tomag. When they reached the *Turk's Heed* he took Malky with him up Cripple Foot Lane to the back court of the ale house. Niall and Davey waited for them on the other side of the way. A quarter of an hour later, Tomag and Malky emerged, each holding a pail of ale in one hand and a pitcher of gin in the other. They'd used Milbourn's ale money and also some of the coin that John McGilvray had slipped Malky.

They marched on, each taking turns with a pail. When they arrived at the Mill Dam they could see McGilvray, and the boy who worked on the keel, sitting in a coble tied up to the quay. They all walked down the path towards the Tyne as though looking out at the river, where a handful of ships were anchored. There were several cobles skimming the waters as Sunday was a popular day for fishing on the river when there was not a lot of other activity. Tomag walked over to the coble and exchanged a few words with John who handed him something, and took the offered pitcher of gin. Tomag came back to his friends. They all stood close together giving Niall the chance to take off his highland blue bonnet to don the homespun fisher's headgear that McGilvray had given Tomag. They didn't want anyone noticing that a Scotchman in a blue bonnet had been seen boarding a coble at Mill Dam. As the others slowly walked away a lone figure in working clothes sauntered across to the quayside, looked around to make sure that no one was looking in his direction, bent down, untied the rope from the bollard, and stepped quickly in to the coble which headed upstream. The boy in the bow put the fish-net over the side and they looked like any other of the fishers out for a Sunday's sport.

It was drizzling hard when they reached Coatsworth's panns. There was no one about, and then Malky saw a fellow come out of one the salterns to relieve himself up against the wall. They walked down and asked him if Alec Duncan was about. The lad turned his head. "Ach, is that Malky? I was wi' ye in the big kirk at Durham. Cam alang in, Alec's inside wi' the rest o' us."

They passed through the door into the fore-house. All the St. Monans lads were there along with one or two others, sitting on benches around a single brazier. Alec stood up with a whoop of joy as he saw Malky, Tomag and Davey.

"Ye'se are a sight for sair eyes," he cried out, slapping them on the shoulders. "We were just sitting here freezing oor ballocks off with nowt else to de, and in ye walk. I knew ye'd cam ane day, Malky, but it's lang *syne*."

"Ach weel, if ye'r ballacks are freezin', I've got just the thing for ye," said Tomag, handing over the pitcher of gin, "but just hae a snifter, and then we can start on the ale. Twa pails each with eight quarts of the best auld ale frae the *Turk's Heed*."

The Scots lads had horns for cups and dipped them eagerly into the ale. Marledane had started adding hops to his ale and it gave it a bitter flavour, but he'd also put in some honey on the second brew to give it strength and a touch of sweetness, and the Scots lads drank deep.

Coatsworth had bought a dozen Scotchmen, and as he had to feed them all, he paid two widowed sisters who lived in one of the cottages opposite the panns to cook for them. When the meal was ready one of the women would bang the bottom of a kettle with a spoon and some of the lads would cross the way to carry it over. Their overseer, Rabbie Dunne, doled out their ale, which they suspected he watered down before bringing it to them. All twelve slept in one of the cottages on the way, and it was so cramped that they preferred to socialize in the furnace room. It was a double saltern and was roomy enough for them all.

Their life was not that different from the highland Scots although they sometimes went to a kirk in West Panns Way on a Sunday morning. They had decided against it that morning as they would have arrived wet from the drizzle, and then would have had to stand through the long prayers and sermons that sometimes lasted until dinner time. Some of them preferred to walk to Jarra's Lake, a large bay that became a mud flat when the tide went out. They had managed to make a primitive bow and some arrows with points hardened on dying coals, and would sometimes take a small bird or fowl. They had to be careful as the fishers from the toon-end who came up the river in their cobles, looked on the lake as their private preserve and would set on any panners they found there.

With the gin and the ale there was soon a festive atmosphere with loud voices and laughter. The time passed quickly and Davey was becoming anxious as he did not want to be late for his dinner.

"Gang on hame, then, Davey," said Tomag, patting him on the back. "Malky and me will no' be lang. We've just a wee bit of business to do. Here, ye tak the cloak."

The ale and the gin were all but gone when they heard the banging of the kettle. None of them was over steady on their feet and Tomag and Malky made their farewells.

As he was about to go, Tomag stood to his full height and called out. "And dinna' forget, lads, that there was four of us here including Niall, ma brither, who wandered aff towards Jarra's Lake to catch some birdies." There were shouts of agreement. Tomag had told them of their plans and sworn them to secrecy.

To give some credence to the tale, Malky staggered along the way in the opposite direction to Tomag. He hunched his shoulders, and pulled his blue bonnet over his ears against the icy drizzle and the now strong winds. There were few folk out, but any that he passed avoided the drunken Scots lad who seemed to be determined to find his way to the lake. After he had been seen by a few folk, Malky doffed his bonnet, turned on his heels and made his way back as quickly as he could, half-running half-walking by the salterns. He caught up with Tomag by the bridge, and donned his bonnet. They looked in at the *Turk's* to return the two pails and the one pitcher, and with the last ha'penny he had, Tomag bought them two gills of gin to warm themselves up.

By the time they opened Milbourn's door, which had been left half ajar for them, they were both well away with the drink. They stumbled over to the hearth, and in doing so woke up Jenett who screeched in panic until she realised who they were. A clearly flustered Peggy came out from the back of the room, and Malky just caught sight of a worried looking Davey moving out of sight under the stairs trying to pull up his trews without being noticed.

Jenett had ratcheted up the pot over the fire so the sassidges and black pudding had kept warm. The two latecomers were so hungry, that they ate them as they were and did not want them heated up anymore. They wolfed down the warm, greasy meat, and complimented Jenett on her cooking skills. Tomag started to become overfamiliar, and Malky's head was dropping on to his barley bread trencher so Jenett shooed them up the stairs to sleep it off, on pain of a flogging from the master. The cook was so flustered by the breaking of her Sunday peace that she did not notice the absence of Niall.

The Milbourns and the Frosts did not return until later that night, and retired to bed soon after. Niall's absence was not remarked upon until the next morning. Frost questioned the three highlanders and got little sense out of them other than they had left Niall by the Coatsworth salterns as he drunkenly headed towards Jarra's Lake. The constable was informed. After their story was confirmed by the St. Monans Scots and one or two passers-by, who had seen a drunken Scot with a blue bonnet headed in the direction of the lake, it was assumed, that in his intoxicated state, he had ended up in the river. No body was found but no further sightings were made.

Lewis Frost went to see his father. They were making little profit from the salt-houses with the competition of the Scots salt makers, and they decided to close the pann in the salt-house where Niall had worked, until trade picked up.

With Niall now gone it was only Malky, Davey, and Tomag left. Malky would often see Molly walking along the way giving her fish-wives' call, and stopping at the doors where she might sell some fish – or some other things in the bottom of her basket that had come in at Frenchman's Bay. She would just look his way and he would look back. He now went down to the toon-end most Sundays when he could. He'd have a wrestle with Geordie Naesbitt and Micky Coulson, and any of the other fishermen who fancied their chances. When he was there, Captain Bowmaker took charge and it was starting to become a regular Sunday morning sport, with men making wagers with each other on who might win. Few bet against Malky, although Geordie had come near to besting him a couple of times. The Vestry court had forbidden all sport on a Sunday apart from archery practice at the butt field on the Lawe, but the fishermen just ignored them and the constable refused to venture to the fishing quarter.

After a couple of bouts and if the weather was fair, Malky would walk out with Molly. They'd do some beachcombing for driftwood, and then go up to her loft for their canoodling which was becoming more and more passionate. When his blood had cooled on the walk back to Milbourn's house for his dinner, Malky was often thankful that Molly was a strong lass who could fight him off when his lust for her body overcame his senses, but he felt that she was weakening, and had as much desire for him as he had for her.

Young Davey had thickened out a lot with the hard manual work and the regular meals. Little Peggy could not keep her eyes off him, and it was becoming so obvious that both Mrs. Milbourn and Jenett made sure that they rarely got within touching distance. Their embrace under the stairs, which had been interrupted by the drunken Tomag and Malky, was now just a dim memory. The only time that Davey could hold her and kiss her was when she came to the salt-house with their oat pudding for their breakfast. As soon as she came in the door, Davey would run over and help her with the pudding kettle. When the meal was dished out he would go with her to the door and hold her tightly up against the wall, feeling as much of her body as she would let him until Jobling's uncouth voice told her to leave the furnace lad alone and get back to the kitchen.

One night, Malky woke up as he felt Davey getting back into bed. His first thought was that he'd got out to piss in the pot, but as he snuck in beside him Malky could hear him breathing heavy. "Ye all right, Davey?"

"Och aye. I've just sneaked doonstairs and got Peggy to touch me with her hands. I didna' last lang, but next time'll be better."

"Did Jenett no' wake up?"

"Ach no. Peggy had waited until Jenett was snoring and then sneaked oot to meet me under the stairs. I nearly groaned when I shot ma bolt, but I kept quiet - just."

Davey and Peggy's night time trysts went on for a while and then, one night, Malky, and everybody else, was wakened by an almighty shrieking. Both he and Tomag dashed down the stairs at the same time as Ralph Milbourn, all with just their shirts on. They could see little in the dark but managed to make out Jenett's bulky form with Peggy in her arms.

"There's a man in the hoose, and he was forcing poor Peggy reet up against the wall. I hit him with the piss pot and he's on the groond."

"It's all reet, Jenett, we're here noo," said Milbourn. "Malky, light a torch and we'll see whe it is."

"Ach, it's only me." It was Davey's shaky voice. "And I wasna' forcing her, was I, Peggy? And noo I've got a sair heid and I'm covered in piss." Malky's rush torch lightened the scene. It was Davey, all right, stretched out on the floor with his shirt barely covering a still half stiff wee man. He was holding the back of his head and you could smell the piss. They had started as usual, but Davey had wanted more than just touching from Peggy, and his own hands had excited the lass so much, that she had very little will to fight him as he took her up against the wall. Davey had not been able to completely supress his moans, and his foot had knocked against the piss pot. Jenett had awakened to see a half-naked man pounding poor Peggy against the wall under the stairs.

"Forcing her or not, ye've broken the rules of this household," shouted a furious Milbourn. "Fetch the cane, Jenett, and I'll tan his arse for him noo." He grabbed Davey by the arm and pulled him to his feet. He turned him so that he faced the wall and pushed his head down. "Pull your shirt up," he cried out as he took the bendy cane from Jenett. It was used when one of the servants needed a beating.

Tomag stepped up to Milbourn. "Ach no."

"He's my servant and I have a right to beat him."

"Aye. But Davey's a man noo. He does a man's work. If ye are to beat him then he'll take it on the back like a man, not on the arse like a boy, or a woman."

Milbourn stood back. "Reet, I'll tan the hide on your back, Davey-lad. Pull your shirt ower your heid. I'll not rip good cloth."

As Davey pulled his shirt over his head, Jenett pushed Peggy away, but a woman's voice came from the top of the stairs. "Hold her where she is, Jenett. She must see the whipping. That's what she'll get in the market place tied to the back of a cart, if she lets him at her again, the immoral bitch. She's got to learn."

"Twelve strokes then," said Milbourn. He looked at Tomag and Malky.

"That's what he deserves, Mr. Milbourn. But do ye want him to work a full day tomorrow in the salt-house, or to be lying on his stomach groaning for a day?" It was Malky this time who had spoken up.

"Give him the punishment he deserves," shouted his wife.

"I can't afford to be a man doon, with things as they are. Six it will be for noo. But if he as much as looks at Peggy, then he'll get the other six."

Mrs. Milbourn stomped down the stairs. "They're animals these men, and you should not have brought them into this house. I've tolt ye before I dain't want them here."

Milbourn looked at his wife. "Ye better watch your tongue, woman, when you speak to your husband, or I'll belt ye as weel. I decide what gans on in my own home."

Mrs. Milbourn shut up. She knew of other men who beat their wives if they spoke out of turn, and so she stood quietly with the other women as Davey took his punishment.

"Hands against the wall, and if ye move, Tomag and Malky will have to hold your arms steady."

"He'll no' move," said Tomag, and he didn't, as Milbourn whipped the cane hard on to his back and shoulders six times. Davey made not a sound. Milbourn then turned to the women.

"Noo put him on the table and rub salt into his wounds."

Mrs. Milbourn took pleasure in the salting of the wounds, and was none too gentle. This time there was a muffled moaning as the salt stung those places where the skin had broken.

When Davey came up to bed he got in beside Malky and lay on his front.

"Was it worth it?" whispered Malky.

"Och aye," said Davey.

The next evening at six o'clock, just as they were finishing their shift, Jenett and Peggy came in carrying a kettle with salt fish cooked in milk and a basket with barley bread.

"Ye'll be eating in here from noo on," said Jenett. "When ye've finished Jimmy'll tyek ye to yer new home." She laughed. "Such as it is."

Jobling had already told them the news. Milbourn had given in to his wife and Jenett, and the men were to live in an empty cottage in Widders Court up Pig Path. Jobling had told them about it. The cottage was more of a hovel with only a single room and a central hearth. It had a garden at the back with a cess pit, but they had to fetch water from the common well in Back Low Way - a good few steps up from the path. There were some wooden pallets with straw mattresses and they could fetch their blankets from the house. They'd eat in the furnace room during the week but they'd have to come down to the house themselves to collect their meals on the Sunday.

They wound their way up a narrow path, with gardens on either side where pigs were kept, following Jobling who was carrying a lantern, and then along a tight alley that led to a small close where half a dozen cottages faced each other round a court. Jobling opened the cottage door and a fetid smell hit them. When the foreman waved his lantern there was a furious oinking, and two large pigs charged towards him. He got out the way quickly and used his stave to chase the screeching pigs out into the courtyard. The door opposite opened and the figure of a tall woman was framed in the doorway.

"Have ye been keeping your pigs in Mr. Milbourn's hoose, Widder Wallis?" shouted Jobling.

"And what if I was," replied the widder curtly. "He said I could let them into the garden, and it's handy to put 'em in there at neet."

"Well he's ganna lodge three panners here. They can't sleep there the neet noo, with it smelling like a shit-hole, or worse."

"Why not," the woman shouted, "if they're them filthy Scotchmen I've heard aboot, a stye 'll suit 'em fine."

"Mr. Milbourn will be up here in the morning with the new constable who'll hev ye up before the Vestry court for trespass and damages, and anything else they can hoy at ye," cried a furious Jobling.

She gave as good as she got and soon the doors of all the cottages were open.

"Come on, lads, let's gan," said Jobling. "Nae one gets the better of Widder Wallis when she starts on. I'll let me master sort it oot."

It took a few days, and in the meantime they slept in the furnace room. At least it was warm and Milbourn gave them fresh straw from his stables. The constable had given the widder short shrift, and she had her scullion, a half simple lass called Alice Ferman, sweep out the cottage and scrub the walls and the flagstones with strong soap. The straw mattresses were full of pig shit and were pulled out of the cottage and put in the garden to dry out and then be burnt. The place still stank and on the Sunday the lads were set to covering the walls with whitewash. A fire was set in the hearth and Milbourn got them to dismantle their bed and carry it up to the cottage. Milbourn was not happy and kept giving Davey hard looks.

They slept there that night. The building was damp and cold despite the fire in the hearth, and they shivered in the dark. There was no chimney, only a smoke blackened cowl that hung from the rafters to take the smoke up and through the thatch. They took turns to get out to poke the coals and put more on to keep the fire going, which woke them all up. They eventually fell into a slumber, but were not up at six and a furious Jobling was banging on their door to wake them. They did not have a timepiece, and he was going to have to arrange for someone to knock them up.

The Widder's Court was not a place you'd see unless you were told it was there. The alley that led to it off Pig Path was narrow and easily missed. It was surrounded by houses on all sides. The cottages were old and dilapidated and they were about the only homes left in Sheels that had thatched roofs, apart from some of the fishermen's hovels. The thick smoke from the salt-panns would hold tiny fragments of red-hot coal or ash, and if the wind blew it down on to thatch then fires would break out. All houses now had slate or stone-tiled roofs. Not all of the cottages were occupied.

Their spirits rose a little as the weeks passed, and the March winds scattered the thick smoke clouds and let the sun's rays through for a while. It was a sunny day when Jobling set Malky and Davey on strengthening the rock walls of the sumps on the foreshore that held the sea water after the tide had gone down, so that there was a steady flow to the wells next to the salt-house. Over the winter some of the stones and rocks had been washed away and needed replacing, and more sand and mud dug over it. They had taken their shoes, socks and knee breeches off and only had their shirts on. They had all but completed the work by the afternoon. The cold waters lapped over their ankles as the tide slowly came in. They were little more than lads, and when Davey kicked some water on to Malky, the other did the same. They forgot their work for a moment and were soon sending large waves at each other. Malky made a rush forward and Davey ran back laughing until his foot slipped and he lost his balance. One foot had mud under it but the other had nowt, and he felt himself falling. He flung himself forward and his head went right under, leaving him coughing and spluttering. Malky pushed himself through the choppy waves towards him and held him up. The water was up to their waists.

"It must gang doon steep," shouted Malky.

"Aye, I thought I was a goner for a minute," replied Davey.

"Can ye no' swim then?"

"Never tried it."

Malky walked his friend to shallow water and then flung himself head first into the stream and started swimming. He would push his arms forward and then bring them back in a half circle, kicking his legs like a frog.

"I learned in the Marlee Loch with the laddies up at Kinloch." He swam back to Davey. "It's best to start swimming like a dawgie," and in just four feet of water he did a dog paddle.

"Ye try it, Davey." Davey pushed himself forward but soon went under. Malky then stood about six feet away and got Davey to do it again. This time he managed to reach Malky without going under. A couple more times and he nearly had the knack.

They heard a shout, "Oot the way. There's nae swimming in the Tyne." Malky looked up and saw a keel bearing down on them. A brawny looking fellow with bronzen locks flowing from under his blue bonnet, a wide smile on his face, and a dimple in his chin, was at the bow. It was Niall.

"We're taking coals to the *Ipswich*. If the skipper agrees we'll drap in at the quay on the way upstream. It'll be a guid five or six hoors. Have a lamp on the quayside."

The two lads finished their work and then it was time for their six o'clock supper. Dograve boiled with milk again - now that they no longer ate at the house their fare was mainly fish and cheap cuts, but they had enough and could not complain. Malky and Davey had already told Tomag that they might see Niall that night. They stayed on in the fore-house and took it in turns to sit on the quayside with the lamp they used to guide themselves back to the Widder's Court. It was a cold night with the usual fresh breeze, and the one who was on watch had the cloak wrapped round him. Tomag happened to be on the quayside when the keel glided gently in, and a rope was thrown up to him. It was slack water and the skipper had had no problem in finding the quay, using the *swape* and the oar and not rigging the sail. Tomag made the call of the night owl, the agreed signal, and Malky and Davey came running down.

Niall jumped on to the quay, followed by the skipper. Tomag grabbed him by the arms and shook him slowly. The other two lads slapped him on the shoulders.

"Weel, ye said ye wanted to be a keelman, and here ye are. It's guid to see ye, Niall," said Malky. "Is yer heid still full of snot?" The others laughed.

"Keep yer voices doon, laddies," whispered Tomag. "We dinna' want anybody coming doon here and finding oor Niall, who's supposed to be away droonded in Jarra's Lake."

"Thanks to John McGilvray," said Niall. "The skipper here's his brither, Angus."

"Ach, John told me what he was planning and I was happy to help," said the skipper. "Niall's living with us noo. It took him a guid two weeks at John's to get his strength back away frae the coal dust and the heat of the furnace. Mind, we hae oor share of dust when we're loading the ships, but there's always plenty of fresh air. He's been on the keel a week noo, and has just started earning some coin. He's taken ower frae ma cousin who wanted to gang back to Scotland. His young lassie's father has died, and if he marries the girl he can tak ower the croft, so he wanted away. He's bonded to John Binks oor *hostman*, but I'm the only ane who deals wi' Binks, sae he'll no' know that Niall's taken his place. But if ye come up to Sandgit' to see Niall ye'll hae to call him Alec. Alec Patterson."

"D'ye work the nicht as weel?" asked Davey.

It was Angus who replied. "We get paid for each *tide*." He sensed the others were a bit lost. "We keelmen call each trip when we deliver a load and return back to the quayside at Newcastle a tide. With the keel fully loaded with eight chaldrons we need the tide wi' us, even if the wind allows a sail. We try to time it so we start unloading in slack watter and then we should be all reet to have the incoming tide behind us. If we have to come to the mouth of the river it can take us eighteen hours for ane tide. It's not the same as a sea captain's tide, is it, Niall?"

"Ach, these keelmen have their funny ways, but I'm getting used to it. And ye have to shout all the time," Niall started to bellow but was quickly hushed by the others.

"We always work together with the other keelmen, and ye have to be able to be heard, especially when it's a black nicht," added Angus.

"I canna' call in here too often. But noo ye know where I live come up on a Sunday. Choose a fine day and ye'll find us on the quayside ha'ing a drink before the Sunday roast," said Niall.

"Ach, we'll do that," said Tomag.

The keelmen were ready to go. Angus sat on the stern holding the swape, a long oar with a large paddle on the end with which he steered the keel. Niall and the other *bully*, pulled on the other oar with the boy – this oar was even longer than the swape and they were soon moving away upstream.

"He seems happy enow," said Malky as they went back into the furnace room. "If we all want to gang up to Sandgit' I can ask Geordie Naesbitt, or ane of the other fishermen, to tak us up there in a coble if they're no' oot fishin'."

Malky was not unhappy with his life in Sheels, but he wanted more from Molly than he was getting. He also wanted to earn some coin for himself. He had an idea what Tomag was cooking up with Marledane and was hoping that he might help them, once it got going. Now that Niall had managed to escape, he had started to think that he might be able to free himself, and look for his real father, John Douglass.

Although Malky himself rarely went to a Sunday morning session down the steps in the *Turk's Heed*, many others did. A new constable for the town had been appointed by the Vestry court on Lady Day in March. To hold the office had once been an honour but was now something of a burden. The job was unpaid, and not every constable was too keen to carry his stave around the streets at night, or to get too involved when the fishers and the panners started fighting in the ways or in the pubs. When the Icelandic and *Westmony* fishing fleets arrived in the town for their salt, some constables locked the front door of their houses until they had sailed away. The previous constable had known John Marledane, who would often supply him with ale or gin at no charge, and so was never curious as to why drunken men were seen emerging from Cripple Foot Lane at noon on a Sunday. The new constable was cut of different cloth. Thomas Puncheon had set up shop as a *cordwainer* before the wars when the Sheels panns were attracting a lot of monied adventurers, who were likely to buy new shoes, rather than have their old ones cobbled up. He was a thick set, fair haired man with a perpetually worried look. From the outset he had been a regular complainant before the manor court at Westoe before the *Palatinate* was abolished by the Parliament. He had managed to have Henry Chisolm, the cobbler, fined for making a pair of shoes from the leather of old shoes that were no longer wanted or repairable. The old King's law was that only cordwainers made new shoes, not cobblers. He was also always the first to complain when his way along the High Street was hindered by waste, or water running from blocked sinks, or by a drunken man or woman lying in the gutter. The last constable had started slamming his door in his face so tired was he of his constant complaints. When the Vestry court had met to consider the appointment of a new constable for the next year it was the outgoing officer of the law who had nominated Puncheon.

"He's always telling me how the job should be done, so let him do it for himsel," he said. It was often difficult to find someone willing to take the constable's stave in a town like Sheels with rough characters who liked nothing better than to drink and fight, but Puncheon was up for the challenge.

He recruited half a dozen like-minded souls to serve on the watch, and it was now a common sight to see the constable with his stave and his lantern walking the streets after dark with one or two of the watch. Although a church-goer, he had decided that once in a while he would forgo the preaching on a Sunday morning to check that all the public houses were closed during the hours of divine service as laid down by the Vestry court. He had decided to take the town's two ale-cunners with him – they not only had to check that ale being sold was of good quality and that the tankards held a pint or a quart, but they were required to report if any house was allowing unruly or disorderly behaviour. The ale-cunners, Thomas Haswell and Nicholas Woolfe, had at first turned him down flat, but he had raised the matter at the next Vestry court and they were ordered to accompany him. They had walked from St Hild's, across the pasture, down the Salt Well Lane, and then along the High Street checking that the doors of the ale-houses were all barred or locked. Some were open as the landlord or landlady used the time to sweep the floors and scrub the tables. If they had heard of any house likely to sell ale on a Sunday, they would knock on the shutters with their staves to demand entrance. They passed along the winding long row and then on to the low way. Their passage had not gone unnoticed and when they neared the fishers' quarter they found their way barred by a group of rough looking lads and lasses, men and women. The ale-cunners turned to go back the way they had come, and, after a bucket of fish guts had been thrown at his feet out of a doorway, the constable followed suit. As they neared the salt-panns, Puncheon said that they should not give up and he banged on the door of the *Orange Tree*. There was no answer. Puncheon was about to bang again when Nicholas Woolfe, the ale cunner, called out.

"It's Nick Woolfe, Dick, We're just checking that you're not full of panners drinking on a Sunda'."

The door opened and a stout one-eyed man wearing a leather apron opened the door.

"Ye kna' I wouldn't do owt like that, Mr. Woolfe. Why dain't ye and yer friends step in." There was a fire in the hearth by the wall, and four men were sitting in front of it with tankards in their hands.

The constable pushed himself forward.

"Ye'll empty those cups doon the drain and I'll hev ye up before the next Vestry court, Dick Redheed, for selling ale during hours of divine worship."

"Weel noo," said Redheed, picking up his own mug, "I'm not hoying good ale away for anybody, even ye, Tom Puncheon. And I'm not selling ale. These are my good friends, a respectable sea captain, a merchant, the toon's chief cooper, and a carrier. I tyek no payment for what they drink as my guests." He looked round at them and said, with a broad smile on his face, "Being Presbyterians, we always meet on a Sunda' morning for a prayer meeting. It's thirsty work saying all those prayers, mind, so it's me best double-trouble."

The seated men laughed. Captain Bowmaker was one of them and raised his tankard. It was to this meeting house that he had brought young Niall those weeks before.

Puncheon was not best pleased. "Ye must think I'm a freshwater mariner if I'd believe for a minute ye'd be saying yer prayers, Will Bowmaker, or ye, Cuddy Heron," he said as he looked at the captain and the carrier.

"Seat yersel's doon and I'll bring ye'se a pint of my best," said Redheed.

Nicholas Woolfe and his fellow ale cunner did not need a second invitation to taste Dick Redheed's double brewed beer. Puncheon demurred. "Weel, I'm not taking strong ale on a Sunday when it's forbidden by law, which I'm supposed to enforce." He stomped out of the door.

As he left Woolfe took a good swig of the ale. "Wye that's good. Hey, noo, I dain't remember seeing the slate ootside yer door, chalked up to say that ye'd just made a brew, so that I could come and taste that it was all reet."

"Aye, and claim your two gallons worth as your fee," muttered Bowmaker.

"It must have slipped me mind, Nick," responded Redheed, "but ye can make a good start on your ale the day. And when it's twelve o' the clock and the others start paying, ye'll still hev yours for free. Wye it's nearly twelve noo."

The two ale cunners were nicely settled when the door flew open and Squinty Johnson, the pot boy from the *Turk's Heed*, came running in. "Mr. Woolfe and Mr. Haswell, ye're wanted at the *Turk's*. Auld Puncheon's in a reet brawl with Jimmy Jobling and his mates. John Marledane sent me."

Woolfe and Haswell were quick off their bench and out the door. "Ye kna' what gans on doon the *Torks* on a Sunda',"

139

Redheed said to Bowmaker.

"I've heard," the Captain replied, "and Marledane isn't too particular who he lets doon his stairs. I'm ganna take a wander along there. Wor ale cunners might need a hand if Jimmy Jobling sets on them."

Puncheon had walked along the way and had stood on the corner opposite the *Turk's Heed*, in two minds whether or not to go back to join the ale cunners at the *Orange Tree* as soon as it was noon. He did not see why they should have all the free ale. He saw the doors of the *Turk's* open ready for business and then he noticed several men in high spirits and talking loudly, walking down Cripple Foot Lane. He couldn't see where they were coming from and he heard one of them say, when he saw the constable, "Wye all those prayers make you thirsty, lads," to much laughter. As the last ones came out of the alley he decided that he'd had enough of prayer meetings and walked over. Jimmy Jobling, a little unsteady on his feet and very red faced, tried to avoid him, but half tripped and put his hand on Puncheon's shoulder to steady himself.

"Unhand me, Jobling. Ye look well away on drink, and I want to kna' where ye got it on a Sunda' morning?"

"Ye got nowt better to do, Constable?" asked one of the men behind Jobling. They were all panners and hard men into the bargain.

Jobling did not need egging on. "Aye, it's nowt to do with ye wharr-a-de on a Sunda', ye blitherin' windbag."

"I'm the constable and ye'll tell me who sold you drink or I'll have ye in the pillory the morrow, ye *swill-belly*." Puncheon raised his stave and pushed it hard into Jobling's bulging midriff. Jobling grabbed the wood and the two of them started pushing and shoving. It was then that John Marledane sent Squinty to fetch the ale cunners. The constable and his two companions had been seen going into the *Orange Tree* and only Puncheon had come out.

By the time the two ale-cunners came running, Jobling and two of his fellow panners had taken the stave off Puncheon and were pushing him this way and that, and every now and again hitting him on the arse with the stave. The ale-cunners ran in but were soon on the wrong end of some well-aimed blows.

Tomag had come to the door of the house to see what was going on.

"Come on, Tomag," said Marledane, and the two men walked into the fray, and, with some help from Bowmaker, managed to extract Puncheon and the other two with some choice words exchanged. Jobling did not want to upset Marledane, and one look from Big Tomag was enough for the others to stand back muttering. The crowd of men who'd been down in the *Turk's* vault were still laughing and jeering, but the arrival of Ralph Milbourn and Lewis Frost walking in front of their wives and children after their morning service put an end to any further outbursts and the crowd drifted away. After they had dusted themselves off, Marledane steered the three officers of the law into the *Turk's*, sat them down and brought them tankards brimming with his best beer – on the house, of course. Puncheon overcame his previous scruples and took a much-needed swig. After they had escorted their families home, Frost and Milbourn arrived at the *Turk's* and joined the others for some Sunday ale and to decide what action was needed.

An assault on the constable and the ale-cunners was a serious affair and a special Vestry court was arranged for the next day. Frost got the names of the other two malefactors out of Jobling. All three appeared before the court and were sentenced to be whipped in the Market Place in the High Street the following day at noon. Milbourn and Frost had already agreed on what action they would take and had told Jobling that he would lose his job as foreman, and salt master, for six months and would work for that time as a servant on eight pence a day. Jobling did not complain. If it were not for the shortage of men to work on the panns he could have been dismissed. The owners of the panns all knew each other and he wouldn't have been taken on by anyone else.

"And ye'll stop drinking gin, Jimmy," cautioned Milbourn. "Ye smell of it all the time."

"Aye, I've got a taste for it all reet. It'll be ale and beer only from noo on." He looked at his feet. "De ye kna' who ye're taking on as foreman for the six months?" Frost and Milbourn said nowt. "It's just that Tomag, the Scotchman, has learned all I can tell him aboot salt making. He's got a knack for it, and a real feeling for the salt. The others respect him and he won't have any problems with them."

"We'll think on it, Jimmy. Get back to the salt-hoose but dain't tell the lads any of this until we've made a decision."

Milbourn looked at Frost. "Tomag's a good worker and I've had nae trouble with him, but he's an indentured servant and I paid twenty pund for him. If we make him up to foreman I should rightly pay him something as a premium."

Frost rubbed his chin. "Jobling gets four shillings for every pann of salt we draw, and we have five drawings every fortnight - the servants eight and sixpence. We'll de well out of it whatever we pay him."

"Aye, but Tomag would have to be registered as a foreman and salt master, and he can't do that while he's still indentured."

"It's only for six months and we shall have to be sure he's up to the job. We'll keep him on indentures so he still gets fed and lodged, and we'll give him a fortnightly premium of ten shillings for the extra responsibility. If Parliament puts a duty on the Scotch salt and the trade picks up, then we can take on extra panns then we'll make him Jobling's deputy."

Whippings always attracted a good crowd, particularly if the culprit was a woman when there was a chance that the crowd could see her titties. Jobling was well known in Sheels, and there would be three whippings, so the Market Place was packed with onlookers. Shops closed and many of the salt-pann workers had been allowed to leave the panns to watch the punishment given out to their fellow panners.

Tomag had no wish to see the flogging of someone who had helped him to learn the trade of a salt maker, and so he stayed at the salt-house to make sure the furnaces were kept at a steady heat while the others went up to the High Street.

The Sheels folk stood three or four deep round each side of the Market Place. There was a horse-drawn wagon in the centre. Jobling and the other two panners stood just behind it. Officers of the watch stood guard and the Curate of Sheels and the members of the Vestry court stood solemnly behind their constable, who was to officiate and who had his stave held high in front of him. At his signal the first to be whipped was manhandled by the watch and had his doublet top and shirt pulled away to leave him bare-backed. His hands were tied to the back of the cart, and Big John Chilton, the blacksmith, who was to give out the punishment, stepped forward. He was holding the whip, a short stick to which were attached nine, yard long strips of leather – it was the cat-o-nine tails that was used on ships.

Malky and Davey had first been standing with the Milbourn family, and Davey had managed to get just behind Peggy. He dared not speak to her but she had sensed his presence and they lost no opportunity to look into each other's eyes, and occasionally touch fingers. Jenett and Mrs. Milbourn were too keen to keep their eyes on the whipping of the half-stripped men to pay any attention to what the scullion might be doing. Malky sloped away on his own looking for Molly, and soon found her standing beside Geordie Naesbitt and Micky Coulson and some of the other fisher folk. He squeezed in beside her, pushing Geordie and Micky good naturedly to one side. They pushed him back.

"Hey, if ye'se lot start fightin', they'll give ye all a good whippin'," cried out Molly.

"Well if they de, it'll give me a chance to show ye me muscles and me hairy chest," said Micky.

"Nae thank ye," replied Molly. "Noo hush yersel, I wanna watch."

Big John had taken up his position. He was tall and barrel chested with thews hardened by daily labour. He stepped back and then forward, bringing his right arm right back before propelling the whip towards the man's back. The tails whipped about in the air before striking the bare skin with a crack that was heard right across the Market Place. The man did not cry out, but those nearest could see the white of his knuckles as he gripped the back of the cart.

"How many does he get?" asked Malky.

"Until the skin breaks and the blood flows freely," said Geordie.

On the fifth lash, the skin broke, and on the sixth there was blood. The blacksmith paused and looked at Puncheon who waved him on. After two more strokes the crowd could see the blood spurting and running down the back. The whipped man was resting his head on his hands and groaning. His hands were untied from the middle and attached to one of the rails at the side of the cart. The next man struggled as he was tied down and then the whipping started again. Once more Puncheon did not stop the flogging until a good two strokes after the first blood was drawn and some in the crowd started jeering.

Then it was Jobling's turn. He was bigger than the other two men and well-muscled. It took longer for the skin to break and Puncheon did not halt the whipping until there was not only a stream of blood, but pieces of flesh that could be seen flying off. Big John stopped. Puncheon urged him on. Big John was a hard man but he knew when he should call a halt. He stood back and spoke in a voice that carried, "He's had more than the other two put together. If ye want the floggin' to gan on, then ye de it yersel."

The crowd were shouting. The fishers wanted more and the panners wanted it stopped. Isaac Frost stood forward and called out. "Let's get the cart rolling." The cartman jumped up to his seat and flicked his own whip over the back of the horse and slowly moved off. The crowd moved back as the cart circled the Market three times dragging the three men behind. They barely held their footing as they were humbled before the crowd and the bairns threw clumps of mud at them.

Malky had got very close to Molly who had enthusiastically cheered as the blood spattered. She had not seemed to notice where he put his hands, and what he was pressing up against her thigh, but when the cart passed them, she pushed him away. "Dain't ye get any ideas, Malky, rubbing yersel against me like a rutting dog. If I were to let ye have what ye want, and ended *belly-up*, then I'd be the one having strips taken off me back."

Geordie and Micky had heard – they'd have had to be stone deaf not to.

"Weel, at least we'd all get a good look at your titties, Molly," laughed Micky, and it was a good job that he had quick reactions or his head would have been knocked off his shoulders if the swipe she gave him had landed. Even Malky had had to jump back.

"Now ye'se lot leave me be as I'm ganna de some sellin'. I was up at five to get an early ferry across to the north side and walked to Tynemooth to collect winkles and mussels, and anything else that folk 'll eat. I've cooked it all up, tossed it in salt and vinegar and should sell it easy enough with all this crood."

Malky put his arms right round Molly and whispered, "Can I come round the nicht. Naebody will know that I'm oot noo we're living in the cottage oot the way."

She looked at him with a sparkle in her eye. "Aye, Malky, but come up the steps quietly and dain't let any of the nosey parkers roond there see ye. They say enough aboot me as it is," she replied, and then lifted a heavy basket that was between her feet and hoisted it on to her head. Molly then opened her mouth and let out a long cry that could have meant anything, but got her noticed and soon there was a crowd around her buying shellfish. It was hungry work watching a flogging. It was a ha'penny a pint and a farthing for two gills, and she had some old pins for those who wanted to eat their winkles straight away, so long as they gave them back for others to use.

The crowds were slowly moving away, some taking the chance to have a quick pint before they returned to their work. Malky noticed Hamish coming out of Salt Well Lane with a pail in each hand. He had been asked by Isaac Frost to tend the backs of the flogged men. They had been untied but still leant on the back of the cart. Hamish took a rag out of his satchel and started washing down their backs with the well-water. It was known for its curative powers, either rubbed on or just drunk as a tonic. After the backs had been cleaned, Hamish spoke to Isaac Frost. Jobling had the worst damage and really needed a poultice, but he'd need some long strips of rag to tie round the torso to hold it together, and then he'd need to check it in two days' time. As Jobling was not one of Mr. Coatsworth's servants then Hamish doubted that he would be allowed to leave his salt-house in the West Panns to treat him. The other two men were sent on their way.

"Do ye have what ye need to make a poultice?" asked Frost.

Hamish tapped his satchel. "Aye, I half expected I'd need some. I've got the dried cow dung and willow bark, but I'll need warm water and somewhere to work – and not in a salt-house where there's coal dust in the air."

"Come on then, we'll gan to my son's hoose and get Jobling put strite. Will he be able to work tomorrow?"

"So long as he keeps his back covered and disna' have to do any heavy lifting."

After Hamish had done his work, the two Frosts, father and son, invited him to dinner with them in the parlour. Isaac Frost then rode back to the West Panns with Hamish following. He left the lad at the panns but went to see Coatsworth at his home at the Lay Gate lane.

Sheels had needed a pothecary for some time and now Isaac Frost decided to act. He bought out Hamish's indenture with Coatsworth, and young Burns was set up as a pothecary in Sheels. He would still treat the west panners but would earn more coin from the merchants and tradesmen of Sheels, who would pay well for his services. He would remain indentured to Frost, but could keep a half of his earnings until the monies that Frost had invested would be paid off. To start, he would work from the salt-house opposite his son's house. They were in the process of taking the single pann out and the house could double as a shop, and also serve as a workshop where Hamish could dry his herbs and make his ointments and potions, and where a still would not be out of place.

That night when Malky arrived at Molly's house he crept up the stairs and quietly opened the door. There were only a few logs in the hearth giving a low light and Molly was already under the blankets in her bed.

"Hey what ye'r deein'?" she whispered as Malky quickly took off his clothes and climbed in beside here. She put up a struggle, but her heart was not in it to resist the desperate young Scot's passions. As he lay on top of her, she lifted the palms of her hands against his chest. "I'll let ye have it the once, Malky, but when ye're ready to spill, ye'll pull yersel oot."

"Och aye," said Malky, ready to agree to anything to at last have the full warmth of a woman's body.

CHAPTER SIX

Marledane, the landlord of the *Turk's Heed*, no longer used the vault under his ale-house for Sunday morning drinking sessions, but it would come in handy in the future as a cellar to store the barrels of usquebah that Tomag's distilling business would produce. Hamish had made a drawing of the copper lid, pipes, and condensers, that he would need for a small still that a pothecary might use to distil potions for ointments, creams or perfumes to treat certain ailments. The vessel in which the mash would be boiled was just a smaller version of the tuns that Marledane used when brewing his ale, and the local smith could provide a suitable vessel. When Marledane went to Newcastle to the copper foundry, he not only ordered the equipment for Hamish, he also asked the master founder to make a larger set that would fit over a traditional vat that a householder would use for brewing ale. John McGilvray would ferry them to Sheels on his keel and make sure that no excise man would get a sight of them.

Tomag used Hamish's small still as an experiment to test the right amount of fermented barley mash to produce the life-spirit.

Tomag had obtained a glass bottle from Marledane to collect the spirit. The liquor was clear and Tomag was the first to take a sip. It was bitter and had a foul taste.

"Gie it a bit mair time," said Hamish, "the first drippings can sometimes take in the bad humours."

They poured away a small amount and then Tomag tried again. He licked his lips and then took a short swig, coughed and tears came to his eyes. "Och, it's fiery."

Hamish coughed even more.

"It disna' taste o' much noo, but it's mair than strong enow," said Tomag. "We'll put it into small barrels and let it stand for a few weeks to give it some flavour."

They waited till they had enough to fill a bottle and then took it next door so that Malky and Davey could try. Tomag then corked the bottle to take to Marledane that night.

Once he was satisfied, the other still was set up. They had first to ferment the malted barley which Marledane had provided, and to decide when it was ready for the boiling that would distil the alcohol. Marledane came over and stirred the mash to check for any bubbles, and then he tasted it before declaring it ready. They decanted into another vessel, and let it stand for a week before pouring it back into the boiling tub. The two stills were heated over small fires that they had made in the old hearth that used to heat the salt-pann that had been taken away. The coal came from the salt-house next door.

The following day the larger still was up and running. Hamish's old master knew something of the dangers of distilling. If the equipment was not air tight then there was the risk of gas seeping out. Explosions had been known to happen when the gas met the open flame, and anyone near to the still might be overcome by the fumes. The copper lid did not fit tightly over the brewing tun and Hamish had asked Marledane to get his wife to make some hard dough – the same she used as *coffins* for minced meat. He rolled it out thin to make a good seal. By the time the stilling was complete the dough was cooked hard. He also bought a wicker cage and had one of the lads he knew at the West Panns catch a linnet on Jarra's Lake. He kept it in the cage near to the stills. If any gas leaked, the bird would die quickly and Hamish could damp the flame and look for the leak. It would take several boilings of the large still to fill one barrel, and with the time needed for the fermentation of the mash, they realised that they were only likely to have enough for their own consumption, or sale to friends, if they only had the one still, but it was a start.

Malky and Davey were both love-lorn. Now that Tomag was foreman of the saltern, Davey was allowed to get close to Peggy for a few minutes in the morning when she brought their breakfast, but they barely had time for some kisses and a cuddle. Having tasted the forbidden fruit once, Davey wanted it again. Malky was still seeing Molly. They could kiss and canoodle, but Molly had made it clear that she had let him have it the once because it was his first time, but she could not risk falling pregnant and it would be cuddles only. The lad kept hoping that she would weaken, but Molly was a determined lass.

As well as Sundays, Malky would sometimes try to sneak round at night in the week. She was normally in bed to save on the wood or the coals and the lad would get in beside her, but one night she was sitting on a three-legged stool beside the hearth. She had a cup in her hand, and when she looked up Malky could see a single damp tear under one of her eyes. Now Molly Hawes was not a lass to shed tears.

"What's the matter, lassie?" asked Malky.

She smiled up at him. "Nowt that ye can fix, Malky lad," but she stood up and let him hold her tight and kiss her warmly on the lips.

"Och, you taste nice the nicht," whispered Malky.

She held the cup to his lips. "Just sip it forst, til ye get used to it."

Malky did. It was strong liquor with a flowery taste that burnt the back of your throat. "It's no' gin," he said.

"It's French brandy from Captain Bowmaker," Molly said, taking the cup and drinking another mouthful down. She went over to the hearth where a glass bottle stood on the floor. "Here, have another." She filled the cup and handed it to Malky. "But dain't tell anyone ye've been drinking it, or where it came from."

"Ye mean the brandy wells at Frenchman's cove."

She laughed, and stood very close to him while she shared the brandy cup. "My man, who's deed and gone, my Daniel - he was a wild one. All the lads roond here used to try it on with me once I'd started me rags, but I was as big as most of them and once I'd clouted them they stayed away. But not wor Danny, he'd come back for more. He was a tall lad but broad at the showlder and strang as an ox, with arms like whipcord. Once he got ha'd of me, I couldn't have got away even if I wanted to. He was a fisherman and worked on his father's coble, but he also did jobs for auld Bowmaker. He would take one of the sea cobles, with another lad to help with the rowing, to Frenchman's cove in the dark, and bring back whatever had been landed. It was cheaper than using donkeys and less risky. But one night two years gone to this very day, he never came back. He'd taken young Joe Coulson, Micky's brother, and neither them nor the boat were ever seen again. We said that they were lost oot night-fishing. The folk here knew different as Danny was nae *fyeul*, and if he was fishing he'd have taken at least one other man with him, as well as the boy. I always mark the day and so does Bowmaker. He gives me a bottle of this rot gut, but it only makes me weep for my Danny. We'd only been wed a few month. I had a bairn in my belly. My wee Gracie – Daniel's family let me live here as I'd nivver seen eye to eye with Dan's Mam. Little Gracie died of a pox when she was just a few months auld."

Malky had walked her over to the bed and they sat down side by side. She looked into his eyes. "But that's in the past and ye're here noo, Malky, with yer eyes of two different colours."

They drank some more, and managed to laugh and joke in between kisses. When at last they lay in the bed together Molly drew the young Scotch lad to her and they gave in to their desires. He never knew whether she was thinking of him, or of her Danny, but she responded to his passion, and when he thought she slept and readied himself to leave, she pulled him to her and rekindled his flame.

The next Sunday when Malky was on the strand wrestling with the fisher lads he saw Molly talking to Bowmaker. After the contest, which Malky won, the captain walked over. He was a plain speaker. "Molly says ye have a taste for the brandy."

Malky smiled. "Ach, it's a bit fiery for me."

"And that she told ye aboot her man, Daniel."

"Aye."

"It would be best if ye say nowt aboot it to any o' the other Scotch laddies. The fisher folk never talk aboot the goods I bring in at Frenchman's cove or at Manhaven come to that. Mind, the toon-folk will always buy anything that's cheaper than goods that have paid customs or excise."

"I'll say naught, Captain. I was gonna hae a word wi' ye anyway after what Molly tolt me." Malky hesitated but then carried on, his bonnet in his hands. "I luv Molly, and I would wed her, but I'm an indentured servant, as ye know, with another six and a half years to gang. I need to make some coin of me own and then I could buy oot my indentures and wed the lass. I just wanted to say that if there's any work ye need a strong back and limbs for, ye could count on me."

Bowmaker did not respond for a while. "Even if I can find the odd job it would never be enough to pay off your indentures, and whatever ye do, dain't get carried away with your feelings for Molly. If ye make her belly-up, she'll be whipped like Jobling was, and your master Ralph Milbourn will have to bring up the bairn, and he'll add extra years to your service to pay for it."

Malky's face fell and nearly touched the gravel on which they stood.

"Ye haven't.." Bowmaker thought better than to say what he was thinking. He was about to turn on his heel and then he paused. "The Good Lord works in mysterious ways, Malky, but ye have to help yersel."

"I've something else to tell ye, Captain. Ane thing that oor Tomag misses is his usquebah."

Bowmaker's face lightened. "I only drank it the once and I couldn't remember owt about it the next morning," he laughed.

"This is in confidence, ye understand, but he's made a friend of John Marledane, and they've set up a still. Me and Davey are helping them oot. We mind the stills when Hamish is oot seeing somebody. I didna' want ye to think that we were ganging into competition wi' ye, and if we make enough ye could help them sell it on."

Bowmaker slapped Malky on the shoulders, bent towards him and whispered in his ear. "We rogues stick together, Malky." He laughed and walked off to his prayer meeting at the sign of the *Orange Tree*.

The river was soon filling up with colliers waiting for coals from Newcastle. Tomag would tell Malky and Davey how the men of Sheels felt hard done by. The coal trade was run by the City Aldermen and hostmen of Newcastle, who had a monopoly on all shipping in the Tyne. All ships with cargo were supposed to berth at Newcastle to load and unload their cargoes, but the Tyne was a difficult river to navigate. The City fathers of Newcastle used none of the money they gained from their monopoly, on dredging or improving the stream. There were sandbanks and even islands on the eight miles from the river mouth to the Newcastle quayside, let alone the wrecks of ships that had attempted the journey and had grounded or collided with another vessel. The ship's masters were forbidden, on pain of fines or imprisonment, to unload or charge ships at North and South Sheels, or even empty their ballast at the Sheels ballast wharves, which were for the use of the fishermen and the salt masters. So they had to use and pay for the services of the keelmen, who were all bonded to the hostmen, to have their cargoes taken to and from the Newcastle quayside. The rules did not apply to the Freemen of Newcastle, who made full use of the privilege, and were also allowed to provision their ships from Sheels, which was also forbidden to others. This is what really upset the Sheels publicans and merchants.

"Marledane reckons that him and his ilk could make a fortune if they could provide ale and victuals for the voyages," said Tomag, "but they have to sit and watch while the keelmen haul it doon the river. They're thinking of putting someone up to opening a brewery for the shipping trade just to see what happens."

"But don't the mariners come ashore for their ale?" asked Malky.

"Och aye," said Tomag, "I dinna' think that even the bigwigs in Newcastle would try to stop a sailor frae coming ashore for his pint, or something else for that matter. They're not gang all the way to Newcastle in a keel to walk up Grope-Kunt alley when they can wander up some of the paths in Sheels were the widders live."

"Ye dinna mean the Widder Wallis?" whispered Davey.

"Nae, not her, but there's many a young widder with bairns, who's lost her man and not found another, who'll give a tar what he wants up a back alley to feed hersel' and her *wee yins*. They say that there's some who only de it when the Iceland and

Westmony fishermen come for their salt. They're away on the ocean for months, and they're all on the lookout for something afore they gan. They say that the women can make enough in three days to last them through the winter." He rubbed his hand over his lips. "Mind, they canna si' doon for a few days either," and he burst out laughing.

The lads didn't know what to make of it, but it determined Malky to try and make an honest woman of Molly.

When he was outside shivering in the April winds, and often soaked in the showers working the pump, Malky would watch the river traffic. He looked out for Niall on the keels but there were many Scots lads with blue bonnets, and he could never be sure if it was him he saw struggling with the long oar with his crewmates. In the middle of the month the winds turned into gales and blew straight from the North rather than off the sea. No ships could sail, and with the cross wind the keels could not tie up alongside the colliers, and so they all made for shore, either on the North or South side. Malky was pumping for all he was worth and only just heard the desperate shouts from the quay. A keel was struggling to land a rope on one of the bollards, but the water was so choppy with the full tide that even with all hands on the oar they could not keep the boat steady. The lad who had been hoyed up to the wharf-side had fallen back down and only just landed on the keel. Malky shouted at the top of his voice through the salt-house door and ran to the quayside. Angus McGilvray was standing on his toes and holding the swape down with all his strength as Niall once again hoyed the rope. This time Malky grabbed it and but for Tomag and Davey, who were now right behind him, would have been dragged into the ice-cold waters himself. They managed to wind the rope round the bollard and the bow was secured - it took another few fraught minutes before they had the stern as well. Then the skipper, Angus, and his crew shinned up the ropes and ran to the shelter of the saltern. The keelmen huddled round the furnace doors to warm up while a muttering Malky went out into the storm to continue the pumping. He had nearly lost his bonnet to the wind twice and took it off and pushed it down his breeches. After about an hour, but what seemed more like a day and a half, the door of the furnace room opened and Tomag waved him back in. The cistern was full, and they weren't due to fill any of the panns again until the morrow.

The drenched lad headed straight for the furnace door and stripped off his clothes to dry them off. Jobling had insisted that they just let clothes dry while they still kept them on, but Tomag had tied some branches together and hung them from the ceiling just above the furnace door so that the pump man could dry his clothes if needed. It didn't take long over the heat of the furnace for them to dry out. Malky stood naked by the open door, and the light from the coals showed off the muscles in his back and arms that six months' hard labour had done for him. He turned his head to look at the keelmen who were passing round a bottle of Tomag's usquebah. Niall passed the bottle to Malky who took a swig.

"Och you're a strapping fella' the noo, Malky-lad," shouted Niall. "Not like the skinny lad we first met at Dunbar!"

"He was no' a weakling, though, he took the heid off a Sassenach ," said Tomag, "and he's no deef either, Niall, you're not oot on the watters noo."

The keelmen were known for their loud voices, as they had to shout to make themselves heard when on the river.

"Ye may be strang, Malky," continued Niall, just as loudly, "but working in here in front o' the furnace and then gangen oot to the freezin' cauld'll finish ye aff. Just like it would hae done to me, had oor Angus and his brither not got me onto the keels."

"It's skipper to ye," shouted Angus back and pushed Niall on the arm. Angus turned his head and saw their boy staring hard at Malky's back and shoulders. "Och, if ye stay wi' us ye'll hae muscles jest like Malky, *Peedee*."

"Aye why don't ye gang and hae a closer look, if ye want to, Peedee," shouted Jockie, the bully. "Yon lad might let ye feel his muscle if ye ask him nicely."

The others laughed coarsely as little Peedee looked at his feet. He could not have been much more than twelve or thirteen, but he was no weakling – the boys on the keels grew up quickly.

"I'll hae no talk like that, Jockie," shouted Angus angrily and walked aggressively towards the man.

"I meant naught, skip," shouted back the man, "but standing here in this heat is giving me a thirst for ale. That usquebaugh just loosened ma tongue."

"Weel, ye've had a good idea for ance," said Angus. He walked over to where Tomag was standing. "I doubt if this wind is gang to blow ower the nicht, and I don't want to sleep in the *huddick* in this gale. There'll no' be any problem if we stay the nicht here, Tomag?"

"I'll have to ask Mr. Milbourn, but I canna see any difficulty. He might have some straw or blankets," replied Tomag.

Angus poked about in the pouch that hung from his belt.

"If we're gang to visit an ale hoose, we'll need some coin. I hae a few pence but not enough for us all. We're getting paid noo in tokens which we can cash at ale-hooses and shops in Sandgit' that the hostmen own, or hae an arrangement wi'. I doubt that they'll tak 'em in Sheels, but your Mr. Milbourn might be able to give us coin for them and he can use them to pay for his coal."

"Ye'll want feeding as well. We eat at six and hae oor food brought to us here. I'll ask if they can make a bit more for you'se all. It would be best if ye came wi' me to see him yersel. We can walk over the noo if ye want," replied Tomag.

They went out into the storm, and although it was only just after noon, the sky was black and it could have been night it was so dark. Ralph Milbourn knew Angus of old as he had often bought coal from him for coin if they had some left over, no questions asked. The keelmen could sleep in the furnace room and Peggy would bring over some straw and blankets. He spoke to his wife and they were going to have salt pork with beans and pease pudding. She would just add more to the pot. He took one of Angus' tokens.

"I'd heard that the hostmen were using tokens for their keelers. There's been a shortage of coin in Sheels as weel, and some of the merchants here are giving out their own tokens. The Parliament doesn't like coins with the King's heed on, but they're not making enough of their own to make up. I'll take the tokens if you sign a note, Skipper McGilvray. I'll give ye ten pence to the shilling."

"Ye'd take money oot of the pocket of a poor keelman, when we're on a laying tide. We'll only get 2s 6d for the stop ower and not the 13s 4d we're entitled to. If we can't sail for more than three days then our families in Sandgit' will gang withoot." Angus tried to keep his voice under control but it was loud enough.

Milbourn sensed his anger. "I'm not charging for the food as ye're friends of Tomag," he paused, "if ye leave me a basket of coals, before ye leave I'll give ye full money for the tokens."

"Och, in a gale like this there's always a few that fly aff frae the top. Ye write the note and I'll make my mark."

Niall had kept himself in the background as he did not want to be recognised. He was not going to the ale-houses, and would take shelter in the keel's huddick for the afternoon. It had a brazier and he would take some hot coals from the furnace to start a fire.

The other keelmen ran to the nearest ale-house, the *Orange Tree*. They were not allowed in as another crew of keelmen were already there drinking ale. The Sheels publicans were used to the keelmen when they had to lay over, and knew from experience that whilst the crew rarely fought with each other, they would nearly always fight with another keel's crew over something. In any case their rough language and loud voices often led to locals going elsewhere, so one crew at a time was enough. Angus led the others along the way to the *Turk's Heed* that Tomag had mentioned, and they settled in there for the afternoon. Peedee had asked if he could stay at the salt-house as he did not want to venture out into the storm, and have to sit and listen to his crewmates shout at each other as they quaffed ale.

He was a wiry lad with a cheeky smile and a mop of black hair that fell over his brow. He asked Malky if he could help and he was soon shovelling coal into a basket to bring to the furnace which Malky was stoking. As they chatted Malky called him Peter, which is what he thought he had heard. "Naw, Peter's not my name. It's Peedee," he said,

"Och, is it short for something?" asked Malky.

"Naw, all the boys on the keels are called Peedee, and divvent ask me why. I've asked the skipper and he just says that the boys have always been called Peedees, and so far as he was concerned always would. We divvent get paid but live with wor skippers' families and have wor food and ale. Me Da's a collier at Winlaton, and we often went withoot so I was happy to gan with the skipper. As soon as I'm strang enough I'll be a keelman mesel."

Both panns would be ready for drawing the morrow so they were letting the furnaces die slowly. Tomag asked Malky to keep an eye on them and he'd take Davey to see if they could find the keelmen and take a drink with them for an hour. The rain seemed to have passed for the minute, but it was still blowing hard.

"D'ye want to come wi' us, Peedee?" asked Tomag.

"Naw, I'll stay with Malky."

At six Peggy came in with a large kettle full of pork, beans, and a pease pudding. She had a two-pound loaf under her arm, and a pail of ale in the other hand. She looked round. "Is Davey not here?"

"Och, no," said Malky. "He's ha'ing some ale wi' the keelmen, but they know when the meal's served."

"I'll leave the kettles here." She seemed to be reluctant to go. "The master's having his dinner with the Frosts at Biddick Hall on Sunda'. I asked the mistress if I could gan to visit my parents at Harton. I've not seen them for a six month and I'm supposed to gan once every quarter. If I went I'd need a lad to come with me as I'd be taking my wages that go to them. I kna' the master wouldn't let Davey gan, but he'd trust ye, and Davey could meet up with us on the way."

"Och aye I could, so long as this weather has passed. I'd no' fancy walking a ways in the wind and the rain."

"It's a few days yet," said Peggy.

As she was leaving she asked if someone could tell her when they'd finished eating and she'd come for the kettles. "And ye'll need to fetch the straw and the blankets." She seemed a bit more cheerful.

"Ye hungry?" Malky asked the boy.

"Wye aye, I'm bliddy starvin'," shouted Peedee.

Malky was so shocked that he automatically cuffed him on the lug, just like his own father would have done had he used intemperate language. "Ye don't use that sort o' language wi' me. Ye're not on the keel the noo." Straight away he regretted his act and his hand lingered on Peedee's cheek. "Ye're only a wee lad, Peedee. I didn't hurt ye?"

"Naw, ye barely touched me, but if ye act like a bairn on the keels ye'll soon be ower the side."

"Run doon to the keel and tell Niall he can come back up. Naebody but us and the keelmen will be in here the nicht."

Peedee ran off and was soon back with Niall.

Malky opened the furnace doors to give them some light and cut three thick slices of bread. They used their knives to cut into the pease pudding and then spooned out some pork. They were hungrily chewing the food when the others returned. There was little talk as they all helped themselves to the meat and pease, and a horn cup passed round for the ale. After the meal, Tomag went up to the house to take the pans and kettles back. Malky and Peedee tagged along. As well as straw and blankets they were given a brazier to warm the keelmen in the night. The rain had all but gone now and the wind seemed to be blowing itself out. When they returned and told Angus of the weather, he said that unless the storm blew up again they would leave after their breakfasts. Tomag decided to sleep there with them.

When Malky and Davey arrived at the salt-house the next morning, the keelmen were all laughing and Peedee was pulling with his hands on Niall's doublet. "Aw tell us what it was like then, Niall."

"Ach, ye're a dirty little arse-worm," shouted Jockie. "If ye come here I'll show ye what it's like," and he made a tugging movement between his legs.

Malky looked at Tomag who was laughing with the rest.

"It turns oot that ma wee brither has become a bit of a beard-splitter since he's been away, and as there's not enow in Sandgit' to keep him busy, he's starting on the Sheels lassies, and oor Alice Ferman of all people."

Malky was none the wiser and asked, "What's a beard-splitter?"

"Och, ye're an innocent ane Malky," cried Angus. "Have ye nivver split a woman's beard then, laddie?"

"But women don't have beards," said Malky walking right into it, and hearing the furnace room rock with the keelmen's laughter, with Peedee nearly hysterical beside him.

"Not on their chins," said Tomag, trying to keep a straight face.

It still took Malky another good minute to grasp what they meant. When he twigged he blushed a deep red, and then clipped Peedee round the ears. "And ye shouldn't be listening to this filthy talk, ye're only a bairn." He looked at Niall. "But wi' Alice Ferman? She's a bit slow, isn't she?"

"Not when it comes to lifting her skirts up," grinned Niall. "I'm surprised ye didn't hear her groaning when I had her up against the wa' of your cottage last nicht."

When the keelmen were settled for the night and most of them asleep, Niall had had to get up to have a piss. He went over to the coal heap and heard a noise. After he'd relieved himself he crept forward, and saw a woman filling a pail with coals from the heap with a small shovel. "I didna' want to scare her so I just said very quietly that she should no' be stealin' the coals. She nearly jumped oot of her skin as it was, but said that with the cauld weather coming on sae sudden, the Widder Wallis had run oot of coals and they were so cauld they couldna' sleep. The widder had said that Tomag, the salt panner, who lived opposite, would no' mind if they took a small pail, and she could let him have something in return." There were some more chuckles from the listening keelmen as Niall continued. "So I said that I would no' tell the constable as she was a neighbour of Tomag, and that I'd see her safe back hame." He paused a moment and rubbed the dimple on his chin. "But I said that she'd ha' to gie me something in return. I carried the pail and had my arm roond her skinny waist, and whispered into her ear as we walked up the alley. She knew what I wanted and didna' say no."

The wind was still blowing but not enough to stop them from setting out. They waited until after they had had their oatmeal pudding and ale before they went down to the keel and filled up a basket of coal for Mr. Milbourn. Tomag saw them off and gave Angus a bottle of his usquebah to keep them warm on their trip, but to bring the empty bottle back. When Tomag had talked to Angus about his plans to distil more of the spirit, the skipper had agreed to take any barrels up to Newcastle and could easily find a place by the boards which held the coal in place.

"Will it take ye lang to get back hame?" asked Malky.

"Most of the day. The tide's low noo so we can get to the collier easy enough, but once we're half way doon this pile," he pointed to the stack of coal held firm by the boards, "it'll be hard hoicking the coal up to the portholes. Once the tide starts coming in then it lifts us up and we can finish aff and still hae' the tide behind us when we heed back to quays in Newcastle. We work by the tides and one trip there and back is seven hours short of twenty-four."

Malky was thinking that if they could manage five or six tides a week then they would earn good money, at 13s 4d a tide. But it was hard work, and dangerous if the wind and waves were against them.

Malky had sneaked round to see Molly on the Friday night to tell her that he wouldn't be coming on Sunday, and he explained about taking Peggy to Harton.

"So as soon as ye're on the road to Harton young Davey-lad will meet up wi' ye?"

"Och aye."

"And he and Peggy haven't done any canoodling for a few month?"

"Och no."

"Weel, you're ganna find yersel on your own as soon as they find somewhere they can…weel ye kna' what I mean, and they won't want ye watchin' them. Why dain't I come with ye, and mebbes we could find somewhere to be alone?" Molly was trying to fend Malky off as they sat on her bed. "Had on a minute, Malky. Ye'd think ye hadn't had it for…"

"Five days," said the young Scot, as he started to take his clothes off.

She didn't get any more conversation out of him until they'd spent themselves and lay together under the blankets. Malky was happy for Molly to come with them, but suggested that she go out as usual on the sands combing for wood, and then meet up with them. She said she'd put some food in a basket in case they got hungry. "Auld Bowmaker was saying that ye want to come in with him on the smuggling. If ye de, ye'll need to kna' the bays and coves on the coast to Marsden. And there's caves there where ye can gan in, and nae one will see what ye're deein'. Why dain't ye get Davey to meet us at Trow Rocks. Ye and Peggy can come across the fields and we can work wor way along the cliffs to Harton."

When Malky left that night and walked as quietly as he could down the steps and made his way down the alley to the way, he heard a door open and the voice of a woman. "There he gans again, the Scotchman and wor Danny only gone two-years." It was Molly's mother-in-law. Malky thought to himself that it was probably a good thing that he wasn't going round on the Sunday.

Malky and Davey were up early that Sunday morning. It was the last day of April and the sky was clear. Malky waited outside the Milbourns' door for Peggy, while Davey ran off down the Low Way. He had been happy to agree to Malky's suggestion that they meet at the Trow Rocks and would head over the sands. He'd keep an eye out for Molly who would be going the same way.

Ralph Milbourn was with Peggy when the door opened.

"Reet, Malky lad, here's a pouch with Peggy's earnings for the last six month. Ye be sure to give it to her fatha' noo. If they ask ye to stay to dinner then ye can come back with her, but if they dain't then she'll be all reet walking back on her own."

Peggy was a quiet and shy girl and had blushed when Malky told her of his plans, but when they met Davey, who had been sitting on a stone near the Trow Rocks, she ran to him and they were hugging each other with passion. Malky heard a shout and saw Molly walking along the sands, a basket under her arm. The sun was up and it was now warm with a brisk breeze off the sea. She looked a real bonny lass with her yellow hair just poking out of her bonnet. Her blue bodice stiffened with *bents* pushed out her bosom and showed off her cleavage and her shoulders, unlike Peggy, who wore a linen collar and long sleeves. Both women wore their best Sunday dress. The two lads, in their grubby working clothes, had only their taut muscular bodies, their bright eyes and their eager smiles to show.

"What time are your parents expecting ye, Peggy?" asked Molly.

"They're not. They dain't kna' I'm coming. But when I gan ower there on a Sunda' I usually arrive after they've had their bait of the morning and then stay for dinna'."

Molly looked at the sun. "Weel, we've probably got an hoor or two. Have ye seen the Fairies Kettle, Davey?"

"Ach no. And I'm not sure I want to - I'm afeared of fairies."

"Weel, Peggy'll have to ha'd your hand, or someitt else," said Molly laughing crudely as Peggy blushed red, but Davey had a crafty smile. They walked down to the sand and Molly pointed to the cave. "Gan up there. Me and Malky'll sit on the rocks and then come in for wor turn." It was Malky's turn to blush. Molly looked at him. "Weel, Malky-lad, if ye dain't want it today, we can just sit here and throw stanes into the watter. The tide'll be up soon."

"Ach, ye know I want it, Molly," he said quietly. "But ye've no need to shout it oot so much."

As soon as he started kissing, and Molly let his hands roam over her soft and welcoming body, his reservations soon left him, and after what seemed to him an age Molly whispered to him that they'd given the other two enough time. As they half climbed the rocks up to the kettle, Malky called out. "We're coming noo."

He could hear groaning and the sound that two bodies make when they're locked together in heat.

"Och just gie me another minute, will ye, Malky," called out Davey in an agonised voice, and the noises grew in intensity until Davey cried out and Peggy moaned. They quickly straightened their clothes and Malky showed Davey how to go up to the top of the cliff. Molly was waiting for him.

When Malky and Molly emerged onto the cliff top, Davey and Peggy were sitting on the green under the gorse bush, holding hands and looking into each other's eyes.

"Weel, I dain't kna' aboot ye'se but I'm feeling peckish noo after fighting off wor Malky," said Molly. Malky just had a sly grin on his face which told its own story. They both sat down and Molly started rummaging in her basket.

"I made some oat *cyeks* mesel last neet, and a pease puddin', and I stopped off this morning first thing at Mrs. Atkinson's up chicken path for some fresh cheese. She had some fresh eggs that she'd boiled so I bought half a dozen of those for a penny. I'm skint noo, so if there's time the day I'll gan ower to Tynemooth this after and pick some winkles."

The two lads had not eaten that day and fell on the food like wolves on a fold. She'd not brought ale but she sent Malky back down into the cave to fill up a pot she'd carried with her, from the Fairies Kettle and he managed to bring it up without spilling too much of the cool and fresh spring water.

After they'd eaten their fill they ambled along the cliff edge. They walked on past Frenchman's Bay.

"Och, why's it called Frenchman's Bay?" asked Davey.

It was Peggy that answered. "It was years ago when a French ship was wrecked there. There was only one survivor, and he managed to clamber up the cliff where the path is noo, and trekked across the fields until he came to Harton toon. Mind that was the auld toon. They took him in as folks did in those days with any stranded mariner, but a couple of days later he started coughin' and sweatin' and geet big black boils started growing all ower his body. It was the plague and when news got oot the men of Westoe and Sheels sent for the garrison at Newcastle. They surrounded the toon and nae one could get in or oot. Everybody died, including the bairns. When they were all deed the troops threw pitch and tar into the hooses and then shot burning arrows onto the thatch and burned everything to a cinder. Some say they heard the screams of some who might not have been as deed as they had thought. They built a new hall and a toon further doon the road and that's why some still call it New Harton. Ye can still see the ruins of the auld hooses but if ye gan at neet, ye sometimes hear the screaming of the burning souls."

"Wye, I nivver knew that," said Molly, "but ye're reet, because auld Bowmaker always calls it New Harton. Ye can show us the ruins when we get to the toon then, Peggy."

"Och, I'm not gangen to anywhere there's been a plague, and wi' ghosties screamin'" muttered Davey.

"We won't pass the toon on the way to me Da's because we live at a cottage by the cliffs. There's a fold there for the cattle that graze on the cliff fields and on Harton Down, and he has plough oxen for the other fields that the Widder Clibbourne holds."

"Ye'll kna' the Manhaven then?" asked Molly.

"Wye aye," replied Peggy, "and the cove before ye get to Manhaven where there's the deep cave. We all have an idea what auld Bowmaker gets up to. Me Da' says he sees nowt, hears nowt and says nowt, but he nivver says nae when the Captain gives him a bottle of that French brandy, or some raisins or spices."

They could nearly see the cottage now, which was set back form the cliffs at the end of a lane that led down from Harton Down home-stall. The cliffs were not as high as they had been and you could see a small cove just below them. Molly took Malky and Davey down but Peggy stayed on the cliff top. "The tide'll be up soon so ye'd better be quick, Molly," she shouted down.

"Dain't worry, hinny, I kna' what I'm deein'."

Once they had reached the bottom of the slope they could see that the waves were coming in fast, but Molly took no notice and led the two lads up a rock ledge to where there was the mouth of a cave. They bent as they entered but they could soon stand up. The cave itself was above the high tide but the sands below would be covered. They couldn't see much but the cave clearly extended a long way back. "If ye put anything in here, it will stay put," said Molly.

They heard a screech form Peggy and made their way back out. The last wave had come right up to the foot of the rocks and more big waves were thundering in.

"It's the bliddy tide," muttered Molly. "Tyek yer shoes and stockings off, we'll need to plodge oot." The lads followed her lead and walked out carefully down the rock ledge. When they felt the sand and pebbles beneath their feet the water was up to their knees. Peggy was shouting at them to be quick. They clambered up the rocks that led up to the top just as a wave much larger than the others thundered in and would have had them floundering.

Davey ran to Peggy who shouted, "I thowt ye knew what ye were deein', Molly."

"Aye, I'm sorry, Peggy, I should have known ye can nivver trust the seas."

Malky had sat himself down and laid his shoes and socks on the ground while he let the sun dry his legs.

It didn't take long and they were soon standing on the cliff top looking down at the bay they called Manhaven. It was a smaller inlet than Frenchman's, but the sandy beach was level and protected by high rocks on either side. You could launch a coble there in rough seas.

"The cottage's just ower there," said Peggy, pointing to a thatched building in a dip. There were a couple of sheds and a farmyard with an enclosed garden.

Davey spoke up. "If ye gie' me the coin, Malky, I'll gan in wi' Peggy and can stay wi' her, and walk her hame."

"Ach, Davey, Mr. Milbourn gave the money to me and said that I was to gie it to Peggy's parents. When I get back I'll hae to tell him that I did what he asked," Malky replied apologetically.

Peggy looked at the crestfallen Davey. "The master was adamant that it would have to be Malky to bring the money, and if he sees me Mam and Da' and asks them they'll have to say it was the Scotch lad Malky. But why dain't ye wait here with Molly, and I'll ask me parents if ye can come in and stay for dinna'. I'll say ye're a friend."

"Aye," Molly agreed, "but if they agree and Malky comes back with me then he'd better gan his own way once we get near Sheels. Folk doon the toon-end are starting to gossip aboot Malky sniffing roond - me auld Mutha'-in-law included."

When Peggy led Malky into the cottage, followed by a half-crazed hound that was yelping and jumping up in joy at seeing Peggy, her mother looked up.

"Aw Peggy, ye couldn't have come at a worse time, hinny."

She was of the same build as Peggy, skinny as a rake and with wispy hair poking from under her woollen cap. Her face was sharp featured and haggard. The cottage was old and had one room with a central hearth and no chimney or cowl. A lad who looked a couple of years younger than Peggy sat on one of two settles that made a corner by the fire, but he did not look well and spent most of his time coughing.

"Young Hal is bad with his chest again. He gans doon to the sea every day when the tide's gannen oot to tyek away the humours, but it hasn't done him any good, and the walk takes so much oot of him that all he can de is sit by the fire and cough."

"Where's me Da'?" asked Peggy.

"His back's bad, and he decided that he'd rest it, what with it being the Lord's Day, but it wasn't that bad that he couldn't hoist himself up onto the donkey to tyek him to the Ship for his ale. He says the publican got ha'd of some French brandy, and a good cup will ease his pain. Ye'll be lucky if ye see him today and then if the donkey comes back on its own I'll have to walk up the lane to where he's fallen off and half carry him back. It's nae use ye coming here with a fancy man and expecting dinna'…"

"Aw, shurrup, Mam," said Peggy, "and he's not my fancy-man. He's Mr. Milbourn's servant and the master asked him to walk with me here, as he's got me wages for the last six months to give to me Da'."

Her mother looked up sharply to Malky. "Weel, ye're not giving it to him or it'll gan strite doon his gullet. Ye can give it me."

Malky did not demur and he handed the pouch to the woman. She poured the coin out on to the table. "The Lord be praised. Ye're a good lass, Peggy. I can mebbes buy a bit of ox-tail and make some good broth for Hal to build his strength up.

"We were just ganna' have some green cheese and oatcakes for wor dinna', and the auld man would have warmed up pottage from yesterday. There's work on the farm to de, and I haven't got time to cook as well. In any case we're oot of coals, and wood'll need chopping for the fire."

Peggy spoke quietly to her Mother. "Ye look worn oot, Mam. Malky's gan' strite back and canna stay with me, but one of his Scotch friends, Davey, came with us and he's not in a hurry to get yem. The master's oot for dinna' so there'll be nowt for me when I get back. Ye can stay by the hearth and me and Davey'll do any work. Have ye got any once-cooked beans and any salt pork and I can quickly put it in the pot while

Davey chops the wood? Then we can have a proper dinna' and Davey can gan and get me fatha'."

Her mother was too tired to argue and pointed to a large chest by the back wall where her provisions were kept, while she slumped into the settle next to Hal.

Malky just left, and in a minute or two they heard Davey's steps in the yard. Because Peggy wasn't with him, the hound went for him, hackles up and barking. Davey just went down quick onto his knees and held his open palm out to the dog. Still growling and baring its fangs, the dog pushed its snout aggressively into Davey's hand and nipped it with his teeth. Peggy had run out and knelt beside them and Davey was soon patting and stroking the beast.

"Come on in," said Peggy. Davey followed her in. "Me Da's bad with his back and so ye'll have to do his work the day while I cook the dinna'."

Davey nodded to Mrs. Blayre and Hal.

"We'll need some wood choppin' for the fire first," said Peggy.

Davey looked round and found an axe and a basket by the door which held a collection of hoes, rakes, spades and scythes.

Hal called out, "The hound'll show ye were to gan," and then went into a coughing fit. He put his hand in front of his mouth and when he took it away there was black blood on his fingers. His mother wiped it away on her pinny.

"Ye should gie him some auld ale wi' honey for his cough. Me Ma swore by it," said Davey before going out to the yard with the dog leading him round the side of the cottage. He found a lean-to shed where there was a pile of logs and dead branches. The stump of a tree was used as a chopping block and Davey set to work.

He carried in enough chopped logs to build the cottage fire and then he filled a pail from the well, and took it in for Peggy to boil the pork and drain away the salt water before cooking it with the beans and lard. He then had to fill the troughs in the night pound. As the donkey would be waiting outside the ale-house at Harton, he had to fetch two of the oxen that were grazing in the old quarry and harness them to a cart. After he'd replenished the troughs he was sent up to the old quarry to carry some loose stone that was needed to repair the wall in the pound nearest to the cliffs where the recent storm had done some damage. Robbie Clibbourne, the widder's son who now ran the farm, had been on to his tenant to do the work, but George's back had stopped him. As Davey was unloading the stone he saw a man coming towards him from the home-stall. He was a well-built man in his early thirties with red hair poking out from under his black hat. As he neared, he shouted in a gruff voice, "And who are ye, working on the Lord's Day?"

Davey stood up and doffed his bonnet. "I'm Davey Finlayson, a servant of Mr. Milbourn of Sheels. I came here wi' Peggy who was bringing her wages for her parents, and then I'll see her safely hame. Her Da's back's bad so I'm doing a bit of work that he could no' manage."

"D'ye kna' what ye're deein?"

"Och aye, I was a dab hand at building wa's on me Da's croft. I've got a hammer, but I coudna' see a stone pick in Mr. Blayre's tool basket."

The man rubbed his chin. "Wharraboot ale? It's thirsty work repairing walls."

"I didna' see an ale barrel in the cottage, and if there was then young Hal should hae' it, warmed up wi' some honey, for his cough," said Davey.

"Come up to the hoose wi' me, then, and I'll give ye a pick and some ale. I'm the Widder Clibbourne's son Robbie and I de most of the work roond here. Me Mam's been a bit touched since me Da' passed away. If she comes oot and starts talking to ye as though ye're somone she kna's, just gan alang with her."

The Harton-down home-stall was a good-sized stone-built hall with a chimney. Davey could see that there was a big chunk of fat beef roasting over the fire, and Robbie's wife, a tall woman in her Sunday best, was poking it with a skewer. A much older woman with straggly hair and a wild look about her eyes was sitting in a settle by the hearth muttering to herself. Robbie had found a stone-pick, and Robbie's wife came out with a quart jar of ale for him.

"I'll come doon to inspect the work when ye're done," said Robbie. "Is George up the *Ship?*"

"Och aye."

"And on the brandy nae doot."

"Aye, I've got to gang and fetch him when ma work's done and bring him back for his dinner. Thanks for the ale, master, and I'll de a good job for ye."

"Call me Robbie, lad. We're all equal under the eyes of the Lord."

A couple of hours later Robbie Clibbourne walked down to where Davey was just finishing up. He looked closely at the repair and gave it a couple of hefty pushes but it stood firm. "That's good work. Are ye one of the Scotch lads that the salt masters bought from auld Haselrig?" Robbie asked.

"Och aye."

"Is that reet that you're bound to him for work, but get no pay?"

"Aye, seven years hard labour. But he feeds us well."

"Seven year, and nowt to show at the end of it," mused Robbie. "Can ye work for anyone else?"

"I've never asked, but we work twelve hoors at the panns and only have the Lord's day off," replied Davey.

"If auld George's back gets any worse I might need someone to do a bit of work, and I dain't mind someone, apart from me, that is, working on a Sunda'. I usually pay a penny a day, but if it's work that George should have done, I'll give ye a ha'penny and Mrs. Blayre can feed ye."

He opened a small pouch that hung from his belt. "Here's a ha'penny for the day. Ye can buy yersel some ale."

When Davey walked into the ale-house at the sign of the *Ship*, the conversation stopped as everybody looked round at the stranger with a blue bonnet. He went over to a tall, thin man wearing a leather apron who stood by the open fire against the back wall. "I'm after George Blayre," he mumbled and held out a quart jug, "and a ha'pennorth of auld ale, please."

A red faced, barrel-chested man, who was sitting very straight in one of the settles by the hearth looked the lad over. "Did the auld hinny send ye?"

The conversation started up again.

"Och aye, I came wi' Peggy to bring her wages frae Mr. Milbourn. Peggy's cooked the dinna', and they thought you might want to come hame for it."

"Weel, I could de with another cup of brandy before I gan, if ye've got some coin."

"Ach no, I only have the ha'penny for the ale and that's for Hal for his chest, he was coughing awfu' bad, and auld ale wi' a bit of honey's the best thing for him."

The landlord gave Davey the jug of ale. "Ye say young Hal's chest is nae better..?"

"He was coughing blood just noo."

The landlord went over to a big wooden chest, opened the lid an pulled out a pail. He took an empty cup and dipped it in. "That's from the Widder Clibbourne's hives. It'll de the lad some good." He could see that Davey was hesitant. "It's a gift from me, lad." He then whispered, "I kna' that George spends coin here that should be spent on victuals, so tell Hal's Mam that this is for the lad."

George was unsteady on his feet and Davey only just managed to keep him on the donkey's back as well as hold on to the honey and ale. After their dinner Davey and Peggy brought the cows and oxen back to their pounds and then made their way back to Sheels.

CHAPTER SEVEN

When Malky woke the next morning he remembered the May Day festivities at Blairgowrie, but today was going to be just like any other at the salt-house. He'd remembered feeling miserable on his first Christmas in Sheels. There had been no staying up for midnight on the eve of Christmas, and he had worked as normal on Christmas Day when most of the shops and ale-houses were open and the church closed. Nobody liked it but the Parliamentarians were in charge and were down on all sorts of enjoyment. It hadn't stopped Mr. Milbourn from having a goose for his dinner, and the salt-house servants had had theirs when they'd finished their work and were given extra ale.

Stoking the furnace, when he would rather have been dancing round a May-pole, his thoughts would drift to the time he'd spent with Molly the day before, but he was wondering when he would see her again. Peggy came in with their dinner a bit early, looking flustered. For once she didn't run over to Davey.

"I dinna' what's gannen on, but there's a big crood coming along the way from the toon-end, and folk are shouting and making an awful row." The panners forgot their dinner for a minute and ran out up to the way. Malky could see a group of the fishermen he knew, leading the crowd and carrying a long pole on their shoulders. They had ribbons on their hats and carried ribboned sticks. Those following were shouting and singing and making rough music, beating on kettles and pans – one or two had drums and horns and there was even a couple of fifers. As soon as Malky reached the way, Geordie Naesbitt, who was in the front of the gang with Micky Coulson, shouted, "There he is, let's grab him, lads," and dashed forward. Before Malky had a chance to ask what was going on, strong hands grabbed him, unbuttoned his doublet and tore it off him, then his shirt was pulled over his head. They put his blue bonnet back on, pushed him onto the pole.

"Had on tight, Malky," shouted Geordie into his ear, "and look as though you're enjoying it or they'll hoy all sorts at ye." His hands were tied to the pole with fisher's twine, and he was hoisted up in the air as the pole was lifted on to the shoulders of four men - two at the front and two at the back.

"What are they deeing to oor Malky?" shouted Tomag.

Jimmy Jobling who was standing beside them answered, "They're making him ride the stang. I'd heard that the fishers were ganna de something for May Day, but I'd nivver thowt it would be a stang-riding. I've not seen one since I was a bairn when they rode the stang to auld Mutha Muschamps' who'd broke her husband's heed, or so they sang. I dinna' what young Malky-lad's been up to, but we'll soon find oot. Haway," he shouted, throwing his hat into the air, "haway, for the stangers."

Tomag looked at Davey. "De ye kna' what oor Malky's been deein' that he should na'." Davey's face must have given him away. "With that Molly the fishwife?"

Davey had gone as white as a sheet and looked over to where Peggy was standing by Milbourn's doorway. Tomag saw the glance. "Well let's hope they dinna' come for ye as well."

The stangers had turned round, and made their way through the crowd that parted for them as they went back along the Low Way towards the toon-end and the fishers' houses.

Not many in the crowd were sure why the bare-chested Scotch lad with the blue bonnet was being stanged, but they shouted and jeered him as they went along. It was only when they neared the fishermen's part of the toon that someone ran forward with a dummy made of straw, dressed like a fisher lass, with two pig's bladders, stuffed with something to make them round and firm and just about strapped into the bodice. The stang was lowered and the straw lass was pushed between Malky's arms and tied round his waist, the pig's bladders were right in his face. He was hoisted up again and the laughter rose to a crescendo. Molly had been in the crowd but when she realised that it was her and Malky that they were stanging, she ran as fast as she could and up the stairs to her loft. Then one of the men in the crowd started shouting out words to an old song,

> *Malky the Scotchman's,*
> *Got a geet lang pole,*
> *And he's pokin' it where he shouldn't,*
> *Reet up wor Molly's .....*

They carried poor Malky up the alley where Molly lived. Then the door of the house below opened and John Hawes, Molly's father-in-law, came out. He was now bald and stooped of the shoulder, but he was still a hard man, and few would argue with him. He pushed himself through the crowd to the stang holders.

"Ye've had yer fun, lads. Noo put him doon and gan drink some ale."

"Weel it was your wife whe put us up to it, John."

"Ye've had your fun. Put him doon."

The two big lads at the front looked as though they might want to argue, but Geordie Naesbitt put his hands on their shoulders.

"Aye, let's put the poor bliddy Scot doon. We've still got the bonfire yet, and we can burn poor Molly."

Malky was unhitched, but as he put his feet on the ground he stumbled and nearly fell, clutching his groin. Sitting on a pole is not good for the thighs, or the ballocks for that matter. But the crowd had lost interest in him, and they all stood round on the strand where a pile of driftwood was being lit. A good stang always ended with a bonfire, and when it was blazing, the effigy of Molly was thrown onto the fire and the dry straw shot flames up into the air. Most of the local publicans had rolled barrels of ale out onto the strand and were selling it to anyone who had a pail or a horn to drink it out of. There were no ale cunners to check the measures, but nobody cared. The flames were seen by the mariners on the ships waiting for their coals or other cargo, and there were soon shouts to the watermen to bring a coble alongside to bring the sailors ashore.

The constable and the watch arrived but when they saw the numbers of folk who were enjoying themselves and who were well taken in ale, they decided to retreat back along the Low Way. They had heard, however, that the stangers had ridden a lad for what was described as fornication out of wedlock, which was, under the Parliament, an offence, meriting three months' imprisonment. When they started asking who it was, they only got, "I dinna'." People began to realise that if a lad was going to end up in prison for having it off with a fishwife, then half of the young lusty men in Sheels might be at risk. No more was said about Molly and Malky, apart from the odd snigger behind their backs, but there was always something else to talk about.

Malky had half staggered back home with the pain in his groin, and when he took his breeches off that night he felt some blood on his thighs and his balls were twice as big as normal. The next day he asked Hamish if he had any ointment he could put on. Hamish said he did, but that he'd have to have a look for himself before deciding what was the best treatment. The others sniggered as Malky went into the pothecary's shop. Hamish was doing well and his treatments were talked about, but he was getting a reputation for taking special care of young lads – any injury that was below the chin would require the patient to pull up his shirt and lower his breeches while Hamish had a good feel round. It was not long before they heard Malky shouting in panic to Hamish that he'd been rubbing the ointment on long enough and that he could do it himself. He came back in a few minutes later, pulling his breeches up, red in the face and covering his groin with his hands. There was stifled laughter but they all felt that Malky had put up with enough and nowt more was said.

Malky sulked for the next few days, but Hamish's ointments worked and he decided that he was not going to be bullied by the fishers. That Sunday he went down to the toon-end as usual for the wrestling and asked Tomag to come with him, in case there was trouble. Davey was away again to Harton – Peggy had managed to smuggle out a cup of honey and Davey was to take it for Hal. He would do any heavy work that was needed and hope that he might be paid for his labours by Robbie Clibbourne.

When they reached the wrestling ground, Malky strode up to Geordie Naesbitt and asked him if he was ready. "Wye aye," was the answer. Malky went in hard. There was a cold look in his eye, and whereas in the past he had tried not to hurt his opponents, this time he showed no mercy. When he threw Geordie to the ground he did nothing to stay the fall, landing on top of him with all his weight. He won all three rounds and by the finish Geordie was breathing heavily and half limped over to the edge of the green and sat down. Malky sought out Micky Coulson next, and any others that he remembered from the stang. Although they were big men, they stood little chance against the angry Scot. He won all his bouts and the others, who usually sparred with him, drifted away. He stood alone for a minute and then he walked over to where Geordie was sitting, and said in a loud voice.

"I'll see ye next Sunday, Geordie, and we'll hae a few more practice sessions, then." He put his hand out and helped Geordie get to his feet. The lad stood up with a look of relief on his face.

"Aye, we'll see you, Malky-lad, but ye might gan a bit easier on us." There were a few laughs. Malky had made his point and joined up with Tomag to go back up the Low Way. He looked over and caught sight of Molly standing by the opening to her alley with her empty basket at her feet, and with Micky Coulson standing beside her. He waved and she gave him a smile but he did not go over. He'd have to find other ways of seeing her. Captain Bowmaker was at her side and he followed the Scots lads along the way.

"Ha'd on a sec, Malky," he called out. He caught up with them and put a hand on Malky's shoulder.

"A word. Ye did well, lad, to make it up with Geordie. He helps me oot noo and again with me little side line - him and Molly both, and his mate Micky Coulson, who had ideas of his own aboot her until ye came alang. Why dain't ye come with me to my prayer meeting, lad. Ye look as though ye could de with some prayers." He chuckled. Malky knew about the so-called prayer meetings at the sign of the *Orange Tree* and could do with a drink so he said he would come. "And ye Tomag?" asked Bowmaker.

Tomag didn't reply at once. It was not unusual as he always thought things over without hurrying himself.

"Ach, I've got a little business with John Marledane at the *Turk's*, but it won't take lang and I might have something to show ye."

"Well if ye come, it's up the side alley and in through the stable yard by the malting shed. Just open the door and come along the passage by the scullery. We'll be expecting ye."

The prayer meetings at the *Orange Tree* were nothing like the old sessions in the *Turk's* vault when anyone came in. It was a select few only, known to the landlord, Dick Redheed, and to each other. The odd guest was allowed, and no one took exception to Malky as he came in with Bowmaker and sat beside him in one of the settles by the hearth. The three men there were middle aged or old, and like Bowmaker were dressed respectably, but not too fancily. One of them, a thin faced, sharp-featured man, looked hard at Malky.

"Are ye the Scotch lad who rode the stang the other neet?"

Malky looked back without demur and nodded.

"Ye're Ralph Milbourn's bonded servant?"

As Malky nodded again, Bowmaker chipped in. "Malky's a good lad and is my guest, Abe Taylier, and we'll all make him welcome."

"So we will," replied Abe, "so long as he tyeks his hat off in the presence of his elders and betters."

Malky blushed a little and doffed his bonnet.

"Ach, I'm sorry, I dinna' normally bother in ale-hooses."

"This is a private gathering this morning, Malky," said Bowmaker, "but nae harm done, eh, Abe."

"Nae harm done, Malky," replied Taylier, less sternly. "I'm having some trouble with my son who's been talking to the Quakers and thinks that nae one needs to show respect to anyone else."

"Weel, we're just waiting for Cuddy," said Dick Redheed.

Malky looked anxiously between Bowmaker and Redheed. "It's no' catching. You'se two only having the ane eye?"

The two men laughed. It was Bowmaker who replied. "I'm a ship's captain and master mariner, although I dain't de much sailing noo. Young Dickie here was mate on John Coatsworth's *Ffortune* until he took the *Orange Tree*. When ye're at sea ye have to take yer bearings, and in wor day ye used the *Jacob's cross*. It's a stick aboot an arm's length lang, with a cross piece that ye move up and doon. Ye'd put the bottom of the stick to your cheek, line it up with the horizon, and take a sighting of the sun over the top of the cross piece. Like this." He held out his right arm out in front of his face and put his left forearm over it to form a cross. "The markings on the stick would give ye the latitude."

"Aye," added Redheed, "but staring at the sun lang enough to take the reading gets ye bedazzled, and in time ye lose the sight of the eye. Ye'll see a few auld sailors with eye patches."

"Ach, weel I'll not gan to sea then, and lose an eye for it," replied Malky.

"Weel, ye won't the day," said Bowmaker. "Most mariners noo use the back staff. It's the same principle, but ye turn yer back to the sun and tyek the reading from the shadow."

"Aye, and they were aboot when I was on the *Ffortune*," commented Redheed with some bitterness in his voice. "I asked John Coatsworth to have one made for us, but he said it was a waste of money when he had a perfectly good cross staff."

"Weel, the Coatsworths dain't like spending their coin," muttered Abe Taylier.

They then heard the sound of a stick hitting something and the ee-aw of a donkey. They laughed. "That's him then," said Bowmaker. The last of the group came in. He was a stout little man with a red face, a wisp of grey hair poking out from under his hat, and a twinkle in his eye. Although he had his roast-dinner clothes on, there were bits of straw on his breeches and mud on his shoes. Malky knew him by sight. He was Cuddy Heron, the carrier, who had a steading by the brick fields where he kept his donkeys.

Redheed put out a small table with a pack of cards on top. "Ye just watch, Malky lad. They always have a game before the drinking starts." The game was *Losing Lodam* and although Malky had never played it, he soon worked out the rules. Highest cards or trumps, loaders, won the trick and you had to follow suit. Aces counted eleven, kings ten and so on. The catch of the game was that if you won a trick with a loader, a scoring card, then those points counted against you, not for you. Once a player got to thirty-one he was out and the game continued until there was only one player left who claimed the kitty. The main catch in the game played at the sign of the *Orange Tree* though, was that the last player paid for all the drinks. There was a lot of talk between the players who tried to put their opponents off. Taylier was the first out, soon followed by the other stranger to Malky. He was Charles Robinson, the town's chief cooper. It was Cuddy Heron who won, and therefore lost, much to the amusement of the others, and he had to put his hand in his pouch for four pennies – two quarts of ale each. Bowmaker was going to put a penny in for Malky, but Cuddy stopped him. "A guest of one of us is a guest of us all. I'll pay my dues."

The tankards full of ale were brought in and the drinking began. It was a dark ale and much to Malky's taste. The landlord, Redheed, was known for the quality of his ales. "I used to call this brew Best Scotch, when the Scotch soldiers were here, but after the army left the toon with all those lasses pregnant with bairns that we're ganna have to keep, and then bornt and wrecked the panns, there were no takers, so noo it's just Redheed's Best."

"How's the brewery gannen, Dick?" asked Taylier.

"Canny. Michael Coatsworth's ganna lease me the auld warehoose on his quay, and Will Guby's deeing the building work. It should be ready in time for the first harvest ale," said Redheed.

"Aye, and I'll have your brewing vats and your barrels ready by then," added Robinson. "Mind, I'll have to get the barrels stamped by the excise man in the presence of the ale cunners, and that Coultheard won't give ye a drop or two either way. If the barrel's just a fraction more or less than it should be, then I have to work on it till it's reet. It's 36 gallon for beer and 32 for ale. And I expect ye'll be wanting *kilderkins* and *firkins* as well."

Redheed nodded. "Aye I will. They're easier to carry in a coble or a wherry."

"Weel, I'll get my captain to buy ale from ye," stated Bowmaker, "but aren't ye expecting any trouble from the high and mighty in Newcastle? They won't like ye selling ale to the ships in the harbour. They make the ship's masters send up to Newcastle for ale and victuals, and then they have to pay the watermen and the keelmen for the transport. Newcastle has the monopoly, and they'll try to enforce it."

"Ha, I'll be ready for them," said Redheed angrily. "I'll have some stout lads working for me and I'll arm them with staves and pikes if need be. Mr. Coatsworth's told me that the Parliament has no truck with King's monopolies, and he says that if I have any trouble he'll see to it that there's a petition in Parliament."

Malky enjoyed the company, and Cuddy Heron in particular seemed happy to natter with him, on this and that. The sound of someone coming in through the back door silenced the conversation, but it was only Tomag with a pottery jug covered with a cloth.

"I thought ye might be interested in this, Capn' Bowmaker, and yer friends too," he said, doffing his hat to the company.

"Do ye have any small cups, Mr. Redheed?" And he pulled away the cloth, letting the landlord smell the liquor inside. Redheed sniffed approvingly.

"The usquebah frae my own still. It's been in a wine barrel for two weeks more than a month and has a bit of colour." Two cups were quickly brought out and filled by Tomag. "It's got a kick sae just sip it at first."

Redheed, Bowmaker and Malky shared one cup and the other passed between Taylier, Robinson and Heron. There was plenty of coughing, then lip smacking. Tomag drank from the jug. The cups were filled up again.

"Weel," said Redheed, "I can understand noo what those Scotch soldiers were gan' on aboot when they said they missed their usquebah, and that gin and brandy were nae substitute. Can ye let me have a small barrel? I'd keep it away from prying eyes and only serve it to special customers, like this lot."

Bowmaker chuckled. "Ye're too late, Dick, I've already agreed to help them shift any that's surplus to their needs. And we kna' someone who can carry it up to Newcastle where it'll fetch more than it would in Sheels."

"Ye have yer own still then?" asked Redheed.

"Och aye, but I reckon I'll need at least another ane, before I hae enow to sell any on, and I have to find somewhere to put it where the excise won't spot it. It won't be that difficult in Sheels with all the smoke blawin' frae the salt-hooscs." He drained the last of the usquebah from the jug.

"I'll be aff back to the *Turk's* and fill me jug. I'll bring it back up the hoose, Malky, for when we have oor dinner. Ye'll fetch it frae the Milbourns'?"

Malky was a little fuddled from the ale and the liquor, and just nodded.

As they finished their beer, Redheed readied himself to open the doors at noon, Bowmaker and Cuddy accompanied Malky outside. They went through the back yard and all three had a long piss up against the wall.

"Malky-lad," said Bowmaker. "Me auld Mate, Nick Frampton's noo the Master of the *Pole Star*, and he should be coming in from Amsterdam any neet. He's carrying Strasbourg brandy, Dutch gin, lace, raisins and spices. He'll offload some that's not on the manifest at Frenchman's Bay, and Cuddy here'll carry it doon to Sheels. He'll need a strang lad to help him with the load. One of the fellas that used to help is away at sea noo, so ye can help him oot. He'll need to kna' where ye live, so ye show him noo."

Tomag and Davey said nowt when Malky told them that he was going into the smuggling business. Malky had grown up since they had first met him, not only physically with the hard labour, but after the ride on the stang pole his face had hardened and he was less easy going. Malky himself was now determined to find a way out of his indentures and also to find a way see more of Molly. He slept in his clothes the next night but nothing happened, and then the night after a tapping at the door had wakened Davey, who was a light sleeper, and he pushed Malky out of the bed.

"Haway, man, we need to be off sharp," whispered a rough, inpatient voice. Malky was half asleep but pulled on his bonnet and stepped out of the door.

"Naw, man," an exasperated voice whispered, "everybody'll kna it's a Scotchman if ye wear yer bonnet. Put this on." And he was handed a woollen fishers' cap. Malky followed the lad who had come. He was taller than Malky and well built. He didn't carry a lantern, but found his way without any problem along the back row to the long bank where Cuddy was waiting with his donkeys.

"Aboot time," he said. He had a small lantern on a stick and held it out in front of them as he pulled on the reins of the first donkey in the train and they set off over the path by the docken field.

"Did ye bring a stick?" asked the lad.

"Ach naw," said Malky.

A whippy cane was put into his hand. "And if ye try it oot on me, ye'll get one back."

Malky grabbed the figure and dragged it close to him. In the dim moonlight he could just make out the yellow curls under the cap. "It's no' ye, is it Molly?"

A gentle laugh told him the answer.

"Stop *clartin' aboot* ye'se two. Ye'll have plenty of time for prittle-prattle when we get back to Redheed's and he lets us taste the goods. For noo, ha'd yer tongues."

The donkeys fell in behind the leader, and only needed an occasional touch of the whip to keep them in line. Malky could just make out Molly ahead of him. She was wearing a doublet and breeches and her shapely behind brought thoughts to his head, that he shouldn't have been having, and which took his mind off the job. They were passing the night ox-pound and one of the beasts suddenly appeared poking its head over the wall and bellowing. Malky nearly jumped out of his skin and the donkey he was walking beside eee-awed, and made to run away. The strip of hide that was tied to its harness from the donkey in front held it back, but Malky had to be quick to grab its ears, and beat it hard with his cane to get it into line again. Cuddy said nowt so as not to disturb the donkeys any more, but Malky heard him muttering under his breath, and he tried to keep his eyes on the job and away from Molly's behind. Once they had passed the wattle walls of the rope walk, they headed down onto the sands and it was easy going then, with nothing likely to cause an upset.

They were soon on the cliff-top by Frenchman's Bay, and Cuddy led them in a full circle so that they were pointing in the right direction for the way back. He then tied the harness of the lead donkey to a gorse bush. He stood on the cliff top with his lantern held high and waved it back and forth. If you looked hard you could just see a ghost-like ship a few hundred yards out. He took a coil of rope from the donkey's baggage saddle and went down on his knees and felt around under the branches of the gorse bush. "Got it," he said. There was a stout iron spike fixed firmly in the ground and he slipped the noose at the end of the rope over it.

"Reet, Molly, ye stay up here with the animals and me and Malky'll see what's what doon in the cove."

The way down to the beach, partly formed by a natural cleft, was as rocky and steep as Malky remembered. Cuddy went first with both hands on the rope and then Malky followed. As they reached the bottom they saw the barrels and boxes that had been brought ashore in the ship's boat that was run aground on the beach. A group of sailors were standing by them.

"Well met, Cuddy," said one of them who stepped forward and shook the carrier's hand. "The skipper 'll see Bowmaker and settle up. Here's a list of what we've brought ower." He handed over three small slates with writing in chalk on them. All ships carried the slates, and they were used at sea for any notes that needed taking. They had the advantage that anything untoward could be wiped off after the captain had written in his log what the official story was to be.

Cuddy handed them to Malky. "Reet, Malky lad, ye're the one who can read, so ye call oot what's written and I'll check it's here and ye put a cross agin' it." Cuddy gave Malky his lamp to read the slates as he counted each barrel and box. It didn't take long and then Cuddy asked the mariner, "Can ye lend me a couple of lads to help bring them up the cliff?"

"Naw. We bring 'em in here, ye take 'em oot. The Capn' doesn't want any of his crew linked to what ye're deein'. We'll up anchor noo and then just wait for the tide to get us ower the bar." He turned his back and the boat was pushed off the sand and they rowed back to the ship.

Cuddy poked about among the cargo. "Aye there'll be aboot the reet size. Noo the hard work'll start. Ye stay here and I'll come back with the baskets." Cuddy clambered up the cliff slope using both hands on the rope with surprising agility for his size, and minutes after reaching the top he came back down again, a basket dangling on each shoulder. When he got to the bottom again he gave one of the baskets to Malky. They had loops half way up which fitted over the hooks on the donkey's pack-saddle. Cuddy showed Malky how to put his arms through the hooks, and then he put the baskets on the sand and they started to fill them.

"We dain't put too much in, as it's nae good if ye conk oot before ye get to the top. We can always put more in when we load up the donkeys." When Cuddy thought that the baskets were full enough, Malky knelt down and put his arms through the hoops. Malky stood up carefully as the basket was high on his back and he needed to lean forward to get the balance.

"Does that feel aboot all reet?" whispered Cuddy. Malky nodded and then the carrier loaded the other basket on to his own back. "Ye can gan forst, and if ye're having any problems I can give ye a push."

What would have been a mildly tricky climb of itself, became a real challenge with the heavy basket on his upper back and shoulders. His arms met the strain, but he had to keep his balance which was not easy with his feet slipping on the soft limestone and the loose rocks. He fell to his knees twice but managed it. Molly helped him lower the basket to the ground, and to put another one on his back.

"Ye'll do one more lift, then Molly'll take ower, then ye'll spell me," muttered Cuddy. It seemed an endless task but Cuddy finally brought the last basket up. Molly had worked as hard as the two men and was breathing no heavier. Cuddy had brought a skin of ale and they all drank deeply before loading the baskets onto the donkeys. Cuddy and Malky lifted the first basket on to the lead donkey. Malky found it tricky to make sure that the loops slipped over the hooks. Molly held the donkey's head to try and stop it moving too much. Once the basket held firm, Cuddy moved over and put his hands under the bottom to take the weight while Molly and Malky lifted the other basket on. The ale-skin was passed round again when they had finished, and then they moved off. The sky was just starting to lighten as they took the donkey train onto the sands towards the toon-end of Sheels.

"Have ye been doing this lang, Molly?" asked Malky.

"Wye aye, wor Danny got me into it when we were forst courting. I'd always gone oot on the river in the coble with me Da, or me brothers, and could row as well as any of them. Dan was short of a lad and asked me to come with him. At that time we normally brought the goods in by boat, but after he didn't come back that neet, Bowmaker got Cuddy to carry the stuff back on land with his donkeys. The coin that I get from helping and from selling the odd thing, means I can just aboot manage to put a bit aside for when the weather's bad and the fishers dain't gan oot."

They rounded the headland and soon passed the fishers' houses. Those that were up and about paid no attention. Cuddy was often seen with his donkeys carrying all sorts, and as it was just starting to become light no one thought owt about it.

"Have ye ever been stopped by the customs?" asked Malky.

"Wye naw," replied Cuddy, "Newcastle keeps all the customs dues to itself. There's a customs hoose on the quayside there for ships that gan upstream, but for those that dain't there's the customs boats. They've got their own quay in Sheels and meet all the ships that anchor in the harbour. The boat stays for aboot a week then sails up to Newcastle with all the coin they've collected and another comes doon to replace it.

"And they've nivver worked oot that ye can bring goods in by boat or donkey from Frenchmen's, or anywhere else come to that. But there is a custom hoose in Sheels ye kna', Malky-lad. It's a way up from the *Orange Tree* so we dain't pass it."

"Take no notice of him, Malky," said Molly, "it's the ale-hoose reet opposite the quay where the custom boats moor, and the customs men spend all their time in there when they're not oot meeting a ship. Everybody calls it the customs hoose, but it's the sign of the *Three Tuns*."

"Had yer tongues then, we're nearly there." Cuddy turned the lead donkey up the alley by the *Orange Tree* and they were soon unloading the baskets with the help of Dick Redheed and his pot boy. As each basket was emptied, Redheed put a line through the entry on the slate. When the last one was marked off he said, "Reet, that's the business done. Come in for a minute then, for some ale."

"I'll tyek the ale, but dain't ye need to taste the brandy to make sure it's not gan off," commented Cuddy.

Redheed looked at him, and then laughed. "Ye'd drink the profits before we've made any? All reet then I'll open one that's got my name on it, but ye'll only get a taste."

Redheed's idea of a taste was a good gill each. The brandy was light in colour, but strong in taste and brought an immediate blush to Molly's fair cheeks. Malky coughed as the fiery heat slipped down his gullet, but Cuddy just swigged his back. Redheed savoured his.

"Wye, that's good stuff. I think I'll keep a barrel for mesel," and he topped their cups up.

While they were taking their ease, Malky said to Cuddy and Redheed, "It was lucky that I can read, for the checking of the slates doon at the beach."

"There's any number of fellas who would come in with us," answered Redheed, "and the fisher lads are stronger and nimbler than ye, Malky, but as Cuddy can't read we needed someone who could."

"Well ye didn't think that auld Bowmaker took ye on for yer good looks," cried out Cuddy and they all laughed.

When they left the *Orange Tree* their ways parted. Cuddy was happy to drive his donkeys back on his own. "Once they realise they're gannen' yem and will get their feed, they're nae bother."

As he left the yard, Malky took Molly's hand, pushed her against the stable wall, and kissed her on her brandy flavoured lips. There was no hiding the lad's state of excitement as he pressed against her. "I canna' do without ye, Molly," he gasped.

"Calm doon, Malky. I miss ye as well, but I'm not ganna' let ye have it. Not standing up against the wall in a stable yard, anyway." Molly gently pushed him away, and they parted with a long look at each other. It was nearly six so Malky had to run to the salt-house and start his twelve-hour shift.

Malky stopped going down to the toon-end on Sundays as he wanted no more gossip about him and the fish lass. He could still see Molly whenever a ship stopped off at Frenchman's cove, to offload some surplus goods while waiting for the tide to cross the bar at the mouth of the Tyne, but it was more seeing than touching. Molly seemed reluctant to give him more than a brief embrace and a quick kiss.

He and Davey would often go out for a walk on a Sunday morning, and one day when they were standing by the mill pond behind the dam, Davey asked Malky if he could teach him to swim like he had started doing some months ago when they had been splashing about in the Tyne.

"Och aye, I could. It's a hot day and a dip would do us both some guid. I'll gang in first and see how deep it is," answered Malky. There was a clump of willows and elders further along the path by the mill pond and they quickly undressed. Malky jumped in but had to wade a few feet before the water covered his waist and it did not get much deeper. "Cam on in, Davey," he shouted and they were soon splashing about. It did not take Davey long to get the knack of the 'dawgie' paddle, as Malky called it, and then he was soon swimming confidently like Malky, kicking his legs like a frog and pushing his hands forwards and bringing them back like paddles. Their Sunday morning dips came to an end when some of the churchgoers who saw them splashing about and laughing, on the holy day, complained to the constable who lost no time in telling the lads that their swimming had to stop. Malky explained that he was teaching Davey to swim as he had nearly gone under in the Tyne.

Puncheon pulled on his whiskers. "Well gan doon to the sands and swim in the Ocean. Nae one will see ye there."

The next Sunday the two lads walked up the long bank and across the Docken field to the sands. They stood and watched for a while as the fishers were laying out their nets for the salmon. Hauling in nets on a three-man sea coble could be dangerous if there was a heavy swell, so two cobles would work together. The long salmon nets were laid out on the sand and then each end tied to the stern of a sea coble. The fishers then rowed out a good way offshore. As soon as they felt the nets starting to pull with the weight of the fish, they slowly rowed back to the sands, pulling the full nets behind them, and landed them on the beach, where the women waited with their baskets to carry them to the toon-end.

Malky and Davey walked on until they were well out of sight and then swam in the sea. It was cold and they had to jump over the incoming waves, but once in they could swim and splash to their hearts' content.

It became a regular routine for them, and after their swim they would often walk over to Harton. Davey had become quite friendly with Peggy's family and he would occasionally help with the farm work, either in the evening or on a Sunday.

If George's back was bad he might be given a ha'penny by Robbie Clibbourne. Hal was a little better now that the sun shone for a few days, but he still could not do any heavy work. One day when there were no jobs for Davey, he and Malky decided to walk over the Harton Moor to Biddick Hall to see if they could see Dougie. He still worked in the kitchen turning the spit on a Sunday morning, but could be found in the stables with the other lads who worked there in the afternoon.

They had heard from Lewis Frost that Dougie had settled in well. He did all the work asked of him in the kitchen, but he had also taken to working with the horses. The stable lads always put the new boys in with the stallions to see if they would get a chunk taken out of them, but Dougie had not flinched. He had talked to the horse in the erse, and had a quiet way about him that seemed to calm even the most highly strung of Isaac Frost's steeds. As well as the working horses, the master had started buying good blood stock, which he took pride in riding over the Harton moors and the Cleadon hills, when his son and his younger friends were visiting. The horses needed to be exercised every day by the grooms, and it was soon apparent that Dougie had a natural gift in the saddle. Although he was still growing, he was slightly built and wiry, rather than big muscled.

When he heard Davey's voice in the yard, he ran out of the stable with a smile on his face.

"Och, Davey and Malky. It's been an age since I've seen ye. Cam in to the stables wi' me. The master was sae pleased with the fat beef he had for dinner, that he sent us lads some of the meat and a pail of beer. The meats all gan' but there's still some drink. I'm sure we can spare ye a pot."

There were two other lads sitting on the straw bales. They were both older and bigger than Dougie but welcomed his Scotch friends and did not begrudge them a pot of beer.

The talk was all about the master's new stallion, *Lightning Lad*, that was reckoned to be the fastest in all of Durham county. It was a three-year-old, and only the master and his son were allowed to ride it apart from the grooms who exercised it. The master would not hunt with it, as it was too valuable to risk over walls and hedges, but would gallop it on the sands at Sheels. Race meets like all other sports were no longer allowed by the Parliament, and Mr. Frost was just waiting for the chance to race it against some of the other horses in the county. Dougie took Davey and Malky to its stall in the stables. *Lightning Lad* was a superb specimen, black with white ankles and a white blaze on his head. Whilst Dougie patted its nose, the other two lads stood well back as it whinnied and snorted.

"Ach, he's nae harm. He just disna' like strangers," chuckled Dougie. "I tell ye, when ye get on his back on the sands, and let him run, ye feel as though ye're gangen like lightning yersel'."

"He'd be likely to win any race he's in for, then?" asked Davey.

Dougie rubbed his chin. "Ach, with me riding, he would, but Mr. Frost and his son are big fellas and would slow him doon too much. But if there is any race then it's only the gentlemen that are allowed to ride, not their grooms or servants."

"Ach weel at the moment we'll nivver find oot," said Malky, "wi' the Parliament banning all sports and anything else that folk enjoy."

When they arrived back to their cottage Tomag was already there, and had been down to Milbourn's to collect their dinner. A kettle with a whole cooked salmon in it was on the table, with a pot of salad leaves in vinegar, a loaf of barley bread and two quarts of beer. They ate with relish. It was salmon again four nights that week. When the tide was up they could see the river cobles out with their small salmon nets hoiking a salmon, or two at a time, into the boat. The ship owners, or the fishers with five men boats were out on the ocean with their large salmon nets and could land hundreds at a time. The smaller boats used a line or drew nets on the sands, as Davey and Malky had witnessed. A lot were salted in barrels for sale onwards, but folk would salt their own and hang them from the rafters over the hearth to smoke them, and they would keep for months, like ham, bacon, or cheese.

Of an evening they would sit on the step of the cottage. The Widder Wallis and Alice were usually there with their spindle or their weaving frame while it was still light, unless it was raining. The widder's husband had died years ago, but she kept his sixth share in a fishing coble, and a quarter share in a chicken run further up the alley. She had had two sons to bring up, so had started weaving for Gerritson, the tailor, like a lot of single women who did not want to go hawking fish or salt round the streets. Her sons were both sailors and might turn up for a week or two and then were away. She had not seen one for a twelve month now although his ship had come back. He had probably found a woman in another port – it was often the way.

Tomag would sometimes walk over to her and talk of this and that. She was a tall woman with a stooped back and watery eyes that were becoming weaker as the years went by. She had a sharp tongue and was forever shrieking about something to Alice. After a while she seemed to take to Tomag, and would sometimes give him a cup of her ale. Like most folk she brewed her own, and would only buy from the toon brewery, or from an alehouse, if her own brew had soured. She would normally blame that on Alice for having come too near to the mash tun while she had her rags on. She normally had enough coin to get by on, but she suffered in the cold winters. Coal was not dear but she couldn't always afford it. She'd send Alice out at night with a pail to see what she could get from the coal heaps outside the salt-houses. Lots of lasses did it and if you were caught you'd be fined by the Vestry court, or if a salt worker caught you then he might ask for something in return for the coal, as Niall had done. Angus and his keelmen had not had to lay over much lately with the summer weather, but if they did then Alice would be down there with her pail, waiting for Niall to catch her.

Tomag had decided with Marledane that if they were going to start making some discreet sales of his usquebah, they would have to invest in another still. Two big stills in Hamish's shop would be noticed, and so he would need somewhere else to locate it. Their cottage would be ideal as the Widder's Court was hidden away and there were no passers-by, and no tell-tale chimneys with smoke coming out all day. The problem was that the still needed watching all the time. One evening when the widder was outside her cottage weaving, Tomag went over with a bottle of his usquebah. He offered the widder a drink and he stood talking and topping up her cup as well as his own. When he came back he told the two lads that his problem was solved.

"The widder's gang to let me put oor still in her cottage in exchange for free coal and a bottle or two of the usquebah. She or Alice will watch it and we'll let her have a caged bird for the gas."

"Niall won't be happy," said Davey, "he'll no' be able to let oor Alice have her free pail of coal and something for him in return."

"Dinna worry aboot oor Niall, frae what Angus was telling me there's plenty of lassies in Sandgit' who'll gang for a walk wi' him up a dark alley." He handed the nearly empty bottle of usquebah to Davey and Mallky to finish off.

Keelmen Playing at Cards

CHAPTER EIGHT

When the herring season started the whole town knew it. The sighting of the first shoals off Cullercoats in late June would give rise to shouts of, "The harrain's here, the harrain's here." The shoals would swarm in the German Ocean until September and the Sheels fishers rarely had a poor season. The sea-going cobles would be out in mass but rarely stayed out for more than two or three tides. The larger fishing doggers, and the five men boats, would go further north at the start of the season and south when it was ending, and could be out for a week. They'd carry their own salt to cover the fish until they returned to Sheels. Some of the larger vessels would take two or three sea-going cobles with them that would bring their catches back each night, and tie up alongside the mother ship.

Women folk from the Scottish borders, from Tynedale and Riddesdale, would arrive in the town and seek lodgings with the fisher families. They would work alongside the Sheels women along the shore, gutting the fish, and then packing them into barrels, covering each layer with salt. Of an evening when the day's work was done they would sit round open hearths feasting on the fresh fish, roasted in pots with lard, or boiled in kettles, and eaten with pease pudding, bread, and ale. The fisher lads waiting for a tide would join them, but rare was the lass who gave in to a lad before she had a promise of marriage, and not all the lasses that came in June went back in September. Those that did had enough pennies in their purses to see them through the winter.

The Milbourns often bought a whole basket of fresh herring from Molly, which Peggy had to clean and salt and lay in their own fish barrel. When Peggy knew that Davey was going to Harton one Sunday, she had wrapped three good sized fish in a cloth so that Davey could take them to her parents. Her Da's back was bad again and he'd not worked for a week after the hay harvest. Hal had helped with the mowing, but the dust had got onto his chest and he had coughed so much that he had vomited up a whole lot of blood, and had had to be carted home.

As she tried to sneak out of the door to take the men's dinner on that Saturday evening, she bumped into Mrs. Milbourn who was coming out of the parlour, and the cloth with the fish inside slipped from under her arm.

"Ye're not stealing wor fish for your fancy man then?" she shouted. "Ralph, ye'd best come oot here, there's a thief in the hoose."

Mr. Milbourn came out of the parlour, a look of thunder on his face, and they all marched into the kitchen. Jenett was at the table, stoning some raisins for the Sunday dinner.

"Did ye kna' aboot this, Jenett?" cried out Mrs. Milbourn, putting her hand on Peggy's back and pushing her into the kitchen. Jenett did not see the fish that Mr. Milbourn was picking up from the floor and jumped to the wrong conclusion.

"I'm sorry Missus Milbourn, I knew she'd missed her rags twice, but she's only just starting to show and I didn't think it was my place to say owt."

Mrs. Milbourn shrieked and fell back against her husband who dropped the fish again. He helped her to the settle by the hearth. "Calm doon, pet," he said, looking as shocked as she was. Jenett had quickly grabbed a cup and filled it with ale for her mistress.

Mr. Milbourn looked sternly at Peggy. "Ye'd better explain yersel'," he said.

"Weel, me Da's bad with his back and poor Hal's half deed with the coughing sickness, and I thowt that Davey could take the herring up to them when he gans to see them tomorrow. I didn't think ye'd mind."

"Ye mean Davey, wor servant's, gannen to your parents?"

Peggy nodded. "He came up with me last time I went to see them and helped oot on the farm."

"And do they kna' that ye're pregnant by him?"

"I'm what?" cried Peggy. The lass had had no one to talk to about the small changes in her body, and it had never occurred to her that she was with child.

"Ye little slut," cried Mrs. Milbourn, re-invigorated by the ale, "ye've been letting him at ye, under wor noses, and ye're pretending ye dain't kna' ye're belly-up?"

Peggy went white as a sheet and held on to the table. She looked at Jenett. "I didn't kna', but I've been feeling sick these last mornings when I have to pour the fish blood into the puddings. I just thowt it was the smell."

"Weel, we can't have ye working here in that state. I'll make up your wages and ye can gan yem tomorrow. Your Davey can take ye with him." Mr. Milbourn had no choice. Her condition would soon be noticed and he'd be shamed for having a loose woman in his employ.

"She's not getting away with it that lightly," said Mrs. Milbourn coldly. "Nor is the lad. She's with child and unmarried. The Vestry court should know about it, and the Scotch lad who's taken advantage of her should be punished as weel. He's an indentured servant and can't marry her, let alone support her and the bairn."

Although he would rather just send Peggy packing back to Harton, Ralph Milbourn looked at his wife and knew that she would not back down.

"Are ye sure that ye'd want the gannens on in wor own household made public?" he asked in one more attempt to keep the peace.

"It's wor duty, husband, and must be done. We cannot let the servants get up to immorality and fornic…. There I can't even say the word without feeling ashamed."

Milbourn sent for the constable. Jenett took the workers' dinner to the salt-house and told Tomag that he shouldn't let Davey out of his sights.

"What's the lad done noo?" he asked.

"He's only got poor Peggy belly-up, and Mrs. Milbourn insisted that her husband tell the constable. They'll be up before the Vestry court," said Jenett, her voice shaking.

Davey and Malky who had come over for their dinners heard what she said. Davey just stood there and said nowt.

Malky looked down at his feet, knowing that he could very well be in Davey's shoes.

Constable Puncheon was in his element. Immorality and fornication were heinous crimes, and he was more than happy to take it on himself to report it to the Vestry court. A special sitting was arranged for the Monday. Puncheon required Ralph Milbourn to ensure that his servants did not seek to flee the town. It was no problem. Peggy was not allowed to leave the house and Tomag gave his word that he would keep Davey by him all the time until the court appearance.

Malky walked down to the fishers' strand on the Sunday with a pail and bought half a dozen fresh herring for a penny. He walked over to Harton and gave them to a thankful Mrs. Blayre. Hal was so weak that he just lay in bed, lathered in sweat and coughing.

"I dain't think he's lang left," whispered the tearful mother, "and George's back is so bad that he can't even gan to the pub for his Sunda' ale. And he's started to cough and wheeze himsel'. I dain't kna' what I'm ganna de."

When Malky told her that Peggy was with child and that she and Davey were going to be up before the court the poor woman looked lost in despair.

"Weel, at least if she comes yem, she can help me with the work, but how could we feed another mouth when the bairn is born?"

Malky had no answer. He chopped some wood for the fire, took a cup of ale and then walked back to Sheels.

Word had soon spread and crowds were about on the Monday morning as Puncheon marched the two unhappy lovers along the Low Way and then up the High Street to St Hild's. They were jeered and booed and few seemed to have any sympathy for them. A horse and cart were waiting in the Market Place. Puncheon had spoken to the Curate and a flogging was inevitable.

The court hearing did not take long. No one spoke for Peggy or Davey and they looked forlornly at each other as they were both sentenced to be flogged in the Market Place that very morning. There had been some concern about the constable's actions in letting the floggings of the three panners go on long after the blood was drawn, so this time the court itself prescribed the number of lashes. As a woman Peggy would only be given six strokes, but Davey would receive a dozen. As Davey's master, Ralph Milbourn was ordered to pay for the upkeep of the bairn when born, unless Peggy married before then. He had not expected to bear that burden, and cursed the lad under his breath. Outside the Church, Milbourn told his wife that her insistence had cost them dear, and that he was in two minds over whether to give her a flogging as well when they returned home.

Not long after Davey had been taken out of the saltern by Puncheon and his henchmen, two strangers had walked down from the way towards the salt-house. Malky was working the pump and they bade him good-day. They were dressed well, but plainly and with no ribbons or feathers in their hats, or showy belt buckles or brooches. Malky doffed his bonnet to them.

"There's nae need for that, my friend," said the older and taller of the two, who had an air of natural authority. "We're all equal in the eyes of the Lord and no man need uncover his head or bow his knee to another."

"Ach, I was scolded the other day by an elder man, Mr. Taylier, who upbraided me for not doffing ma bonnet. He didna' think I was his equal," Malky replied, putting his bonnet back on.

His companion, who was not much older than Malky, with a fresh, innocent looking countenance, blushed a deep red. "He's me Da', and I'm not surprised he scolded ye. It's not long since I met Bob here and joined the Society of Friends. As we believe all men are the same in the eyes of the Lord, I called him by the name that Christ gave him, Abraham, instead of father or sir. He became so angry he struck me aboot the heed, and said that if I didn't show him proper respect he'd knock the teeth oot of my mooth, and he would have done had I not got oot his way quick. I'm Nathan Taylier."

"And I'm Robert Linton," said the older man. "Bob to ye."

"Och, I couldna' call gentlemen like ye Nathan and Bob..."

"Weel, ye should, Malky," said Bob.

Tomag came out of the salt-house. He had heard the voices. "Can I help ye, gentlemen?" he asked.

The same conversation the men had had with Malky ensued. "Ach then, Bob and Nathan it is, and I'm Tomag, salt master, and what can we do for ye?"

"We heard aboot young Davey Finlayson who's been charged with fornication."

Malky looked blank. "I thought it was aboot the *skullduddery* he'd gotten up to with Peggy."

It was the turn of the Sheels men to look bemused.

"It's the same thing, Malky," said Tomag. He looked at the strangers. "I dinna' want to be impolite, but what business is it of you'se two?"

"One of wor friends is Robbie Clibbourne of Harton," said Bob. "He told us that Davey is an indentured servant and cannot marry Peggy, whom he loves, as he gets no pay for his work."

"That's reet," said Malky. "All of us Scots who were captured at Dunbar by Cromwell were sold aff by auld Haselrig as indentured servants, for twenty poonds apiece. We'll have to work for seven years for no pay."

"But that's slavery," cried Nathan.

"It might as well be," said Tomag. "We're fed well, and Mr. Milbourn's a fair enough man so lang as we work oor twelve hoors a day, and mair sometimes. But we're not free. If Davey was paid a panner's wages, he could marry young Peggy, and he has eyes for naebody else. But he canna', and there's naught we can de aboot it."

"Weel said," cried out Linton. "In the Society of Friends we condemn slavery and indentured servitude and we speak frankly to all men. We shall speak oot aboot poor Davey to wor friends when we preach the word of the Lord."

Tomag muttered to Malky, "Back to your pump, laddie, they're *ranters* or *dippers*, and if they make trouble it'll only be the worse for Davey."

Malky did as Tomag said. Robert Linton smiled at Tomag's words. "It is only by speaking out that the Lord's word will be followed. But we are not *dippers*, and certainly not *ranters*. You may have heard of us by the name of Quakers, *'As the Lord saith; but to this man will I look, even to him that is poor, and of a contrite spirit...'*"

"Ach, *'And trembleth at my word'*," called out Malky from the pump. "The number o' times ma Da' drilled that into me. It was his favourite verse frae Isiah."

"Aye," said Linton. "We believe all men, however high or low, should tremble, or quake, at the word of God. Ye kna' the scriptures then, Malky."

"My father was Archibald Dalgleish, a Covenant minister. He was training me to be his clerk."

"Ye can read and write then?" asked Nathan, in surprise.

"Och aye."

"Then you're wasted pulling a pump handle," commented Linton. "Another injustice for us to dwell upon, Nathan. Come, we must away to hear the verdict. Thank ye for your time, Malky and Tomag."

News of the punishment laid down by the court soon spread and a good number of folk lined the streets around the Market Place. Malky and Tomag were there. Jimmy Jobling had agreed to keep an eye on the furnaces, as he had no wish to attend the flogging. Many had taken the opportunity to visit an ale house and there was a festive atmosphere. The street vendors were out, and Malky caught sight of Molly with her basket of fish with Micky Coulson at her side, but did not go across to her. They heard the sound of shouts and cries long before they saw Puncheon striding ahead with his constable's stave, leading the two culprits who hung their heads in shame. As they approached the Market Place, Malky saw the two men he had spoken to earlier walk out from the crowd, move directly to the cart, and then young Nathan knelt and held his hands as a stirrup so that Robert Linton could climb up onto the back of the cart.

He stood there with his hands raised as Peggy and Davey were marched up, then he cried out to the crowd to be silent as he wished to say a few words.

"You have no business here," shouted Puncheon, but his voice seemed only to aggravate the crowd.

"Let him speak," shouted someone, and the call was taken up.

Linton managed to make himself heard as the crowd slowly quietened.

"I'm Robert Linton, from over by the Lay Gate, Bob to ye." There was laughter. "And I wish to speak as a grave injustice has taken place. I ask ye to pity this lad and his lass, Davey Finlayson and Peggy Blayre, not to condemn them with your angry voices. They have committed nae sin in the eyes of the Lord." Linton had a deep baritone voice and it carried across the Market Place. "They are condemned because they have lain together out of wedlock–" cries of shame– "and I would be the first to condemn them myself if I did not know that they wished to marry, and would marry tomorrow if they could. But young Davey is one of the Scotch prisoners sold by General Haselrig for coin to the salt-pann owners of Sheels. He was sold for twenty pounds and is an indentured servant and must do his work in the panns for twelve hours a day and receive no payment. He is little better than a slave." Cries of shame, shame. "If he was paid, he would earn his share of each salt drawing, and could afford to wed his Peggy. But those who make the laws will not bend, and they are both to be flogged in front of ye." He paused and once more raised his hands to the heavens.

"I ask ye to witness this cruelty in silence. And I also ask that when the flogger strips bare the shoulders of young Peggy, that you avert your eyes and do not look on her nakedness." There was silence now, but some were not happy as they had only come at the prospect of seeing the lass's bare titties. Linton walked to the side of the court and jumped down.

Puncheon pushed Peggy forward and prepared to untie her bodice. As he did so Davey stood between the constable and Peggy and cried out at the top of his voice. "I beg ye no' to whip ma Peggy. It was ma fau't. I'll tak the punishment for her."

Puncheon shoved the lad to one side. "Oot the way, the law must take its place."

Nathan Taylier stepped forward. "It's a fair request. The lad admits his guilt. Man is strong and woman is weak. Let him take her punishment."

The crowd were not sure about this, as it was a rare spectacle to see a woman whipped. Then Linton spoke up. "The constable is only the arm of the court. I have heard of other cases where the man has taken the woman's punishment. The court members are all here. Let them consider this plea." This time there were shouts of support.

Henry Ashburne, the court clerk, came forward and then turned to face the members of the court who were all standing together. "Mr. Linton is right to state that there are precedents of cases where a court has agreed that the man who has committed the sin of fornication could offer to take the woman's punishment. I did hear only a six month ago, where the court at Auckland, of its own volition, ordered that the woman's punishment be given to the guilty man." He paused. The Curate was looking daggers at him, but the other court members seemed sympathetic. "In this case the lad would wed the lass if he was not an indentured servant and can earn no money. I would advise the court that it certainly seems to be a case where they should spare the woman, a frail lass, from the rod."

Henry Ashburne was a well-liked personality and his little speech had brought cheers from the crowd, not many of whom had understood all his long words. The court members had a quick conference and agreed by a majority to accept Davey's plea. The Curate, who had wanted the sinful woman flogged and shamed, stalked angrily away.

Jenett ran over, put her arms round Peggy and walked her quickly away. "Ye dain't want to see what happens next, pet."

Ralph Milbourn was alarmed at the prospect of Davey having eighteen lashes, which could very likely render him unfit for work for some days. He walked quickly over to where John Chilton, the blacksmith was standing, whip in hand. He took some coin from his purse.

"Tuppence for ye to lay it on light, John." John Chilton pushed the hand away and looked straight into Milbourn's eyes.

"Your wife gave me thre'pence to put all my strength into it. I took the coin and I dain't gan back on my word for anyone."

Milbourn looked across to his wife who had a look of triumph on her face, as she guessed what was going on between her husband and the blacksmith.

Puncheon and his henchmen roughly took off Davey's doublet and shirt and tied his hands to the cart tail. There were murmurs from the crowd. He was a handsome lad with his black wavy hair and olive skin – he had broad shoulders, well-muscled arms, was thin at the waist, and strong shanked. As his hands were being tied, Linton raised his arms. "May the Lord give his subject, Davey, courage to support this unjust punishment. Let us witness it in silence and respect."

Davey looked across to where the Quakers were standing and he saw Nathan's gaze upon him. The lad was looking straight at him, his eyes bright, and his mouth half open. Davey cast his own eyes down.

Big John Chilton, the blacksmith, came forward. The crowd hushed as the flogging began. The blacksmith was putting all the strength of his back and arms into each stroke and everyone in the crowd could hear the whistling of the nine tails through the air, and the smack as they struck the bare skin. Blood was soon seeping from the cuts. It seemed an age before Puncheon cried out, "Stroke the twelfth!"

John Chilton stood back. "That is the man's punishment. I'll noo give the six strokes he is taking for his lass. When I whip a woman, I only tyek my arm halfway back. That is the punishment this lad'll get."

Even with the last six strokes given as though to a woman, Davey's back was little more than a patchwork of raw flesh when Big John had finished.

Davey, whose knuckles were white where he had gripped the cart tail, had not cried out once. He was then dragged behind the cart as it passed round the Market Place, and it was only then that the jeering started up. When the cart stopped, Davey's hands were untied and he half stumbled to his knees. Tomag and Malky rushed over to help him to his feet, but he was not in a good state. Although his back was red with blood, his face had lost all its colour and his eyes looked dead. Hamish was on hand to wipe his back and rub it down with water from the salt well. Davey groaned for the first time and fainted away.

Ralph Milbourn came over to look at the damage to the lad's back.

"How lang will he be off work?" he asked the pothecary.

"His back is red raw and he has some deep cuts. I'll need to rub more salt in when he is face down in his bed. He will need some strong liquor for the pain and the shock. As soon as the cuts start to heal I can apply some of my ointment if you wish." Hamish looked up at Milbourn. "Tuppence for a large pot and a penny ha'penny for linen to dress the wound." Milbourn nodded, and Hamish said, "I'll look in on him every day, but it'll be a good week before he can do any heavy work. The wounds will have to be healed dry before he gangs back into the furnace room. If coal dust gets into the cuts it will aggravate the humours and the wounds may fester."

A miserable looking Milbourn pulled thre'pence ha'penny out of his purse and gave the coins to the pothecary.

Davey was coming to, his face wracked with pain.

"Will ye be able to get him to the Widder's Court?" asked Milbourn. In answer, Tomag knelt down and Malky gently pushed Davey onto the big man's back. "Ha'd on tight roond his neck," he whispered to Davey. As Tomag slowly stood up, Davey wrapped his legs round his cousin's waist. "I'll be reet behind, Tomag, and ha'd his arse so that he won't fa' aff," said Malky.

Milbourn had already headed off but he turned his head and called out, "Stop at my hoose on the way, and I'll give ye a pitcher of brandy and a pail of ale - and some salt for ye, Hamish."

They crossed Peggy on the way to the Milbourns' house. Sha was holding a cloth bundle which contained her few belongings. As she saw Davey, she gasped and would have put her arms round him had Tomag not shaken his head. "We'll let ye know how he fares, Peggy." The forlorn look in her lover's eyes brought tears that flowed down her cheeks as she hurried along the way to the long bank - she would trudge alone to Harton.

When they arrived at the Milbourns', the place was in ructions. Jenett let them in looking flustered.

"The master's giving his wife a whipping in the parlour. He came yem in a furious state, as he said she'd given his coin to Big John to lay the lash on Davey. Mrs. Milbourn's got a gob on her, and she shouted back that he should never have let the Scotchmen into wor hoose, and the lad deserved all he got. Mister Ralph then said that she'd cost him a week's work by the lad at the panns, which he'd now have to pay someone else to do. She just laughed in his fyece, and he went mad. He grabbed her by the showlders, turned her roond and pushed her ower the parlour table telling me to get the cane. Weel, I dashed off and when I got back he had her skirts up showing her arse. She was struggling and screeching, but Mister Ralph's a strong man, and he told her that the mair she struggled the mair she'd get it. I gave him the cane and made to shoo the children into the kitchen, but he said they'd have to watch to learn what happened to wives who didn't obey their husbands. Then he whipped her. They must have heard her screams in Tynemooth."

Tomag and Malky could hear the woman's sobs, and then Mr. Milbourn came out of the parlour door. He was red-faced but with a mischievous glint in his eye.

"I should have done that years ago," he said as he noticed the Scots lads. "Ye've come for the brandy, then, lads. Come into the kitchen. Jenett, draw a large pitcher for them. It's for Davey-lad to ease the pain." He looked at the lad, who Tomag had put down, and who was standing very unsteadily between Malky and Tomag.

"He looks like deeth warmed up. Four cups as well, Jenett, we'll all have one noo. Ye look a bit shocked yersel' hinny, so ye better have one."

"And the Missus, master?" Jenett spoke very quietly.

He ignored her. "I dain't care, but bring oors as quick as ye like, or ye'll get a taste of the whip yersel'."

Davey coughed and spluttered as the first cup was poured down his gullet, but after the second his cheeks showed a little colour. Malky and Tomag joined in, and Milbourn did not stint himself.

"Reet, ye better be off noo Malky, ye'd better stay with him at the cottage and de whatever Hamish tells ye, but I'll expect ye at work tomorrow. If he needs someone to look in then ye can ask the widder or her scullion to help. Tomag, ye get straight back to the salt-hoose and work oot with Jobling what ye can do the day. And ask Jimmy if he kna's anyone who can take Davey's place until he recovers – sixpence a day. If he can't get a man, then a boy or a woman at thre-pence ha'penny a day. They can rake oot the ashes and carry the coals ower." He paused. "And if either of ye get a lass belly-up then I'll give ye double whatever Big John gives ye and I'll make ye work whatever state yer in."

Peggy received scant welcome from her mother, as although she could help around the farm it was another mouth to feed. Hal died just two weeks after Peggy arrived. George had started coughing not long before Hal passed away. He was also in constant pain with his back, and the only thing that relieved his pain was the French brandy which Peggy had to fetch from the sign of the *Ship*, when they had any coin. Robbie Clibbourne had been to see Mrs. Blayre. He was now having to pay one of the village lads to help out with work that George could not do. He gave her until after the harvest and then she would have to leave the cottage unless George recovered.

"If your Peggy had not disgraced hersel with young Davey, then one of the farm lads from roond here could have married her and taken the cottage," he told the nearly broken woman.

Malky went occasionally on a Sunday and kept Davey informed of any news. Malky talked to Tomag about putting the money they now earned from their little sidelines towards buying out Davey's indenture. They had nowhere near enough and it was unlikely that Milbourn would let Davey leave and replace him with someone he would have to pay. Cheap Scottish salt was starting to come on to the market and whilst it was not as good as Sheels salt in quality, merchants would buy it and pass it off as genuine. As Scotland was now part of England, the Parliament did not levy customs due on produce from Scotland as they had done before.

Davey's back took a good week to heal and for another week he was on the pump only. But after that he was back to the long days at the salt-panns, with herring or salmon for their evening meal. Once in a while they might have umble pie, or sassidges, and on a Sunday they still had boiled beef or occasionally roast fat beef if there was enough to spare. One Saturday evening they were walking back to their home with the large pot holding their roasted, rolled up herrings and pease pudding, when they heard the sound of shouting coming from one of the merchants' houses they had just passed. Tomag and Malky just kept walking on, but Davey stopped. He recognised the lad Nathan who, with Bob Linton, had helped him and Peggy when they were flogged. The young fellow was in a furious row with an older man, whom Malky recognised as being Abe Taylier, Nathan's father, who kept grabbing at Nathan's hat. Davey went to walk towards them.

"Dinna' interfere wi' other folk's trouble," muttered Tomag, but Davey ignored him and ran over. As he was approaching them the old man struck Nathan a vicious blow in the head with his cane. The lad fell to the ground and his father bent over him and struck him repeatedly on his back and shoulders until Davey grabbed him by the arm and pulled him off. Davey then snatched the cane from the man, and held him firmly to prevent him from further hurting his son.

"Unhand me," shouted Abe at Davey, who let the man go. Malky had come down the way and stood with Davey. Nathan managed to sit up but there was a deep gash to the side of his head which was bleeding profusely, and he seemed dazed.

"If you do not show me respect in my own house then it is no longer yours," cried old Abraham. He looked at Malky whom he recognised. "He stood in front of me in my own parlour with his hat on his heed and refused to take it off in my presence, his own father." He looked down and saw Nathan's hat on the ground and stamped on it vigorously, breaking it into a misshapen mess.

"I respect all men equally," said a very pale and shaken Nathan, slowly rising to his feet, "but as we are all equal in God's eyes, then I will not doff my hat to you, Abraham."

The father would have started on him again had Davey and Malky not stood between them.

"Then leave this hoose, and never darken the door again!" The old man was red in the face and spittle was flying from his lips as he spoke.

Nathan was very unsteady on his feet, and Davey wiped away some of the blood from his face and put his arm round him to steady him.

Malky spoke quietly but firmly to the old man. "I think ye'd best gang in hame noo, Mr. Taylier. Folk are watching and ye dinna' want to draw attention to yersel' just noo. We've got a big shipment coming in the nicht, and we need to store some in your warehouse. Davey'll look after Nathan."

"Weel, he's nae longer a son of mine so he can do what he pleases." He patted Malky on the shoulder. "Good luck the neet," and he went into his house, slamming the door behind him.

Davey was walking slowly with Nathan and was heading down to the old salt-house. "Ye gang on hame, Malky. I'll get Hamish to tak a look at him."

Malky was anxious to get home and have his meal so he could have some sleep before anyone came tapping on his door, but he walked quickly over to Davey and whispered in his ear, "When ye see Hamish tell him we might hae something for him the nicht or early tomorrow."

Hamish was in his shop, making up some ointments. He wiped away the blood from Nathan's head wound. The gash was deep and the pothecary pressed some dried leaves into the cut before binding it tight with some strips of linen. With Davey's help he took Nathan's doublet and shirt off. No skin was broken but there were deep red bruises to his shoulder and to his ribs. Hamish gently felt the bruised areas. "I canna' feel any breaks in the bones, but somebody's given ye a right beltin'. I'll rub some ointment on and gie ye a pot to take wi' ye. It should stop the evil humours from festering. Ye'll hae some pain for a few days until the swelling gangs doon."

Nathan was listening to Hamish, but looking at Davey who was kneeling beside him. "If ye hadn't stopped him, he might have killed me. I've never seen him so mad. You're the lad who they flogged at the market?"

"Och aye, ye and yer friend helped me and Peggy then, so it was the least I could do," said Davey, a little embarrassed.

"And do ye still want to wed the lass?"

"Och aye I do, and if I could, then I could tak ower the cottage frae her fatha' and make a living of it. Rabbie Clibbourne would hae me, but there's no way I can buy oot ma indentures."

"Robbie Clibbourne's their master?"

"Aye, and he's a guid man."

"I kna' him," said Nathan. "He's one of the friends who come to wor meetings. After the floggings, we all spoke aboot the evils of bonded servitude and all condemned it."

He sat there quietly a moment thinking on Davey's problems. Hamish's hands were smoothly rubbing in the ointment and seemed to be working their way slowly further down Nathan's back. Davey remembered Malky's experience.

"Hae ye not rubbed him enough, Hamish?"

The pothecary gave Davey a sideways look, but finished his attentions and helped Nathan put his shirt on.

"William Maud, the grain merchant, has a hoose in the High Street, and is also a friend. I'm sure he'll take me in until I can find somewhere to stay permanently. Could ye walk along with me, Davey? I could still do with a helping hand." He gave Hamish a half groat for his cares and the ointment, and he and Davey walked off. After a few paces Nathan half stumbled and fell against Davey, who once again put his arm round him as they walked along the way.

As they neared Mr. Maud's house, Nathan spoke again to his friend and helper. "How much did Milbourn pay for ye, Davey?"

"Twenty poonds for seven years' labour."

"I'm ganna see if my friends are prepared to act on their principles. I'll talk first to Robbie Clibbourne, and then ask Bob Linton to call a meeting. I'll ask the friends to each give what they can, to buy out your indenture and then ye can wed Peggy," said Nathan in a calm but serious voice.

Davey stopped and looked at Nathan. "Do ye think they would?"

"Some will certainly give, but it depends on how much," replied Nathan. "I do have some money of my own, and I could make sure that your servitude is ended."

He was looking at Davey now, in the same way as he had done, when the lad was half naked behind the whipping cart.

"I could na' gie ye anything, in return, Nathan. I luv ma Peggy," mumbled Davey.

"I'd expect nothing in return, Davey, just your friendship."

"That I'll gie gladly."

Malky was busy that night. It was well after midnight and it wasn't Molly that called for him but Geordie. "Wor Molly's not coming the neet, she's getting tired what with working all day with the harrain'."

Malky said nowt but thought that Geordie was not telling him something. Molly Hawes never got too tired to earn a penny or two.

They met up with Cuddy, but the shipment could not all be carried in one journey. Although Frenchman's Bay was near to Sheels, it had the disadvantage that there were no deep caves where the goods could be left, and everything had to be moved in one night. Cuddy did not want to over-tire his donkeys as they would be working the next day. After they had helped unload the cargo at Redheed's, Geordie took Malky with him to the landing where they took out a sea coble. The lads each took an oar and headed out of the Tyne. There was a high tide and they crossed the bar with little trouble. Geordie knew the waters well and headed out far enough so that they would not drift back to the shore. He had a lantern tied to a pole at the bow, but it was a cloudless night, and as it was mid-summer there was already a glimmer of daylight in the sky. They passed the ship that had discharged its surplus cargo at Frenchman's Bay, and which was heading into the Tyne, and a little later they pulled into the cove. It was hard work lifting the cases and barrels into the boat, and they drank deep of the ale-skin that the fisher lad had brought. The tide was slowly beginning to turn when they reached the mouth of the Tyne and they had to row hard to make any progress. It was almost light now but they had no fear of any custom craft as they never bothered the fishers' boats. When they pulled up to the quay by Taylier's warehouse, old Abe was there himself with two of his men and they had soon unloaded the cargo. Cuddy had taken all the slates with him so Redheed was sent for, and came over to check that it was all there. When they had finished, Redheed opened one of the cases and heaped the contents into a basket. "That's tobaccy for the pothecary," he said to Malky. "I'll carry it to the *Orange Tree* and ye can tyek it along to him after ye've had yer brandy. We' hoy a few coals on top so ye won't look oot of place. Ye'll come as well, Geordie, for a tot?"

"Wye aye, I will. We'll just tyek the boat back forst and then we'll call in."

The sea cobles were larger than the river cobles and also had higher bows to give protection against waves and swell, and it was heavy work to pull it aground and up the coble landing. After they had finished they walked along the Low Way to the *Orange Tree*.

After his early morning brandy and ale, Malky walked a little unsteadily back to the salt-house, with the basket on his shoulders, which would look like a basket of coals to any casual observer.

It was a good two weeks later that Robert Linton and Nathan came to the salt-house on a Saturday afternoon. Malky was outside on the pump, and he walked over and took the two men into the fore-house. It was a hot day and Davey had his shirt off while he stoked the furnaces. Malky shouted over and the lad stood up, stepped back from the fire door, and wiped the sweat off his brow and chest with a rag. In the half light of the furnace room, the light from the fire gave his muscled body a golden glow. Malky happened to glance at Nathan and saw that the young man was open mouthed and looked smitten. Davey had told Malky that the young Quaker had made little secret of his feelings for him, so Malky had a bit of fun.

"While ye've got yer shirt aff, cam and show the friends yer scars."

"Ach no'," said Davey looking angrily at Malky.

Robert Linton's voice boomed out. "I'd like to see the effects of the inhuman punishment inflicted on ye, Davey. I can then speak at first hand of the degradation suffered by those like ye who are whipped for no good reason."

Davey reluctantly walked over and turned his back. Although the wounds had healed the scars were still ugly and the coal dust on the lad's back made them stand out the more. "Ach ye can feel them, Nathan," said Malky, putting his own calloused paw onto Davey's back and rubbing it roughly. Nathan could not restrain himself, and put his own delicate fingers onto the scarred flesh. While Malky took his hand away with a smirk on his face, Nathan moved his own slowly across Davey's shoulders and then downwards, as though he was caressing the lad's body. Even Bob Linton noticed the look on Nathan's face.

"Put yer shirt on, Davey, we've some news for ye."

Davey moved away, but turned and looked at Nathan. "Ye've got saft hands," he said, "like a la…"

"What's gang on here?" It was Tomag who had come out of the boiling room a moment before.

Nathan was snapped out of his reverie. "Ye're free, Davey," he cried excitedly. "Wor friends have raised enough money to free ye, and Mr. Milbourn has agreed to accept eighteen pund ten shillings and a penny ha'penny to cancel the indenture. We worked oot that that takes into account the wages he's saved for the work ye've done so far. He's made a condition, however, that Tomag and Jobling find a lad who can take Davey's place before ye can be freed."

Davey tossed his bonnet in the air with a whoop and did a jig, shouting out a Gaelic battle cry. Tomag and Malky joined in the celebration. Tomag then went over to the corner of the room where he kept his bottle of usquebah and raised it in the air.

"We canna' thank ye enow, Bob and Nathan," he cried out. "Hae a swig o' this. It's hame made, sae dinna' tell the excise man." He made to pass the bottle to Mr. Linton who said, "It's Nathan who should have the first drink, it was his idea and he's very persuasive when he wants something. He will not take naw for an answer."

Malky shot a glance at a worried looking Davey, and then they both broke out laughing as Nathan took a long swig, went red in the face and coughed something terrible.

"He's not used to strong liquor," said Bob as he carefully sipped the usquebah himself, and smacked his lips. The two Quakers left not long after. As soon as Tomag had found someone to take Davey's place they would arrange a meeting with Mr. Milbourn and the clerk to the Vestry court to have the indenture cancelled.

"I'll gang ower the nicht to tell ma Peggy," said Davey, half sobbing with emotion.

"Och aye," replied Tomag, "and we'll all gang up to Sandgit' tomorrow to give oor Niall the news."

Tomag and Malky went down to the fishers' quarter that evening to see if anyone could take them upstream. Geordie Naesbitt was there checking his nets over, and letting them dry. He was out every day now in Micky Coulson's sea coble, taking herring.

"I dain't work Sunda's, but I was thinking of taking the river coble oot for a couple of hoors, and gannen to Jarra's Lake with me bow to see if I could take some fowl. I'm getting fed up with eating harrain' all the bliddy time. If one of ye'se 'll give me a spell rowing the boat, then I can tyek ye to Woolington Ballast Quay, that's half way up the Tyne to Newcastle."

The next day, and despite their sore heads after all the ale and usquebah they had drank in celebrating Davey's freedom, the three Scots were down at the fisher's landing early, and Geordie was ready for them. The river cobles were flat bottomed so that they could land on the shore without the need for a quay. They could be used for fishing for salmon in the river, but more usually for taking passengers from a ship to the shore or to another ship. Tomag and Davey stepped into the grounded craft and Malky helped Geordie to push away. The tide was just coming in and rowing was not difficult, but Geordie gave Malky a turn at the oars. The river was quiet as it was a Sunday, and they soon passed Jarra's Lake. Geordie took over as he had to cross the channel and then steered them into the inlet by the Woolington ballast wharf. There were a few ships anchored there, and where they grounded their boat on the public landing there were several cobles and wherries on the shore.

"I dain't kna' how lang I'm ganna be, so I won't come back for ye'se, but if ye walk here from Newcastle on the way back ye should find someone whe'll tyek ye across to West Panns for a ha'penny."

They pushed him off and then headed west along the shore. As they walked by the banks of the Tyne they realised why so many ship's masters anchored near the mouth of the river rather than venture upstream. They could see stretches of shallow water where there was only a narrow navigable channel. There were also wrecks which narrowed the channel even more. If a large ship, or even a fully loaded keel, was coming in the opposite direction, then the risk of a collision was high. It took them a good two hours to reach the city walls, but before they did so they saw the many great houses where they made glass, but which today were not pumping out the black smoke like the salterns of Sheels. When they crossed the wooden bridge over the Ouse burn they were not alone, but many of the folk went on into St. Anne's Church. They gave the three men in working clothes on a Sunday curious looks, but the Scots lads paid no regard and carried on through the Sand Gate and on to the quayside. When they had first arrived in Sheels, the number of houses up the bank to the Lawe had impressed the Scotchmen, but that was nothing compared to Sandgate. Big houses, mansions and storehouses fronted onto the quayside, but behind them was a mass of dwellings, all crammed in between steps leading up the hill from the river, with darkened cross passages. "I wouldna' like to gang up there," whispered Davey, "ye might get lost and never cam oot again."

Although it was a Sunday with little movement on the river, the quayside itself was thronging with the keelmen enjoying their Sunday morning, in their Sunday best. They all had tall, black, wide brimmed hats, and most of them wore bright yellow waistcoats. They were all big, stout chested men with broad shoulders and sturdy legs. Some were just standing talking, but others were seated on large wooden blocks, playing cards. No constable or watchman had dared to seek to enforce the Parliament's ban of any form of gambling on these hardy fellows who lived by their own laws.

Davey was beginning to feel jittery as the three strangers drew fierce stares from rough looking men who clearly resented the intrusion of strangers. Tomag and Malky ignored the glances and walked on, shoulders back, and fists clenched. They heard Niall's whoop of joy, before they saw him emerge from a group standing round some card players. He was not wearing his blue bonnet, but was attired the same as all the other keelmen.

"Ach, it's ma brither and ma pals frae the salt-panns at Sheels," he shouted. The keelmen all knew his story, and the suspicious looks changed to more friendly glances of curiosity. Young Peedee came tearing along and jumped up to fling his arms round Malky's neck, gave him a slap round the cheek with alternate hands and then jumped down and did a jig. Angus McGilvray and Jockie, the bully, joined them as well.

"We came to see ye, as we've promised many a time, but to tell ye some guid news," said a beaming Tomag.

"Och aye, I'm ganna be free, at least frae ma indentures, but if it all gangs through, I'll be not sae free, as I'm gang to marry ma Peggy," cried a joyous Davey.

Niall slapped him on the shoulders. "Ach, weel, ye better tell us all o' it."

"He will, but first you'se 'll whet yer whistles wi' some o' ma usquebah," said Tomag, holding out a large stoppered earthenware jug and a small cup, and pouring out the amber liquor. "Ye first, Niall, this lot has been in a barrel for a guid three month and it tells."

Niall smacked his lips as he emptied the cup and it was passed round. Peedee was the only one to say no as he'd burnt his gullet last time he'd tried any. They all listened intently as Davey told the story of what the Quaker friends had done.

"And the master wants Tomag to find a lad?" shouted Peedee.

"Ach, I'll soon find ane," said Tomag.

"Wye aye ye will. I'll de it. I'm fed up with the river, but I'll gladly come and work for ye and Malky. Ye kna' I can de the job from when we've had wor lay-owers and I've given ye a hand when the others have gone to the boozas." Peedee was more of a lad than a boy now. He had grown a little in height, his shoulders were now broadening, but his mouth was just as big.

"Ye tak him, Tomag," shouted Jockie, "we'll be glad to see the back o' him, the mouthy little arseworm."

"Are ye sure, Peedee?" asked Niall. "It's no' for everybody, and ye might get the panner's sickness like I did."

Peedee was not to be dissuaded. "And I might fall owerboard and droon if I stay on the keel."

"Angus?" asked Tomag.

"If it'll help Davey oot, then I won't stand in yer way, but ye'll need to give me a day or two to find another boy."

Tomag looked at Peedee. "He'll de, but I'll hae to tak him to Milbourn first, but that will no' be a problem. Drap him doon when ye've got anither boy," said Tomag, passing the bottle to the skipper.

"Ach, we never have trouble taking a boy aff a poor family's hands. We'll drap him off during the week."

"What about his fatha'?" asked Malky.

"The auld man was glad to see the back of me," shouted Peedee, "and I've not seen him since I went to live with the skipper. He'll only want to kna' if I get any wages that he can take off me for his beer."

"If Mr. Milbourn taks ye on, he'll give ye food and lodging like us, so I doubt if ye'll get any coin to start wi', but as ye get aulder ye'll get a share of the salt drawings. Malky and me work for nowt so ye can buy us ale." Tomag's remarks were greeted with laughter, as the others patted Davey on the back, and swigged their usquebah.

Angus went off and came back with a couple of keelmen, whom he introduced as skippers like him, and both Scots. "These are pals o' mine and might be interested in taking some of the usquebah aff yer hands if you start to sell it. I said ye'd gie them a taster." The cup was filled and the two big men took sips and then swigged it back and put down the cup for more.

"Ach, that's better than the rot-gut ma Uncle Eck used to brew. I'll tak a bottle any time." The other nodded in agreement, and they sat down to join the others and take their turn at the drink. Anyone else who came by in the hope of having a snifter was sent packing.

Davey was telling his tale a third time to the two newcomers, when Niall suddenly ducked his head down beneath Tomag's shoulder. They all looked round and saw a gang of about six or seven tough-looking characters leading a girl along the quay as she looked carefully at the faces of the keelmen. As they came nearer, the man who was holding the lass by the arm looked over at them. He was a stout, red-faced fellow of middle age, with greasy black hair poking out from under his hat, and he was respectably dressed.

"Is that ye, Angus McGilvray?" he asked.

"Och aye," said Angus. "And what can I de for ye, Archibald?"

"Ye could ask that lad opposite ye to show his fyece so my lass can have a good look at him."

"And what if he disna' want to show his face?" replied Angus, pleasantly enough.

"Then I'll ask Little Jake here to stand him up for me whether he wants to or not," said Archibald.

Little Jake was a massive man, with a broken nose and a swollen ear, testimony to his fighting past, and he rubbed his huge hands together as he readied himself.

"There's nae need for that." It was Niall who spoke as he got to his feet and stepped away from the benches to show himself.

"That's him, Da'," cried the girl, "but he was wearing a blue bonnet like the lads sitting there, and ye can see the dimple in his chin. He said his name was Alec."

Angus lent across to whisper to Tomag and the others, "It's Archie Ridell, the landlord of the *Shoulder of Mutton* off Penny Pie Steps, and not ane to cross."

"I am Alec Patterson, and I do know the lassie," called out Niall.

"Weel, she's my daughter, Kitty, and she says ye took her up one of the alleys, forced yersel on her, and noo she's pregnant by ye. Ye're ganna come for a walk with us and tyek

241

yer punishment, and then we'll discuss the marriage."

"How many weeks gone is she?" asked Niall.

"How de I kna'," replied Archie, "but me wife says she's missed her rags twice already and she's starting to show."

"Weel, I did tak her up an alley, but I dinna' force any of the lasses who came wi' me for a bit of fun. I dinna' need to. I went wi yer Kitty the ance, aboot twa weeks ago, sae it's no' my bairn."

He looked Archibald and his daughter straight in the eyes and shouted out in his keelman's voice, "I'm no' gang to cam and tak any punishment, and I'm no' gang to marry yer Kitty." As he spoke he took two steps to the side and stood beside a large stone in the quay. He looked round at his accusers and at the keelmen who were now all watching and hoping for a brawl, and he spat on the stone.

"What's he deeing?" Malky asked Angus.

"It's what a keelman does when he's ready to fight, and his friends do the same to show they'll back him up."

Malky stood up quickly, walked over to where Niall was standing and spat on the stone. Davey followed. Archie and his men did not look worried, but then Tomag stood up, walked slowly and deliberately towards where Little Jake stood, looked him in the eye and then went to the stone, and spat. Little Peedee was next, much to the amusement of all, but then Angus and Jockie followed and the two skippers that had taken of the usquebah. Other keelmen started to rise.

Archibald realised that there would be no fight. One keelman could take any other three or four men in a fight, and he and his crew were already outnumbered.

"Divvent worry, Alec Patterson, I kna' whe ye are and ye'd better watch yer back when ye're sneaking roond the alleys looking for young lasses." He looked angrily in Niall's direction and the lad himself spoke.

"Can I hae a word wi' ye, private like?"

Archie looked dubious.

"Bring Little Jake wi' ye to watch yer back and Tomag'll cam wi' me." Niall's voice was quiet but determined, and he walked a few yards away from the others with Tomag by his side. Archibald nodded to Jake and the two of them came over, Archie still keeping ahold of Kitty.

"Ye might not like what I'm gang to say but it's well meant, and just stay calm til' I've had me say." Niall paused and then spoke. "Your Kitty was not a maid when I had her," Archie moved as though to strike Niall, but Little Jake put his hand on his shoulder. "I like lassies, but I'd nivver get ane belly-up, and I have a wee trickie to mak sure that ma seed disna enter their belly, sae I kna' it's not me." He looked over to the group of men Archie had brought with him. "Who's yon blond, guid looking fella at the back?" Archie said nowt. "It's just that oor Kitty has been looking back at him all the time we've been talking."

Archibald looked towards the man. "It's wor Johnny, Kitty's sister's husband. He runs the *Crown* for me at the Side. Wor Annie's just had a bairn and Kitty's been staying…" Archibald stopped dead.

"Tell Kitty to point at him noo, and see what happens," Niall said quickly.

"Point him oot, Kitty," barked Archie menacingly. The lass started sobbing and Archie squeezed her arm hard. She yelped and pointed her hand at Johnny. He took off at once and ran up the first steps he came to.

Archie was beside himself. "After him, ye lazy sods," he shouted to his men. "It's him the…" He was lost for words.

"He said he loved me," sobbed Kitty, "and that if I got someone else to tyek the blame, I'd be wed and he could still see me afterwards."

Archie looked at Niall. "Ye still took advantage of wor Kitty sae divvent think ye've nowt to worry aboot. But not as much as wor Johnny for noo." He turned on his heel and marched his daughter away. "Ye've made a bliddy fool o' me," he was shouting, "and given someitt that the keelmen and their women 'll talk aboot for months."

They stood together finishing the last few drops of usquebah while Niall told them all what had been said.

Malky took it all in. "What was that wee trickie ye use to mak sure ye dinn'a get a lassie wi' child?"

Niall laughed. "Ach, ye'r too young for that sort of thing, Malky lad, and ye a minister's son an'a'." They all laughed and Malky blushed, thinking of his Molly.

Angus had a word with one of the watermen and a coble took them down the Tyne to Jarra's Lake by West Pann's Way. They gave the man a ha'penny and started heading off.

"It's not too far aff frae' Biddick Hall. We could tell oor Dougie that I'm gan to be free."

"Guid idea," said Tomag. "We'll be late for oor dinner though."

"Ach," said Malky, "we could heat it up ower oor fire when we get back. And if we wake Jenett up when we barge in, at least there'll be naebody having his wee man pulled under the stairs." He ran off as Davey chased after him shouting blue murder. Tomag chuckled to himself as he walked on.

When they arrived at Biddick Hall, Isaac Frost and Thomas Haselrig were in the yard admiring *Lightning Lad*, who was held by one of the grooms. They both had cups made of glass in their hands and were drinking a deep red wine. Although Tomag and Davey held back, Malky, emboldened by the usquebah, strode forward. As he approached them Isaac Frost looked up. "Can I help you, lad? Ye're one of the Scotchmen who work in the panns?"

Malky doffed his bonnet. "Och, aye. Ye may not remember it, but my name is Malcolm Dalgleish, bonded to Mr. Milbourn. We were hoping to have a quick word with Dougie, yer kitchen servant and groom. We hae some good news aboot his cousin Davey there," he pointed to the lad, "that he'll want to hear."

"Dougie's roasting the fat beef for wor dinner, and then he'll help serve it. But if ye tell us the news then I'll pass it on."

"Thank you, master." Malky now tried to speak in the educated Scots that his father would have insisted upon, but his nerves soon got the better of him. "If ye could tell him that his cousin, Davey Finlayson here," Malky pointed to Davey who doffed his bonnet, just as Malky had done, "is gang to be freed from his indentures with Mr. Milbourn, and will be a free man again."

Thomas Haselrig who had been drumming his fingers on his fine striped knee breeches in impatience at the Scot's words, now looked up with interest. "And how is that?" he asked peremptorily.

"Davey was whipped for *skulduddery.*" Malky realised his mistake as he saw the expressions on the men's faces. "Ach, I mean fornic..."

"You mean fornication, Malcolm," said Frost. "I remember the case, and he bravely took the scullion's punishment as well."

"Aye, weel, two Quakers, Robert Linton and Nathan Taylier, had spoken up for him in the Market Place and a few weeks after, he saw the lad Nathan being beaten in the street by his father. I was there and auld Abe..."

"You mean Mr. Abraham Taylier," interrupted Frost sternly.

"Och aye, I'm sorry, master. Mr. Abraham would have killed him if Davey had not cam between them, and taken Nathan away to be seen to by the pothecary. Mr. Nathan was so grateful that he spoke to his Quaker friends, and they've all given their coin so that the indenture can be cancelled. They also did it so that Davey could marry Peggy who's carrying his child and he can work the holding noo."

"And has Mr. Milbourn agreed?" asked Frost.

"Aye," Malky replied.

"Could I hae a word wi' Mr. Haselrig?" Malky asked.

"Those who want to address me usually call me Sir Thomas," said Frost's companion, a little haughtily, but he wanted to hear what the Scotch lad had to say.

"Sir Thomas," began Malky, "ye may remember when we Scotch lads were sold to the Sheels pann-owners, that I read my indenture before I signed it, as my Da', the Minister Archibald Dalgleish, had aye tell me to read anything that I was to give ma name to."

"I do," chuckled Sir Thomas, "and I seem to remember that the Curate was none too happy."

"Weel, I'm just thinking back that at the end of the indenture there was a condition that it could only be discharged before the end of the term if Sir Arthur Haselrig or his representative agreed."

Sir Thomas just inclined his head as if to agree.

"I was wondering, as ye are here noo, whether ye could give yer agreement, and it would save the clerk, Mr. Ashburne, the trouble of having to send somebody to Newcastle to ask ye."

Sir Thomas looked at Isaac Frost. Neither of them had taken the trouble to read the indentures but would not admit it to the young Scotch lad. Frost looked at his empty glass, and walked over to the open hall door. He shouted for some wine. "And a pail of ale for wor visitors." He turned and looked at the groom. "Ye can take him back to the stable noo, lad."

It was Dougie who came out with a jug to refill the wine glasses, and then brought a pail of beer and gave his friends cups, which they eagerly dipped into the foaming brew. Davey took the opportunity to gabble away in Gaelic and Dougie clapped his cousin on the back, and went back into the hall.

"There is a good reason for such a condition," said Sir Thomas, licking his lips as he sipped the wine. "Cromwell had freed the old, the young and the wounded as they would not have been a threat, but he could not return able bodied and trained soldiers to return to their homeland, in case they took up arms again. My father had incurred considerable expense in caring for the prisoners."

Tomag looked as though he was going to say something but Davey put his hand on his arm. He wanted nothing to jeopardise his freedom.

Haselrig continued, "And by selling the prisoners into bondage as indentured servants, it meant they would not be free to go back to Scotland for seven years. I could only agree to a discharge of his indenture if the lad remained in Sheels."

"Could he gie his oath?" asked Malky.

"He could but it would be better if he was bound to another master for the remainder of the term. It would be the usual sort of bond where a servant agrees to serve a master, but would be paid for his work, on the terms of the bond."

Davey now stepped forward, his cap in hand.

"Can I say something?" he asked very nervously.

Frost nodded.

"Robbie Clibbourne, who runs the Harton Down home-stall for his mother, who's not reet in the heid, is happy for me to take ower at the Marsden Cottage if I marry ma Peggy. He said something aboot it being a bondage ten..e something."

Isaac Frost smiled. "Then there's your answer, Sir Thomas. It certainly is a bondage tenement and young Davey here would be tied to the land for the term of the bond."

"Well you're a lucky fella, Davey-lad. I'll give my consent to the cancellation of the indenture if you enter a bond with this Robbie Clibbourne which keeps ye in Sheels for at least the length of the indenture. I'll write a note to that effect if you, Isaac, see the clerk of the Vestry court and make sure that everything is set to writing. Let us go in, I'm starved, and tired of talking." He stalked off.

Isaac Frost was more friendly, and slapped Davey on the shoulder. "I'll make sure everything is settled, Davey, and congratulations on your freedom."

The three Scots made their way back through the West Panns and stopped off at the *Turk's Heed* for more ale and usquebah before picking up their cold dinner from Jenett. She was not as unfriendly as usual, and told Davey that she was glad that Peggy was to be wed, and hoped that he would look after her well.

On the Wednesday of the next week, Angus pulled up against the quay on the way back from discharging a load of coal on a waiting collier, and put Peedee ashore. The replacement Peedee was in the keel, a skinny ginger-haired lad of about twelve, who would soon have to toughen up or be sent on his way. Angus did not stay, as he was to take off some ballast from a newly arrived ship and they would have to work fast to catch the incoming tide.

Peedee was under strict instructions from Tomag to keep his gob shut when he was taken to see Mr. Milbourn. He was to work for only his lodgings and keep to start with, but as he learned the work and pulled his weight, then he would get his share of the salt drawings. He was glad to be off the keel – Jockie, the bully, had taken against him, and had started knocking him about a bit too much.

Nathan Taylier was a frequent visitor to finalise the talks with Ralph Milbourn. On one of his first visits he broke the news to Davey that George Blayre had died in his sleep and so Davey could take his place as the bonded tenant straight away. He then called in on the Friday afternoon to tell an anxious Davey that all was now settled and they would go up to St. Hild's on the Saturday morning. Robbie Clibbourne was coming over from Harton and everything would be signed and witnessed.

"And can I gan straight to Harton afterwards?" asked Davey.

"Aye ye can," said Nathan, "and Robbie Clibbourne is bringing Peggy with him so you can give your particulars to Mr. Ashburne, and he'll arrange for the banns to be read." He paused and looked embarrassed. "There is a problem with the Curate. He's not prepared to allow a pregnant unmarried woman into the church, so ye'll have to stand in the porch while the ceremony is conducted."

Davey said nowt, as it made no difference to him. When they went to collect what would be Davey's last meal, they found that Jenett had made them a mutton pie with raisins, and some of the fried apple cakes that they had had on their first day at the Milbourns'. She also gave them two pails of ale. They had a memorable farewell night. Malky, Tomag and Peedee were off to work at six, and Davey made his farewells. He would wait in the Milbourns' kitchen, until it was time to go up to the church.

CHAPTER NINE

At one of Angus's next drops, he pulled in at Milbourn's quay and unloaded the parts for Tomag's new still, covered in canvas sheets. The two Scots carried them into the salt-house and came back for them that night, so as few as possible would see them being carried to the widder's cottage. Cuddy Heron would keep them supplied with malted barley from the *Turk's* when he was on his rounds. Hamish supplied a bird in a cage – a robin that one of the panners had caught for him.

The two stills in the pothecary's shop bubbled away when the mash was ready and no one took any notice of them. Tomag would take away the distilled liquor to the *Turk's* when it was ready. The former salt-house premises were large and airy, and once Hamish started making his coffin seals on the copper lids over the mash tun, he had had no problems with gas leaks. He came up to the widder's cottage to help install the still, and he was there when the first malt came over and explained carefully to the Widder Wallis and Alice how important it was to keep an eye on the still at all times when there was a boiling. The flour seal was applied and the still was soon bubbling away. On Hamish's instructions the first drops were tasted and spat out until the clear spirit no longer had the early unpleasant flavours. One of Marledane's barrels was ready for the spirit to be poured into it as soon as the receiving pot was full.

Peedee very quickly made himself as annoying to the panners as he had been to the keelmen, but he was a hard worker and pulled his weight, despite his young age. Although he paid little attention to Jobling and Tomag, even when he got a clip round the ear, he always listened to Malky.

Malky looked at Peedee one day and said, "Ye telt me a while ago that they call all the boys on the keels Peedee."

"Wye aye, they de."

"Ach, well, we'll call ye by your proper name noo, Pee…" He stopped and they all laughed.

"Naw," mumbled the boy. "Ye'se can just call me Peedee. There's nae other keel-boys in Sheels."

He would follow Malky around, but he made himself useful. He went with Malky to the toon-end on the first Sunday and watched as Malky wrestled. He'd never seen the back-hold before, but was soon shouting and whooping for Malky. After his bouts, Malky sat with Peedee and watched the others. As he looked round he caught sight of Molly standing with her basket by the alley. He whispered something in Peedee's ear and the lad sped off. He came back in two ticks and said she'd be there.

"Come on then, Peedee, I'll need ye as a look-out."

They walked quickly to the sign of the *Orange Tree* and went up the side alley. Malky went into the pub and had a quick word with Redheed and then came back into the stable yard. Not long after, Molly came in. Malky held out his hand to her and led her into the stable. He called quietly back to

Peedee.

"Dinna' let anybody cam in. Redheed knows we're here so he won't cam oot. When we've finished I'll gie a whistle. Ye whistle back if the coast's clear."

"Wye aye," shouted back Peedee.

Once inside, Malky pushed Molly gently against the wall away from the open doors. He kissed her on the lips and let his hands run over her full bosom and then down to her shapely behind. She gently pushed him away.

"Dain't get too excited, Malky, ye can't have it. I'm pregnant with yer bairn."

Malky moved his left hand onto her stomach. "Ach, Molly. I did wonder when ye didn't cam the other nicht when Geordie called for me to gang to Frenchman's. Does Geordie know?"

"Aye and he's the only one. I didn't see much point in telling ye, as there's nowt ye can de, and we can't wed with ye being indentured. I was daft to let ye have it in the forst place. I decided to wait until I knew what I was ganna' de.

"Even though I've not needed me rags, I've been washing them and putting then oot on the bushes to dry so that auld Mutha Hawes wouldn't twig. I've made mesel a bigger bodice but I can't hide it for much longer. I telt Geordie so he could gan to see wor sister in Cullercoats. She's ganna' take me in, and we'll say that I'm a widder who's just lost her man at sea. Noo I've seen ye I'll gan as soon as I can. Mebbees this week. If Geordie and his mates are gan' oot in a sea coble for the harrain', he'll drop me off there. I can still de some work for her, gutting and salting the harrain', and I've some coin put by from the smuggling."

"Can I come and see ye?" asked Malky who was now gently pressing himself against her and becoming more and more aroused. Molly seemed more fresh and beautiful to him, than ever.

"I dain't think so. Not to do owt like this. But if ye came with Geordie on the boat ye could say hello."

Malky was not really listening, and gently steered Molly on to the heap of dry straw on the floor.

Peedee heard Malky's whistle. There was no one about so, he whistled back, and Molly came out first, looking a little red and flustered. Malky then came out, his face flushed, and brushed away the bits of straw on his trews.

"Did ye have it, then, Malky?" Peedee shouted.

"*De'il haet*, Peedee, can ye no' keep yer voice doon for ance." Malky raised his hand to cuff the lad, but when he saw the look on Peedee's face he stopped.

"Ach, I wouldna' hit ye, Peedee. Ye're not to know. I did hae it ance wi' Molly and folk foond oot and they made me ride a stang in front of Molly's hoose. If they see us oot togither then I might get a whippin' like Davey did. And ye're ganna have to try not to shout all the time, Peedee, ye're not still on the watter." Malky put his arm round Peedee's shoulder. "Anyway ye're too young to talk aboot that sort of thing."

"Naw I'm not," Peedee shouted and then put his hand over his mouth. "I'm sorry," he said in what he took for a whisper but it was probably heard on the other side of the river. "I've got hairs growin' roond me thing, and I'd dee it with a lass if

I got the chance."

Malky needed his ale. He took Peedee with him through the back door of the Orange Tree. Redheed took one look at the lad and said, "Oot the door. It's select company only on a Sunda'."

"Gang outside, Peedee," said Malky. "I'll hae some ale and then come and find ye."

Cuddy Heron was there with Abe Taylier and Charles Robinson, the chief cooper. Auld Abe was looking his age and was quite red faced even though it was still early. Redheed brought Malky his pint, and did not seek any payment. He was in a good mood. The final fitting out was underway at his new brewery and Charles would be installing the vats and tuns in a few days.

"I was ganna wait until the new harvest, but if I can get some of last year's barley I'll start a brew of strong ale. I'm not spreading word in case the news travels to Newcastle too soon. I'm just ganna get the watermen to take barrels to the ships. Once the trade catches on, it'll be a good front for selling any brandy Cuddy brings in ower the sands, or Tomag's usquebah. I'll have to get the ale cunners and the excise involved for the ale, but keep the nebs of the customs men oot of it. They're hand in glove with the hostmen and the aldermen."

It was a quiet summer evening at the Widder's Court. Malky and Tomag were sitting on the step outside their cottage and puffing on their clay pipes. News of Hamish's tobacco had quickly spread from those to whom he had recommended it as a heal-all. Angus had ferried a couple of cases of clay pipes from Newcastle, and they were selling like hot cakes. Hamish made a gift of some plugs of baccy to his friends, and after some coughing fits they had now taken a liking to the fragrant vapours. The widder Wallis was outside on her weaving frame and Alice was inside, keeping an eye on the still. Peedee had got hold of a hoop and stick from somewhere, and was running up and down the close, whipping the hoop along at breakneck speeds. Alice came out of the widder's cottage, holding a long piece of blackened pastry in her hand. She bit an end off and chewed it. "I've been givin' some bits to poor Robin. He's not been chirping much. I tried some mesel and it's quite tasty."

Peedee had stopped his running and took a small piece. "Wye it's canny," he said. "I'll give a bit to Robin." He was always in the widder's cottage talking to the bird and poking it with sticks to make it sing. As he popped his head through the door he shouted, "Ye've killed it, Alice, it's lying deed on the floor." The next minute Tomag flew across the yard, grabbed Peedee, and dragged him out of the doorway. He was just in time. There was a mighty bang and a flash, as an explosion rocked the cottage. Minutes later, flames were shooting out of the thatch.

The widder shouted in terror and started dragging her weaving frame away from the flames. Tomag grabbed their own pail of water and flung it on the flames to little effect.

"You'se two, tak two pails each and run up to the well. We'll need to damp doon the thatch on the other cots to stop the fire spreading."

Malky and Peedee ran off, followed by Alice. Peedee kept shouting fire, and soon there was a chain of men, women and boys, passing pails from the common well on the back row down to the close. Tomag had pulled out the table from their house so that he could stand on it to throw water on the roof. Others did the same, and as soon as a spark lit up some thatch on a neighbouring roof they flung water on it or knocked the flames back with brushes. The constable and the watch arrived and gave their help too. Puncheon had noticed Peedee's hoop resting against the cottage wall. When Peedee passed him with a pail of water the constable muttered to him, "If that's yours, son, then keep it in the close. If I see ye running aboot along the ways then I'll hoy it on the nearest fire and give you a stroke or two of my whip. It's ungodly to play frivolous games with balls and hoops." Peedee said nowt and walked away.

By the time the dusk was drawing in the fire was out, but all the thatch and most of the roof timbers of the widder's cottage had burnt away. Almost all of her furniture and belongings had been consumed in the fire when the burning thatch fell into the inside of the cottage. None of the other roofs had caught, but it was decided that a watch would be kept during the night in case any embers might flare up if there was a wind. The widder and Alice would have to share the panners' cottage for the time being. Tomag gave Malky a few pence to go down to the *Orange Tree* with Peedee and fetch back some pails of ale for those that had helped fight the flames. They all had their share. It was the end of any ideas of expanding the distilling business, but Tomag would continue to have his little sideline with the still in Hamish's shop. If there was any spare to sell to anyone, then the profit went straight to Marledane who had lost the money he'd paid out for the second still.

When the harvest started, Tomag, Malky, and Peedee went over to Harton on the Sunday and spent a day in the fields. Davey looked well and fit with his face and arms well-tanned. The Sheels men were still pale – little sun penetrated the thick clouds that hung constantly over the town. Tomag and Malky had both used the scythe during the harvests in Scotland and worked well with the other men, taking their share of the ale when they rested. Peedee helped the women and the lads and lasses, stacking the sheaves. He had never seen a harvest before and took in eagerly everything that was new. He came into his element when they were scything the last square of corn in the centre of the field, and along with the other lads and lasses he was given a stick with a nail driven through its head to chase and kill the rats, mice and other wildlife that now had to run over the stubble to escape the scythes. He ran like a demon and whooped with excitement each time he made a kill. They shared the harvest supper of mutton stew with dumplings, and returned home to Sheels weary but content.

Peedee took no notice of what the constable had told him, and took his hoop with him down to the saltern each morning. There was plenty of room on the quayside to have a good run, and if there was a break in their work, he'd be out tearing up and down. Some of the other panner boys might ask a turn and if they were lucky he might let them try it out. If any overzealous adults – and there were one or two killjoys in Sheels – spoke to him, he'd just disappear round the corner of one of the quayside sheds.

It was a fine but blustery day at the beginning of September and the latest batch of Milbourn's salt was to be weighed out. When the salt in the drabs was dry, then Tomag or Jobling sent for the excise man and the salt measurer, and the dry salt was shovelled out of the drabs either into a wey-case, or a bowl. On that day it was all the best fine white salt which was going into bowls, which each held a bushel, and would sell at 2s 4d. On a weighing day, the panns would be left to simmer very slowly as the panners would need to do the shovelling and carrying. Malky whispered into Peedee's ears to keep the boy informed of what was going on, as it was his first salt-weigh. All the bowls to be filled were checked by the town salt measurer to be sure that they had the chief cooper's mark – he held the brazen measure and ensured that all new wooden bowls would hold exactly a bushel, not a grain more nor less.

In the weighing shed a bowl was first checked then filled, the lid was tacked on with pins, and then the excise man would affix his own seal, and add it to his tally on a slate which would be used to work out the final bill. Each bowl paid 3d excise duty. The full bowls were carried to a separate shed where they would be stored until carried to the salt merchant or sold directly. There were women who would buy a bowl, and then hawk the salt to those who could only afford to buy a gill or a half pint at a time.

Henry Coultheard was there. As well as his two guards, he had brought his son Christian with him. He was a well-built lad with a mop of fair hair sticking out under his cap, a snub nose, and a cheeky grin. "As ye're here ye might as weel do something," said Coultheard. He handed him some slates and a chalk. "Ye can keep the tally for me. Make a mark after each bowl has been sealed and then ye can work oot how much I'm owed."

The lad looked surprised but took the slates with the confidence of youth.

Peedee had been looking sideways at the excise man's son with his clean face and hands, and his fine clothes. He was about the same age as the panners' lad. Peedee was helping to carry the sealed bowls out of the weighing shed, and as he passed Christian, who was standing by the door, he pushed into him, making his chalk slide over the slate.

"Sorry," shouted Peedee in the keelman's voice he now reserved for strangers. The next time Peedee passed him he did the same, but this time, Christian looked at him, poked his tongue out, and barged him back, laughing and shouting, "Ye didn't say nae returns."

Malky, who was standing nearby with his own slates, put a hand on Peedee's shoulders as he guessed that he was going to respond in turn.

"Ach, ye must no' bother the tallyman, Peedee. And ye, Christian, should concentrate on the tally. Have ye marked that ane?"

Christian looked down and made a mark. Malky was keeping the tally for Milbourn to make sure that there were no mistakes by the excise man. He looked at Christian's slate.

"Ye're just marking each ane aff?" asked Malky.

"Aye, that's what me Da' said."

Malky showed him his own slate. After the fourth mark he had drawn a line and written in 1s. "Each bowl is thre'pence, and four are a shilling. If ye mark it like this it's a lot quicker to add up at the end."

Christian looked at the slate. "Ye're reet. Ha'd on a minute," he said to Peedee who was bringing another bowl over. "I'm just ganna mark-up me slate like Mr. Milbourn's clerk has shown me."

Peedee laughed. "Malky's nae clerk. He's a panner just like the rest of us, but he can read and write and does all the tallying."

Christian looked at Malky. "Weel, ye're daft, Mr. Malky, to work in the panns if ye can read and write. Ye'd get paid twice as much if ye worked as a clerk."

"He's not daft," shouted Peedee with a smile on his face, "he's a slave," and he walked off with the sealed bowl. His voice had carried and Henry Coultheard walked over.

"Nae slacking noo, Christian," he muttered.

"Malky-lad here's not a slave," said Milbourn who had followed the excise man and had heard Peedee's words. He'd have had to be deaf not to. "He's an indentured servant. He's one of the Scotch prisoners captured at Dunbar that General Haselrig sold to the pann-owners of Sheels."

"Ye're a soldier?" asked Christian.

"Ach, I was for four days, and I've lost my freedom for seven years because of it."

Nowt more was said and the weighing continued. There was no more pushing and shoving between the boys, but they poked their tongues out, and made faces as they passed each other. When all the drabs had been emptied and the tallies justified, Ralph Milbourn invited Coultheard to settle the account and to take a glass of brandy. Coultheard went with him, but let Christian stay outside with his two guards, and Milbourn sent ale out for them. As soon as they had gone, Peedee dashed across to the saltern and came out with his hoop and stick.

"I bet I can gan faster than ye," he shouted to Christian.

"I'm not sure I'm allowed," muttered the lad. "Me Da' took mine away and broke it. He said the Parliament had forbidden frivolous games, and that he'd whip me if he caught me playing owt like that. He had to set an example."

"Ach, hae some fun, Christian," said Malky. "I'll keep an eye oot, and as soon as I see yer Da' coming oot o' Milbourn's I'll gie ye a shout."

"Thanks, Mr. Malky," said Christian, running over to where Peedee stood with his hoop.

"It's just Malky. Short for Malcom," the Scot replied.

"And ye let Peedee call ye by yer first name."

"Ach, and why should I no'. But if he gives me any cheek he gets a beltin'."

"So it's all reet if I call ye Malky?" asked Christian.

The Scotchman nodded.

"Me Da' calls me Christian but everybody else calls me Kit."

"Weel, Kit it is, eh, Peedee."

"Wye aye. D'ye want a practice forst?" he asked.

Kit did, and it took him a while to get used to whipping the hoop, but after a while he was away. Then the two lads were tearing round the quayside, whipping and whooping.

Tomag was standing next to Malky. "He seems a braw young lad, that Kit. It's guid that Peedee's making friends his own age."

"Ach, until his auld man comes oot," said Malky and turned his head to see Milbourn's door opening and a slightly red-faced Coultheard coming through it. Kit had just started a run down to the quayside with Peedee beside him and was beginning to pick up speed. They heard Malky's cry of warning and Peedee shouted, "Roond the corner oot o' sight." They darted towards the last shed and Peedee who was in front to show the way took the turn quickly, but Kit's feet got tangled up and he went head first over the dock side with a shriek followed by a splash.

Malky kicked his shoes off, threw down his bonnet, and was away quick. He was only wearing his shirt and his breeks, and threw himself headlong into the river. As he surfaced he could see Kit's fair hair just downstream. The tide was turning and the current had him. He was holding on to the hoop but struggling to keep his head above water. Just as he started to go under, Malky kicked with his feet and dived down. The sun was high and the waters were clear, and Malky saw Kit still holding the hoop but sinking. He pushed hard with his legs and his hand managed to grab the hoop. He pushed up and broke the surface, a spluttering and coughing Kit coming up just in front of him.

"I've got ye," he shouted.

"I canna swim. I'm droonin'," shouted Kit, putting both arms round Malky's neck. Malky was struggling to keep afloat with the weight of the boy round him. "I've got ye, Kit," he said again. "I'll try to swim ye ashore." The lad seemed to calm and then Malky gently prised his hands from round his neck, but still held him firmly by the arm. The current was strong and Malky knew that he'd need to kick very hard to get to the riverside. He wasn't making any way against the flow, when he heard an ear-splitting yell from the quayside.

"Ahoy the keel, swape to starboard, man adrift." It was Peedee yelling with a voice like a fog-horn.

"Swape to starboard," answered an equally loud man's voice. Malky looked up and saw a keel bearing down on them. A bully in a blue bonnet threw a rope that hit Malky on the side of the head but he managed to hold on. The man and a boy pulled them in as the other crewman held the long oar steady. They hauled Kit over the side and then a strong hand gripped Malky's and he clambered into the keel.

There was little room for them as the keel was packed full of coal. The skipper who was holding the swape shouted impatiently, "Back to the oar, lads, I'm not gonna try to pull into a quay with this load on, we'll gang to the *Twa Brithers* to tie up, and see if they can put them ashore in one of their boats."

The keel carried on, with the two bullies and the boy lifting up the oar, walking back to the stern, then dipping it down as deep as they could, pushing with their right feet for all they were worth to drive the keel on. As they closed on the *Two Brothers*, the bullies pulled in the oar, and propelled only by the swape, the heavily laden keel came alongside the ship and the boy threw up the rope from the bow as a bully cast the other rope aboard from the stern. Malky had seen keels come alongside ships before, but had never appreciated the skills of seamanship required.

Even with the sun on their shoulders, the rescued lads were both starting to shiver as the cold of the water crept into their bones. Malky held Kit to him and tried to keep him warm. After the ropes were secure and they were finally tied up to the larboard of the *Two Brothers*, Malky called out to the crewman who had thrown the rope. "Thank ye, friend. I dinna' whether I could have got this ane ashore on my own. The watter's no' friendly and there's a terrible undertow."

"Ye'd ha' done the same. I can tell ye're Scotch, are ye a boatman as weel?" asked the keelman.

"Ach no," replied Malky. "I work in the salt-panns. I was captured at Dunbar and sold as an indentured servant to work in the panns at Sheels."

"I'm Matty Coutts frae Ridsdale. Ye'll know Alec Patterson then, who works on McGilvray's keel?"

"Och aye I do. His brother Tomag still works here with me. When I saw your blue bonnet I thought it was him throwing me a line," said Malky.

"Ha'd your tongues you'se two, we've got work to do," shouted the skipper. He pointed to Malky and the lad. "The Cap'n of the *Twa Brithers* 'll look after ye until he can put oot a boat to tak ye ashore." He held a hand over his eyes to shield them from the sun. "But I think those fellas there might organise something." He pointed to a landing just opposite them where Coultheard and Milbourn were standing, waving, and shouting.

"It's me Da'," said Kit, trying to put his feet on the narrow boards along the keel's side and nearly going in the water again.

Malky held him firm.

"We won't pull ye oot a second time," shouted the skipper, now anxious to put his unwanted passengers aboard so that the crew could get on with the unloading. Malky and Kit slowly and carefully crawled along the narrow footway around the hold. Kit was still holding onto the hoop.

The keel's Peedee, who could not have been much more than eleven or twelve, looked on and asked in a normal voice, "Is that a hoop? I've always wanted to have one."

"If ye'r gang to become a keelman then ye'll need to learn to shout like that young'un' on the quay, and ye'll no' play with toys," chuckled Matty. He looked at Malky. "The boy's only been wi' us a week or two."

Kit looked at the boy. "Ye and the others saved wor lives, so I'd gladly give it ye, but it's not mine, it's Peedee's."

"Weel I'm Peedee too," said the boy.

"Ach, let him have it, Kit. I've nae doot that oor Peedee will have mair things on his mind than the hoop when yer Da' and Mr. Milbourn give him a whipping for letting ye fall in the Tyne."

Kit gave the peedee the hoop. "Ha'd on to it if ye fall in the watter. It helped me keep afloat just long enough for Malky to reach me."

The Captain of the *Two Brothers* was a big bluff man who hailed from Norfolk and was glad of an excuse to open his brandy bottle to give the two lads a drink to warm them up. He had a good swig himself, and then gave his hosts a thick blanket each to help them dry out. Although the sun was out there was a keen nor'-easter blowing off the German Ocean and the rescued lads were shivering, with Kit's teeth clattering.

It was not much later that a boat pulled alongside and Malky and Kit clambered over the side into the welcoming arms of Henry Coultheard and Ralph Milbourn. Once they were ashore they were taken straight away to Coultheard's house in the High Street. The women were chased out of the kitchen while they took off their wet clothes and wrapped blankets round themselves, as they sat on a settle in the hearth. They were given more Strasbourg brandy by Henry Coultheard, who helped himself to several cupfuls, while the two who had been in peril just sipped the fiery liquor. It had its effect on Kit who soon dozed off, his head resting on Malky's shoulder. Malky soon followed and it was sometime later that he was shaken awake by a strong hand on his shoulder.

"C'mon, Malky lad." It was Ralph Milbourn. "Ye've had your dip in the river, noo put your claes back on and get back to work."

Mrs. Coultheard, a grey-haired matronly type, would not hear of it. "He's staying to dinner. It's the least we can do since he saved young Kit. Henry, you tell Mr. Milbourn."

Kit was still half asleep but he had heard what had been said. "Aye, ye should stay for some dinner. I'm starvin' mesel. I hope it's not fish again, Mam."

"Wye no, it's mutton chops with barley broth and peas, and we're having wheaten bread from the new grain, as well as first harvest ale. It can be ready in a tick if ye want an early dinner, Henry, and then Malky can be back to work."

"Aye well, I suppose another hoor won't harm," said Milbourn.

"And ye'll think ower what I said?" half whispered Coultheard.

"Aye I will." Milbourn left them to it.

Malky and Kit put their dried clothes on and then sat down at the table. Malky and Kit wolfed their food down to the amusement of Kit's sister, Anna. The mutton chops were juicy, with thick yellow fat, which was soon dripping down their chins. Anna was herself fair like Kit, and was a little older than her brother. She could not help herself from looking at the young Scotchman with his wavy chestnut hair, his odd coloured eyes, and his manly features. Malky paid no attention as he was concentrating on filling his stomach.

Once the mutton was finished they were served sweet apple dumplings with butter and honey. As the meal came to an end Henry Coultheard tapped the table with his large signet ring.

"When I saw wor Kit fly ower the quayside at Milbourn's saltern, I thought he was a goner. He can't swim and the river was full. But then I saw Malky lad here jump into the Tyne withoot any thought of his own safety. He kept Kit's heed above watter until they were saved by the keelmen. Mind, if that keel had not come alang when it did, they could have been washed ower the bar and oot to sea, and we'd nivver have seen them again." The French brandy was having its effect and tears dribbled down the excise man's cheeks. Mrs. Coultheard dabbed her eyes with her napkin.

"Ach, weel ye've got Peedee to thank for that," said Malky. "He's only a lad but he's got a keelman's lungs on him. They telt us, didn't they, Kit? They wouldn't have seen us if they hadn't heard him shouting."

"Aye, I was there mesel'," added Coultheard. "Milbourn wanted to give him a whipping because of his tomfoolery in causing Kit to go ower the side, but I wouldn't have it.

"Noo then, Malky. The excise business is very profitable at the moment. I would like to do something for ye, for saving Kit. Is there anything ye'd like, anything at all."

Malky was already half dazed by his efforts in the river, together with the brandy and his full belly. He looked round the table. He knew what he wanted but he did not want to ask for something that might be beyond their means. He was saved from his dilemma by Kit.

"I kna' what he wants and if he doesn't, he's daft. He wants his freedom. We'll buy oot his indentures."

"We will then," roared Henry. "I've already spoken to Milbourn and he's agreed in principle, but needs to kna' whether you'd keep working for him as a paid man or whether ye'd leave. If ye do, he'll need time to find another salt worker."

"He'll leave," cried Kit. "He can read and write and he'll get a job as a clerk."

"Ye can read and write?" asked a surprised Coultheard.

"Och aye, me Da's a Minister in the kirk and a covenanter. That's why I was at Dunbar and was taken prisoner."

"Weel, auld Milbourn's been hiding yer light under a bushel. Will ye look for work here or gan yem to Scotland?"

"I have to stay in Sheels. It's a condition of the indenture that it can only be cancelled if Sir Arthur Haselrig agrees. We were sold as indentured servants not only for the coin, but also to keep us frae ganging back to Scotland as we were prisoners who'd fought against the English. Sir Arthur agreed to the Quakers buying oot ma friend Davey's bond, because he was gang to work at Harton as a bonded tenant at Marsden cottage."

Coultheard rubbed his chin. "But ye will still be a free man, and can work for coin, but ye have to be bonded to a master?"

"Och aye. I'm not gang to stay a minute langer than I have to in the salt-panns, but I'll need to find a new master. I should find a work easy enough with a merchant, they're always after clerks and sic like. I canna thank ye enow, Mr. Coultheard," said Malky who was almost overcome with emotion.

"Could ye not give him a job with ye, Da'? Ye're always saying how good men are hard to come by," asked Kit.

"And whether ye work for Mr. Coultheard or not," exclaimed an animated Mrs. Coultheard, "ye could always come and live with us here, Malky. We've plenty of room and Kit's bed is big enough for two."

"Aye and ye could have mutton chops every day," cried Anna, not wanting to be left out. They all laughed.

"I'll ha' to think on it," mumbled Malky, "this has all cam as a surprise and a shock to me." As he stood up to leave and get back to the salt-house, Malky shook Mr. Coultheard's hand and then, as an afterthought, he asked, "Ye've done mair than enow for me, Sir, but can I ask for something else? Not for me this time. Only Peedee loved playing wi' his hoop. I know that it ended up badly the day, but Kit and I gave the hoop to the boy on the keel as he had helped save oor lives and the boys – they're all called peedees - have an awfu' hard life."

"Aye, I was wondering what came of the hoop. I can get one of the carpenters to make one, but we'll have to keep quiet aboot it as the Vestry court have banned all sports." Henry Coultheard looked at his son and anticipating what was forming in the lad's mind, said, "And I suppose we better have one made for Kit here as well. But ye're to take it doon to the sands oot of sight and not gan anywhere near the quayside."

Before he finally parted, Malky spoke again. "As ye've been so guid to me, I could do something in return. Me and Davey used to gang for a swim on the sands on a Sunda' morning after I'd taught him to swim. I could tak Kit wi' me and teach him, in case he falls in the river again."

Kit was standing in the doorway and shouted out, "Please, Da', and would Peedee come as weel, Malky?"

"Och, he would. He gangs everywhere that I do."

"But it will mean him missing church," said a doubtful Mrs. Coultheard.

"Weel, I'd rather he learned to swim and stayed alive, than drooned and went strite to heaven," cried Coultheard.

Malky had a long talk with Tomag after he got back to the salt-house. That evening he walked along the Low Way and called at Captain Bowmaker's house to tell him the news and to seek his advice. Malky wanted to keep involved with the smuggling business and play a larger part, but he'd need to have a proper job as a front.

"I need the coin if I'm to marry Molly and look after her and the bairn." Bowmaker knew of course of Molly's pregnancy, and of her stay in Cullercoats.

"Tyek one thing at a time, Malky-lad. I'll need to talk things ower with the others in the business. Dick Redheed wants to keep his nose clean for a while. He's heard that the Newcastle hostmen are not happy at all aboot anyone supplying the ships and selling ale to the mariners on board. Only the other week, they sent doon a troop of men from the garrison in Newcastle and closed Ralph Gardner's brewery in North Sheels. He was selling to the ship's masters and he's noo in prison at the Castle Garth. So Dick's only brewing for himsel and other publicans, but doesn't want to draw any attention to the brewery. Auld Abe might be yer best bet. He's said nowt, but he misses his son Nathan. He didn't realise how much help the lad gave him, and so he might be happy to take ye on. But ye'll need to get yersel settled forst, before ye can think of bringing Molly back. Auld Mutha' Hawes won't be happy if she finds oot her Danny's widder's expecting yer bairn."

PART III

CHAPTER TEN

Malcolm Dalgleish, dressed soberly in a black coat, and wearing a black, wide brimmed hat, instead of his blue bonnet, walked purposefully along the way, and then turned down the path that led to the merchants' quay that served several warehouses and sheds. He was a regular caller at the premises of Maud and Taylier. Young Nathan had been taken into partnership by William Maud, who had long been trying to encroach into Abraham Taylier's agricultural trade, and the use of the Taylier name of itself had been reason enough for Maud to welcome Nathan into his business.

Malky had now been working for Abraham for nearly a month. The old man had been a little wary at first, but had soon given the Scots lad his full confidence. Malky was officially Mr. Taylier's secretary, as designated in the six-year bond that he had sealed in front of Henry Ashburne. This enabled him to openly talk to Bowmaker, Dick Redheed, and Cuddy Heron about the arrival of new shipments at Frenchman's Bay, and the selling on of the merchandise. At the same time he would learn all about Abe's business, spending time at the warehouse with Abe's chief clerk, who kept the ledgers and who would arrange for the payment to ship's masters and foreign merchants of bills of exchange that Abe had issued to buy merchandise at the

Baltic ports. Abe himself owned one ship outright, the *Jacob and Sarah*, and had shares in five others including an eighth *thirty second* share in the *Old Providence*. Abe's son, Nathan, had dealt with the ship's masters, but Malky now took on this role and was often out on the river, meeting ships when they arrived and representing the owners when the customs claimed their dues. He would usually come back with a bottle or two of Dutch brandy in his satchel, which the captain would hand to the customs men and the merchants, from his personal supply of course – no duty paid. More than once he would stagger along the plank from the waterman's coble to the landing when a ship's master had insisted on his tasting the goods first.

Abe also specialised in providing anything that the local landowners might need, from cart wheels, to leather goods, ploughshares, and tools. Whilst a farmer might need to wait weeks or months to order something from a Sheels craftsman, Abe would always have some in stock. Malky would become a regular sight, riding his pony along the paths by the side of the fields to make courtesy calls on the leading farming families in Sheels Heugh, Westoe and Harton.

It was as a result of a call on Bob Stote of Horsley Hill earlier that week, that he had been sent by Abraham to confront Nathan once again. Farmer Stote had always sold his grain to, and bought his seed from, William Maud, but he had told Malky that he was now buying two ploughs and four yokes from him as well, as he had always got on well with Nathan, Maud's new partner, who was not as sharp in the tongue as Auld Abe.

Malky would go through the motions and sit down for a cup of ale with Nathan, who would always welcome him warmly. The talk would often turn to Davey Finlayson out at Marsden Cottage, and Malky would take pleasure in teasing Nathan.

"Ach, oor Davey enjoys the fresh air and he looks braw noo, with his wavy black hair and his sun burnt, *sonsie* face. He has a bit of a desperate look on him, noo though, of course, as Peggy won't let him on her because o' the bairn in her belly." Malky leant over and whispered into the eager faced lad's ear. "Ye'll no' know much aboot married folk, Nathan, but when the woman's pregnant and the man can't gan all the way, the wifie 'll ..." Malky made a pulling movement with his hand over his groin and watched the mouth of Nathan dropping open and his eyes widen. "Ach, ye'll no' be interested in that sort of talk."

It was an easy job to persuade Nathan to ride over to Harton with him the next week to visit Davey. Malky had business to discuss. He had soon realised that brandy, and also the new but expensive tobaccy, were the most profitable goods that they smuggled in. Ship's masters had to pay for a licence to carry brandy, and this added to the customs' dues made it a luxury item. It would never be as cheap as gin, but the smuggled brandy was much sought after. It was bulky though and to bring in a high volume the smugglers needed a cave where they could store it for a day or two, or longer, without anyone discovering it. The deep cave just next to Manhaven was ideal for this purpose. Davey, and possibly Robbie Clibbourne, would need be in the know as they were so close to the cove. Marsden Cottage could also be used as a way station for the donkey or pony trains. Nathan came into it as they needed storage on the quayside near to the long bank so that any pack-ponies would not need to pass the customs boats. Malky hoped that if Davey was willing to be involved then Nathan would need little persuading if it meant that he might see more of the Scots laddie.

Malky returned to Abe Taylier's house, where he spent much of his days when he was not out and about. Abe had wanted him to live there, and take over Nathan's rooms on the upper floor, but Malky had explained that he needed a dwelling of his own so that no one else would see his creeping out at night, or be disturbed by his nocturnal callers. Bowmaker had also told the old merchant about Malky's dalliance with Molly, and that the lad wished to marry her as soon as he was well established. Just along from Abe's house was Stony Steep Lane and Abe held the lease on a rank of half a dozen two-storeyed houses which had wooden stairs leading to the upper floor at the back of the premises. One of the houses was let to a cobbler who had his shop on the ground floor, and, as a single man, slept in his workshop and did not need the upper floor, which he was happy to let to Malky. Abe halved his rent and Malky had his own rooms.

Abe was half way through his daily bottle of Strasbourg brandy, and already red faced, when Malky arrived. Abe greeted his secretary with his usual rant against unfaithful sons. Malky told him that he had spoken sternly to Nathan, but it was difficult to get the lad to see reason. They were disturbed by a voice shouting through the half open door.

"Are ye in, Malky?" It was Geordie Naesbitt.

Malky came out as Abe would not welcome a fisher lad into his home.

"It's wor Molly," said a worried looking Geordie. "It's my fault an' all. I went to see her the other day in Micky Coulson's boat and he wanted to come alang to meet her. He didn't knaw she was belly-up, and was very quiet on the way back, which isn't usual for him, as he's normally gabbling on. Weel, he only went and tolt auld Mutha' Hawes, and she was strite off to the constable. She says he's ganna' gan and see the Vicar of Tynemooth and have her brought back. They won't want to have to give relief to an unmarried mutha' and a bairn who's not from their Parish. And he'll put her up before the Vestry court here so she can be whipped in the Market Place. That's what Mutha' Hawes has wanted all alang."

"I should have sent for her earlier, Geordie. I've got ma own hame, and I'm earning enow frae auld Abe to be able to marry Molly and keep her and the bairn."

"Will ye gan to see Constable Puncheon?" asked Geordie.

"Ach no, I've nowt to say to him. I'll speak to Mr. Ashburne, the Vestry clerk. He knows what's what."

The result of Malky's talk with Henry Ashburne was that when Molly was brought over on the Sheels ferry by the Tynemouth overseer she was met, not by Puncheon, but by Malky and Captain Bowmaker, who had agreed to lodge her at his house until the Vestry court had made a decision. Ashburne had been quite firm with Malky – she could not live at his home until they were wed.

On the day of the Vestry court, several interested parties were there who wanted to hear the fate of the pregnant fish wife, and the court would sit in the church itself. No charges had been laid against Malky as there was no evidence that he was the father of the child apart from gossip stirred up by the Hawes family and Micky Coulson.

Henry Ashburne stood up before the Curate could open the court.

"I have an announcement to make, members of the court, that may affect your considerations. I have received application, and the usual fees, for the banns to be read to proclaim the proposed marriage of Malcolm Dalgleish, secretary to Abraham Taylier, to Mrs. Molly Hawes, widow of the late Daniel Hawes, currently residing with Captain Bowmaker."

Loud murmurs ran round the Church with looks of surprise on many faces.

The Curate then spoke. "Weel, if the lass is to be wed then we cannot in all justice deal with the charge against her today." He then paused for a moment. "But even if there is a marriage there is still the fatherhood of the bairn to consider. Is Malcolm Dalgleish in the church?"

Malky stood up. The Curate recognised him at once and give him a stony stare.

"Do you admit to being the father of this child, to have committed fornication out of wedlock?"

Malky had been briefed on the response to make by Henry Ashburne.

"I admit to no impropriety with Molly Hawes, but if we are wed, and the bairn is born alive, then as a matter of law I

279

shall be recognised as the lawful father, and will undertake to be responsible for the upkeep of mother and child."

There were more murmurs, and then an angry woman's voice rang out as Mrs. Hawes sprang to her feet.

"He canna marry her – she's already wed to wor Danny. She's been up to all sorts with the Scotchman and we want the skin flayed off her back!"

The Curate banged his gavel and stood up. "Silence," he called out. "We shall not have our meeting disturbed."

John Hawes angrily pulled his wife back to her seat and then stood up himself. "May I speak, Sir?"

"We rarely see you in Church, John Hawes, and now your wife disturbs our peace," spouted the Curate.

"I'm sorry aboot the Missus, Fatha'. What she meant to say was that we would object to the marriage as the lass is still married to wor Danny."

The Curate sat down and looked at the clerk who then said, "The first reading of the banns will be this Sunday and you can certainly object then, but we all thought that Molly Hawes was a widder after her husband was lost at sea."

"His body was nivver found. We dain't believe that he's deed, and we never came to ye, Mr. Ashburne, to report him deed," was John Hawes' response.

"Weel if he's not deed, then where is he?" shouted Molly, unable to control herself.

The gavel hammered again and the Curate shouted out 'silence' once again.

Henry Ashburne rose to his feet again. "It appears that the charge against this woman is not well founded, as she is either engaged to be wed to Malcolm Dalgleish, or is still wedded to Daniel Hawes. I advise the court to dismiss the current charge and ask Mr. and Mrs. Hawes to see me in the Vestry and I can help them put their objection to the banns in writing."

The next day Molly was asked to go and see Mr. Ashburne. He told her what the Hawes had said about the circumstances of Danny's disappearance. Molly could only give the same story. He had gone night fishing in a sea coble with Joe Coulson, Micky Coulson's brother, who was only fourteen at the time. They'd never come back. There was a light breeze that night, but no squall nor storm. No wreckage was found, nor any bodies. Neither the Hawes nor Molly mentioned that the real purpose of the trip was to collect a load of merchandise that had been dropped off by ship from France. When Danny did not show up, Captain Bowmaker himself had gone out to Frenchman's Bay and there was no sign of any goods on the beach. Equally puzzling had been the fact that the ship had not entered the Tyne, and had not been heard of again.

After the banns had been read that Sunday, the Curate had announced that an objection had been made which seemed to have substance, and would be considered at a special meeting of the Vestry court, which had been convened for the next week, and to which all the interested parties had been called.

Malky had kept in touch with the Coultheards since he had been freed from the indenture, and he had sought Henry Coultheard's advice. Coultheard had been so disappointed when Malky had declined the offer of lodgings that Malky had told him all about Molly and his hope of being able to marry her. Coultheard had put his arm round the embarrassed lad's shoulder, and said that he himself had been young once.

"Ye're clearly a headstrong young lad full of vigour, Malky. We'll do all we can to help ye and yer lass." He paused, looked thoughtful, and chuckled. "I was just ganna say that ye should sometimes stop and think before ye do something that might put ye in peril, but if ye'd stood on the quay thinking things ower when wor Kit was in the watter, he wouldn't be here the day."

He went with Malky to the court.

The hearing was over quickly. The decision had already been made at a private meeting, and Henry Ashburne announced that there was no Parish record of Daniel Hawes' death and in the absence of a body they could make no presumption of death. The rule of the English common law was that seven years should lapse after the disappearance, before death could be presumed.

"This means," he continued, "that Molly Hawes is still, in the eyes of the law married to Daniel Hawes and when she gives birth he will be named as the father."

There was a cry of rage from auld Mutha' Hawes. "It can't be wor Danny..."

Mr. Hawes elbowed her hard in the side. "Shut yer gob, hinny, or I'll shut it for yer."

Henry Ashburne continued. "The court believes that the intentions of Malcom Dalgleish to seek to wed the lass are honourable, but we must warn him that as she is now regarded as a married woman, then any improper conduct on his behalf could lead to a charge of adultery, which the Parliament has ordained is now punishable by death."

Ashburne's words were followed by a deathly silence. "In these unprecedented circumstances, at least for Sheels, the court would like to be satisfied as to the arrangements for the lodging of Mrs. Hawes and the bringing up of the bairn, in the absence of any involvement of Dalgleish."

To Malky's surprise, Henry Coultheard stood up. "My family have known Molly Hawes for a lang time, and my wife is always singing the praises of the fresh fish she hawks. We were only saying the other day that, as the excise business is very profitable at the moment, with the reopening of the salt-panns, that we should perhaps contribute to the poor and needy of the parish. We'll take the young woman into wor home, and if she is unable hersel to care for the bairn we undertake to be responsible for its upkeep. If Dalgleish wishes to visit the lass, then we shall ensure that one of the household is always present so that no impropriety takes place."

Molly looked shocked and glanced in Malky's direction. He smiled and nodded his head. He had been surprised when Mr. Coultheard had stood up, but it was an ideal solution to their problems. The only ones who were not satisfied were the Hawes. They had little sympathy from anyone else, as it was Mother Hawes' hatred towards her daughter-in-law that had been the cause of all the trouble.

Malky was out on a trip to Frenchman's Bay that week with Geordie. It had not been a large cargo and one trip with Cuddy Heron's donkeys had been all that was needed. As the contraband was mainly woollen cloth, fine linen, threads and candlewick, they went straight to Taylier's warehouse – the

Rhenish wine went to the *Orange Tree* and a jug was shared before Cuddy and the lads made their way home. Malky no longer needed to rise as early as he had for the salt-panns and would go home first for some sleep before going to Abe's for breakfast. The mornings were becoming darker as Summer was gradually giving way to Autumn and it was still dark as he clambered up the wooden steps to his rooms. He stumbled against something and a voice he knew well shouted, "Hey, can ye not watch whe yer stepping on."

"Ha'd yer tongue, Peedee or ye'll wake the whole street and folk'll want to know what I'm doing creeping in before dawn," whispered Malky. "Ye should have just gone in, the door's not bolted."

"Weel, I didn't kna'," whispered back Peedee as he followed Malky in. The Scots lad poked the fire in the grate and poured on some more coals. "What ye're doing coming aroond here at this time o' night?" he asked.

Peedee said nowt but just sat on the floor near the fire warming himself, and Malky said, "Ach, I'll find oot soon enow from Tomag." He caught sight of Peedee's face in the glimmer from the flames and saw that the left side of his face was swollen.

"Tomag wouldn't clout ye like that unless ye'd really riled him."

"I only got up to de a piss oot the door, but I got lost on the way back to bed and ended up next to wor Alice. She didn't say owt as I got on top of her, and she just let me de it to her. She was pretending to be asleep but I could hear her groaning a bit and calling me Alec. Then I started gannen' a bit quicker and bliddy Tomag must have heard. He grabbed me by the hair, pulled me oot from under the blanket and slapped me so hard that I hit the wall before I went doon. He flung me oot the door, throwin' me claes behind me, and said not to come back."

Malky was lost for words. He'd always looked on Peedee as a young boy but he was now a lad and doing what lads did with lasses. He remembered what he'd said to Davey after he'd been whipped by Milbourn. "Was it worth it then, Peedee?"

"Wye aye it was, even If I didn't get to shoot me bolt. Can I stay with ye noo, Malky?"

"Och aye, but ye'll ha' to say sorry to Tomag when ye gan into work."

"It's not the same without ye there, Malky," muttered Peedee, "and Jobling's back on the gin."

"Ach weel, ye've got to stick it. If ye don't work, the constable 'll send ye back hame to yer auld man in Winlaton."

Malky was tired and wanted to sleep. When he awoke, Peedee was still there. He poured them both some ale and then talked to the lad.

"I've been thinking, Peedee, I might need a lad at the warehouse. There's plenty of work. We already have a counter where folk can buy frae us direct, and if we made oor own deliveries then we would increase oor sales."

Peedee's face brightened. "Wye aye I can work for ye, Malky. Ye kna' I'm a good worker," he laughed, "and I promise not to shout at the customers."

"Cam on then, I'll gang and talk to Tomag. He might want ye to work until they find somebody else."

When Peedee had not turned up for work, Tomag had been to see Mr. Milbourn and said he would not take him back. He'd had enough of his antics. Since Malky had left, the lad had become difficult, and both Tomag and Jobling had had to give him a whipping. Jobling knew of a couple of panners at the West Panns who were looking for work after their owner had closed their saltern. "That lad's too wild, Malky. He tolt ye what he was deeing last neet with oor Alice?"

"Ach, I feel responsible for him, Tomag. He came to work here because of me. But I can gie him a job in the warehouse and we'll see how he gets on."

Malky took Peedee along to see Abe and they had breakfast at his house. Peedee ate his on the kitchen floor by the hearth, while Abe and Malky sat at the table. The old man was happy for Malky to take the lad on. He now had confidence in Malky and gave him very much a free hand.

Later that week Malky and Nathan rode over to Harton. Peedee now tagged along behind Malky wherever he went unless he was out driving a donkey along the narrow ways of Sheels, delivering household goods. He ambled along behind the two men on one of the donkeys.

It had surprised Malky that Nathan was more than happy to be involved in the smuggling operation, but Quakers were not in favour of Parliaments lording it over the people, and he saw no reason why he should be forced to pay customs dues.

Davey was harder to convince. After nearly a year in the salt-panns, marrying Peggy and having his own holding was enough for him. He dared not risk any of it by involving himself in smuggling. When they had arrived he was out in the yard working on the plough, and the oxen harnesses, in readiness for the first ploughing of the harvest fields.

"Robbie Clibbourne is gang to gie me a hand as I've nivver stood behind a plough before, but he says it's not hard to get the hang of it, so lang as ye have a strang back."

They were standing in the yard taking a cup of harvest ale that Mrs. Blayre had brewed. Peggy had come out with the pail, but she was moving slowly. Her belly was full and she did not look well.

"Is your Peggy all right, Davey?" asked Malky.

"It's the bairn. She's tired all the time, and I think she's gang to have to tak mair rest until the bairn is born but we're not expecting it until the end of the year and I can no' do withoot her help. Her Mutha's not been the same since George died, and just wants to sit by the hearth, stoke the coals and stir the pot. Ma Peggy's having a job wi' the milking and I'll need her to lead the oxen while I hold the plough, and if she can't I'll have to pay ane of the village lads or lasses with coin I do not have."

"I could de it," shouted Peedee.

"Aye ye could, but I need ye working for me and ye'll be doing a bit of night work soon." Malky looked at Davey. "If we land the goods at the creek by Manhaven ye'll turn a blind eye to Peedee shouting at the donkeys in the deed of nicht, Davey?"

"Ach, of course I will. And I can gie ye a hand at nicht wi' the hefting, but I will no' keep anything on the steading."

"We'll manage, Davey, and we'll let ye and Rabbie hae the odd barrel of brandy and sic like. We'll just tak a look at the caves again, and we'll be away."

Nathan said he'd stay a while with Davey as he had not seen him for a while. He would catch up with them.

Malky called round at the Coultheards' that evening to see Molly. In contrast to Peggy, she was in bloom. Her belly was as big as Peggy's but her height made it a lot easier to carry. She was having no discomfort, and looked as pretty as a picture. Things were not going well with the Coultheards, though. The other servants resented her presence, and Mrs. Coultheard had not been happy when Molly had started street hawking again. The lass had said that there was nothing wrong with her and she was not going to be cooped up, when she could be earning a penny or two. She would not go back to the fishing quarter, but she had bought a bushel bowl of salt from the salt merchant, and also had a few thing in the bottom of her basket that she had obtained from Bowmaker, and was out on the ways again. Mr. Coultheard had heard wind of her dealings and had spoken to Malky. As an excise man he couldn't be seen to be condoning any irregularity in trade.

Malky had a long chat with Molly as they sat on a settle against the back wall of the kitchen and spoke in whispers. When he told her about Peggy and how Davey was worried about how he could manage on his own, she did not hesitate.

"I dain't mind giving up the hawking, but I can't stand being cooped up inside. Nae one can object if I gan an' live with Davey and Peggy, and I can certainly do the milking and walking alang beside a couple of oxen doesn't sound like hard work." She looked across to the hearth where the cook and the scullion were sitting and quickly put her hand on Malky's thigh. "When ye come ower to the Manhaven at neet ye can gie me a whistle, and I could sneak oot and give ye a hand." Her own was moving up the young Scot's thigh into dangerous territory. "And I dain't mean with any heavy lifting."

Within a month everything was in place. The ships with only a few cases of contraband still hoved to at Frenchman's Bay, and Malky and Peedee would be off to join Cuddy at the top of the long bank. No one now came down for Malky as he now knew in advance when a ship was coming in. Peedee proved himself to be a natural driver of donkeys, not being afraid of giving them a whack with a stick to keep them moving.

Through his connections with the sea captains, Malky would arrange for ships coming from Amsterdam or Bordeaux to bring in brandy together with smaller quantities of tobacco, lace, raisins, dates, and spices which would be stored in the cave not far up from Manhaven, and then they would take the donkeys over at night when it suited them. They would come back down the long bank and straight into Nathan's warehouse. Geordie Naesbitt would pull in with a coble and take the brandy barrels down the river to the quay just opposite the *Turk's*. They would then be unloaded, and rolled to the trapdoor of the vault and then down a ramp to Marledane and Tomag below. The vault was an ideal place to keep any spirits or wine until it would be sold on. Peedee would put a small barrel, or bottles that they had filled themselves, into the bottom of a large basket and put his other goods on top, and then would be off to his customers.

Davey helped out, as he would get a message to Malky or Cuddy when a ship anchored near the cove, and gave the agreed signal. Malky would come that same night as he needed to check the delivery and pay the agreed amount in coin or diamonds - smugglers not using bills of exchange. Molly would sometimes help with the loading, and she and Malky would usually find a few moments to be together out of sight of the others. Peedee once tried to sneak up on them to spy on what they were doing, but Geordie Naesbitt came after him and gave him a good punching, so he limited himself to the odd wise-crack about what Malky had been up to, as they trudged back to Sheels.

Both Abe and Nathan had strong-boxes in their homes for the large amounts they were now amassing. Malky did not want to store any of his at his home as he was not often there. When he was living at the cottage, he and Tomag had taken one of the large stones out of the wall and made a hollow inside the rubble-filled cavity between the inner wall and the outer. Malky now asked the cooper to make him a wooden box with a lock that would fit in the space they had, and he hid his coin there, alongside a pouch that contained some shillings that Tomag had made from his usquebah.

They had agreed that once they had enough, they would try to buy out the indentures on Tomag himself and on Dougie. Tomag was now quite happy working very much as a salt master, but wanted to be his own man. They had also made an oath that if either of them passed away or was otherwise taken, then the other should use the money as they had intended or such other purpose as they felt the other would have agreed to.

It was soon December, however, and as very few ships would venture out of a safe harbour into winter seas, the smuggling trade died away. But Malky would find excuses to go over to Harton to see Davey and, more importantly to him, Molly. Although celebrating Christmas was still officially banned, Robbie Clibbourne had given Davey one of his geese for their dinner, and Malky and Peedee had been invited, along with Hamish who would close his shop with a note saying he was visiting a patient at the West Panns. Malky brought a small brandy barrel, and Hamish some clay pipes with tobaccy, so that they could all have a smoke, which was not only pleasurable, but said to be good for the health.

When the guests arrived in the mid-morning, the cottage was welcoming and warm with the well-banked up wood fire, which had been blazing since early morning. The goose was roasting on a home-made spit, which Davey had fashioned with help from Robbie and the Harton smith, as the Blayres had rarely used one. Molly was in charge of the roasting and had made some sweet pies with chopped meat, raisins and spices which she had fried the night before over the fire. Mrs. Blayre had brewed a Christmas ale with honey, but otherwise sat on a bench away from the hearth, spinning wool. Peggy lay on her cot which had been pulled near to the hearth to keep her warm. She looked very pale and was in serious discomfort.

Davey would sit beside her and spoon some ale into her mouth to keep her spirits up. Hamish was worried, and whispered to Davey and Malky when they had a moment together, "Your Peggy must be nearly due but she looks very weak. She's gang to struggle when she starts her labour."

291

"Ach," replied Davey, "she'll be all right ance the bairn cams. She's always been a strang lass."

The goose was succulent and greasy, and Molly had roasted some neeps and cabbage in the goose fat in a pan, and they all licked their chops at the good fare. While the men started on the brandy, Molly fried the sweet cakes in butter to warm them up and they all ate heartily of them apart from Mrs. Blayre, who only nibbled away at one, and Peggy who had managed a slice of goose but had no appetite for any more.

After their meal they slumbered in the settles until Molly got up and went out to do the afternoon milking. Peedee went with her and when they came back he was licking his chops, as Molly had squirted him with milk. He had tried his hand at the milking, and had even drunk from the teat.

Davey produced a pack of cards and a stack of small splinters of wood that they used for counters. The cups were filled with brandy and they played the Queen Nazareen. As Davey dealt the five cards to each player, Peedee carefully examined his cards.

"They're all reet," he said, "it's not a lang card deck." The others looked at him, as folk often did when he came out with one of his odd utterances.

"Ye've nivver heard of it?"

The shaking of the heads gave the answer.

"Ye hev an auld deck, but the aces and kings are just a fraction langer than the other cards. Unless ye kna' ye'd nivver guess. If ye hev to cut the cards ye win for certain. Some of the keelmen used to try it on, until young Sebbie Greene got caught out, and they nearly killed him before hoying him in the river. He was lucky that a waterman was passing and hoiked him oot."

"Ach, Peedee, after all that goose that I've given ye and the milk, ye had to check my deck to see if I was cheatin' ye," cried Davey with a smile on his face.

"Weel, Malky's always telling me to double check everything, as ye canna' trust nae one," cried the lad.

They played well into the night. Whenever Molly played the Queen of Diamonds (the Nazareen), the man who laid the Knave Nnocker (the Jack of Diamonds) on top of the Queen demanded a kiss from the lass.

None of the guests were in a fit state to make the journey home, and Peedee was sent out to the barn to bring in straw for their beds. It was in the dead of night when Peggy gave her first scream as her contractions started. Davey was already about, putting more wood on the fire as he had left their bed when Peggy's waters had broken. The young Scot had thought that she had wet herself. The others now stirred and Mrs. Blayre sat by Peggy's side, holding her hand.

Molly looked concerned. "She's screaming mair than she should at the beginning of the labour, God kna's what she'll be like at the end. I think ye better gan and fetch the midwife, Davey."

"Who is she?" asked a bleary-eyed Hamish. He knew most of the licensed midwives in Sheels and some of the 'auld women' who charged less for the poorer folk, who often lost the bairn as a result.

"It's Miss Linton, Bob Linton's sister," replied Molly.

"Och, I know her," said Hamish. "She's unmarried and does it out of the kindness of her heart. She used to be licensed, but the Curate took her licence away when she left the Church and became a Quaker. They canna' stop her, though, from helping folk, and she disna' ask for any coin from those who hae none."

"Nathan asked her to cam to see Peggy last time he was here visiting," said Davey. "She wasn't happy with her state and said to call her straight away ance she started.

"Ach, I'd better gang noo. They live all the way doon West Panns Way, so it'll be a guid hoor before I get back," said a worried Davey as he started putting his clothes on.

"Take ma pony," said Malky. "I'll gang and saddle it up for ye."

As he opened the cottage door there was an icy blast and a flurry of snow blew in. "Ach, that's all we need," he muttered as he wrapped his cloak round him and went out into the night. He came back in a few seconds later.

"I canna see a thing. Hae ye got a lantern, Davey?"

Davey pointed to a shelf by the door and Peedee ran over to light the wick of the candle. "I'll come with ye, Malky," he shouted and lit another lantern for himself. When they came back Malky said that Peedee should go with Davey on his donkey. There was no moon and it was as black as pitch. Even with a lantern it was hard enough to see more than a few feet in front of you with the snow, and with the wind blowing then a single lantern could go out. Davey might have difficulty finding his way on his own.

For those inside the cottage it was a long wait. Although Hamish tried to help to keep Peggy calm, he had little knowledge of the workings of a woman. Brandy for the pain was all that he knew. Molly had lifted Peggy's skirts up and had a good look at her. She was very worried when she came to stand beside Malky and Hamish. "She's very narra' doon there, and it's a big bairn. She's ganna' have trouble. I only hope the midwife gets here soon."

Peggy's contractions kept on, and she was soon too weak to scream and just lay groaning. When she looked as though she would faint away, Hamish forced a sip of brandy into her mouth to keep her awake.

The morning light was just breaking through the gloom when Davey and Peedee returned accompanied not only by Miss Linton, but also by one of her grooms who had been sent along to make sure she made the journey safely. It had taken the two lads nearly two hours to make the journey. They had been fortunate that they could keep to the cartway that led to Westoe and then along the Casten Dyke to West Panns Way. With the snow on the ground they would have certainly wandered off the trail had not the lanterns shown the hedges and trees by the roadside. Peedee's lantern had been blown out as they met the full blast of the wind by the Casten Dyke, but he seemed to have a sixth sense for travelling at night and stayed in the lead to guide Davey.

Davey was not sure of the Linton house and they mistakenly woke the Coatsworth household first before arriving at the Lintons'. The barking of the dogs had already raised the grooms who came out armed with their staves to see who troubled the peace on Christmas night. Robert Linton himself opened the great door to the hall, and got the grooms to take the two mounts into the stable for a rubbing down and a feed. One of the maids made up the fire with fresh coals to help warm the two lads who were chilled to the bone and Linton himself offered them brandy. Peedee declined and he was given ale instead. Linton looked twice at him. "Are ye the lad that brings us wor deliveries from Nathan's stores?"

"Wye aye," said Peedee, "but it's easier to find when it's not blawin' a gale and snawin' as well."

The Lintons liked their cut price Strasbourg brandy and tobaccy.

Even though the snow had almost died away when they left, Bob Linton insisted that one of the grooms accompany his sister, and he could escort her back when the babe had been born.

It had not taken Miss Linton long to realise that it was going to be a difficult birth. Despite the heavy contractions the bairn was not moving downwards as it should have done, as Peggy was too weak to push hard. The midwife was not too pleased with all the men standing round. She was happy for Hamish to stay as he could be of help, but she wanted the others outside. They all put on their cloaks and went into the yard where Davey made a bonfire with old wood to keep them warm. Molly came out with a pail of cold goose meat and bread, and another with ale so they came to no harm. They heard no more and at noon Miss Linton came out to say that the labour would be a long one. She did not think they'd see a birth that day, and it could well go on into the night. She told the groom that had come with her that he should return to the Linton household and tell them not to expect her until the morrow. She looked at the others who were starting to feel the cold in spite of the fire. "I really don't want ye in the house. Can ye not ask Robbie Clibbourne if he'll shelter ye until the bairn is born?"

Davey was about to answer when there was a shriek from inside the cottage. It was a woman's voice and then Hamish came to the door.

"Miss Linton, ye'd better cam in, Molly's waters have broken and she thinks she's starting as weel."

"It nivver rains but it pours," muttered Miss Linton as she turned to the door. "Just ha'd on here a minute till I see what's what. Is her husband among ye?"

"No, he isna'," said Malky angrily, "he was lost at sea twa years ago, but his parents objected to me marrying the lass and sae I could no'. I'm the bairn's father, but dinna' tell anybody or the Curate 'll have me hanged for adultery."

She went inside and it was a good hour before the door opened and Hamish came out. He beckoned the three lads over.

"Peggy's in a bad way, but there's naught we can do until the bairn starts moving, which it's showing no signs of doing. Molly's contractions have started, but she's doing fine so far, and as she's already had ane bairn, Mrs. Linton thinks it will be straightforward. She can probably manage with the twa of them if I help her, but she disna' want anybody else in the room." He looked at Davey. "Can ye and Malky gang up to Rabbie Clibbourn's? Peedee can cam into the cottage so lang as he sits in the corner and keeps quiet. He can gang and fetch ye or take a message back to the Linton hoose if she needs

297

anything fetching."

Rabbie Clibbourne was happy to have some company and poured the ale out as soon as they were seated by the hearth. Mrs. Clibbourne said that birthing was no place for a man, but that Miss Linton would need a woman's help.

"Have ye had yer dinners yet?" she asked. When they shook their heads, she smiled. "Weel, we've got some cauld goose left ower from yesterday and some onions and pears pickled in vinegar, and plenty of breed and butter. Ye kna' where it is, Rabbie, when they're ready for it. I'll gan doon to the cottage. They may need some food cooking doon there and I doubt if Mrs. Blayre is up to much."

It was late in the evening when Malky and Davey were slumbering in their settle by the hearth, when an excited Peedee burst in through the door.

"Molly's had a boy, Malky," he shouted, waking all in the Clibbourne hall and probably most of Harton village as well. The two Scots rubbed their eyes and then stood up. "Miss Linton says ye can come and see the bairn. She wants ye as weel, Davey." Peedee's excitement died down and his voice became serious. "Your Peggy's not deein' too well and the midwife wants to talk to ye."

The night was cold and although the snow had stopped there was still a driving wind off the sea. There was a glimmer of light from a crescent moon as they hurried down the path to the cottage. On one side of the hearth a tired but smiling Molly was lying on a bed, with Mrs. Clibbourne beside her holding a crying bairn.

On the other side of the hearth Peggy was in a piteous state. Her head was propped up by a pillow of straw and Mrs. Blayre was sitting on a three-legged stool holding her hand, and looking as nearly as exhausted and worn out as her daughter. Miss Linton was kneeling between the lass's open legs with Hamish beside her. She had taken her bodice off and rolled up the sleeves of her shirt. She stood up as the men came in, with blood on her hands. She was a stout woman in early middle age with dark brown curly hair, a rosy cheeked face, and a washerwoman's arms.

"Ye, Malky, gan and see your bairn. He's a healthy boy and came oot nae bother. Mrs. Clibbourne did most of the work, but I was on hand for any difficulty. Ye can hold him a bit then give him to Molly who can give him a teat to keep him quiet. I want ye to stay with us as I'm ganna need yer help in a minute." She wiped her hands on her apron, stood back a bit, and looked at Davey. "There's nae easy way of saying this, Davey, but the bairn won't come oot. I tried to make a cut to make the opening wider but it did nae good. The bairn's heed's where it should be but the bone isn't loosening up as it should do. If we dain't do owt then they'll both die. We might lose your Peggy anyway, her heart's barely beating and I doubt if she can last much longer."

She let her words sink in and then spoke on. "The bairn's got to come oot. I've seen surgeon pothecaries who've put a knife up into the womb and brought a bairn oot in pieces, but if you're not careful you can snick something inside the mother and she'll die in agony days later. The only way I can see, is for us to break the bone, prise it apart and let the bairn come through. If the mother survives she'll be crippled for life but we can save the bairn."

Davey just stood there. His swarthy skin was pale and his eyes moist. He tried to speak but his tongue would not move. Malky, who had heard it all, handed his bairn to Molly. He went over to Peggy. Her face was white and convulsed in agony and she was barely breathing. Malky knelt beside her, she looked up and for just a moment a small glimmer of something came into her eyes. "Save the bairn, I'm done for," she managed to whisper before closing her eyes and fainting away.

"She said to save the bairn, Davey," Malky shouted.

The Scot lad looked completely lost, but he nodded his head.

Miss Linton went into action. "We're ganna have to be quick." She looked at Davey. "I'll need a hammer. A wooden mallet will be best." Peedee ran over to the tool basket by the door and found a mallet. "That'll de," cried the midwife. "Noo take the husband oot of here. I dain't want him having second thoughts when we start on his wife. Wrap him up in a cloak and walk him oot to a barn. We'll call ye back when it's ower."

As Peedee hurried Davey out the door, she then turned to Malky who was now holding the mallet. "Ye're the strongest here so ye'll have to de it. I'll push my fingers inside to try and keep the bairn's heed away." She knelt down again between Peggy's open legs and looked up at Malky, "Noo give me yer left hand." Malky did so. She gently pushed one of his fingers, along with one of hers into the opening. "Can ye feel the bone?"

"Och aye."

"Ye'll have to catch it reet in the middle where its weakest. Tap it first then hit it as hard as ye can from the front. And dain't think of Peggy and stay the blow. It must be done quickly with one strike."

She looked over to the other side of the heath. "Mrs. Clibbourne, stand in front of Molly and put yer hands ower her ears. She doesn't want to get the vapours noo when there's a bairn to feed, and another here if God's on wor side."

She looked again at Malky and moved over to give him room. "Gan on, lad, noo."

Malky half knelt and gently tapped the mallet just above the midwife's fingers. He then lifted the hand holding the mallet and brought it down with force. There was a loud crack, a half-strangled scream from Peggy, who then gave the death rattle and lay still.

"Reet noo, ye, Hamish, put yer hand on your side of the hole and ye, Malky, on the other and prise it open as gently as ye can. I'll try to get my hand up and bring oot the bairn."

There was still some resistance, but then there was a squelching sound as the ligaments gave and the bairn slipped out into the waiting hands, a cawl over the head. Miss Linton worked quickly to cut the cord and tie it and she then lifted the still body up by its feet and slapped it on the back. A hesitant cry came out, followed by a full bodied one.

"It's anither boy," cried Malky.

Just then the door banged open as Davey ran in. He had heard the cry. He dashed forward and looked at the bairn in the midwife's arms. "Oor Peggy said it would be a lad," he half shouted in joy, and then he looked at the bed where a lifeless body lay.

"She's deed, I'm afraid," whispered Miss Linton.

Raising her voice over the babe's cries, she spoke again in a solemn voice. "Let us all kneel." They all went down on their knees apart from Molly, who bowed her head. "We'll give a prayer to the Lord Almighty and thank him for saving the life of this wee bairn, and ask him to welcome his poor mother into the Kingdom of Heaven. Amen."

She stood up and then carefully took the cawl off the head of the newborn child. "Are there any mariners in the hoose?" she asked. There were one or two blank faces, so she added, "If a sailor takes a cawl with him to sea then he'll never perish in the wave."

"I'll have it then," cried Molly. "My brother Geordie could de with someitt like that."

Mrs. Clibbourne had earlier made a broth from the goose carcass and the left-over flesh in a large kettle over the fire when things had been relatively calm. She now grated a loaf of bread, poured it into the kettle which she put back on the fire. The savoury smell was tempting and it would put some strength back into all those who had lived through two days they would never forget. There was still some brandy left in Malky's barrel and the men drank thirstily. Peedee ran up to the Harton home-stall and brought Robbie back down.

They kept a wake of sorts that night and Peggy was buried the next day in the small Harton burial ground. Davey was in a state of shock and Molly had her hands full with the two bairns she was now nursing. Malky agreed to let Peedee stay at the cottage to help with the milking, and any other jobs that could not be put off. He returned to Sheels, although it was a quiet time for merchants, and he himself spent a good many days visiting at Marsden cottage. Davey had called his bairn Hal, as Peggy had said that if it was a boy that's what she wanted. Molly thought George was a good name for a lad and Malky was happy to go along with it, but there was a problem. The two babies were like two peas in a pod with little to distinguish them and after the first night when they were both put in the same basket, Molly could not tell them apart. "Dinna worry, pet," laughed Malky. "The ane with eyes of different colour will be oor Geordie!"

CHAPTER ELEVEN

Peedee had come back from the cottage after about six weeks. Molly was helping Davey and one morning Mrs. Blayre had suddenly stood up from her settle, a smile on her face and started talking as though nowt untoward had happened. For the first time she started taking interest in the two bairns, and was now happy to watch over them if Molly was out helping Davey. She would call the mother in when they needed a feed. It was a problem for Davey. He missed his wife and the attentions she had given him. When he rose in the morning Molly would often be feeding the bairns both at once and Davey could not stop himself from staring at her bare titties.

Abe's chief clerk was letting Malky help with planning the voyages their ships would make in the next month or so, depending on the weather. Lewis Frost had decided to take up the captaincy of the *Old Providence* once again, and voyage to the Baltic. Coal and salt from the Tyne were always wanted and in return he could bring back timber, iron, leather goods and anything else that was on the market and would sell in Sheels. The family had ventured into the salt-panns as a surer and risk-free way of making money, but the slump in the salt trade had made them change their minds. Two or three voyages to the Baltic could earn them more coin in a year than salt would at the present prices. Lewis also wanted to get away. He was still a youngish man and liked to think of himself as a merchant adventurer. Even Ralph Milbourn was muttering about going back to the seas. Since he had whipped his wife she barely spoke to him, and gave him the cold shoulder at nights.

The great storm in the first week in March put everything back as the sudden dangers of the deep were brought sharply to mind. The Monday was blustery and a few white clouds scudded across the sky. Half a dozen colliers had made the journey from Yarmouth and London. They would keep close to the coast, and when they had to tack, they would not venture too far out into the Ocean. The masters all had their *kennings*, knowledge of the time it took from one headland or cape to another, and so, at any sign of the wind rising or a storm coming they could head for the safety of a harbour or sheltered cove. They were taking on coals from Newcastle and salt from Sheels. The keels were starting to be seen more now, and by the morning tide on the Tuesday several were coming down the Tyne to the waiting ships. The first keels came empty, or with a light cargo of provisions, as they had to take off the ballast. They were supposed to take it to the ballast hills just before Sandgate, but some would take down their sail and hoy a load over the side into the Tyne as they headed inland. They would have more time to pick up their coals and get back on the next tide.

The storm came in from the North East, before dawn on the Wednesday, as the tide was on the turn. In Newcastle itself they only had the odd light gust and so the keels set off, those with sails, lowering them using the hinged metal cup that held the mast in place, but enabled it to fall backwards so the keel could pass under the Tyne Bridge.

By the time they reached the river mouth the dark storm clouds were as black as those coming from the saltern chimneys and the gale was on them. Angus McGilvray had been one of the first away, and had managed to tie up to the *Ann of Yarmouth*, but it was soon clear that unloading the coal would be too dangerous. The *Ann*, without most of its ballast, was bobbing up and down like a cork, and the ship's hull was thudding hard against the keel's timbers, with the top-heavy heap of coal at risk of sliding over the side and taking the keel down. The collier's skipper came to the rail and Angus shouted up to him that they would have to untie the ropes. The ship was moored in a channel close to the south shore and Angus would tie the keel up to a quay and lay over while the storm blew itself out. The rope to the stern was undone and the keel drifted away to the larboard until the bow was pointing upstream.

"Rope away," shouted Angus. "Oar oot and ready," cried Niall as the crew readied themselves to move the keel onwards with the long oar, as Angus pushed the swape hard to port. The manoeuvre was working and the bow was heading slowly towards the river bank when a vicious blast of wind and wave hit them side on. Niall grabbed the boy who had lost his footing and they just held on. He then heard Angus' high-pitched yell of warning and looked up to see another keel bearing down on them. One of the other keel's bullies had been trying to take the sail down and the wind had caught them both and he was dangling dangerously over the side. The keel's skipper was shouting in fury, and had not seen Angus's craft in front of him, but heard the cries of warning and put all his weight on the swape. Although he avoided a head on collision, the two keels came together side on. The bully on the sail was cast into the water going straight down, and the oar on Angus' keel was smashed away. With the sail flapping wildly in the wind, the other keel was caught up by the tide and lost all chance of tying up to any of the colliers, or of putting into the shore. The craft was pulled relentlessly towards the harbour bar by the outgoing tide. It would not last five minutes in the raging waters of the German Ocean.

Their fate was not on Angus' mind as his own craft had been shunted round and was now beam on. Jockie joined Angus on the swape, and with the two men using all their strength, they managed to turn the boat but were now heading towards the bar. Niall still had the boy in his grasp. He had seen the terrified look in the eyes of the lad as the other keel had been pushed on out to sea, and Niall knew that that would be their fate too. He quickly pulled his knife from his belt and cut free one of the planks that held up the coal. He looked at Angus. "We're ditching, skipper, I'm not gang to droon oot there." And holding the plank in one arm and the boy in the other he jumped into the wind-whipped waters of the Tyne. The cold nearly took his breath away, but he managed to get the lad to clutch onto the plank alongside him and he started kicking with his feet and paddling with one arm to head them towards the river bank. The current had them though, and he was finding it hard to make any headway.

Malky had been down in the fishers' quarter visiting Bowmaker, and both he and the Captain had ventured out to see the effect of the storm on the moored ships and the keels. There was a large group of folk watching helplessly as the drama before their eyes unfolded. They had seen the one keel dragged over the bar by the undertow, and vanish beneath the monstrous waves. The other keel now seemed doomed as well, and they had gasped as one of the bullies and the boy had jumped overboard, and were now struggling against the tide and current in what looked like a desperate but doomed attempt to reach the shore.

Without thinking, Malky ran forward across the strand and started pushing a coble into the stream. Geordie Naesbitt and Micky Coulson tried to stop him, but Malky shouted out, "You'se ha'd on to the rope, I'm just gang to cut them aff." The two strong fishermen saw the sense of what he was saying and helped him float the coble off, but held on to the mooring rope. A dozen at least of brawny fisherman joined them as the coble was caught by the tide, but they held firm. Malky was holding on to the bow of the boat and for a minute thought he would be too late, but Niall had seen the craft and gave a desperate lunge of his arm and a wild kick of his feet and then felt Malky's strong hand on his shoulder. Time froze for a moment as a wind-whipped wave nearly swamped them, but the men on the line were now reeling them in. Malky had one hand now on Niall's shoulder and with the other had pulled the boy over the side. Niall had nothing left and just held on until he felt the rough hands of the fishermen, who had waded into the waves, hoick him out. There were shouts of joy as the drenched bully and the peedee were dragged more dead than alive, but still breathing, out of the coaly Tyne. They were both carried into the *Coble*, the nearest ale-house, where their soaking clothes were pulled off and they were wrapped in homespun blankets, and sat in front of the fire. Malky himself was drenched, although not frozen quite to the bone, and joined them.

"Angus," whispered Niall.

"Taken," was all that Malky could say. The skipper and Jockie had hung on to the swape, and refused to abandon their boat. It had seemed for a minute that they had managed to make a little headway towards the sands just inside the bar where they could ground the keel, but a furious gust had forced them away over the bar to their watery grave.

The two who had been rescued, and Malky, had started to warm up and take some ale when the door opened and Lewis Frost and Ralph Milbourn walked in. Niall made the mistake of turning his head to see who had come in. Even in the gloom inside the ale-house there was no hiding his sandy hair that reflected the flames from the fire, and the dimple in his chin.

Frost called for ale and cried out for all to hear, "Weel, we heard that a keelman and a boy had made it ashore saved by the fishers, but nae-one tolt us that it was a miracle. This lad," he pointed at Niall, "went missing a good year ago, and was said to have fallen into Jarra's Lake."

He took the pint mug that the landlord had brought over to him. "Have ye been swimming aroond all that time?" There was laughter from the other drinkers but Malky and Niall's faces were serious.

"Ye've made a mistake, Mr. Frost," said Malky. "This lad's Alec Patterson and he's bonded to work as a keelman to Mr. Binks, the hostman."

Frost and Milbourn came over to where the lads were sitting on a bench by the fire. Frost was in a good mood and did not seem threatening. "The last time ye rescued someone form the Tyne you were rewarded for your bravery by Mr. Coultheard, Malcolm."

"Och aye I was, but I did no' do much this time, Mr. Frost. Nia…I mean Alec was the ane who decided to save himsel and the peedee by jumping owerboard with a plank to keep them afloat. I just went oot a few yards in an empty coble to help them to land."

"Will ye be gannen back to keep yer bond with Mr. Binks then, laddie?" asked Frost.

Niall thought for what seemed a long moment. "I dinna' think so. If a bully abandons a keel without the skipper's permission, he breaks the keelmen's code. If I went back to Sandgit' they'd shun me, and Angus' kin could do what they wanted with me without hindrance."

"My Da' cancelled Niall Dewar's indenture to him after he fell in Jarra's Lake," replied Frost, "but I'm looking for crew on the *Old Providence*. I'll write ye doon as Alec Patterson. We were ganna set sail this week for the Baltic but I think I may wait a while longer. Ye can stay with yer brother Tomag until we sail. I'll find yer ale and yer food, and ye'll be paid sixpence a day, with a bonus of an equal share with the rest of the crew in one thirty-second of the profits when we return to Sheels."

He stuck out his hand, and after the briefest of hesitations Niall grasped it in return. He had little choice.

"What of the boy?" asked Frost. The ginger haired peedee looked up.

"I dinna' want to gan back on the keels. Nae one'll tyek me on anyway."

"What about yer Da'?"

"He's deed," said Niall, "and his Ma has two younger bairns and just hawks what she can roond the streets." He put his hand over his mouth and leant over to whisper into Frost's ear, "Including hersel."

"Ye'r a bit on the young side, boy, but if ye've worked on the keels then ye'll be strang. Ye can come as a cabin boy."

The lad just nodded.

Once their clothes were dry they walked back along the way and went into the salt-house. Tomag was overjoyed to see Niall. Word had already spread of the rescue, but Tomag had not realised that the keelman was his brother. He went over to Milbourn's house and asked Jenett if she could put a bit extra in the pot. When the Milbourns were away he would call in and sit with her and would slip her a bottle of his usquebah, so she was happy to return the favour.

Malky could not wait to tell Davey of the news and headed over early the next morning to the Marsden cottage, with Peedee just behind, on his donkey. When he arrived and dismounted from his pony, Mrs. Blayre saw him from the barn where she was milking the cows. She rose quickly from the stool and came out into the yard almost shouting out his name in greeting, in an attempt to forestall him. Malky went quickly into the cottage. Molly was sitting on the edge of her pallet with both breasts bare and the bairns in their cribs. Davey, who had heard the door creaking, was coming away from her, his hand trying to cover what was sticking out under his shirt.

Malky said nowt. He then looked at Molly who had tears in her eyes, and he remembered that it was a year almost to the day that he had last seen her in tears for the anniversary of her man's death.

He looked at Davey. "Find a wet nurse for Hal and send Molly back to Sheels." He looked at Molly who had not thought to cover her breasts and felt a hot rush of desire himself.

"I'll find a room for ye near mine, and ye can gang back to yer hawking. A'body's forgotten aboot ye and me noo."

He turned back to Davey. "I came to tell ye that Niall's back but not for lang. If I see anything like this again I'll draw ma knife, Davey." He turned on his heel and left, knocking into Peedee who was standing in the doorway. "Ye tell him aboot Niall," he half shouted and left.

Lewis Frost had another motive for taking on Niall as crew as the Scot found out over the next few days. Ralph Milbourn and Lewis Frost knew all about Tomag's little side-line, and Ralph Milbourn had guessed that the explosion at the widder's cottage had been a still exploding. He had had a quiet word with Tomag and agreed to turn a blind eye to the still in Hamish's shop in exchange for the odd bottle of the home-made usquebah. He had realised that there would be a ready market for the Scotch spirit, and that it would not be too expensive to import from Scotland now that Scottish goods did not pay customs dues when entering English ports. He himself had a share in the *Old Providence*, and had talked to Lewis Frost about whether they might be able to import some legitimate usquebah from one of the Sottish ports on the return from the Baltic. Having a Scot on board who could speak the Gaelic might prove useful. Lewis Frost decided to take Niall with him to see his father when he discussed the idea with him, and made the final arrangements for the voyage.

He had invited Abe Taylier in view of his share in the ship, but Abe was not well. He had suffered a seizure a few days before. He had been talking business with Malky, and had launched into one of his tirades against his son. His face had become scarlet and all of a sudden his eyes had shot up in their sockets, and he had half stumbled against Malky who had helped him onto a settle. The right side of his face seemed to have collapsed, his right arm hung limp at his side and he had difficulty talking. He had been in bed now for two days and was slowly starting to put a few words together. A pothecary from Newcastle had been called in and had recommended two pipes of tobbaccy a day which would have a calming influence on the old man. Malky and Abe's chief clerk had decided to carry on as before, and hope that no important decisions would need to be made.

It was Malky who went with Niall to accompany Lewis Frost to Biddick Hall to see his father. Isaac was in the yard talking to his chief groom and to Dougie who was holding *Lightning Lad's* reins. They had just returned from an exercise run over the Harton moor.

Isaac Frost, who normally had a sparkle in his eye, looked distracted. He only half listened as Lewis told the story of Niall's rescue from the Tyne. He did not seem interested in the fact that the lad, who was thought to have drowned, was now alive, and would be a crew member on the *Old Providence*. Dougie, on the other hand, could hardly contain himself and was hoping that the serious talk would soon finish so that he could have a proper natter with Niall and Malky. Auld Isaac's ears pricked up, however, when Lewis mentioned the possibility of importing usquebah from Scotland.

"Is there profit in it?" he asked.

"Aye, there would be," said Lewis. "There's little market noo for brandy that comes in through the harbour, as ye can buy the best Strasbourg Brandy from Abe's delivery lad at a low price with nae questions asked. We'd be the only ones importing the usquebah, and we'll sell it on with nae bother.

"You're looking a little troubled, Father."

"It's the horse," Isaac said, pointing to *Lightning Lad*. "Sir Thomas was doon here the other day for dinner. He's noo the owner of a stallion called *Drummer Boy*, that he reckons could beat *Lightning Lad* any day, and over any ground. He kept goading me to agree to a race. I was adamant that nae other horse would beat *Lightning*. Weel, we were on wor second bottle of that Strasbourg brandy ye were talking aboot, and I stood up and tolt him that the race was on. 'And the wager?' he said looking me in the eye. I said nowt as I wanted to think, and then he said, 'Then a hundred pounds it will be'."

There was a stunned silence. Even Dougie went google-eyed. "You refused, of course, Father."

Isaac looked angry. "Of course I didn't. I couldn't back down to that little shite. The wager stands. And if *Drummer Boy* wins then I'll be in difficulty, and ye too."

"Weel, if the Sheels constable gets wind of it he'll get the Vestry court to stop it. The Parliament has banned all races along with any other form of what they call frivolous entertainment," said Lewis.

"Aye, we discussed that the next morning when Sir Thomas was leaving," replied the father. "We're to tell nae one aboot the race. It will be held on the sands early one Sunda' morning. He'll come doon the day before with some friends and we'll all gan oot on the horses for a ride. When we reach the shore, the two horses will walk off together towards the Trow Rocks, and then turn and race back. A course of one mile four furlongs will be measured out the day before, and we'll have a starter ready for the off. The rest of us will be at the finish line."

"Have ye fixed a date?"

"Late April or early May. He wants some time with the horse to make sure it's in good fettle, and there's more chance of some decent weather. We'll need a morning when the tide has been oot for a while and the sands are firm and dry. He's not riding the horse himself and has a rider in mind, but any jockey must be a gentleman. In other words nae grooms or servants."

"So that rules oot wee Dougie," said Lewis Frost.

The head groom coughed. "Can I say something, Master?"

"Wye of course, speak yer mind, lad." He laughed. "Ye usually do."

"Can ye not get him to change his mind? With Dougie in the saddle wor *Lightning* would beat anything ower that distance. He understands the beast and talks to it in his own tongue, that the *Lad* understands. He's also lighter than any gentleman would be, with them eating fat beef and drinking that brandy all neet lang."

Although Isaac did not see the funny side the others chuckled quietly.

"Ye kna' it's the rule for any horse race, lad," said Lewis. "I used to ride for me Da' when they had the beach races in Sheels before the wars. But I'm too heavy noo, and I'll be somewhere in the Baltic Sea."

There was a silence, then Niall nudged Malky and whispered into his ear.

"Niall's got an idea," said Malky.

Niall had not expected to speak and started off in his keelman's voice. *Lightning Lad* jumped about a bit until Dougie had calmed him down.

"Yer not on the river noo," said Malky.

"Ach, I'm sorry," the former keelman muttered. "Ye'll jest have to switch him."

There were blank faces but Isaac Frost was interested. "Gan on."

"Ye find a gentleman, or mair like a gentleman's son, frae roond here, who's aboot the same age and build as Dougie. Ye let him ride the *Lad* to the sands, but just before the race he has to gang and have a piss. He'll have to be wearin' some bright claes – a yeller waistcoat would de the trick. When he cams oot o' the bushes, it's no' him but Dougie in the yellow coat. He jumps on the *Lad*, and off he gangs. After he's won, he jumps doon, and ye'll hae to find a way for the other fella to jump back up in the saddle wi' the yellow coat on withoot anybody noticing."

Isaac Frost looked sternly at the young Scot. "And do ye think that I would stoop to such a low trick to win this wager." There were some worried looks. Then his face broke into a wide smile. "Weel, if it means putting one ower Sir Thomas, then wye aye I would! Let's have some ale."

It was no more than a few weeks later that Malky was walking behind the cart that was carrying Abe Taylier's body along the Low Way on his last journey to St Hild's. Auld Abe had passed away after another seizure. He had taken no steps to disinherit Nathan, who now planned to return to live in Abe's mansion house on the Low Way. He was walking beside Malky, and had been the one to take charge of the funeral arrangements. The windows of the house had been draped in thick black curtains, and all mirrors and any reflective surfaces had been covered so that the spirit of the dead man would not be attracted by them and lose its way to paradise. The night before the funeral there had been a wake at the house, and friends and neighbours, and often those who just hoped for wine or ale in the black hours of the night, had watched over the body. The funeral procession had headed off the next day as soon as it became dusk as night was the proper time for a funeral. Malky and other servants, as well as close friends of the merchant, wore the silk crepe scarves that Nathan had given them in their hatbands, and would be expected to do so for three months, the mourning period.

The open coffin of black painted oak lay in the back of the cart, which was bedecked with the pall, and lit by silver candlesticks attached to the sides. Walking beside the cart were Geordie Naesbitt and half a dozen brawny fishermen bearing torches. It was not out of respect for Abe, but to make sure that no one would make a grab for the pall, and the silver ornaments - a common practice in Sheels. Abe was well known and there was a good crowd following behind, many banging pans and kettles, or blowing horns and fifes to keep the evil spirits at bay.

The funeral cortege slowly wound its way along the narrow ways to the High Street and then to the Mill Dam quay and up the narrow path to the church. Night had now fallen and the Church stewards carried tallow candles to light the way. The Curate's sermon in the cold and gloomy church was long and tedious, and Malky, like those who had sat up for the wake the night before, felt their eyebrows drooping. They then all trooped to the grave-side. Abe had bought a plot for his wife, when she had passed and the coffin was lowered in. The expensive silver handles, which had been hired for the funeral along with the pall and the candlesticks, were unscrewed first, and the coffin sealed. But at least Abe would lie in the coffin in the ground, unlike the less fortunate, whose family used the parish coffin from which the dead body was lifted and placed in the ground with their winding sheet only, with the coffin available to be used again.

The funeral party then returned to the house where they were served with wine and biscuits. Geordie and his torch carriers were taken to the back of the room and given ale with bread and cheese. There was no shortage of wine and then a small barrel of brandy was brought out. It was not until well after midnight that the last of the mourners staggered home along the way.

Davey had found a wet nurse for young Hal. She was the daughter of one of the farm workers on the Lay Gate farm estate. She was unmarried, and it was generally thought that the father of the bairn was Thomas Coatsworth, the youngest son of William, one of the owners of the estate, which was why she had not been brought before the Vestry court. Miss Linton had delivered the baby girl and when it was known that Molly would be leaving, and as the mother seemed strong and healthy, she was sent over to the Marsden Cottage to nurse young Hal as well as her own bairn.

Malky had found a room for Molly above a shop in Stony Steep Lane where he lived and the amorous Scot had already started creeping up the back stairs to her room at night. His desire for her womanly comforts were such that he had put to the back of his mind what he had seen in Marsden cottage.

After the funeral, Malky had carried on much as before learning the business, although Nathan now liked to deal personally with the negotiations with the ship's captains, and other merchants on all the legitimate business.

Molly was soon back down to the shore where the fishing boats came in, filling her basket with fresh fish which she would hawk round the streets with her George in swaddling clothes strapped into a wicker basket on her back.

Malky and Peedee were starting to become busy again with Cuddy Heron and his donkeys on the way to Frenchman's Bay or Manhaven. They now used their smuggler's cave near Manhaven, and the barrels of Strasbourg brandy and the cases of tobaccy were stored there until they could transport them to Nathan's warehouse and then to Marledane's cellar.

Malky tried to keep a low profile looking after the custom-free trade, with Peedee and Molly as his main distributors in Sheels. John McGilvray was more than happy to carry any goods to Newcastle, where Malky had paid a visit to Archie Ridell at the sign of the *Shoulder of Mutton* and built up a small network of publicans ready to sell off his spirits and baccy.

It was in the first week of May that Peedee came running into the Taylier warehouse in Low Way where he knew he'd find Malky.

"The race is on this Sunda'," he shouted, "and Auld Isaac wants to see ye." Peedee had been on a delivery to Biddick Hall, and had been collared by Isaac. Together the two of them went up to the Hall and Isaac Frost laid out his plans and where Malky would come in.

On Sunday the fifth of May, a crowd of folk were to be seen on the sea front by the Hogshead Well at six o'clock in the morning. Although no one was supposed to know about the race, word had got round. Malky, Molly, Tomag and Davey, and Peedee were there along with Geordie Naesbitt, Micky Coulson and a dozen or so big fisher lads. Captain Bowmaker, Dick Redheed and John Marledane were also present, and a barrel of ale was ready to be broached. It was not long before they saw the horsemen appear, coming down off the Lawe pastures and heading towards the well. There were two parties: Isaac Frost with his grooms, accompanied by the Coatsworths, the Lintons and Nathan Taylier, and Sir Thomas Haselrig and about a half dozen officers from the Newcastle Garrison. When they arrived Isaac shouted at the crowd in mock anger and told them that they had no business to be there. Sir Thomas rode over.

"Do I see ale?" he cried out in a voice that carried.

"Wye aye, Sir Thomas," shouted back Dick Redheed. "A barrel of me best dark ale, twice brewed. For the refreshment of all. Exercising the horses must be thirsty work."

Isaac rode to where the barrel was and dismounted, handing his reins to one of the grooms. "The ale will wait until we've had the race." He held his open palm over his eyes and peered into the distance. "The starters are there." He gestured to his grooms. "Tie the ribbon to the posts, lads." The finishing and starting posts had been put up the day before when a mile and four furlongs course had been laid out with a *chain* measure. Robert Linton was the starter, and one of Haselrig's officers would stand at the finish line.

"Let's have the horses," Isaac called out.

Lightning Lad was the first to walk over. He was in a lively mood and his rider was having difficulty in keeping him calm. "It's young Tommy Coatsworth," said Peedee to Malky in a

321

whisper that was heard at the back of the crowd.

A rider in a military uniform rode out next on a chestnut mount that was not as big as *Lightning* but was bright eyed and sleek. Sir Thomas was just behind.

"May I present Major Robbie Colquhoon, former owner of *Drummer Boy* and the best rider in the regiment." The Major tipped his cap and guided his horse towards the other stallion. He was a young man, slim of build and keen of eye, with a clear control over his mount.

"Well met, Coatsworth, I hope ye can control him better when we're racing, than ye did on the way ower here. I dinna' want any barging frae ye."

"Dain't worry, Major," said Thomas good naturedly. "It's just nerves. Once we're away ye'll only see his back hooves so I wouldn't worry aboot barging."

"A cup of ale for the jockeys," shouted Redheed.

A cup was taken over. The major drank his from the stirrup, but Thomas couldn't keep his horse still, so he dismounted with the aid of a groom, and thirstily drank his ale down asking for a refill. He was slight of build with only a few strands of blonde hair poking out from under his cap. He had discarded his coat and wore a bright yellow waistcoat, with a silk scarf of the same colour round his neck. He seemed to be enjoying his ale and chatting away with Redheed and Marledane.

As Colquhoon sipped his ale, he looked over into the crowd of men around the well. His heart skipped a beat as he saw a young man in sober dress, solidly built and with chestnut curls poking out from under his black hat. He moved his mount forward and the lad turned his way and looked his straight in the eye. 'De'il haet' he whispered to himself as he saw the odd coloured eyes of Malcolm Dalgleish, who he had last seen on the Dunbar field. The Major turned his horse and pulled away.

Isaac Frost feigned impatience and called on the Coatsworth lad to mount up. He and Colquhoon should have already been trotting their mounts along the sands to the start line. Tommy was helped back into the saddle and they were both starting to make off and then Tommy shouted to the major.

"Ye gan on, I must have a piss," and turned *Lightning* with some difficulty. There were mutterings from Sir Thomas's bloods, as their confidence in their own man grew at the ineptitude of *Lightning's* jockey. Young Tom jumped from the saddle, just giving the groom time to catch the reins and ran behind the well. He was lost among the crowd of big fisher lads who had started on the ale, but was out in a minute, jumped in the saddle, and cantered off, now in full control of *Lightning* who seemed altogether calmer. As he rode along he pulled his scarf up over his mouth as protection against the biting sea wind.

Those clustered round the ale barrel watched as the two riders took their mounts all along the sands, nearly to the Trow and then stood at the start line under the orders of Robert Linton.

Tomag was standing next to Malky and said, "Was that the Colquhoon who took yer pony, and left ye to fight the Sassenachs on yer own?"

"Och, he's the ane all reet, and I'll be having words wi' him when we've won."

They heard the bell ring and could just make out the horses as they galloped over the hard sands, kicking up little sprays as they went. The red jacketed Major had a clear lead, but then the yellow waistcoated jockey on *Lightning* leant well forward in the saddle and seemed to be whispering to the *Lad*. They passed the mile post neck and neck and had come close together, when the arm of the red-coated Major lashed out, and caught the face of the *Lad's* jockey full on. He fell forward onto the neck of his mount and *Drummer Boy* edged forward, but the yellow waistcoated rider recovered himself, half stood in his stirrups, whipped his horse hard and the *Lad* responded. With two furlongs to go it was neck and neck again, with *Lightning* giving the other horse and its jockey a wide berth. Another flick of the whip and the *Lad* surged on, reaching the finish line a length in front.

The crowd round the well were in a turmoil. Redheed and Marledene had shouted themselves hoarse, cheering the *Lad* on. While Tommy had been relieving himself, they had walked across to Sir Thomas' men and made several side wagers.

As the jockey pulled the *Lad* up, he was immediately mobbed by the fisher lads who pulled him from the saddle and threw him up in the air. He was set on his feet, surrounded by the big lads. It was wee Dougie, who had taken Coatsworth's place when he had pretended to have to take a piss. He also had a yellow waistcoat, and his black hair had been all but shorn away, with what was left drenched in flour. Tommy Coatsworth was there and ready to take his place, when Dougie put a hand on his arm.

"Ach, sorry, Tom, but ye'll need this," and he pulled his arm back and slashed the lad's face hard with his riding whip. Pulling his waistcoat off, he disappeared into the crowd. Blood was starting to seep from the wound, but Tommy was a game lad, and pushed himself out of the mob to clamber up on to the back of *Lightning*. The horse didn't like it and he was nearly thrown. As soon as the groom had managed to hold the stallion's head firm, the line judge declared him to be the winner. All the while a furious Robbie Colquhoon was talking angrily to Sir Thomas.

Young Coatsworth now dismounted, to the relief of himself, the *Lad*, and the groom, and walked over quickly to the well and to the ale barrel. He was standing talking to Isaac Frost, the proud owner, when an angry Scot's voice called out from behind him.

"Turn yourself, laddie, and let me see your face."

Tommy stood his ground. "Weel, I dain't want to see yours."

"Ye'll see there's no' a mark on him," shouted Colquhoon as he roughly handled the lad's shoulders and turned him round. An angry welt, seeping with blood, ran from his left ear, under his eye and over a nose that was not the same shape as it had been earlier that morning.

"The devil, Robbie, ye could have put his eye oot," exclaimed Sir Thomas.

The young Coatsworth then looked at Sir Thomas. "I was on the *Lad*, as ye had agreed with Mr. Frost that only a gentleman should ride in the race. Did ye dress up one of the grooms in a red coat then, Sir Thomas? A gentleman would never have done this to a fellow rider."

Colquhoon went at young Coatsworth and would have no doubt strangled him if Sir Thomas had not grabbed him, and then with the help of some of the other soldiers dragged him away. Haselrig came back a few minutes later and apologised to Isaac Frost and to young Thomas.

"He's a sore loser. He doesn't believe that anyone but a skilled groom, who was riding for payment, could have beaten him. He thought that ye had switched riders at the last minute, and that young Coatsworth would have been unmarked. My apologies again, and my congratulations to ye, Thomas Coatsworth. Ye must come up to our hall and have a ride yersel on *Drummer Boy*. If he takes to ye, then ye'll ride him in the next race.

"I'll see ye back at your hall, Mr. Frost, for the breakfast ye promised us," said Haselrig.

"Aye and we'll settle up," replied Isaac Frost.

Colquhoon had dismounted while one of the grooms rubbed the horse down and joined Sir Thomas. "Could I ask ye, Mr. Frost, did I catch a glimpse just now of a lad I know by the name of Malcolm Dalgleish, and who I last saw on Dunbar battlefield?"

"Young Malky?" replied Isaac. "Aye, he came to Sheels as an indentured servant to work in the salt-panns, but was freed after he'd saved the life of Henry Coultheard's son who'd fallen into the Tyne. He's a brave lad is Malky, and is now working for a merchant, and doing well."

"I'd like to renew my acquaintance wi' him. Ye couldna' invite him alang to the breakfast?"

Isaac agreed, and Malky made his way with the others to Biddick Hall.

The breakfast was a boisterous affair with roast ham, veal and fowl, and wine for those who preferred it to ale. Care had been taken to get Dougie back to the stables without being seen, and he was under strict instructions to stay in the hay loft until all the guests had gone, so that no one would notice the red weal on his cheek, just like the one on Tommy Coatsworth's. Isaac Frost made sure that his guests did not linger as he and his family would be going to their chapel in West Panns Way later that morning. As the last remaining few left the table, Robbie Colquhoon tapped Malky on the shoulder and sat down beside him.

"Ach, it's good to see ye again, laddie, but I nearly had a turn when I saw yer odd coloured eyes doon at the well. Yer poor father Johnny Douglass had a tear in his eye when I told him how ye had bravely given yer life fighting aff the Sassenach s, and that I had nae chance but to leave ye and try and rally the troops.

"Yer Da' and I split up when he decided to gang wi' King Charles to France and I stayed hame, and gave ma oath to Sir Arthur. Ye should gang to France. I'll try and get a message to your Da' to tell him that you're alive and weel."

Malky had said nowt, and was not sure whether he was going to answer Colquhoon when Sir Thomas and Isaac came over.

"It's time we were leaving, Robbie," said Sir Thomas. He was not in the friendliest of humours having paid over one hundred pounds to Frost, whose steward had laboriously counted out all the *crowns* and *double crowns, angels,* old *ryials,* and *unite* coins that made up the one hundred pounds, before himself shaking Haselrig's hand. Sir Thomas then turned to Major Colquhoon.

"Had I bought the *Drummer Boy* from ye and not won it at cards, I'd have asked for my money back from ye."

"Ye lost it in a game of cards?" asked Isaac.

"We had both taken liquor," muttered the Major, "and I had lost money in a game, but Thomas said he'd gie me a chance to win it back on a turn of a card. We cut the pack. I lost and lost again until I had only the *Boy* to wager with."

"It was my lucky deck," said Sir Thomas, and he reached inside his coat and pulled an old set of playing cards from his pocket. "I carry them with me always, and seldom lose."

"Ye lost the *Drummer Boy* cutting the deck?" asked an incredulous Malky.

Robbie just nodded sheepishly. Peedee who had been out in the stables with the grooms sharing the leftovers from the master's table, had come in to find Malky. He was standing just behind him and had heard Sir Thomas's words. He nudged Malky and whispered in his ear.

"Could I hae a look at them?" asked Malky. "They look awfu' auld."

"Handed down for generations," said Sir Thomas, untying the blue ribbon that held the cards together and handing them to Malky.

The others talked of this and that while the young Scot handled the well-worn cards. After a while he looked at Peedee and then laid the deck on the table. "Can I cut them wi' ye, Major Colquhoon, to try ma luck. But no' for race horses," he laughed, "just for a bit o' fun."

He won three cuts in a row, drawing a king, an ace, and when Colquhoon drew a Queen, Malky pulled an ace. He set the cards down. Haselrig made to grab them but Malky pulled them away.

"It's a lang card deck, Robbie," he said.

"A what?"

"A lang card deck. Because the cards are auld, or made to look auld, it's not easy to spot, but the aces are langer than the other cards, only by a fraction, mind, and the kings are a little bit shorter than the aces."

Colquhoon took the cards from Malky and looked at them closely.

There was a deathly silence.

"Ye can write, Malky?"

"Och aye."

"Could ye let us hae some paper, a quill and some ink, Mr. Frost?"

When the writing material was brought over from one of the wooden cupboards by the wall, Malky readied himself.

"Tak this doon," said Colquhoon.

"'*Whereas Sir Thomas Haselrig is disappointed at the running of his horse Drummer Boy, he now hereby agrees to sell the same back to Major Robert Colquhoon, for the sum of one guinea.*'

"Then put in the spaces for the signatures, including yours and Isaac's as witnesses, add the date and melt some sealing wax."

It was done quickly and then Robbie looked a little embarrassed. He glanced at Isaac Frost. "I'm sorry to say I hae nae coin on me. Lost it at cards last nicht. Ye could no' lend me a pound and a shilling?"

Lewis Frost pulled the coins from the bulging pouch in front of him and handed the coins over. "I'll give it ye, as a present."

He took the bill of sale and passed the coins to Sir Thomas, who just muttered, "And no more said?"

"Nae mair said," replied Robbie, who looked in turn at Malky, Peedee and Isaac. They all nodded.

Sir Thomas reached out for the cards, but Peedee beat him to it. "I'm not a gentleman, so I can cheat as much as I like," he shouted as he ran out the door.

"Dinna' worry," said Malky, "I'll get them back but they're no' gangen to ye, Sir Thomas, I'll ask Mr. Frost to hae them for safe keeping."

Sir Thomas stamped out of the room. Robbie Colquhoon patted Malky on the shoulder. "Another debt I owe to ye, Malky, which I will repay tenfold when the chance arrives."

Sir Thomas paused on the threshold and shouted back over his shoulder. "And don't think that I'll agree to any more Scotchmen having their indentures cancelled."

CHAPTER TWELVE

As the summer nights became shorter, the unloading of any cargo at the smuggler's cave or Manhaven had to be quickly done, and Molly took to the work again. When she knew that a ship was arriving, she'd walk over to Marsden Cottage with George in his basket. When Cuddy's donkeys arrived there, Malky or Peedee would make the hoot of a night owl, and she would join them, leaving George sleeping in his crib. If he woke, then the wet nurse would give him a teat to keep him quiet, and if she was short of milk the next morning, Molly would give Hal his feed. She helped with the unloading of the ship's boat, filling the baskets for the donkeys, and then stacking away any barrels or boxes that they would leave in the cave for another day. She would then let them make the journey to Sheels and return to the cottage.

Bowmaker had heard from one of the ships' captains who sailed out of the Kent ports, that a French ship's master he knew, who was bringing wine and brandy, and some general cargo from Bordeaux to the Tyne, would be happy to offload most of his wine and brandy at Marsden. It would be one of the largest drops they had taken, but there was room in the cave and their new operation was working smoothly, so the arrangements were made. As it would be the French vessel's first trip, it was agreed that someone would be on watch and ready with a light on the cliff over the cave when the ship was expected – that was Peedee's job. Malky took on a couple more fisher lads and both Molly and Davey were to help as well.

Malky and Molly went straight to the cottage, as soon as Peedee had ridden over on Malky's pony and warned them that the ship had arrived. They called in at the cottage and then went down to the cove with Davey. Peedee gave the signal that they were ready for the boat to come in and they waited. Cuddy would not be long, with the donkeys and the other lads, but they could make a start.

They were standing on the bay in front of the cave, Peedee holding his lamp high, when the heavily laden boat was gently driven onto the sands. A young lad jumped out first with a rope and Peedee pointed him to an outcrop of rock that they used to moor the craft. Another man came right behind, a sword in one hand, and a lantern in the other, and strode purposefully towards them. The lamp light reflected on to his wavy blond locks billowing from under his head scarf, and the gold ring hanging from his left ear. With his massive shoulders, thin waist and long shanks, he looked a menacing figure.

"Ach, there's no need for that," said Malky pointing to the sword. There was no reply as the man shone his lamp backwards and forwards to light up the faces of the welcome party. In the silence Malky spoke again.

"Do ye no' speak English?"

The stranger's gaze returned to Malky.

"Wye aye I de, and that's a bonny lass stood ower there. That's nivver ye, Molly?"

There was a shriek that made Davey and Peedee jump six inches from the ground, and Molly then let out a high-pitched cry, "Danny, Danny, Danny," before hurling herself forward and throwing herself onto the man. Encumbered as he was with his sword and his lamp, he nearly fell over backwards but his strong legs saved him. He dropped his sword to the sand, held his lantern out for the ship's lad, and then wrapped his arms round her. Then the kissing and the slobbering started, and the sailor with the Sheels accent let his hands run down Molly's back to take a firm grip on her rump.

"She kna's him, then," said Peedee.

"Ach, her deed husband was called Danny," replied Malky.

"Weel, he disna' look deed noo," muttered Davey.

At last the couple parted, and a tearful Molly looked back to Malky. "It's Danny," she said, "back from the deed."

Malky was stunned and his mind was whirling.

The sound of Cuddy's donkeys was heard on the cliff top. Peedee ended the awkward silence on the sands with his keelman's voice. "Nice to meet ye, Danny. If ye can let gan of Molly and start yer lads on the unloading, then we might be finished before day break. Malky here'll check the goods and give ye the coin."

"Danny Hawes, husband of wor Molly," the stranger said holding out his hand to shake Malky's.

"Malcolm Dalgleish, father of Molly and mine's son, George."

The man just nodded, and asked, "Ye married then?"

"Ach no. Yer parents objected when we posted the banns. As nae body was found, and as ye'd no' been missing for seven years, the Curate would no' marry us."

"Aye, I was captured by a *Dunkirker* when its captain decided to steal the cargo that had been landed. Joe and me fought hard, but Joe was killed and I got one of theirs in return. The captain was short crewed so they pressed me on board, and here I am.

"Let's get the business done then, noo we all kna' each other," said Danny.

After the first load was piled on the sands, the boat went for another, and light was just starting to break through when all the cargo had been checked, and most of it stowed away in the cave. The tide was now nearly fully in and Danny was going to have to leave.

"I'll have to gan, hinny," he said to Molly. "The ship's putting in to the Tyne to unload the rest of what's on board and take a load of salt and coal back doon to Folkestone, and then back ower to France. I'll see ye in Sheels, but dain't tell anyone that I'm back yet. I'll have to talk to my skipper before I decide what to de." He jumped into the boat that was half afloat, and was away on the seas.

The next day Danny Hawes was ashore and went straight to Molly's room, where she welcomed him as she had done at the cove. They remained in the room for days as they made up for their two years apart. Molly would just pop out for food and ale. The French skipper sent his men to look for Danny but they did not know where to look and no one talked. It was only after the ship left that Danny Hawes was seen again, on the ways and in the ale-houses of Sheels. He went to Malky's warehouse and told him that now he was back he wanted the

Scotchman to stay away from Molly.

"I dain't blame ye or her, for what ye did. She thowt I was deed and so did ye, but I'm back noo, and I'm her husband."

"And what aboot wee George?" asked Malky.

"He's a canny lad. I'm tolt that as Molly was still married to me when she had him, that I'm his Da', so I'll bring him up reet. It's probably best if ye dain't try to see him or ye'll just confuse the bairn."

Danny had brought his money purse with him when he jumped ship and he had a good amount. He moved into a house in the toon-end, and as well as taking over his father's boat he bought a half share in another sea coble. Molly stopped hawking and worked with Danny in their fish business, gutting and salting, and mending lines and nets, with little George lying in a crib beside her.

Malky missed Molly and was hurt that she had given up on him so completely. But Danny had been her first love and he could not think too harshly of her. In any case he was now very busy with the selling on of the large quantity of brandy and wine that was being brought over from Marsden, as well as dealing with new shipments. He was in regular contact with Captain Bowmaker and the amount of coin coming in was considerable. He would often spend the evening with Tomag at the cottage in Widder's Court. Widder Wallis and Alice had now moved into one of the other cottages in the close that had fallen empty, as Milbourn who held the lease of the burned one was not prepared to spend any coin on its rebuilding.

Tomag had heard that Lewis Frost had agreed to cancel Dougie's indenture as a reward for his riding *Lightning Lad* to victory, but the Haselrigs would not give their consent. Isaac had therefore taken Dougie with him to see Henry Ashburne. When Henry had given him the indenture to inspect, Isaac had explained the situation, and then ripped the indenture into pieces, and flung it onto the clerk's coal fire. It made little difference to Dougie as he loved his work at Biddick Hall both in the kitchens and with the horses. Since the race he had been moved into the house from the stables, and his duties with the horses were now to train and ride them, and he was excused the more burdensome jobs of mucking out and polishing the harnesses and saddles. He was also now given a wage of six pence a day.

As for Tomag, he had talked to Malky about his own plans for the future. He was now more or less accepted as the salt master for the Milbourn and Frost panns, and loved his work. Jimmy Jobling was kept on by Milbourn and Frost even though he was rarely now sober for more than a few hours a day, and they let Tomag run the panns. He hoped that if Malky's money kept coming in then his friend would agree to use the money to buy a salt-pann or two. With the downturn in the price of salt, many owners were thinking of quitting the trade, as it was not bringing the returns they had expected.

Lewis Frost had returned with the *Old Providence* after a successful trip. Not only had they sold the coal and salt for a good price, but they had brought back a dozen barrels of usquebah. Two or three distilleries had been willing to provide them, and the agent they had talked to in Aberdeen had agreed to recruit more if they were assured of a ready purchaser. When he called in to the port on his next Baltic trip, Frost had agreed that he would take up with him empty brandy and wine barrels that would give the spirit a smoother flavour. Niall had been of great help, not only when they had met the distillers, who still preferred to speak in the erse, but also in tasting the product. They did not reject any, but paid less for three barrels that were of inferior quality and would need ageing, or blending with others.

It was on one of his meetings with Bowmaker that Malky learned of the fears that there would be a war with the Dutch.

"If there is then it will hit wor trade," said a worried Bowmaker. "The colliers and the other merchant ships will only sail in convoys escorted by warships, and there'll be nae chance of any of them stopping off at Frenchman's or Manhaven.

"I've heard that the Navy is organising itself for a hard press in all the major ports. They need more men, and if they dain't get enough from incoming ships and from the keelmen and the fishers, they'll send their gangs into the streets and tyek anyone they can, and they won't be ower particular."

Henry Coultheard had maintained contact with Malky and was not averse from taking a small barrel of brandy off Malky's hands now and again. It did not seem to concern him that the spirit had avoided customs dues, saying as he often did with a smile on his face, "I'm an excise man, nowt to do with the customs." Malky was over their house for dinner one day and Henry asked if the Scot could do him a favour.

"It's young Kit," he said, looking sternly at his son. "I have tried to take him under my wing, and he has been coming along with me as my tally man now for a good few months. To put it plainly, it does not interest him, and he finds it difficult to concentrate. He says he does not want to become an excise man, but wants to see something of the world beyond Sheels. He wants to be a merchant adventurer!"

"Like Mr. Frost and your friend Niall," exclaimed Kit. "Peedee has told me all about it. How they sail to the Baltic and to Scotland to trade with the distillers who make the usquebah." His eyes had lit up with excitement.

"Now I kna' he's too young for that, but I wondered if you might ask Mr. Taylier to take him on as an apprentice, or such like, and he could learn the trade of a merchant. As he gets older he would be able to travel on one of their ships as an agent. I might myself be willing to invest in the business or take a share in a ship."

Malky looked at Kit. Like Peedee he had grown from a boy to a lad in the last year. He was bright and lively enough, and he had little doubt that Nathan would be happy to do a favour for the excise man.

"Och, we can always do with another pair of hands. I'll take him along to see Mr. Taylier's chief clerk and if he's happy with the lad, then to see Nathan himsel," replied Malky.

Captain Bowmaker's fears over the forthcoming war proved grounded and the arrival of the frigate *Centurion* in the Tyne with two sloops, the *Ruby* and the *Polly*, as naval tenders, more or less put an end to their smuggling. The three ships would patrol the German Ocean from the Humber to Leith on the lookout for incoming vessels which they could board. They would impress the able seamen, but not always the officers unless it was a hard press, and they were close to their port of destination. When they returned to the Tyne, the *Polly* and the *Ruby* would ferry the pressed men to the *Centurion* which would then transport them to the Nore.

A new Captain Regulator of the *Impressment Service* had set up his *Rendez-vous* in the Side at Newcastle, and with two Lieutenants and four *Midshipmen*, ran a gang of twenty of the roughest thugs and villains he could recruit, and who would live in, all found, and be paid five shillings for every man pressed.

"The gangs have so far been oot only in Newcastle and Gyetesheed," said a worried Bowmaker as he puffed on his clay pipe. "I've heard that they take anyone wearing a sailor's jacket, but that they're not particular. They started on the keelmen but they would lose three or four of their own, injured, to every keelman they took, so they dain't bother with them so much noo. When their drummer boy is heard they say that any boy or man in the streets scatter yem, but they'll gan into the pubs where sailors drink and drag them oot. They all carry *hangers* and cudgels and aren't afraid to use them." He paused. "They'll be in Sheels soon and after the fishermen. If the tenders catch a fishing boat at sea they'll usually take only one man and one boy from a coble, but if the land-press come to Sheels they'll tyek as many as they can."

Little more than a week later, Malky was in the Taylier warehouse when he heard the sound of a drum beating. When he looked out, and up to the way, he saw a drummer boy walking beside an officer and two mid-shipmen, who were followed by about a dozen rough looking men, with swords hanging from their belts and cudgels in their hands. Peedee came running round the corner.

"It's the press gang, Malky. I saw them coming off the customs boat that's just pulled in. The customs man was pointing doon to the toon-end. They'll be after the fishers."

He ran past Malky and came back in a few seconds, carrying an armful of the *capstan-bars* that they kept in stock for ships that might need them.

"Ach, what are ye doing, Peedee?"

"The fisher's knives 'll be nae good against that lot. They'll need something to fight them off with. Are ye coming?"

Malky took half of the bars and followed Peedee down the way. When the press gang reached the fishers' cottages by the strand, the lieutenant waved his warrant at the fishermen, who were standing by their boats or working on their nets.

"Any man who volunteers to serve the Parliament and fight the Dutch will get his shilling," he shouted, at which the gangers ran forward and started grabbing volunteers. The first two they manhandled put up little resistance as they had been taken by surprise, but the others scattered and those that were caught fought back.

Malky and Peedee ran along the way and started giving out the capstan-bars. Malky then heard a shriek when Molly Hawes was knocked to the ground, as Danny fought with three of the gang and was getting the better of them. Another gangsman came behind him and hit him hard on the shoulder with his cudgel. Malky gave out his highland war-cry and ran forward with his capstan-bar in his hand, followed by Peedee. They set upon the men now trying to pull the half-dazed Danny to his knees, and had floored two when the others backed away. Molly grabbed ahold of her man, got him to his feet, and helped him to safety. Geordie Naesbitt used his bar to good effect to rescue Micky Coulson, and other brawny fishermen now came forward holding their capstan-bars at the ready.

The press-gang slowly backed away, holding only three fishermen. One of the midshipmen had drawn his pistol and pointed it at Malky. "We'll have ye," he cried out.

The quarter-deck voice of Captain Bowmaker was heard next as he stepped forward from the way, holding his musket pointing directly at the armed sailor.

"And if ye do, then I'll have ye. Put your pistol back into your belt, man, or I'll plug ye between the eyes." He looked squarely at the now very nervous looking Lieutenant. "Ye kna' as weel as I do, that your warrant doesn't let ye murder honest men minding their own business."

The midshipman holstered his pistol and stepped back beside the lieutenant.

"Ye're not welcome here," continued Bowmaker, lowering his musket. "Gan' on back to Newcastle noo or I won't be able to ha'd these lads back for much langer."

The gangsmen were already well behind the Lieutenant and heading along the way. With a snarl and an angry look at Bowmaker, he turned on his heel and followed his men. The drummer boy struck up the beat and they marched back to the customs boat. Two or three unfortunate sailors in blue jackets were grabbed unceremoniously before the rest of the onlookers on the way dashed off down lanes and up alleys.

Danny Hawes walked unsteadily over to Malky.

"Thank ye, Malky."

"Ach, there's no need for thanks. It wasna' for ye but for Molly and wee Geordie. They need ye to look after them and protect them."

"Aye and so I will," said Danny and walked slowly away.

They all feared reprisals but no more customs boats carrying gangs were seen, and things seemed to go back to normal. But about a week later the gang returned.

Malky had kept his word to Henry Coultheard and Kit had spent a couple of hours with Nathan's chief clerk, who was very pleased with the lad. The Scot was now taking young Kit to see Nathan at the warehouse at the merchants' quay. They had passed the Market Place and were walking along the high way close to the river when they heard the drum beating and the gang came round the bend before them, followed by a dozen red coated soldiers carrying muskets. Malky quickly pulled Kit's arm and dragged him up an alley and into the first public house he saw, at the sign of the *Jolly Tar*. He heard a cry of 'there's two,' and they had only been inside the tavern a few moments, when the doors were pushed open and half a dozen brawny ruffians came in after them followed by a midshipman – the same one that had drawn his pistol when confronting the fishermen.

"I have a warrant," he cried, "and we're after volunteers for their shilling." He looked round the bar and cried out to his men, "That one," he said pointing to Malky. "He was carrying a capstan-bar the last time I saw him, and the lad with him, those four by the hearth," he gestured to where four sailors were sitting, "and the pot boy ower there looks a strapping lad."

"Ye canna take wor Jacob," shouted an irate publican, a one-legged man with a bent back holding himself up with a stick who pushed himself forward. "I canna' run the hoose on my own, and I canna lift the barrels."

"I can take any able-bodied man I choose. Get out of the way or I'll take ye, stick and all."

The gangsmen roughly handled the 'volunteers', pushing a shilling into their hands or pockets and using their cudgels on the sailors who fought back. As he was being dragged towards the door, Malky shouted to the landlord, "The lad's Henry Coutlheard's son, the excise man. Get word to him and he'll do his best for your lad as well."

Once subdued, the men taken were walked back to the Mill Dam quay by two of the gang and put aboard the *Polly* that had brought the gang and their escort down the river. Seated on his horse on the quayside was Sir Thomas Haselrig, talking to the Regulator Captain who had made the journey himself and who would personally inscribe the names of the taken men, who he planned to transport straight to the *Centurion*.

"Well done, Captain Evans," called out Haselrig in a voice that was intended to carry. "That's the Scotchman I wanted taken. He's a trouble maker and leader of riots. I've let ye have the troops, so keep your word. No appeals to free him to be allowed and no substitutes. He's crossed me once and will not do so again. Eh Dalgleish," he chortled.

"And the lad?" asked the Captain.

"Don't know him, but if he's anything to do with Dalgleish we'll be well shot of him."

The gang did not venture down to the toon-end, and by the time they had combed the High Street pubs and alleys they had taken enough sailors and landsmen to earn themselves a good pay day. News travelled fast and there was a crowd of folk on the quayside begging the Regulator to release some of the men. It was no use.

"I'm taking every one of these without exception. It's a hard press to-day, because of the violence shown to my men by the fishermen the other day. They're all going straight to the *Centurion* and will be off and away on the next tide, or the one after, as they'll soon have their quota."

Henry Coultheard with Peedee at his side waited until the crowd started drifting away, and approached the quayside where the gangplank was being withdrawn.

"Captain?" he called out in his best manner.

"Captain Will Evans at your disposal, sir."

"Captain Evans, there's been a mistake. I'm the Parliament's excise man for Sheels and I've been told you've taken my son, Christopher Coultheard, and his employer Malcolm Dalgleish."

Captain Evans who had waved to the men to put the plank back into position, walked on it to the quayside. He had a leather-bound book in his hand, and opened it.

"Aye, I have their names. Both landsmen, but young and fit for service."

"I'd ask that they be released. I'll pay a premium so that you can replace them with volunteers," said Coultheard quietly. He leant forward and whispered, "And twenty pounds for yourself, of course."

Evans looked at him. He was a youngish man to be captain, small of build, but with shrewd eyes and an air of natural authority. He spoke slowly with a drawl, that gave away his west country origins.

"I have been transferred to the Impressment Service by those anxious to take me from the ships of the line so that their relatives and friends can have the best commands. I am not like the other washed-up Regulators who seek to make the most they can of their last posting, and are venal and corrupt. I am neither, Sir. I have put your son on the list of those going to the *Centurion*. I cannot take him off. All you can do is to try to see the frigate's Captain. He alone will be able to release your son. I doubt if he will take payment. Like me he is under orders to get as many men aboard, whatever their rank or status. As for Dalgleish, Sir Thomas Haselrig lent me his troops on condition that if I apprehended the man he would not be released under any circumstances, and I have annotated his entry accordingly.

"Good day, Sir." He crossed back over the plank which was then withdrawn, the mooring ropes unwound and thrown aboard. The *Polly's* sails caught the gentle breeze and headed out into the Tyne towards where the *Centurion* was moored.

"Haway, Mr. Coultheard," shouted Peedee, "let's get back and find a boat to take us oot to the frigate before it sets sail, or we'll nivver see 'em again." It turned out to be not as easy a task as they thought. All the watermen they approached refused point-blank to row out to the *Centurion* in case they were pressed themselves when they pulled up alongside the naval vessel. The press-gang took all able-bodied men and if you could row a coble then you could be dragged out of the boat and pressed. Even Henry Coutlheard's offer to pay a shilling for a trip that would normally cost a penny found no takers. Peedee then had an idea and ran off to find auld Gummy Jack. He was a local character who was one of the oldest men in Sheels. He had been pressed into the navy as a young lad in the reign of Good Queen Bess, and reckoned that he was five years short of eighty. He had lost his teeth years ago and now lived on broth made from fish heads, bone, and blood with barley bread as a sop. But he owned a river coble and still had the strength to row it. He was bald, blind in one eye, and so thin that you could see his ribs, so there was little chance of the navy pressing him into service. He took the shilling that a desperate Coultheard offered him and ferried them out towards the *Centurion*. They pulled alongside and the midshipman on watch poked his head over the ship's rail.

"If ye've come aboot the pressed men, then ye can turn away, the Lieutenant's seeing nae one."

Henry Coultheard stood up, nearly fell down again as the boat bobbed about, and was then held up by Jack.

"I'm the Parliament's excise man and the lad Christopher Coultheard is my son. I ask most kindly of ye to let me see the Captain."

"I'm sorry Sir, I have my orders. Nae boarders before we weigh anchor."

Peedee stood up. The frigate was low in the water and the gun hatches were just about level to where he was. "Did the Regul...what's it, not tell ye aboot the substitute for the lad?

On order of Sir Thomas Haselrig." He had used his keelman's voice and it rung out loud and clear. While the midshipman was thinking this over. Peedee whispered to Henry Coultheard who hoisted him up as high as he could. Peedee's foot landed on the top of the gun hatch and in a second he was clambering over the rails. A tall man came over.

"What's this?" he asked.

"I'm the substitute for Kit Coultheard, pressed the day. But I'm here on General Haselrig's orders. And I'll be of some use to ye. I've worked on the keels and I'm strang and nimble," shouted Peedee.

"Aye and we'd hear yer voice in a sea battle. I'm the Lieutenant in charge of the impressment detail. Hold on a minute."

Henry Coultheard had sat back down in the boat, his spirits low. He could not believe they would take Peedee in place of his son. Auld Jack was struggling to keep the boat hove to near the frigate as the tide was starting to turn and the water was now choppy.

The Lieutenant came back, holding a register in his hand, accompanied by an able seaman who was leading Kit.

"Well he's down here all right. Where's your order from Haselrig?"

"He'll send it ower."

"I doubt if it will reach us before we depart."

Peedee looked at Kit. "Had yer hands oot." Kit did so.

"White as yer sails. He's nivver done a day's work in his life. Look at mine." He held out his calloused mitts.

"Well, be that as it may, I can't see as how I can change the register without the order in writing, sorry, lad."

Peedee went towards Kit, put his arms around him as though to bid him farewell. He then pushed him hard to the rails and straight over the side. He was so quick that the Lieutenant and the Midshipman just looked on open mouthed. Kit gave out a scream which was followed by a loud splash as he fell into the Tyne. Luckily he was just in front of the coble, and when he surfaced his dad's hands hoiked him out of the water. Auld Jack used one oar to push the boat away from the side of the frigate, and pulled away. A drenched Kit sat forlornly beside his jubilant dad on the coble, looking back up to the deck of the *Centurion,* where Peedee was surrounded by seamen. There was nowt the Lieutenant could do, but he was not happy for the record to show that a pressed boy had made his escape from under his very nose.

He looked at a defiant Peedee. "We're taking no substitutes," he said angrily. "Yer down in the register as Christopher Coultheard and that's what ye'll stay.

"Take him away," shouted the Lieutenant as he clipped Peedee round the ears.

Down in the hold, Malky Dalgleish, resigned to his fate, stood up in shock as Peedee was roughly pushed down the ladder into the hold.

"De'il haet," Malky exclaimed. "What yer deein', Peedee?"

The lad ran across, jumping over the pressed men sitting miserably on the planks. "Keep yer voice doon. Ye call me Kit noo. He's gan' ower the side and I'm here in his place."

Malky looked at him. "Ach, and I went to all this trouble to get away frae ye?"

HISTORICAL NOTE

Sketch of England in 1650

After the defeat of the royalists in 1546, the English Parliament ruled supreme and abolished the episcopacy. The lands of the bishops were sold off, including the County Palatine of Durham. In 1649 the King was tried and executed, and the monarchy and the House of Lords abolished. The Rump Parliament established the Commonwealth, a puritanical republic. The Scottish covenanters who had been allies of the English Parliamentarians in the Civil Wars, did not condone the execution of a King appointed by the Lord God, and accepted Charles II as King of Britain. Oliver Cromwell led the invasion of Scotland with his New Model Army and against all odds defeated the Scots under General David Leslie at the Battle of Dunbar. (The war with Scotland continued until the Scots were finally defeated in July 1651 and in October the English Parliament declared Scotland to be part of the Commonwealth. The Parliament was dissolved in 1653 and Oliver Cromwell became Lord Protector.)

Sheels' salterns

The salt trade in South Sheels

South and North Shields (written variously as Shiels, Sheels, Sheals, and Sheilds) take their names from the fishermen's huts that were scattered along the shore. The settlement of South Sheels gradually increased in size to form a township with a way along the riverside. The production of salt by boiling sea water may have started as early as the thirteenth and fourteenth centuries as a natural development to support the fishing. The first direct reference to iron salt pans used to produce salt was in 1489. By the 1600s salt production was a major and very profitable industry, and as such heavily taxed by the King. The stretch of the foreshore between the Mill Dam and Jarra's Lake was given the name West Panns. In

1635 there were between 150 to 250 salt-panns in North and South Sheels, and a Thomas Horth paid £9,000 per annum to the King to 'farm' the salt duties. Sheels' salt was made up of fine white crystals and was far superior to any other made in England or Scotland. Scottish salt imported into England had at that time to pay customs dues and could not compete either in cost or quality with the Sheels salt. The Icelandic and Westmony fishing fleets, of 200 vessels at a time, would come to Sheels to fill up with salt. The town of South Sheels was little more than a riverside settlement with a long and narrow series of ways (some parallel) along the river frontage, with fishing, salt making and other riverside trades as the main occupations. Before the Civil War, the town's laws were laid down by the Court Leet (the Manor Court) at Westoe and the Vestry court at St Hild's, both under the jurisdiction of the Bishop of Durham, who owned all the farm-land around Sheels (Sheels Heugh) and all the land on which the salt-panns stood.

On the abolition of the episcopate the township of Sheels came under the jurisdiction of the Vestry court.

In the Civil War, Sheels was taken by the Scottish army, fighting on the side of the Parliamentarians, and on their departure the Scotch army dispossessed many salt workers of their panns and destroyed many others to give an advantage to the Scottish salt makers. Worse was to follow as the English Parliament annexed Scotland into the Commonwealth in 1651 and stopped taking customs dues for Scottish salt imports. This hit the Sheels salt-pann owners hard. When the war with the Dutch broke out in 1652, the waters of the German Ocean (North Sea) were not safe for shipping, and ships carrying salt and coal had to leave in convoys under escort by the Parliament's Navy.

After the restoration, 1662, with Scotland once again becoming an independent kingdom, customs dues were restored and the salt industry revived. In 1768, Daniel Defoe, on his journey to the North, recounts seeing the great smoke clouds over Sheels during his ascent of the Cheviots, some 40 miles away. Without a contemporary Dickens, one can only imagine the lives of the salt workers of Sheels, and the conditions under which they lived and worked.

Newcastle and the keels

From the 1450s onwards the King had granted exclusive rights over the trade on, and the navigation over, the Tyne, to the burgesses of Newcastle. All ships could only unload goods or discharge ballast at Newcastle quayside. Any unloading anywhere downstream was prohibited, including at North and South Sheels. Nor could ships be provisioned from these towns, or repaired. There was an exception for the fishers, the salt trade, and for vessels owned by Freemen of the City of Newcastle. In the days of sail the Tyne was difficult and dangerous to navigate: there were narrow channels where ships would collide, and the Newcastle burgesses did little dredging or clearing despite the revenues they received.

North and South Sheels were not, therefore, ports of the Tyne, but ships moored at the mouth of the river who would not make the journey to Newcastle were obliged to have their cargoes and their ballast taken upstream to Newcastle on keels and wherries, and any goods for export brought downstream in the same way. The bulk of the export trade was coal, and all coals were ferried down river by keels crewed by the keelmen. The coal keels were 42 foot long and 19 foot wide and of shallow draught (4½ ft). Each keel load was 8 Newcastle chaldrons or 21½ tons. The keels had a mark on the side, made by a nail, to indicate when it had eight chaldrons on board.

The keelmen were hardy souls and a breed of their own, doing a hard and dangerous job and not afraid of anything. They mostly came from the borders, Tynedale and Ridsdale, or from Scotland. As the coal trade died off during the winter months, many worked for nine months and returned home to over-winter. They lived in Sandgate and are celebrated in the famous Tyneside song, the *Keel Row*. They were bonded to a hostman, an agent, who organised the delivery and shipping of the coals.

Keels sailing from the Old Tyne Bridge in the 1650s

SELECT BIBLIOGRAPHY

The Borough of South Shields – George B Hodgson – Facsimile Edition, South Tyneside Libraries 1996

Water Trades on the Lower River Tyne in the Seventeenth and Eighteenth Centuries - Peter D. Wright - A thesis submitted in fulfilment of the requirements for the degree of Doctor of Philosophy School of Historical Studies, Newcastle University March 2011

The Art of Making Common Salt – William Brownrigg – Scholar Select

The Keelmen of Tyneside – Joseph M Fewster – Boydell Press

The Press-Gang Afloat and Ashore – J R Hutchinson – Good Press

The First Dictionary of Slang 1699 – The Bodleian Library

Life in Stuart England – Maurice Ashley B T Batsford Ltd, G P Putnam's sons

In a Free Republic – Life in Cromwell's England – Alison Plowden, Sutton Publishing.

Cromwell's Convicts – John Sadler and Rosie Serdiville – Pen & Sword Military

ACKNOWLEDGEMENTS

A big thankyou to Dave Kerr of Jesmond who drew the maps for me, and not only discovered an authentic looking font but also managed to have ships sailing in the watters!

Heartfelt thanks also to Bill Evans, Marilyn Gordon, Albyn Snowdon, Robert Colls and John Gray for their support, and also my particular gratitude to Robert and John for their endorsements.

A special word for the team at UK Book Publishing: Ruth, Jay and Judith. They have helped me with my three previous books and it was a pleasure to work with them again on Blue Bonnet.

GLOSSARY
– OLD AND DIALECT
WORDS AND PHRASES

Ane – one.

Ance – once.

Angel – eleven shillings.

Back-hold (the) – A Scottish style of wrestling where the wrestlers rest their chins on the opponent's shoulders and grip their hands on their backs as shown in the illustration.

Bahn – the fair.

Ballack knife – long dagger so called because of the two oval swellings at the guard.

Bannock – a flat bread or scone cooked in a skillet.

Belly-up – pregnant.

Bents – reeds used to stiffen bodices instead of whalebone.

Bittern – watery residue of brine produced when the salt dried.

Brigid's plant – dandelion.

Bully – crewman on keel.

Capstan-bars – wooden levers used to fit in the holes of the capstan and used to turn it to winch ropes.

Chaldron – A measure of coal, one Newcastle chaldron weighed fifty-two and a half hundredweight, equivalent to just over two and a half tons.

Chain – a measure of 22 yards – there are 10 chains to a furlong.

Clartin' aboot – playing the fool

Coffin – a hard pastry case to contain minced or other meat for cooking – the pastry was not always eaten.

Cordwainer – shoe maker, as opposed to a cobbler who only repaired old shoes.

Crowns and double crowns – a crown was five shillings, a double crown ten.

Cyek – cake

De'il haet – Devil have it.

Dippers – slang for Baptists.

Dochter – daughter

Dograve – large cod, mainly salted.

Drab – stall that held the damp salt and allowed the last of the bittern to drain away as the salt dried.

Dunkirker – privateer from Dunkirk.

Erse – Gaelic.

Fyece – face.

Fyeul – fool

Groat – four pence (half groat – two pence).

Hangers – small cutlass like swords.

Harrain' – herring

Hasty pudding – wheat flour boiled in milk – honey, butter, raisins, spices might be added.

Heid – head.

Hostman – Newcastle agent who arranged the transport of coal from the collieries to the ships waiting at the mouth of the Tyne.

Huddick – small after cabin on keel.

Impressment Service – the department of the Navy that dealt with the pressing of men.

Jacob's cross – a navigational tool consisting of a stick with a cross-piece, that, when aligned with the sun and the horizon would give the ship's latitude – see illustration.

Keel – boat, 42 ft long and 19 foot wide of shallow draught (4½ ft) used on the Tyne primarily to carry coal - the standard coal weight was 8 Newcastle chaldrons or 21½ tons.

(pann-keel – keel used exclusively to carry small coal to the salt-panns.)

Kennings – landmarks along the coast known to mariners whereby they could judge their distance to the next port or shelter.

Kilderkin – half a barrel (18 gallons).

(Firkin – quarter a barrel (9 gallons)).

Losing Lodam – card game where the winner of tricks with high scoring cards, loaders, lost.

Lus-lus – plantain.

Midshipman – in the seventeenth century this was a senior seaman, and not a cadet officer as it would become in the eighteenth century.

Neep – any root vegetable.

Nicht – night.

Palatinate – County Durham was ruled by the Bishop who owned all land and the Manor courts.

Pant – storage facility for water.

Peedee – name given to the keel-boy. The name is thought to have developed from an earlier use of 'peedee' meaning "footboy", or "groom", from Latin *pede*, "on foot".

Plaid – the belted plaid (or a plaid worn belted) is a large blanket-like piece of fabric which is wrapped around the body with the material pleated or, more accurately, loosely gathered and secured at the waist by means of a belt.

Porritch – porridge.

Pothecary – apothecary (old spelling).

Poudin' – pudding.

Puoy – 18 ft long pole used to propel keel in shallow water.

Ranters – non-conformist sect.

Rendez-vous – the press gang's headquarters on land.

Ryal – a Scottish coin worth sixty shillings.

Scian doo – a little black knife.

Skeel – large wooden buckets for carrying water. It cost a farthing to fill a skeel.

Skullduddery – (Scots) fornication.

Slops – sailors clothing.

Sonsie – comely, jolly.

Swape – long oar used on the keels for steering.

Swill-belly – drunkard.

Syne – since.

Thirty second – it was the practice, on the ports on the East coast of England, for shares in ships to be taken up in thirty-seconds.

Tyek – take.

Tide – in keelman's dialect a trip there and back from the Newcastle Quayside to the collier or salt-pann.

Umble pie – pie made of offal.

Unite – a pound coin worth twenty shillings.

Usquebah – whisky.

Wain – cart.

Wee yins (or wains) – young children.

Westmony – modern Westman Islands – south of Iceland

Wey – 40 bushels of salt, each weighing 56 pounds.